TETHER

WORKS BY JEREMY ROBINSON

The Didymus Contingency

Raising The Past

Beneath

Antarktos Rising

Kronos

Pulse

Instinct

Torment

Threshold

Callsign: King

Callsign: Queen

Callsign: Rook

Callsign: King 2 – Underworld

Callsign: Bishop

Callsign: Knight

Callsign: Deep Blue

Callsign: King 3 – Blackout

The Sentinel

The Last Hunter – Descent

The Last Hunter – Pursuit

The Last Hunter – Ascent

The Last Hunter – Lament

The Last Hunter – Onslaught

The Last Hunter – Collected Edition

Insomnia

SecondWorld

Project Nemesis

Ragnarok

Island 731

The Raven

Nazi Hunter: Atlantis

Prime

Omega

Project Maigo

Refuge

Guardian

Xom-B

Savage

Flood Rising

Project 731

Cannibal

MirrorWorld

Hunger

Herculean

Project Hyperion

Patriot

Apocalypse Machine

Empire

Feast

Unity

Project Legion

The Distance

The Last Valkyrie

Centurion

Infinite

Helios

Viking Tomorrow

Forbidden Island

The Divide

The Others

Space Force

Alter

Flux

Tether

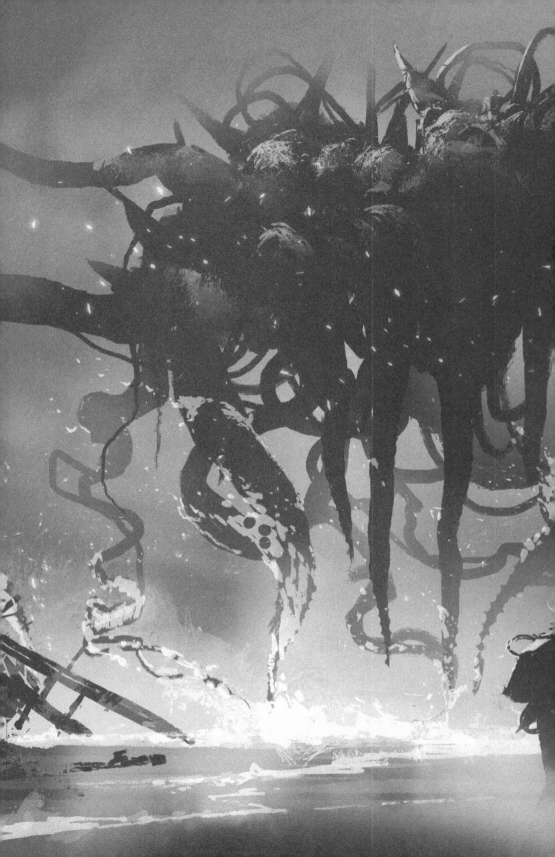

TETHER

JEREMY ROBINSON

BREAKNECK MEDIA

For all you Nemesis fans.
Buckle up. This is going to get weird.

1

Darkness inspires me. Calls to me like a siren. It kindles my imagination and sets it alight to possibilities far out of my reach during the daylight hours. That's all good, and I've made a living from it, but inspiration and the conjurings of an overactive imagination come at a Faustian cost: sleep.

And if the deal isn't renegotiated: the soul.

Because without sleep, the mind breaks.

Anger takes the steering wheel, guided by frustration.

At first, it's the big things that get to you. The world's great injustices. Then it's the little things, like not being able to find a battery for your damn electric toothbrush—who brushes their teeth with normal toothbrushes anymore?

Neanderthals and Philistines. That's who.

Without rest, the mind grinds and then breaks.

At my worst, I averaged two hours a night...taking 12.5 milligrams of time-released Ambien every day for two months. I pushed through my declining health, and focused on deadlines and my ambtion to someday be editor-in-chief of the *Boston Globe*, for whom I write. *Wrote.*

The first thing that goes when you're sleep-deprived is your ability to spell. Memory follows. Common sense brings up the rear, its overweight hands raised, its flabby bingo-arms waggling in the air, enjoying the mad rollercoaster that is your emotional state.

Within a few weeks, I'd botched five articles, missed three dead-lines, and barked at my boss. I wasn't fired. My editor was kind and for-giving. Instead of canning me, he suggested I quit while my reputation was still intact.

I did. And it is.

Which is to say, I didn't have much of a reputation then, and still don't.

Turns out, the job wasn't right for me. Writing under the pressure of daily deadlines turned my nighttime imagination into a monster. Free from the daily grind of crime reporting, my thoughts turned from the things that go bump in the night, to the things that make me smile.

Like my wife.

I'd been on the brink of losing Morgan, too. I hadn't even realized it.

Happily, like my editor, she's a forgiving woman.

And now she's thrilled that I'm following my passions and writing about New England outdoor adventures...on my own blog...which at least one person reads every day. I'm pretty sure it's my mother, but I'm also sure I can make this work.

Morgan's job—something with a lot of letters and an 'ologist' at the end—pays well. So money isn't a concern. While some guys might find it emasculating to have their wives be the breadwinner, I find it a great source of comfort. She has been a beacon for me, a North star, shining the way toward smoother shores.

When I left my job, I was broken. Half chewed up and spit out by the night.

She put me back together again.

It took time.

Took a damn year.

But she stayed by my side, soothing, encouraging, and best of all, making me laugh—and that's no easy task. After years of covering mur-ders, terrorism, and violence of all sorts, my sense of humor had been locked away in a Siberian labor camp, chipping at rocks and living off pine needles.

Now, I can smile.

I'm on a regimen of supplements and drugs, including melatonin, magnesium, Calm CP, Seriphos, and just 2.5 milligrams of Ambien. I sleep an average of seven hours a night. I don't fall asleep until 1am, but my 'job' allows me to roll out of bed at 9am. I miss seeing Morgan in the morning, but evidence of her passing still lingers by the time I rise.

The smell of her shampoo in the still shower-warmed bathroom.

A smoothie left in the fridge.

A note.

Or a chocolate.

Or a fresh photo of her face on my phone's start-up screen.

Even when she's not with me, she is.

Even when I don't see her for days, because, like now, she works the kind of hours that broke me.

But her job is different. It enthralls her. Energizes her. She'll come home from a three-day work binge, walk through the door, and spend the next two hours telling me all about it—what she can tell me about it, without breaking her NDA—with a smile on her face.

SpecTek is a small, but well-funded lab with a government contract. I'm not allowed to know what they work on, and I know not to ask. It's the only secret between us, and that's okay by me. Odds are, I wouldn't understand it anyway. And work is good for her.

And that's good for me.

I miss her, obviously, but we've never been better.

The only downside is that when she's gone, I don't sleep as well. These days that means bumping the Ambien up from 2.5 milligrams to 5, and trying not to think about anything serious if I have to get up to pee.

Tonight is a 5 milligram night.

She's been gone for three days, and she isn't sure when she'll be able to come home.

Some people might worry that there's something screwy going on, that she's refreshed after several days at work because she's actually with her Spanish lover, Esteban. Or something. But we FaceTime. A lot. I know she's at the lab. And if she's getting busy on the sly, it's with one of her middle-aged, kind of overweight, and definitely not handsome co-workers. So I guess kudos to him. While my inner workings pulled a Humpty-Dumpty, I'm not too shabby on the outside, like Matt Damon with a dad-bod...except I'm not a dad.

Last I checked, it was 2am. That's when I took the second hit of Ambien. Now I'm curled up under four heavy blankets—the weight helps—and listening to the drone of a fan, whose symphony of white noise drowns out the world beyond.

Until it doesn't.

A quake runs through my body. I barely notice it in my Ambien stupor, and the beginnings of a dream lure me deeper into sleep. There's a vague image of a woman with a bleach blonde perm—a Golden Girl?

And then shaking again. This time, it's violent enough to rip me from the warm embrace of the drugs, the supplements, *and* my blanket lasagna. Confused and annoyed, I sputter and attempt to shout an expletive. What comes out is, "P-Peterson!"

I don't know anyone with that last name. Haven't watched any TV or movies, that I can remember, with characters named Peterson. The surname comes from the depths of my mental *somewhere*, accessible only through a combination of sleep aids, confusion, and a half-dream state.

Arms outstretched and reaching, a baby emerging from darkness into light, I fumble for the lamp.

By the time it clicks on, the shaking has stopped.

I look around the room for the rhino I'm sure someone set loose, but I'm still alone, and the hardwood floors show no signs of having been stomped on by a two-ton animal. Bathed in light and squinting, I slide to the side of the bed, feet planted.

I glance at the clock.

3:33am.

Wasn't there a horror movie where 3:33 was important? I wonder, my mind waking up.

Don't think about it! My sleepy-self shouts.

If I can't settle down, and soon, this will become a 7.5 milligram Ambien night. Technically, there's nothing wrong with that, but I don't like being dependent on drugs. What if there's a third World War? What if drugs are suddenly unavailable? Will I never sleep again?

Damnit.

I'm awake.

Really awake.

Might even be a full 10 milligram Ambien night. It's been a year since I had one of those.

A tremor shakes the floor beneath my feet.

Not a dream.

Not a hallucination.

Something real is happening.

My first thought is a terrorist attack.

My second thought is that Morgan's not here.

I reach for my phone, intending to check the local police scanner app. Whatever's happening, they'll be talking about it. I pluck the phone off the night stand, but before I can tap in my passcode, the house shakes again.

Dogs howl.

Car alarms whoop.

A loud twang rips through the air. It's electric, like the Faraday cage show at the Museum of Science. And it has a direction.

Southeast.

Boston.

I yank open the light-blocking curtains and lift the double-thick accordion blinds. On a clear day, Boston's skyline is impressive from the second floor of our modest Cambridge home. Tonight, the view is obscured by what can best be described as a blue explosion of electricity surrounding a column of luminous ether stretching up into the night sky.

It's horrifying, and beautiful. I can't help but smile at it.

Then I realize SpecTek isn't too far from the glow's source. I lean forward until my forehead touches the cool glass.

SpecTek isn't just *near* the light's core.

It *is* the light's core.

Heart pounding, I look down to my phone, tapping in my six-digit passcode with a shaking thumb. With five numbers punched in, the phone comes to life in my hand, loudly booming DMX's *Gonna Make Me Lose My Mind*—my wife's personalized ring tone.

I blink down at her name, Morgan Signalman, and the photo of her face, sticking out her tongue. She looks goofy in her lab coat and safety goggles, but I know what kind of person—and yeah, what kind of body—is hidden under that nerdy façade. I swipe to accept the FaceTime call.

A shaky, blue-lit image fills the screen. The electric buzz emanating from the strange, distant explosion is mirrored by the sound coming out of my phone. Old journalist habits guide my fingers, swiping and tapping through menus until the phone is taking a screencap video of everything I'm seeing.

"Morgan?"

A crackle of electricity is followed by a scream. Not Morgan. It's a man.

And then I see him run past the lens. He's blurry, but not because of the camera. It's like he's being stretched out, leaving a slug-slime trail of himself hovering in the air.

Arcs of blue light twist through the lab. I can see an octagonal room with walls of glass in the background. Inside it is a woman, her black body-suit and stark white skin and hair easy to see. But what stands out most are her eyes.

They're glowing.

Blue.

When she rushes the glass wall, slamming her fists into it, I flinch back. She's shouting something. I can't hear her, but her lips are easy enough to read.

Let me out!

The man screams again, off camera until he sails back into view, trailing himself again, this time glowing...no, *burning* with energy.

"Morgan!"

The camera's view 180s. A close up of Morgan. Eyeliner-streaked eyes burrow into my heart. I've never seen her afraid. It takes all my fortitude to keep from sobbing.

"They lie—to u—!" she shouts, her voice crackling in and out. "I'm sor—...—idn't know."

"You need to get out of there!" I say. "Get away. Now!"

She shakes her head, face becoming a frozen mask of pixelization. For a moment, I think I've lost her. Then the image clears and her voice comes through like she's standing next to me.

"Don't be afraid, Saul. I'll be with you, no matter what, okay?"

Oh God...

This is goodbye.

This...

"No..."

"Baby, you can do it. You can live. You can be bold. You don't need me. Never have."

The last of my defenses implode, releasing a trapped bubble of anguish. It pops from my lips as a sob.

"Find peace," she says. "That's all I want for you. Find—"

Outside, the distant laboratory explodes, blue light forcing my eyes shut. The electronic twang slams into my ears a moment before a shockwave shatters glass, lifts me off my feet, and throws me into the wall.

Somehow, Morgan's voice reaches my ears, escaping the phone as a distorted whisper. "Love you..."

For a moment, I feel her there with me. Moving through me.

And then, I feel nothing.

I feel empty.

A wailing of people and animals rises up across the powerless city. I join the chorus, screaming my pain toward the luminous blue night sky, knowing that despite my still-breathing lungs, still-beating heart, and still-functioning mind, my life is over.

2

She can't be dead.

Those four words repeat in my mind as I push myself off the floor.

She can't be dead.

The drywall is dented where my body struck it. Twin divots from my shoulder and my head mar the light blue paint that Morgan so carefully applied last summer. She'd wave it off, bust out some spackle, and in a day, you wouldn't even know I'd been thrown into the wall.

But I'll know, because I can't fix things like that, and because I'm still going to be hurting, and not just physically.

She can't be dead.

I stumble out of the bedroom, while some invisible force grips my heart in its gnarled fingers and squeezes, making each beat a painful labor.

The railing supports my weight as I stumble down the stairs. In socks, the smooth hardwood steps are a slippery deathtrap. But I'm still barefoot and dréssed for bed in red boxers and a black Bob Marley T-shirt. Yesterday's socks are in the hamper. Today's, in the drawer.

I don't care. Not about socks. Or what I'm wearing. Or much of anything.

I'm on autopilot, like a stunned fish. Breathing. Moving. Unaware of where I'm going or why.

I miss the last step. Everyone does it on occasion. I've done it in the past, thinking I was stepping out onto the floor, only to discover another seven-inch drop. Normally, it's not too hard to catch yourself.

Normally.

In my numbed state, I flop forward and slam into the front door, before I can even think to reach out my hands.

The sharp pain in my forehead simultaneously stuns me and wakes me up. I stumble to the side, one hand to my head, wincing. But now I know where I'm going, and why.

I need to see.

She can't be dead.

I twist the door handle and pull, nearly falling back, overcorrecting myself, before stumbling out onto the front porch. Warm summer air greets me, along with the smell of rhododendrons planted on either side of the porch—also Morgan's handiwork, three years ago.

I'm not sure how I make it to the bottom of the steps, but my feet soon slap on cool concrete.

Despite the complete lack of artificial light inside or outside, I have no trouble seeing. Electric blue light flares in the distance, pulsing into the sky where a vortex of shimmering clouds swirl.

She can't be dead.

The desperate argument is losing steam, giving way to the reality that whatever is happening, Morgan is at ground zero.

No way she's alive.

The scene blurs as my eyes tear over.

My knees burn, scraped when I dropped down in the road.

"Saul?"

The voice is familiar, but almost not there.

"Saul. The hell are you doing, guy?" A hand grips my shoulder, snapping me back to full awareness.

It's my neighbor, Randy. Father of two. Uber fan of all Boston sports teams, often spotted in the wild wearing multiple logos and color schemes at once. He's a local, born and raised, and he has the accent to prove it.

I wouldn't say we're friends, but I wouldn't say we're not.

We're New Englanders. If there's a game on, he shouts his excitement, and I pretend to share it. If there's a storm, we check on each other. But it's not like we're watching *Game of Thrones* together, or having backyard barbeques. I mean, he's invited me a few times, so maybe we are friends, but I've never gone because there's only so much sportsing I can take before I'm revealed for the non-sports fan I am, which in Boston—nay, all of New England save for Vermont—is akin to blasphemy.

I look up into Randy's concerned eyes, and he flinches back. Something about my face frightens him. He looks to the house. "Where's Morgan?"

My head lolls to the pavement.

There's a cricket there, hiding in my shadow, perhaps watching the glowing storm.

Morgan liked crickets. Their songs. When the thing chirps, I let out a little laugh, sniff in a deep breath, and find a trace of resolve.

She can't be dead.

I push myself up and stand.

"Damn, guy, you're bleeding." Randy is eyeing me now with something approaching suspicion. "Saul, where's Morgan?"

I lift a finger and point.

At the storm.

Right at its bright core.

"You're shitting me..."

"She called when it happened," I say. "She's..."

She's not fucking dead!

"Hey!" Randy shouts after me, as I sprint inside the house. The blood running down my legs stretches out, tickling my feet. I move through the front hall, the living room, and the kitchen, instinct guiding my hands to each and every light switch as I go, not a one of them working. Luckily, Morgan was a minimalist—*is* a minimalist—and everything is in its place. Navigating to the bowl holding my car keys on the kitchen counter is simple.

Keys in hand, I push through to the garage, slapping the door opener.

When nothing happens, I'm thrown for a moment. It's like I've suddenly lost the ability to move a limb. Then my mind catches up.

No power.

I fumble in the windowless garage, bumping into the RAV4 and following it around to the back. When I find the bumper, I place a hand on the roof and hoist myself up. My arm flails in the dark, like some hungry tube worm at the bottom of the ocean, searching for elusive prey.

There's a gentle tap against my hand, and then it's gone.

I force myself to resist desperation for a moment. To slow down.

The plastic handle taps the back of my hand. I let it slip over my skin and into my palm, where I grasp hold and pull down, unlocking the garage door from the automatic door opener. Then I'm off the bumper and shoving the grinding door up. I would normally cringe at the noise it makes this late at night, but everyone is awake. I can hear them inside their houses, panicked. I can see them lighting candles, fending off the darkness.

"Saul," Randy says, still in the street watching the lightshow. Like me, he's in boxers and a T-shirt, but he thought to throw on a pair of slippers and a bathrobe that's billowing in a growing wind, coming from the explosion's core.

I ignore him, hopping into the RAV4. The vehicle is two years old, and thanks to the fact that I'm something of a neat freak, and I barely drive, it still has that 'new car' smell.

It's familiar, and calming. My own private quiet place.

A fist pounds on the window, drawing a shout from my lips.

Randy. "What are you doing?"

I turn the key.

Nothing.

"No power," Randy says, voice muffled. "It's not just lines. It's like one of those things or something."

"Electromagnetic pulse," I say to myself, but he somehow hears me.

"Right. One of those."

I glance in the rearview, into Randy's yard. His kids are slobs. If they take it out, they leave it out. Tonight, that includes his son's ten-speed mountain bike.

I push the door open, forcing Randy to move behind it. Then I'm out and hauling ass across the street.

"Hey!" Randy calls out. "Damnit, Saul, slow down for a second."

I yank the bike up from the perfectly maintained lawn. The slender seat is uncomfortable under my butt, but I barely notice. The sharp pedal grips on my bare feet stand out a little more, but they don't stop me from putting my weight on them and propelling myself forward.

Randy doesn't try stopping me. He kind of just raises his arms in defeat and steps to the side.

"If you need me," he says, now behind me, "I'm not going anywhere."

Maybe he is *a friend,* I think, as the bike rolls downhill, picking up speed.

I glide down the center of the road, not worried about cars. At this time of night, there won't be many vehicles stalled in the center of the road, and most people are hiding in their homes, no doubt mourning the loss of their power and devices.

Air rushes up my nostrils with each breath. Smells like ozone. Like just after a summer lightning storm. But the air is dry despite the gathering clouds.

When the hill levels out, I pedal hard, grinding through gears until I'm moving at a steady thirty mile per hour clip. It's been a while since I rode a bike like this. Despite my anti-sportsing standpoint, I was an avid biker through high school and college. Marriage and a full-time job changed that, but riding a bike really is like *riding a bike.* All of my old instincts come back to me, guiding me, as I follow the familiar path through Cambridge's tight network of neighborhoods.

Ten minutes later, I'm both unnerved and exhausted. The city's rising panic is becoming palpable, even though I'm only catching conversations in bits of Doppler waves. But I hear things like 'terrorist attack,' 'nuclear explosion,' and 'radiation' as I pass. A sixty-something-year-old woman, in a frilly pink night gown, shakes a fist at me—not in anger, but in warning. "You're going the wrong way!" she shouts.

And she's not wrong. I really don't know what I'm riding toward, aside from a sliver of hope.

She can't be dead.

As I approach the base of the hill upon which SpecTek sits, I stand up and put my weight into each pedal push. By the time I reach the incline, I'm doing forty. As the climb begins, my speed drops by half, and then as my legs weaken, by half again. I downshift and work my way up the hill in switchbacks. It's slow going, but faster than walking.

Near the top, I slide off the bike and hold my ground.

Not because I've run out of energy, although I have. Or because I'm terrified, which I am.

But because the hill comes to an end thirty feet sooner than it used to.

And then I see why.

3

A volcano of radiant energy spews from where SpecTek once stood. There are bits and pieces of the building's outer wall still standing, but the rest of it is just...gone. I thought the structure had exploded, but the complete lack of debris covering the surrounding area suggests otherwise.

Moving closer is probably a bad idea, but logic isn't behind my steering wheel.

Desperation is.

I creep closer to the crater, eyes widening as I expect to see a foundation, but instead I find striated layers of multiple sub-basements, the middle carved out. Fragments of concrete outer walls remain. Severed water pipes drain into the abyss. The cut is clean, like a giant ice cream-scooper took the building away.

I shuffle closer to the edge, toward the blue light, expecting to feel heat. Instead, I feel cold.

My breath turns to vapor, rising into the bright, swirling sky.

What the...

I'm directly beneath the otherworldly hurricane that's absorbing the rising light like a black hole, spewing it out through the surrounding cloud cover. The shimmering pulses move out and away in all directions, but the brightest of them streak toward neighboring Boston.

I've been to the Grand Canyon just once. When I walked up to the edge and looked out over its depths, I felt a strange sense of nausea, not because of its size, but because it feels unreal. How could something like that exist? It's almost incomprehensible.

I feel the same thing now, as I slide my feet toward the precipice and look down. The incline is a smooth forty-five-degree angle, dropping six stories into the Earth. Farther down, large portions of the floors are intact, carved away at an angle. On the periphery, I can see hallways, offices, labs, desks, and debris.

But no people.

That doesn't mean there aren't survivors.

"Morgan!" I shout into the abyss.

My voice is swallowed by the whoosh of skyward energy.

I lean forward. The bright blue grazes my skin.

An unbidden scream pops from my mouth as I flinch back, not in pain from hot or even cold, but because, for just a moment, I feel the dry husk-like grip of death on my body.

Hooks slip and twist through my flesh, tugging my soul from its mortal coil.

I gasp and scramble back, body twitching, a degree or two short of a full seizure.

A final burst of bright blue light billows out and above.

I cringe away from its chill, my hands over my face, eyes clenched shut.

The scent of ozone becomes intense.

And then, for a moment, the scent of night-blooming jasmine. Of Morgan.

Time loses meaning.

When I open my eyes and lower my arms, all trace of the strange phenomenon has vanished. The column of light. The swirling clouds. The pulses of energy moving into the distance.

It's all gone.

I crawl back to the crater's fringe.

There's not much to see in the darkness that follows the lightshow's retreat. But there is something, at the crater's core. The glowing blue octagonal enclosure is easy to spot, because it's the only thing I can see. Its shape is familiar. I've seen it before.

In Morgan's FaceTime.

At the same moment that I recall the blonde woman with the glowing blue eyes, she slams her body against the glass. I can't hear her voice, but the bong of fists on the window gives me a start.

She pounds hard. Angry and violent. Or is it terrified and desperate? It's hard to tell from six stories above, in the dark.

But how am I seeing her at all?

Does the room she's in still have power?

"That's not it," I say to no one, recognizing the residual supernatural glow flowing around her.

No...not around her.

From her.

Her pale white skin is incandescent. Her eyes shine like LED bulbs. She pounds on the glass again, this time with open palms.

Definitely desperate.

But not my problem. Not my concern. I'm here for, "MORGAN!"

My scream echoes through the crater.

The woman ceases pounding. When I look back to her, she's staring up at me, her bright eyes impossible to ignore or look away from.

She was there, I realize. Would have seen Morgan after the phone connection was lost. Would know what happened.

But she's six stories down, in a dark hole and—

"Yo, that shit was on fleek!"

The loud voice spins me around with a shout.

"Ho! Damn, man. Chill." The young man speaking can't be more than eighteen. A red BMX bike lies on the ground behind him. His tilted trucker cap is too big, his clothes are baggy, and every move he makes is with exaggerated swagger, like a bird of paradise in the throes of a mating dance. He's what people of my generation would call a 'poser,' someone who's trying too hard to be something they're not. In this case, a suburban white kid from an upscale Cambridge neighborhood, attempting to look, and sound, like someone with real street cred...in Southern California...ten years ago. He'll stop when he meets the right girl, or when he gets the shit kicked out of him.

The space between us is lit by a lighter in his hand. He holds it out, casting the orange glow on me.

The kid gives me a once over, frowning. "You could'a got dressed before runnin' out here, man."

Loud thumping rises from the crater again.

The glowing woman's light has faded some, but she's still easy to see.

"What the fuck..." the kid says, stepping up next to me, his faux accent gone, his true Massachusetts heritage emerging. "Where'd the building go?" He spots the woman. "Holy shit! Someone's alive down there."

While the kid is stunned, I strike, snagging the lighter from his hand and sliding down into the pit.

"Hey!" he says, reaching out for me in anger, until he realizes where I'm headed. "Oh damn, dude. You gonna save her?"

Going to get some answers, I think, but then I realize that, yes, to get answers I must first save her. I don't really know what that will entail, but I'm going to do it, and then I'm going to find Morgan.

Maybe she's still here.

Maybe she's unconscious.

"Morgan!" I shout, as I slide over the remains of a concrete wall, all cut at a smooth forty-five degree angle. My journey downward is precarious and slow going, lit by the lighter's feeble flame. I brace myself on severed support pillars, cross beams, and pipes, inching my way down.

The woman's banging stops. She can see me coming, lighter in hand, just as clearly as I can see her, though her inner glow continues to dwindle.

Sensing I'm in a race against time, I let myself slide several feet at once. I nearly topple over into empty rooms several times, but I manage to reach the bottom without injury. The floor levels out just a few feet from what I can only describe as a cell. The walls are all clear, though, the woman inside meant to be seen...but not heard.

Meant to be observed...

What were you working on, Morgan?

The woman watches me, the dull blue glow of her skin like a dying fluorescent lamp's bulb.

A chill spasms through my body, locking me in place.

It's the view.

I've seen it before.

With my cellphone. Back at the house. I replay the video in my mind's eye. Morgan. The cell. The woman.

I am standing where Morgan was when...

My eyes turn downward.

A circle of white linoleum around my feet has been charred. I launch away from the spot, revealing two, size-eight footprints.

She was here when it happened.

She was...

I crouch down, tracing my fingers over the darkened floor. They come away clean.

Like the building, Morgan was here...and then she was not.

And that's not nearly answer enough.

"Where is she?" I ask the woman through the glass. "What happened!"

She stares back at me, the glow inside her flickering.

Her eyes flick from me to the floor and then widen with understanding, and what I think is recognition.

Then she goes dark and falls away from the glass.

4

My head thumps against the thick window as I try to peer inside the octagonal cell. The pain barely registers. I press the lighter against the glass, attempting to see inside, but most of the light is reflected. Without the woman's inner glow, she's all but invisible.

I can't tell if she's inside, or even alive.

I glance back at the black circle that might represent all that remains of my wife. Intense pain squeezes my chest. I nearly come undone.

She's not dead.

She can't be dead.

And the only person who can confirm that for me is unconscious, inside this...whatever this is.

I seal off my rising emotions and focus on the cell, moving around its perimeter, inspecting its eight walls in search of a door. If the cell has an electronic lock, there's no helping her. The room could be sealed tight.

"Oh shit," I say to no one. If the room is air tight... Without electricity, the woman might have used up all the oxygen in the small space.

"What're you doing, man?" the kid calls down from above.

I ignore him, moving around the cell.

"I think help is coming," he shouts. "I hear helicopters."

Probably news helicopters out of Boston. I have no idea if surrounding cities suffered the same electromagnetic effect as Cambridge, but if there are helicopters, then that seems unlikely. I haven't heard any secondary explosions. Logan airport must have been spared—thank God for that.

I nearly miss the lock, tucked into the top right corner of the glass wall. It's a sliding bolt and comes free with a tug. There's no door handle, so I grasp the bolt and tug. Nothing moves.

C'mon...

I pull again and the top of the door wobbles outward, but the bottom resists. Crouching, I see the problem. A second bolt in the panel's lower right. The lock snaps up and the door slides open, smooth and quiet, propelled by a resilient rubber seal.

Definitely airtight.

I step inside and fall to my knees beside the pale woman with shoulder length, nearly white, blonde hair. Her wiry figure is revealed by the tight black bodysuit she's wearing. On the right side of her chest is what looks like a serial number:

005-RAIN

I check for a pulse and find none.

"Damnit."

While I'm nothing close to a doctor, after spending time with the worst criminals Boston had to offer, I made it a point to carry a first aid kit in my car, and learn CPR. Until now, I've never had to use it.

I lay her flat, lace my fingers, and place them over her sternum. Hesitation locks me in place. For this to work, to *really* work, I need to push hard enough to compress her chest—which also happens to be hard enough to break ribs.

This is going to hurt.

Both of us.

I straighten my arms, lean over her, and—

The woman lurches up with a gasp, filling her lungs with oxygen-rich air, like she's just escaped the ocean's depths. When she's alert enough to move her head, she notices me kneeling beside her. Her reaction is violently defensive, throwing herself away from me, like I'm

Beelzebub come to collect her soul. She slams into the cell's wall, her head striking the glass with a *bong*.

"It's okay," I tell her, arms outstretched, empty palms exposed.

She eyes me. "I know you..." She shakes her head. "I've seen you."

"I was outside this..." I motion to the octagonal cell. "...before you passed out."

She gives her head a slow shake. "Before that."

"On the phone," I say. If I could see her, maybe she could see me. "Right before...whatever this was."

She shakes her head, confused. "I don't...I don't know."

"Can you tell me what happened? Where did the people go?"

Her suspicious eyes lose their sting when she glances down at my body and finds me dressed in a T-shirt and boxers.

"Please," I say. "Do you know—"

She's shaking her head again, rapid fire. Panic rises.

"Hey," I tell her. "You're okay, now."

"I don't remember," she says.

"You're in shock."

We probably both are. It would explain why I climbed into a six-story deep crater—a possible cauldron of radioactivity—to help a stranger. Not that my motivations aren't selfish. I'm here because she knows something.

She *has* to.

"I don't remember."

"You just need time."

"I don't remember *anything*," she says. She's getting twitchy. Stares at her shaking fingers like they're out of control.

No... It's more than that. She's looking at her hand like she's never seen it before.

She flinches as though slapped. Gasps for air. She looks around at the cell, eyes widening upon seeing the open door.

"A memory?" I ask.

"A feeling," she says, hopping to her feet. "Run!"

She pushes past me and steps out of the cell. For a moment, she's daunted by the steep grade surrounding us on all sides. From the bottom, spotting a path out isn't easy. It's a maze of carved walls, beams, and pipes. A maze with many exits and even more ways to meet a painful end.

She flinches again when I place a hand on her arm. I try to disarm her with a smile. "Over here." She yanks her arm away, but follows me.

When we stop at the straight path I took to reach the bottom, the kid shouts down to us. "Yo! I can see those choppers, man. They'll be here soon." He points east, toward M.I.T., Boston, Logan Airport, and the Atlantic Ocean.

"Go ahead," I tell the woman and step aside. She looks up, trepidation in her eyes, until she hears the *whump, whump, whump* of approaching helicopters. She throws herself into the task, scaling the angled path like an orangutan on a tree branch.

That's when I notice the back of her black body suit. The serial number is there again, this time stretching between her shoulder blades. But above the code is a single word that chills me.

SUBJECT
005-RAIN

What the hell were you doing here, Morgan?

I follow the woman up, struggling to match her pace. Her small frame and light weight make the climb easy, and while I'm not exactly overweight, it's been a while since I've scaled my way out of a crater, and I'm starting to get the adrenaline shakes.

The helicopters are loud by the time we reach the top, just seconds away.

I turn to look and see three helicopters, low to the ground, racing toward us, bright searchlights glaring. I've seen more than my fair share of news helicopters while chasing down stories about criminals. They fly high and slow, depending on their zoom lenses, to get the shot. The pilots of these three helicopters are fearless, hugging the ground and barreling toward the hillside.

The woman grasps my arm, squeezing hard enough to hurt.

"What? Hey!"

I'm angry until I see her eyes.

She's terrified. Whatever misgivings she had about me are gone, now that she's seen the helicopters.

She backs away, eyes darting.

She's going to run.

"They're here to help," I tell her.

She shakes her head, moving farther back.

"Yo, she's buggin'," the kid says. "You need to chill, lady. Be glad you're alive, you know?"

She doesn't hear him.

The helicopters' thunder draws my attention again. The lead helicopter, about to career into the hillside, pulls a sharp turn to the left. The second swerves right. The third goes high. Everything about it—the timing, the speed, the precision—screams 'military.'

They're not here to help…

They're here to check on their investment.

Aside from their bright spotlights, the helicopters are all but invisible, but I'm sure if I could see them, the profiles of three Black Hawks would be easy to make out, maybe loaded with soldiers.

Do I really want to be here?

The Black Hawks slip into a tight formation, doing circles around the site. Spotlights trace their way down the crater until they converge on the cell at the bottom. That seems to hold their attention.

They're looking for her.

I glance back at the woman, whose slow retreat has taken her beneath a nearby tree. She stares at me with pleading eyes. She's desperate to escape, but she isn't stupid. She doesn't know where she is. Doesn't remember…maybe anything. The stranger dressed in his underwear might be her only real chance to get away—

—from the people my wife worked for.

Works for. She's alive.

If I help this woman, am I working *against* Morgan?

Doesn't matter, I decide.

Helping people was why I started reporting crime. Doom and gloom sells papers, but exposing criminals, scams, and schemes serves the greater good. The press can't arrest or prosecute people, but we can help keep them accountable, and on occasion, we can provide evidence that puts real bad guys behind bars. I creep away so the people on the helicopter, and the kid, don't notice.

They're all fixated on the cell right now, but how long will it be before they notice the open door and realize the woman didn't just disappear like everyone else?

Not long, I decide, and I join the woman in the tree's shadow.

"Know how to ride a bike?" I ask, picking up my ride.

She shrugs.

"Everyone knows how," I tell her with feigned confidence. "You might not remember up here—" I tap my head. "—but your muscles will remember." I hand the bike over and pick up the kid's discarded BMX. It's too small for me, but there's no time to trade with the woman. She's already atop the mountain bike and rolling downhill. I peddle after her, picking up speed.

"Yo, man!" the kid calls out after me, his voice nearly drowned out by the thump of helicopter blades slicing air. "That's cold! You could have at least—"

A boom and a bright flash of light from one of the Black Hawks.

The kid's hands slap to his throat. He crumples to the ground.

They shot him...

Oh, God, they shot *him!*

I pedal harder, racing downhill, overtaking the woman I've decided to rescue. I wave for her to follow as I round a corner and do my best to keep up the frenetic pace. The helicopters peel away from the hill and start sweeping the neighborhood with their spotlights.

5

We've entered a strange kind of post-apocalyptic world without electricity. With the night sky blotted out by cloud cover and the streetlights dark, our only source of light comes from the candles and oil lamps held in the hands of neighbors gathered on sidewalks, discussing what they've just witnessed.

The flickering flames lining the streets make me feel like I'm riding my too-small bike toward a Satanic ritual, where I'll be sacrificed to a goat-horned succubus. If I hadn't just seen someone get murdered, the firelight might almost be romantic, but I'm running for my life. Everything feels dangerous, like the Devil himself is holding each candle.

Satanists like to present themselves as just another happy-tappy religion, and I'd like to believe it, but there have been cases of animal and human sacrifices offered up to the dark prince. And Boston is a stone's throw away from Salem, bastion to witches, warlocks, necromancers, tarot card readers—and yes, it's the birthplace of modern Satanism.

I find it ironic that the original witches of Salem weren't witches at all, that those poor Puritan women would find the city's current focus on the occult horrifying. Funny how we can look at a twisted history, twist it some more, and try to fashion something positive out of it. Like the world needs new religions. If one of the ancient ones didn't get it right, God's been kind of a deadbeat dad.

Or mom.

Or tree, if that's your thing.

"Did you see it?" a woman asks me, as I pedal past. "How close were you?"

I barely hear the questions over my dark arts ruminations, which are really just distractions from the fact that I just saw a man gunned down by the people for whom my wife works.

I try to push these thoughts from my mind again, but I think this heavy baggage will weigh on me for the rest of my life.

As more orange firelight fills the streets—from bonfires, tiki torches, and candles—I get a sense that Cambridge is in for the long haul. No one will be going back to bed until they've gotten answers. Which is fine by me.

The helicopters are still looking, their pounding blades keeping me informed about where they are, which is, thankfully, still behind me.

Behind *us*.

I glance back at the woman. Despite her size, she's had no trouble keeping up with me. I think that has less to do with physical ability and more to do with sheer determination. She's a blonde, white woman, whose unexpected facial features look American Indian, but the most captivating thing about her is the intense desperation—or is it deter- mination—in her eyes.

"You okay?" I ask her, despite the fact that she's breathing normally and I'm out of breath.

She gives a curt nod. Says nothing.

For now, that's fine. Save your breath. But when we stop...when there's time, she's going to answer my questions.

She can't remember anything, I remind myself.

She will, my own desperation argues back. *She has to.*

"Almost there," I tell her.

She pedals harder, gliding up beside me. "Where?"

"My place. We can hide."

She glances over her shoulder and up. One of the helicopters sweeps along a cross street behind us. This area of Cambridge is a maze of neighborhoods. Searching them all for two people is slow going, but they're making progress. If we don't get off the street soon, they're going to catch up, and that big serial number on her back is going to make IDing her simple.

Even more so if she starts glowing again.

And what the fuck was that all about anyway?

"Saul!" It's Randy, standing in his driveway beside a fire he's got blazing in a metal trash can. There's a small contingent of neighbors with him, no doubt postulating about what's happening, but his wife and children are still inside, their candlelit faces flickering in the living room window.

Randy's eyes snap to the woman for a moment, giving her a quick up and down, and then back to me. "What did you see?"

I slow and slide off the bike. When the woman stops beside me, I point to my house. "Over there. Door's unlocked."

She drops Randy's son's bike in the street and scuttles to my front door, pausing for a moment before slipping into the darkness beyond.

"Who the hell is that?" Randy asks.

"She was...at ground zero. I think her family was killed. She's in shock."

"Holy shit," Randy says, his suspicion about the woman fading. "What about Morgan. Did you—"

I feel a kind of grim darkness fall over me. I have no idea what I look like, but in the wavering fire's light, I must look like something that's risen from the netherworld. Randy flinches.

"Oh...God... She's...?"

Probably.

"I don't know."

A black stain on the floor.

"The facility is a crater... Nothing left."

No way she's alive.

Tears catch me off guard, as does Randy's meaty-armed embrace. "You need anything, *anything*, just ask. We're here for you."

A single sob manages to sneak through my defenses, but I tamp it back down. I'll mourn later, if I'm still alive to do it. Right now, I need to get off the street and protect Randy and his family by being nowhere near them. I don't know if the men in the Black Hawks could identify me, but I'm not going to take that chance.

"Thanks, man," I say, and I mean it. I want to apologize for not realizing we were friends. I probably should have been nicer over the years. A better neighbor. "I'm going to go inside. Make sure she's okay..." I huff a laugh, somewhat forced. "I don't even know her name."

"Helping her might distract you, but don't forget to take care of yourself." Randy pats my shoulder.

A helicopter thunders down a neighboring street. We watch its rapid progress, Randy with interest, me with terror.

"Know what they're looking for?" Randy asks, as I move across the street.

"Nothing good," I suggest, and then I slip into the darkness that is my house.

The light from the fire outside provides scant illumination. Instead of using it, I recoil from it. A vampire from the sun. I draw the front shades, plunging the house into absolute darkness.

Then, stillness.

I can feel my heart pounding in my chest, the rush of blood behind my ears.

"Hello?" I ask, realizing I should have found my guest before plunging us into darkness. Then I remember I've been clutching the kid's lighter all this time. I give it a flick, filling the living room with dull orange light.

Everything is in place. The black leather couch and recliner are positioned on either side of the fireplace. Framed photos of me and Morgan line the mantle. Morgan's yarn basket sits beside the chair.

I see her in my mind, sitting by the fire on a cold winter day, bundled and crocheting. She was making me a hat. Over time, I will forget much of our time together—the curse of human memory—but the image of her here, at peace, will never fade.

I gasp in fear, and then hope, when I spot two bare feet poking out from behind the recliner. "Morgan?"

My guest flinches when I storm around the chair, hoping to find my wife.

"Sorry," I say, holding out a hand. "Sorry. We're safe."

The house shakes as a helicopter thunders past, trying to make a liar of me. I hold on to the chair's arm, squeezing it until the hunter passes by and fades into the distance.

I suck in a calming breath. "They won't find us here. We're okay." The quiver in my voice lays bare my fear, but the woman manages a subtle nod.

She takes my offered hand. When we're both standing, hands still linked, I say, "I'm Saul. Saul Signalman."

The woman looks about to respond, but then her lips clamp shut.

She can't remember her own name.

"You know what? Doesn't matter. The back of your...uniform...says 'Rain.' Maybe that's your name? It's a nice name."

She gives my hand a squeeze, cutting my rambling short. "Rain is fine."

I'm pretty sure it's not. I doubt it's her name. And I'm not really sure I want to know what it means, because then I might begin to understand what Morgan was wrapped up in, and I honestly don't want to reevaluate my opinion of her now that she's...

I clear my throat and release Rain's hand. "If you want to change, I think Morgan's clothes will fit you." I motion to the mantle, where a photo of Morgan's smiling face breaks my heart. While Rain's form-fitting body suit isn't exactly conservative, it's more concealing than anything you'd find in the average yoga studio. The only thing wrong with it, is that the bold text on the back broadcasts that she's the escaped subject for whom the helicopters are searching.

Rain's reaction upon seeing Morgan's face is more extreme than my sorrow. She reels, thumping the back of her legs into the recliner's arm and falling into the seat. Her fear-filled eyes lock on the photo.

"Do you know her?" I ask, holding up the frame, but not getting any closer when I notice Rain tensing. "Do you remember her?"

After a moment, she shakes her head. She might not have any memories of Morgan, but her body does. Like riding a bike, the body remembers what the mind forgets. And Rain's memories of my wife, it seems, are far different from my own.

We both flinch as another helicopter rushes past.

Sounds like there are more of them out there now.

I return the photo to the mantle. "Clothes are upstairs."

It feels wrong to be leading another woman into my bedroom, in the dark of night, while Morgan is...away. Rain is attractive—high cheekbones, a fit body—but her somewhat albino features are unsettling, and I don't know her. That wouldn't matter to some of my more Cro-Magnon male counterparts, but I'm a romantic, I guess.

Letting Rain dig around in my wife's drawers feels wrong, so I light a few candles and do it for her, looking for clothing that meet three criteria. 1) The right size; 2) Something that is not iconic to Morgan, for my own sanity; and 3) Dark. Despite my assurances, I'm not yet confident we're out of danger. The men on those helicopters could have seen my face. Hell, they could have taken a photo. Could have identified me already. Given the secrecy around Morgan's work, and the extreme vetting she went through, I'm positive there's a file with my name and photo on it somewhere. If that was kept at SpecTek, I might be free and clear. If it's in the cloud...

I find a pair of old black jeans, and an unworn Project Nemesis T-shirt I gave Morgan last Christmas. Despite her claiming it was her favorite T-shirt, she didn't think the 'Goddess of Vengeance,' aka, 'Queen of the Monsters" slogans would go over well at work, or with her family, or with other people offended by the book's main character's penchant for creative foul language. Cool shirt, though. I top it off with a dark blue Red Sox cap that will help hide Rain's hair. I place it all on the bed. "Be out of your way in a minute," I say, snagging my jeans off the bedside chair and my shoes from the floor. By the time I've turned around to leave, Rain has shed her clothing. Her gleaming white skin is in stark contrast to the black underwear and bra, but I barely notice it. Her stomach glows a dull blue. Rain doesn't even notice it. What she *does* notice, is me watching. She slips into the shirt, and I don't bother leaving the room. I've been in my underwear this whole time, and Rain, perhaps because she can't remember who she is, is somewhat shameless.

I do turn my back though, dressing quickly and feeling a little more civilized for it. Sitting on the bed, I tie my shoes and realize I haven't offered any to Rain.

"There are shoes in the closet." I'm about to suggest she get something good for running in, but I'm unsure of how to do that without implying we might not actually be safe. When she steps out of the closet holding Morgan's mostly unused running shoes, I keep the suggestion to myself. The white sneakers with bright pink Nike swooshes aren't exactly stealthy, but they're better than heels, flip flops, or a variety of other footwear not designed for running for one's life.

A car door *thumps* outside.

At any other time, on any other day, I wouldn't have noticed. But tonight...with no cars running...

I step to the window, lifting the light-blocking shade.

Bright headlights carve a path down the street, illuminating the group of neighbors gathered around Randy's trash-can fire. They've got beers now. Making a night of it. Reveling in the mystery of what caused my life's deepest pain. For a moment, I resent them all for finding joy in tonight's tragedy, but then I see two men in dark suits speaking to Randy.

They're rigid.

All business.

Both of them look like they grew up on Krypton and now have super powers, like they could punch the moon out of orbit, or the front of my face to the back.

Their conversation is muffled, but the strangers sound serious, and Randy sounds excited.

Then the pair show Randy a series of photos. He's shaking his head 'no' as he's shown each one, but even from here, I can tell he's lying. He glances up at me, making eye contact.

Too long.

I duck away from the window, just as the two men look toward my house.

"Shit," I whisper, crouching down. "*Shit.*"

That's when I notice Rain staring at me, shoes freshly tied. She looks from me to the window. Then she leans just enough to peek out, and then crouches beside me. She might have no memory, but she's guided by instincts that suggest she wasn't always a test subject.

"Move!" she whispers. "Now! Out the back!"

As we scurry down the steps, into the kitchen, and toward the rear exit, a foot kicks in the front door behind us.

6

A shadow crosses the kitchen window just in time for me to stop short, snag Rain's arm, and swing her into the bathroom. Her light weight makes it easy. I'm surprised and relieved when she doesn't shout.

She must have seen him, too.

I dive in behind her, as the back door is smashed inward. Anger swells. These assholes are ruining my house. I'm not particularly materialistic, but there isn't much about the place that Morgan hasn't fixed, touched up, or improved.

I don't give Rain a chance to ask if I have a plan. I simply open the laundry chute and motion for her to climb inside, which she does without complaint or hesitation. When she ducks inside, I cringe, expecting to hear a yelp and a thump as she falls into the laundry waiting below ...if there is any. I'm in a bad habit of not washing clothes until I hear that Morgan is coming home. Then I slip off my bachelor shoes and tidy up.

Rain's disappearance is soundless, and I don't bother waiting to hear if she's okay. The two men are closing in from both sides of the house.

I'm not looking forward to part two of my three-part plan. It's going to hurt. But I know these guys aren't screwing around. I saw what they did to that kid, and he was just standing around.

I'm the guy who helped their guinea pig escape.

I grip the bathroom counter, hoping the closed door will muffle what I'm about to do, enough to make it look legit.

Ugh...C'mon.

I hesitate.

Do it! For Morgan!

I slam my forehead into the countertop, but miss my target, striking the ceramic sink instead.

My grip on the counter loosens as I lean myself back.

When I feel like I'm falling, I hold on tighter.

I'm barely in control.

And then... A fog. Unconsciousness, I think. For a moment.

A shift in pressure. The door opening.

At the fringe of darkness, voices.

Two men. Serious, but not angry. "Target one is down, Mr. Frank. Appears to have been subdued."

"Asshole didn't know what hit him."

"Lucky she didn't kill him."

"Should we?"

I keep my eyes closed, trying not to panic as they talk to someone not present. I came up with this plan without really thinking it through. I suppose it was instinct. And instinct, in all its non-wisdom, forgot to consider that these men might simply murder their 'unconscious' target. Of course, it wasn't instinct that hit the counter hard enough to knock me out. That was my brain, figuratively, and literally—gray matter colliding with skull.

When one of the men chambers a round, the answer is clear. I need to do something, but what?

It's not like I'm whatever a male version of *La Femme Nikita* is... Jason Bourne? I can't just fight off two men with guns, especially not after being knocked on my ass.

Couldn't win if I tried.

So I don't.

I gasp and sit up like I haven't been listening to the two men casually debate ending another person's life. I open my eyes wide, like I'm surprised to see them, and I do my best to look relieved, despite the gun already pointed at my head. "Out the back! You just missed her!"

The two men snap their heads toward the back door, perfectly synchronized. I can't help but see them as my own personal Agent Smiths, from *The Matrix*. They're not wearing sunglasses—probably because they're human and it's night—but they have that same inhuman, soulless gaze.

The shorter of the two answers an unasked question in the vaguest terms possible. "We'll come back."

And then they're gone, rushing out into the backyard.

My head spins as I try to stand. I need to head to the basement, find Rain, and get the hell out of Dodge. Hopefully she's not injured. That would make getting away even more difficult. Going to be hard enough already. I probably gave myself a concussion.

Before I can stand, the laundry chute door pops open. From my low point of view on the floor, I can see Rain, legs splayed against the chute walls, keeping herself from falling. She emerges from the door the way that creepy chick from the *Ring* movies crawls out of a static-covered television.

I doubt she knew she could do that. The question is, how much else does her body remember how to do that her mind can't recall? Those men didn't doubt for a second that Rain had clubbed me. And they believed she was capable of far worse.

I look at her small form. Probably half my size and weight.

Is this woman dangerous? Is that why she was a guinea pig? Hell, maybe she's a serial killer on death row. Maybe instead of being executed, she donated her body to science. It's a horrible thought, but it's easier to consider than the possibility of Morgan being party to human experimentation against the subject's will.

Even if Rain volunteered, though, it's still an ugly pill to swallow.

She stands and moves to the bathroom door, ready to bolt. When I don't follow on her heels, she glances back at me. The only light comes from the candle I lit in the living room. Deep in the hallway bathroom, I should be hard to see, but when she double-takes, I know she's seen the wound on my head.

"I didn't hear them strike you," she says, reaching down to help me up.

When I'm on my feet, I confess, "I kind of did it myself...to make them think you had." I motion toward the backyard. "They went that way. Looking for you."

"Then we go this way," she says, and she yanks me toward the front door. On the way past the living room, I snag the candle. Hot wax spills onto my hand, but I don't know how much fluid is left in my stolen lighter, or how long we'll be trekking through the dark.

The flame burns out as we pick up speed, barreling out the front door and into the bright beams of a still-running, black SUV.

"Get in!" I tell Rain, who sprints around the back.

"Saul, man, what the— Whoa!" Randy catches my arm. "What happened to you?"

"Get in your house. Get your family inside. Those men are killers."

"Said they were FBI," he explains.

"You see that?" I point to the distant hill where SpecTek used to be. It's lit by a dozen spotlights now, some still furiously circling the neighborhood, some much higher up. The news helicopters have arrived. "Last time I checked, the FBI doesn't do that!"

My wife does.

"But they said..."

"Get. In. Side." The intensity of my glare backs Randy up. He looks to my house, and then the people gathered by his trashcan fire. He waves them away. "Everyone back home! Go!"

I throw myself into the SUV's driver side, slam the car into drive, and hit the gas. Wheels squeal over pavement and we're off. For a moment, I feel the exhilaration of escape. Then windows shatter around me. Cubes of jagged glass pepper the back of my head.

The bullets stop flying when we put a block between us and the shooters.

That's when I notice how hard my heart is pounding...and the three helicopter spotlights growing larger in the rearview.

7

I've lived in Cambridge for ten years. Moved here when Morgan and I got married. My life as a bachelor was lived in Boston, from my time at B.U. to my first assignment as a writer for the *Globe*. And as a writer, I've traveled every nook and cranny of the city and its surrounding suburbs, from Plymouth to Gloucester, and all the way out to Worcester. My knowledge of street layout fades the farther from Boston I get, but here, I'm a human Google Maps.

Without thought, I can plot a course to anywhere in the city and traverse it on autopilot. I've made several trips while daydreaming, unable to remember the journey upon reaching the destination.

Morgan used to say I could run over an old lady and never notice.

Tonight, I'd notice.

I'm noticing everything.

And daydreaming is impossible, because there are three helicopters closing in behind us. The biggest impediment to our escape route is that I don't currently have a destination.

I can't go to a friend. That would be reckless and would endanger people I care about.

I no longer have access to the *Globe's* building.

I need someplace secure. Someplace I'm not publicly known to frequent, like the Dunkin' Donuts on Church Street. If these guys work for the government, and I'm sure they do, we need to go someplace off the radar, or someplace they're not welcome.

"What?" Rain asks, looking at me from the passenger's seat. She's seen the realization in my eyes before I've expressed it with a gasp.

In response, I crank the wheel hard, counter-clockwise, and I cringe as the tires squeal around the bend. I'm a safe driver. A boring driver. I was pulled over just once, because I forgot to register my car. Thanks to modern technology, in the time it took the officer to write up a court summons, I'd registered the vehicle on my smartphone and was free to go. Hell, I play Mario Kart conservatively, so we're about thirty miles per hour outside my comfort zone.

Dark thoughts gather in the corners of my mind, a swarm of spindly legged monsters, ready to impale, gnash, and sever synapses.

They whisper to me.

Your wife is dead. You will be soon. Running is pointless. Fighting, for anything, is purposeless. Just give up.

But the revving engine, shrieking tires, and G-force adrenaline are helping fight back the emotional invaders.

A quick glance in the rearview mirror reveals an empty sky behind us.

Did we lose them?

Too easy, I decide. The SUV is fast, and maneuverable, but the helicopters aren't bound by the confines of streets, which they prove a moment later when a spotlight bathes the SUV in a twenty-foot-wide circle of light. In the pitch dark of Cambridge, we are a beacon.

I'm not sure why, but the scads of people we pass, their faces lit by firelight, cheer as we pass. I wonder if they'd be reveling in the night's mystery if they knew the men in the Black Hawks are murderers, the woman in the passenger seat is a victim of human experimentation, and the driver's a widower whose wife was responsible for said experimentation.

"Stop the vehicle, or it will be stopped for you," a booming voice commands from the helicopter. There's no 'This is the FBI,' or 'Boston P.D.' Just a demand and a threat. Which means these guys aren't law enforcement. Which means I don't need to stop for shit. But I don't doubt his threat.

"Hold on," I say.

Rain grasps the vehicle's ceiling-mounted 'Oh Shit' handle. "What are you doing?"

"Finding some cover."

Another left turn, this one so sharp that the SUV's driver side wheels leave the pavement for a moment. The vehicle bounces, and when all four wheels are planted back on the pavement, it lunges forward.

The helicopter swings far out to the side, disappearing behind tall trees and houses as it comes back around. We have seconds before they're on top of us again. And then...how many bullets will it take to disable the engine?

Depends on what they're shooting, my old reporter's voice replies. I've been to a lot of crime scenes. I've seen what various calibers of bullets do to the human body. To walls. To vehicles. Unless they're firing 9mm rounds, which I doubt, we're screwed. If they're firing a big .50 caliber, mounted machine gun, which is likely given that they're Black Hawks, we're more than screwed. A single round to the engine would kill it. A five second burst would be enough to turn us to paste and the vehicle into a flaming wreck.

The hell am I doing? I wonder, and I pin the gas pedal to the floor.

The SUV roars down the road. I honk my horn for good measure, flashing high beams to let bystanders know we're coming. I can't stop, or even slow down, without risking our lives.

Rain twists around at the thump of helicopter blades cutting through the air. "Here they come!"

The spotlight finds us again, and in the reflected light, I see the unmarked Black Hawk swing sideways, its side door open, a gunner manning the mounted machine gun.

Morgan used to say I 'negatuted.' That I needed to 'positute' more. It was her cutesy way of calling me a pessimist. She might have been right about my attitude, but my worst-case imaginings often come true, making me more of a realist...which is depressing.

The next left turn is three hundred feet ahead. I'm not sure we're going to make it. They must see it. Must know what I'm trying to do.

Rain opens the glove box. The light kicks on, revealing a holstered handgun. She snags the weapon, draws it from the holster, and chambers a round—like she's done it all before. Muscle memory again.

A thundering boom sounds behind us. Pavement to our right sparks into the air. I swerve left around a car that's been abandoned in the street. The machine gun fire saws it in half, kicking off an explosion that the Black Hawk flies straight through.

It closes in again, and this time I have no doubt that the gunner will hit his mark.

One hundred feet to go.

I'm frantic for a solution, wracking my mind. The best I can come up with is plowing into a home or a business, and if we survive the crash, we sneak away in the maze of structures. But that's hardly a solution, and would put other people at risk.

The sound of an automatic window whirring down pulls my attention to my passenger. Rain almost looks calm as she clutches the gun, waiting for the window to complete its descent.

"What are you—"

Rain twists out of the window as a second helicopter flies into place behind us, already turning sideways, ready to light us up. Instead of ducking back inside like any normal person afraid for their life, she pulls the trigger. Over and over.

Sparks ping off the helicopter. The odds of her disabling the vehicle are slim, but when I see a man tumble to the road behind us, I realize she was really just buying us time...with highly accurate, unflinching gunfire from the open window of an SUV moving at high speed.

Who are *you?*

"Shit!" I shout, when the turn catches me off guard. I yank the wheel, squealing tires once more.

Rain's feet fling up. She's falling out the window!

With my left hand on the wheel, struggling to keep us on the road, I clasp her ankle with my right hand. With my limited grip on the wheel, I'm not able to take the turn as sharply as I'd like. We swing out to the far right side of Cambridge's Mt. Auburn Street, a downtown area fringing Harvard's campus, which is lined with tall storefronts and parked cars.

With a shout, I yank Rain back. She bends her body and slides inside the SUV just as we sideswipe a line of powerless vehicles. Shrieking and crunching metal marks our passing, making us an easy target. Two helicopters appear behind us, but the four-story buildings on either side of the street, criss-crossed with power lines, keep them at bay. They could open fire from high above, but not accurately. With the streets full of people, it would be a bloodbath.

It would expose them, I think. Whatever branch of the government is behind this, they don't want the oversight that might come from slaying a large number of Harvard students. I'm sure they've covered up the kid's murder already, and they could probably disappear me and Rain, but if bodies are lining the streets...

The helicopters pull back a bit, continuing the chase from a distance, patient predators. I've seen enough car chases to know how this ends. There is nowhere to hide a car without being seen.

So we let them see us...

The Black Hawks move back a little farther when a pair of news helicopters swoop in to see what all the commotion is about. News crews are trained to see things the rest of us might miss. Over the rumble of their helicopters, they might not have heard the gunfire, but an eagle-eyed pilot would have no trouble spotting it.

Bathed in more light, I speed forward like I'm not going to stop.

And then I do. Hard. A wave of gray smoke billows past us, as the SUV screeches to a stop in the bike lane across the street from Walgreens. I kick open the door and hop out, about to shout for Rain to do the same, but she's already out the passenger's side.

All four helicopters fly past overhead, cutting broad circles as they swing around.

We have just seconds.

I sprint around the SUV, grab Rain's arm, and drag her into the Central T station stairwell. Once we're clear, I let go of her arm, and lead her down into the darkness. We pause to catch our breath, listening to the sound of the helicopters overhead.

I'm sure the Black Hawks are demanding the news helicopters vacate the area, but news crews are very much aware of their rights. They won't take orders from unmarked helicopters unwilling to identify themselves. They'll buy us some time, but not much.

Lighter in hand, I flick a flame to life and hold it to the candle I took from the house. With our meager flames to guide us, I move deep into the bowels of the Boston T system. The air below ground stings my eyes. With the power out, and the ventilation shut down, the air underground is becoming stagnant with the smell of oil and smog—like Boston's South Station in the summer.

"Where are we going?" Rain asks. She's not afraid—I am—just confused about where I'm taking her.

I hold the candle up, trying to read signs. Then I remember, I don't need the signs. There won't be any subway cars coming, and I know which direction we have to go. I slide up over the turnstile. Even if I had my Charlie Card, it wouldn't work. When I turn to help Rain over, she proves she doesn't need me by leaping over with the kind of grace that says she's spent time in a gymnastics class.

"A short walk," I tell her. "It's not far."

And then I lead her onto the boarding platform, pausing at the bright yellow line with the text DO NOT CROSS stenciled in it. On any other day, crossing the line means certain death. Today, the opposite. I lower myself down and turn to help Rain, who once again proves I'm more of a Pippin than an Aragorn in our fellowship of two.

"This way." I strike out southeast, leading a stranger into the dark abyss beneath Cambridge.

No, I correct myself. *I'm Gandalf, leading the way through the mines of Moria, and Rain is—*

She leans forward and blows out my candle. Plunged into darkness, I'm about to complain, when her hand clamps over my mouth. From the stairwell, lights. Voices.

"I can see," Rain whispers, the sound of her voice is the only proof that she exists. The darkness is absolute.

How can she see?

I flinch when her hand takes mine, proof that she can see, and then I'm dragged into the tunnel, desperate for just one thing I can't have.

Morgan.

Rain is Legolas. And I am that pitiful thing.

Gollum.

My precious... Where are you?

I don't get an answer. I'm starting to think I never will.

8

Behind us, lights.

Like the helicopters and the SUV, the G-men tracking us down have working flashlights. The beams carve away the darkness, stretching deep into the subway tunnel.

But not deep enough.

Thanks to Rain's uncanny ability to see in the dark, and my willingness to follow her lead, we make quick time down the tunnel. The only real threat to our escape is the acrid air tickling my lungs, prodding me to cough.

"The tunnel splits ahead," Rain whispers. In the tunnel's tight confines, a voice at normal volume might echo all the way down to the men hunting us.

I imagine where we are, overlaying my internal map of the city over where we entered the tunnel and how far we've gone. "Stay to the right."

As we round the bend, the lights behind us disappear. *We've lost them*, I think, but I feel no relief.

We know nothing about these men, their resources, or their capabilities. And if we find a place to hide, what then? I want answers, and I hope Rain can provide some, but what happens when I get them? Am I going to turn her in?

Just thinking about it gives me a sour stomach.

Despite mounting evidence, I have trouble believing that Morgan knowingly worked for people whose moral scruples match Vigo the Carpathian's.

Even if Rain was once a killer like them, she doesn't remember that life. Should she be punished for crimes she can't remember?

I'm getting ahead of myself. There are too many unanswered questions. Too many variant paths for my internal Choose Your Own Adventure, and most of them lead to death.

Focus on the immediate, I tell myself. Ride out the night. Wait for the search to end.

And then what? They'll be watching my house. My credit cards. My phone... *Damnit, I left my phone at the house!* It might be a useless brick now, but I hope not. So much of Morgan is stored on it, and being paranoid, I don't use the cloud.

I look ahead and see the subway tracks.

Where is the light coming from? It's a dull glow, like moonlight, but there are no lit bulbs. No light from in front or behind. The power is still out. Probably will be for the rest of the night.

"I can see," I say.

Rain glances back at me, revealing the light's source—her face. She's glowing dull blue.

"Can you feel it?" she asks.

"I can see it," I say. "Your face."

"We're not alone."

My arm hair stands on end, as a shiver runs through my body. I search the darkness beyond my personal human-turned-glowworm, but I find nothing beyond endless darkness. *Can those men see in the dark, too?* I wonder, but I quickly discount it. They were using flashlights for a reason.

"I can't see anyone," I say.

"Neither can I," she says, her voice haunted. "I can feel them. Two of them. They don't want us here. We need to hurry." She tugs my hand and leads me deeper into the tunnel.

The glow emanating from her skin flares. She falters. Falls. I catch her and help her move forward. She's crying now, but not in fear.

Like she's lost someone. Like she's remembering.

I decide not to ask. We need to push forward and get the hell out of this tunnel.

After another hundred feet, the glow starts to fade. Rain's emotional state flatlines. She finds her footing, and as darkness consumes us again, she resumes her role as guide to the blind.

Ten minutes later, she says, "There's a station ahead."

If my sense of direction is on the nose, this will be the Kendell terminal, emerging beside the sprawling M.I.T. campus. "This is our exit."

She leads me to the five-foot-tall platform. I plant my hands on the cold concrete, leap, and hoist. For a moment, I'm fluid, recalling how easy this kind of thing was when I was a kid. Then I get stuck. I'm folded over the edge, belly squished, arms struggling, legs not quite flexible enough to reach up and around.

I hear a subtle scrape to my left—the only evidence that Rain is on the move. Then she's above me, grasping the back of my belt and helping me up. The whole thing is somewhat humiliating, so I offer a quick "Thanks," and vow to never speak of this again.

Because you'll be dead, an inner voice taunts.

I flinch when Rain takes my hand again. "This way." She might not have noticed. Might be on task, like I should be. But I can't see her anymore. That otherworldly glow has faded completely.

Questions twinkle to life. Stars shining. Supernovae. So many. Hard to ignore.

I use an old sleeping trick to quash them, imagining a nuclear blast irradiating every image and idea in my thoughts. It's a grim technique, but it works.

Free from pursuit, I pause to light the candle once more. The station glows a horrific orange around me. Without the artificial glow of technology, the underground conjures a primal fear. I need air. I need the sky.

It's my turn to take the lead again, up the stairs, over the turnstiles, and up another set of stairs until—fresh air.

We emerge beside the familiar M.I.T. campus, which is essentially a small city unto itself, except filled with the smartest people in the world, some of whom are no doubt already hard at work trying to make sense of what happened here tonight. They probably won't make much progress without power, but I'm sure they'll have answers before I do.

They're not just smarter, and well-funded. They're also not being hunted.

I scour the dark streets for signs of danger.

Aside from students, gathered in clusters, the streets are dead. No power. No black SUVs or helicopters. The chop of rotor blades echoes in the distance, but aside from a few high-flying news helicopters, the skies directly above are clear.

"Were you stuck down there?" A young Asian woman asks. She's wearing Pikachu footie-pajamas, has her hair put up in twin pony tails like Harley Quinn, and is wearing a pair of thick glasses on her face. She looks ridiculous—*says the middle-aged man*—but probably has an IQ thirty points higher than mine.

"Uh," I say, unsure of just about everything in the universe, never mind how I should reply to the question.

"Hiding," Rain says, turning her head to the sky. She infuses her voice with fear. "Did you see it?"

"Who didn't?" Pony Tails says. "A-plus intense, right? I think the environmental science boys are going to be up all night trying to figure that one out."

I want to tell her it wasn't environmental. That it wasn't a storm. But these aren't the kinds of things I can share without raising eyebrows, drawing attention, or endangering people.

How the hell am I going to get answers?

If Rain can't remember anything, it's possible that even Google isn't safe for me to use. I have a VPN at home. My job—my previous job—required me to search for things that might land me on a watch list, and I've spent more than my fair share of time researching on the Dark Web, but I'm not at home, and I don't remember my password.

"I bet they will," I say before wandering away, trying to act casual. The girl watches us for a moment and then returns to her group of friends, giggling about who knows what.

I try to keep up a fast pace, but the night's insane level of activity is catching up with me. I'm a writer who works at home. My daily activity generally involves walking from desk to kitchen and back, from the desk to the bathroom and back, and from my desk to bed. I was in better shape as a reporter—physically at least—but now... My legs are burning and leaden. My eyes are heavy. My thoughts drifting.

Oh damn.

It's the Ambien.

During the adrenaline-fueled run-for-my-life, the drug's effects were kept at bay. But now that the rush is over, and the body's natural chemical energizers are wearing off, the drug is working again. And now that I'm physically exhausted, it's hitting me hard.

Either that or I have a self-inflicted concussion.

I take a deep breath and push onward, moving through buildings until we reach the Charles River. Across the water is Boston's Back Bay, my alma mater, and Fenway Park, all of it cloaked in darkness. But there is power beyond. To the east, Boston's downtown skyscrapers glow with power. The light is tempting. Calling to me. But I'm in no shape to make that walk, and where will we hide when we get there? Whole Foods? Hotels are a no go.

I turn right and follow the river and M.I.T.'s campus to the west. We move in a zombie-like silence, Rain walking cautiously, me stumbling along like a bona fide member of *The Walking Dead.*

One foot in front of the other, I tell myself. *One foot in front of—*

Holy shit...

Rain is glowing again. The color is faint, but impossible to ignore in the dark night. If she's seen, it won't take long for word to spread.

"You need to shut it off," I say.

"I can't," she says, looking at her hands. "I don't know what it—" She clutches her gut in discomfort, but keeps walking.

I'm wide awake again, scanning the area for interested eyes, shielding Rain with my body.

She grunts, the brightness inside her flaring. I pause with her, and in my search for onlookers, I notice that we're standing in front of the Hayden Library...on Memorial Drive. Visually, the library is nothing special.

All concrete, glass, and angles, like something transplanted from cold war Russia. But I'm transported back in time, to newspaper stories before my time, stories that inspired my article about violence at Boston universities.

A student was murdered here—right here—in 1992. The thief took $33 and the young man's life.

What was his name? He was Norwegian...

"Raustein," I say.

The light in Rain's core flares again. Her back arches, mouth open wide. Gasping. Bent awkwardly, her muscles twitch as she turns to gaze at me with luminous eyes. "Hjelp! Jeg trenger hjelper!"

9

"Jeg blør! Ikke la meg dø! Han stakk meg i magen med en kniv!" Rain reaches for me, grasping my arm while keeping her free hand pushed hard against her chest. Like she's wounded. Like she's trying to stop bleeding...

Details from that decades-old murder surface. The young man was stabbed, twice. In the heart. Right where Rain is clutching her chest.

Concerned voices rise from behind us. Students enjoying the mysterious night.

"Our flashlight is working!" I declare to no one in particular, hoping it will provide a reasonable explanation for the blue glow surrounding us. Several students rush away. A return of power—any power—might mean they're connected to the world once more. Means they might be able to find answers about what they saw, or at least be the first to tweet about it. But there are still a number of people watching us.

And Rain's unintelligible shouting isn't helping.

So I pick her up. She's light enough to fling over a shoulder. "You had way too much to drink," I declare, hopefully loud enough for people to hear, and convincing enough that they don't go in search of security or the police. As I scurry away from the library, Rain goes slack, the glow fading quickly. By the time we reach the mathematics building, Rain is tapping my back and saying, "I can walk."

I put her down and hurry around the building's far side, stepping onto the plush grass of Killian Court. Almost there.

"You want to tell me what the hell that was?"

"Wish I knew," Rain says. "What was I saying?"

I trip over my own foot and stumble for a step. "You don't know?"

"My memory starts in that cell," she says, growing irritated. "I have ...feelings about things from before, but nothing concrete. But I'm sure I don't speak that language, because I know I speak English. And German. And Spanish. I know how to ride a bike. And shoot a gun. I'm pretty sure I know how to fight. But I don't remember learning any of those things, or why. But what just happened..." She shakes her head. "And that language...it sounded...Scandinavian."

"Norwegian," I whisper.

Holy shit.

"Do *you* know what I said?"

I shake my head. "Just...guessing. What was it like? What did you feel?"

"It felt...horrible. Like I was dying. I felt scared. And desperate...but mostly..." She looks up at me. "I felt anger. Rage. And...lost. I wasn't in control, not entirely. I felt my muscles, like I could move if I wanted to, but I felt guided."

Like you were possessed, I think, but I keep that to myself. I don't believe in an afterlife, let alone spiritual somethings capable of taking over a human body. That kind of superstitious mumbo-jumbo has no place in my life, and here, at M.I.T., it feels like blasphemy.

Whatever is happening is beyond explanation, but that doesn't mean it's otherworldly. Morgan's work was scientific. Whatever is happening here is a part of that.

The chop of a helicopter turns both of our heads skyward. The speed and altitude suggest it doesn't belong to a news channel. They're broadening the search area, probably scanning subway exits in both directions, which includes M.I.T.

"C'mon." I jog for the back door.

Most of the doors on campus are the traditional lock and key variety, with security provided by sensors, internal alarm keypads, and a full-time security force. With the whole city in chaos, I'm hoping the security team will already have their hands full.

As I approach the building, a rising sense of dread catches me off guard. Something's wrong, but I can't put a finger on it, like when you leave the grocery store, knowing you forgot something, only to return home and discover the one thing you forgot was your sole reason for going in the first place. Arriving at my destination reveals the mystery.

The lock on the door will be electronic. It's battery operated, so it's independent from Cambridge's power grid, but the electromagnetic pulse took out everything.

Unless...

C'mon, Reggie. Be who I think you are.

I vault up the stairs and pause beside one of the two columns framing the tall doorway. After a quick and very suspicious looking scan of the area, I step up to the entryway. I peer through the windows lining either side of the door, which also stretch a good twenty feet up, and I see no one on the other side—either because they're not there, or because it's pitch black.

But is *everything* in the lab powerless?

I'm about to find out.

I flip up the shield on a digital lock to the side of the door, and even though I'm hoping to see it, I flinch when the screen glows to life. "Yes! I love you, Reg." I place my index finger on the display and swipe out the pattern Reg taught me. But it doesn't matter what pattern I trace out. The display isn't reading the pattern, it's reading my fingerprint. The point of memorizing the movements is to make it look authentic. If someone tries to reproduce it, the security system remains secure *and* records the fingerprint of the would-be intruder, cross-referencing it with law enforcement databases. If it gets a hit, the system alerts the authorities.

The question is, did Reg leave my fingerprint on the approved list? The last time I was here was five years ago. New Year's Eve. A small gathering in a robotics lab. We were served hors d'oeuvres and champagne by a small fleet of primitive robots I later discovered weren't autonomous, but were controlled by a bevy of hidden interns with remote controls. Still, it was close to magical, and Morgan...she was actually magical. I can remember her laugh that night. Her animated conversations with Reggie's M.I.T. buddies, holding her ground with the smartest people in the world, while I sent robots scurrying for more snacks. I was so impressed by the security system that Reg gave me a demonstration, and added my fingerprint so I could try it out for myself.

I haven't been back since. Reggie's party got...rowdy by M.I.T. standards. People didn't take kindly to a naked man riding a Personal Defense Tank being developed for the military rolling down Massachusetts Ave. It was funny as hell. Morgan did a wicked impression of the man, one arm raised, whooping like a wounded bird, cackling as police ran in circles around him, trying to pull him down while suppressing their own laughter.

"Hey," Rain says, holding open the building's door. I didn't hear it unlock. Didn't notice her open it. "You okay?"

I shake the cobwebs of my past away and step toward the door. "Yeah. Sure."

There is another security keypad inside the doorway, but it's fried. Unlike Reggie's personal security measures, the regular security is most likely not hardened against EMPs. So I continue past it, move into the stairwell, and descend two flights to a dark and windowless lab that Reg calls home. The candle guides us the rest of the way. We pause at a second door, windowless and hardwood. It would take a battering ram to get through it. Or the right fingerprint. The door opens for us a moment later, and we step inside the lab...still glowing with the life of modern electronics. I don't know if all of Reggie's gadgets are hardened, but the lab appears to be fully functional.

I sit down at a computer terminal and open Chrome. No connection. A few more attempts on different machines net the same result. The lab is operational, but the systems, lines, wireless networks, and cell towers it might use to connect to the outside world are all down.

When I turn away from the computer, I find Rain standing by a workbench, looking over what appears to be a robot dog...or something. I'm not sure. It has four rigid legs with black, padded feet...and no head. It's a robot. It might not need a head, but it's still creepy.

And probably worth a small fortune.

"I wouldn't touch that," I say, and then I remember the first rule in breaking and entering 101. No fingerprints. I've already left two.

Doesn't matter, I decide. There's no reason to look for us here. No one will know.

But that's not true.

Reg will know. The system will record that someone entered, and will have the fingerprint log of whom.

I'll leave a note, I decide. I trust Reg.

Rain puts the robot down. "Your friend made all of this?"

"Some of it. The students do a lot of the work, but the designs are Reggie's. The patents."

"Huh," she says, giving herself a tour of the lab, which is an odd mix of old and new. The future is being designed and tested in a lab that looks like a cross between the Enterprise and a Gold's Gym, all of it lit by fluorescent rectangles embedded in a water-stained, drop ceiling.

I watch her for a moment. She seems almost innocent as she scours the lab. The world is new to her. She might know what things are, but she has no memory of them. Then again, there are several contraptions here that no one, myself included, in the world outside has seen or even dreamt of yet.

As interesting as all that might be, my thoughts drift.

I settle into the office chair, leaning my head back and closing my eyes.

I replay the night in snippets. The explosion. My phone. The kid being shot. Rain collapsing. Rain glowing. Rain...

I think the Ambien is still working...

A rainbow. It's huge in the sky. I'm home. With a crush from college. She's holding my arm. The affection feels good.

Then she squeezes my arm, turns to me, and says, "Someone's here."

I blink out of the dream. Rain's face is inches from mine. "W-what?"

"Someone. Is. *Here.*" She motions her head to the lab door, which is somehow now on the far side of the room. I look down at my chair. It's on wheels. Rain pushed me here.

When the lab door opens, we duck down together, watching through a shelf covered in metal limbs and body parts, a robotic catacomb. We duck down deeper when someone steps inside, dressed in all black, like some kind of assassin. Or an actual assassin.

How did they find us so fast?

I turn to whisper to Rain, but she's no longer beside me.

10

Rain stalks through the lab, low and predatory, moving on all fours. She's silent, closing in on her oblivious prey.

And me? I'm locked in place. A real chickenshit. My plan was to hide. To hope we were overlooked. Rain's aggressive push has me off balance. Or is that the Ambien? Or the knock to the head?

I should help, but how? I don't know what Rain is doing. She clearly has some kind of plan, and she's executing it. Anything I do could throw a monkey wrench in whatever it is she's up to.

Let her do her thing, I think.

I don't know her. Her past. Her beliefs. Her moral compass. I don't even know her real name. But I have a feeling about her. About what she can do. But it's an ignorant feeling. Will she subdue the maybe-assassin? Will she kill? If so, how? I don't want Reg to find the lab covered in blood.

Stop her, my conscience tells me.

But all I do is crouch and squeeze the shelf supports.

The assassin scans the lab, face concealed by a black mask and shimmering goggles. Intimidation flicks my heart, setting off a palpitation and a surge of adrenaline that focuses my senses.

I notice things I'd missed before. Body language. Body type. Circumstances.

The assassin's stance is casual. Relaxed.

And she's a she...not to say women can't be assassins. Rain's predatory advance leaves little doubt that she's capable of violence to some degree. Or maybe her lack of memory makes her immune to the fear of loss.

My stomach sours.

Don't think about it.

I focus on the assassin again—the assassin who entered this secure lab without kicking down the door.

Her fingerprint is in the system.

And then I understand.

I stand and step out of my hiding spot, as Rain scurries closer. She's hidden behind a crate, easily within striking distance.

Please be right, I think. *Please don't be an assassin.*

"Reg?"

The person I took for a fearless killer yelps at the sound of my voice, throwing up her hands. My would-be assassin is Dr. Regina Adisa. 'Reggie' or 'Reg,' if you're pals. Call her 'Gina,' though, and you'll be on the bad side of someone with an IQ to match Einstein's.

Then she sees me. "Saul?"

Rain stands up from her hiding place just a few feet away from Reg. She's no longer on the prowl, but her sudden appearance draws a scream from Reg, who stumbles back and falls into the arms of a hand-less robot strapped to the wall.

"It's okay," I say, hurrying over to her. "You're okay."

Reg lifts her future-goggles from her eyes, does a double-take at Rain, and then turns to me, reeling in her confusion. "Saul, what the hell?"

"I can explain," I say.

Her fear morphs into suspicion. She gives Rain a once-over. "Why is she wearing Morgan's shirt?"

The Nemesis shirt. I'd shown it to Reg, who also happens to be a fan of the Goddess of Vengeance.

Reg peels her facemask off, revealing dark skin and pulled-back black hair. And suddenly she looks like she could be an assassin. She grips my shirt and forcefully directs me a few feet away from Rain, who's watching us with curiosity.

"Please tell me you are not using my lab as a secret fuck-shack," Reg growls.

"What? No. I—"

"You know that's not what he's doing. Quiet. *He's here for a reason. Find out.* Fine. Fine."

Reg has an odd habit of having conversations with herself. Swears she doesn't have a split personality, but even if she did, I don't think anyone would care. Genius comes with quirks. And Reg often finds solutions to problems by verbally sparring with herself. Her head twists back the other way, and her eyes gaze into mine. "What *are* you doing here?"

"Reg..."

"Do you even know what's happening out there? Or have you been—"

"Reg!" I shout.

The anger in my voice is like a slap in the face for her. She's never even seen me angry, let alone been on the receiving end of it. For a moment, she glares, defiant. Then she sees the pain in my eyes and falters. "What... Why are you here?"

"Hiding," I say, and I quickly follow that up with, "There are people chasing us—"

"Hunting us," Rain adds.

Reggie's eyes flick to my mysterious counterpart, but then home back in on me. *"Hunting you?"*

"They already killed someone," I say. "A kid."

Her expression darkens. She takes a seat, the heaviness of what I'm about to tell her weighing her down in advance. "Who?"

"I don't know his name, but he helped me—"

"I mean, who is hunting you?" Reg says.

"The people who... You saw it. The sky. The power outage."

Reggie's head hangs heavy for a moment, like she's reliving the moment she saw Cambridge enveloped in blue light. "Yeah, I saw it. People in New Hampshire probably saw it. I was in Salem when...but you were here..." Curiosity power-lifts some of the weight away from Reg. "You were at ground zero. What happened? What did you see?"

"What you did, but closer."

I'm trying to get around saying it. Knowing I can't, I look for something to hold onto. I grip a desktop cluttered with metal parts.

"He looks pale," Reggie whispers to herself. *"Not as pale as his friend. I don't trust her. I know. But I trust him."* She nods. When she looks back to me, I wonder if she even knows that little debate was said aloud. "Tell me."

"Ground zero was at SpecTek," I say.

Reg shrinks in on herself. "Morgan..." She doesn't need to ask. If Morgan wasn't there, I wouldn't be here without her. "Have you been to the site?"

"First thing I did," I tell her. "It's gone." Emotion roils up from some dark abyss. I attempt to contain the rising leviathan. My lips tremble. Then my arms. Tears pool. And then, it comes in a moment of monstrous rage. I scream so hard that my voice cracks and fizzles down to a hiss. And then I scream again, the sound of anguish transporting me to another place, where nothing exists.

Human touch snaps me back.

I open my eyes to find the desk overturned, its contents spilled across the floor. "Sorry," I say, embarrassed by what I've done.

"Oh, honey," Reg says. She's kneeling across from me. Tears in her eyes, afraid to ask.

I spare her the discomfort. "She's gone."

"It's a big building, Saul," she says. "Maybe Morgan—"

"The whole building is gone," I say, wiping arm across nose. Blinking away tears. Making room for anger. "There wasn't any debris. It's just gone. Everything above ground, six stories below, and every single person. The only thing left in the whole place..." I turn to Rain, who's looking on with sympathetic eyes. "...was her."

"And she is?" Reggie asks.

"We don't know," Rain says. "But you can call me Rain."

"It's not really her name," I say. "It was on the back of her clothing. Subject 005-RAIN. All caps."

"Subject?" Reg says, eyebrows rising. She's been a scientist all her life. Knows that Morgan was a scientist as well. Might even know more about her work than me. She understands the significance of that word.

What it implies.

"Do you know anything about what she was working on?" she asks.

I shake my head. "She didn't say, and I didn't ask."

"You gotta love NDAs," Reg grumbles. "When was the last time you saw her?"

"Few days ago," I say, and then I correct myself. "She called. FaceTimed. Right when it happened."

"Did you see her..."

"The connection was cut before the final blast."

"What did she say?"

"I...I can't. That—that was for me."

She dips her head, understanding. "What did you see?"

I smile a little bit. Reg is the consummate problem solver. Emotions make her uncomfortable. She did a great job responding to my distress, but I'm sensing her discomfort and her eagerness to move the conversation toward solvable problems, which is fine with me. If I dwell on Morgan, I'll be useless. There will be time for that later. Right now, I need to help Rain and...

Damnit...

...I need to protect Reg. Now that she's seen us. Now that she knows what I do, she's part of this. If they track us here...

Damnit!

"Saul, I can't help you if I don't know everything," Reg says.

I didn't come here for your help, I think, but I keep that to myself. She's part of this shitshow now. Might as well see if her brilliant mind can make sense of what happened tonight.

So I lay it all out for her. Waking up. The shaking. The lights. I tell her what I saw in the FaceTime. The stretching-out man. Rain in the cell. Her body glowing. I tell Reg about the hollowed-out SpecTek facility. The helicopters. The shot kid. Running back to the house. Narrowly escaping the G-men—explaining that it's a loose term for the men-in-black chasing us. And I top it all off with our subway flight, and the circumstances surrounding the two times Rain's body has glowed since all this began— once in the subway, and once outside the library.

"And you were in the subway tunnel during the initial experience?"

"That mean something to you?" I ask.

She shakes her head. "Aside from the glowing, did anything about that event stand out?"

"We weren't alone," Rain says. She's perched on a chair the way Spider-Man crouches on a rooftop, ready to spring into action.

"You saw people?" Reg asks.

"Felt them," I say.

"Two of them," Rain says. "They didn't want us there."

"You *both* felt them?"

I remember the chill. My hair standing on end. "Not really."

"To a scientist," Reg says, "'Not really' is essentially 'Yes.'"

"I didn't feel it like she did." I motion to Rain. "But that was nothing compared to what happened in front of the library."

"Where the student was murdered," she says. It shouldn't surprise me that in Reg's vast treasure trove of knowledge she has information about the one and only M.I.T. student to be murdered at the college. It happened long before her time. She would have been in middle school in San Diego when that went down, but if she reads something, she retains it.

"Murdered?" Rain says, reeling back a little.

"Mugged and murdered," I say.

"You *knew*?" Rain asks, offended that I kept the information from her.

In my defense, she's a complete stranger who was present at the moment of my wife's...disappearance. And Rain freaking glows. I don't really have a solid reason to trust her, and I didn't see how telling her about a murder that happened more than three decades ago would help keep her, or me, calm.

I don't say any of that, though. Instead, I offer, "Hjelp! Jeg trenger hjelp!"

Reggie's curious gaze flinches. "What?"

"I said that," Rain says. "When it happened."

"You speak Norwegian?"

Rain shakes her head.

"*Help*," Reg says. "*I need help*. That's what you said."

Rain gives me a worried look. Spontaneously speaking another language would be enough to freak out anyone. It's the kind of thing that happens in the Bible, not the twenty-first century. But we need all the information we can get, and I have no doubt that Rain's...condition is directly related to what SpecTek was working on.

"What about..." I try to recall the words. "...Jeg blør. Ikke...la meg dø! Han stakk...meg i magen...med...en kniv!"

I feel like I've done a bad job enunciating the phrase, but the look on Reg's face says I got close enough. *"I'm bleeding,"* she says, her dark brown eyes burrowing into me. *"Don't let me die! He stabbed me in the stomach."* She turns to Rain. "And when you spoke that, you felt another presence?"

Rain nods. "He was...angry."

"That's because he was murdered, in 1992. What you felt in the tunnel could have been homeless people. I can only guess how many have sheltered and died down there over time."

"Wait," I say. "Hold on. Are you saying—"

"That they're ghosts?" Reg leans forward, not a trace of humor in her eyes. "Yes."

11

Cambridge is in chaos. Killers are chasing me. I'm partnered with a mystery woman who glows. And my wife is missing, maybe...probably dead. I'm having a shitty night. But when Reg says, 'Ghosts,' I can't help but laugh.

Not just because the notion of ghosts is ridiculous, or that Rain is some kind of living soul detector, but because the suggestion is coming from Dr. Regina Adisa, whose belief system includes only that which can be proven via the scientific method. Cold hard facts. Even scientific theories largely regarded as true—like the Big Bang theory—she doesn't consider as fact until they can be proven beyond a reasonable doubt... until they are no longer just theories.

"You're not serious?" I say.

"Let me be clear," Reg says. "I am in no way claiming that ghosts, defined as the supernatural remnants of some angsty soul trapped on the mortal plane, are real."

Reg walks across the lab, opens a mini-fridge that blends in perfectly with all the robotics equipment and gear, and returns with three bottled waters, which she hands out. She cracks her bottle open, chugs a quarter of it, and wipes her mouth. "However, that is a hypothesis. While science has yet to prove a supernatural realm exists, it also hasn't *disproved* it. Believing alternate dimensions exist requires the same leap of faith. And there are alternatives, which are likewise unproven."

She takes another swig. Rain and I hold our waters, but neither of us drink. We're like two dogs, focused on the treat that is Reg's supernatural diatribe, unable to think about anything else.

"Some think that ghosts are interdimensional beings that we experience when whatever veil between dimensions exists grows thin. This isn't my favorite hypothesis, because it doesn't explain why people see relatives or events from the past. Also, a prerequisite to this hypothesis is that other dimensions of reality exist...which we're nowhere close to proving.

"My favorite hypothesis is what I call chronological residue; events from the past somehow, perhaps because of their intensity, affect time and space—which we know for a fact isn't linear. Ghosts might be nothing more than echoes of past events. Think of it like a streaming movie from thirty years ago, and somehow your mystery friend here—" she smiles at Rain, "—is tuned into whatever frequency is flickering its way through time. That still doesn't explain why people see Granny in her old rocking chair, but there are plenty of other hypotheses to explain those encounters. Mold exposure. Carbon Monoxide poisoning. Acid flashbacks. Hell, too much NyQuil could probably do it. But the hallucinations of some people don't mean all ghost sightings *are* hallucinations. In the case of Rain, get an umbrella."

Reg laughs at her own joke, but it peters out when she notices neither Rain nor I are joining her. Reg takes another swig. "In...your situation. You both saw and felt the same thing. Rain's body was reacting to something outside of her, and she spoke a language she doesn't know how to speak...all of this after surviving an event that defies explanation. She's either totally in tune with a frequency of chronological residue, which would be fascinating and a Nobel-worthy discovery, or..."

I lean forward, eyebrows raised. "Or?"

"Ghosts." Reg smiles. "Of the more traditional variety. As you move forward, I suggest keeping all ideas that haven't been disproven on the table. After all, what we now call science has traditionally been treated as supernatural until someone has figured out how to understand it. Billions of people hold the supernatural realm to be quite real, including many scientists in fields that society assumes are made up of atheists. There are plenty of physicists, biologists, and geneticists who believe not just in the supernatural, but who go to church every Sunday and pray to a deity whose existence will likely never be proven by science. Not because it doesn't exist, but because something that can create the known universe would be beyond our ability to comprehend."

She looks back and forth between Rain and me. "I'm rambling. Sorry. None of this helps your current predicament."

"I'm not sure about that," I say. "Understanding motive almost always exposes the criminal." I crack open my water bottle. Take a sip. Then another. "So, spirits of the dead or not, would it be safe to assume that SpecTek was working on some kind of supernatural science?"

"That's an oxymoron," Reg says. "Something cannot be both supernatural *and* science. Something can metamorphose from the former to the latter, but it cannot be both, and it cannot reverse course."

"You know what I mean," I say. Reggie has a tendency to take things literally. I once said 'Holy shit,' in front of her, and she spent twenty minutes explaining why shit can't be holy, and how 'bullshit' was a better term to use.

She takes a moment to collect her thoughts. While she does, I glance at Rain, who has fallen silent. She's probably wondering whether or not she's a believer in the supernatural. With no memory of her past self, her beliefs and biases might have been erased, too.

"Was SpecTek researching the science behind supernatural phenomena?" Reg says, attempting to consume and regurgitate my question in a more accurate format. "It's...possible. But improbable. I was under the impression that SpecTek's primary benefactor was the U.S. government, which, in case you didn't know, in the science world, means DARPA."

"DARPA?" Rain asks.

"Defense Advanced Research Projects Agency," I say. "They're a government agency that figures out how to make awesome science into deadly weapons."

"That's a...crude description of their mandate, but not inaccurate," Reg says. "Not all of their programs kill people. Most are focused on saving or improving lives."

"But you don't work for them?" Rain asks.

"God, no," Reg says. "I don't want my robots killing people!"

I throw my hands up. "But you just—"

"Saul. When it comes to robots, there are generally only two things people think to do with them—put holes in other people, or fill them."

I groan.

She waves her hands. "Just...bad joke. Sorry. But you won't find any silicon in this lab. Or guns. I want my creations on other planets. In surgery suites. At the bottom of the ocean. I want to expand the world's knowledge, not...you know."

"Killing people," Rain says, with a nod of approval.

"So, what then?" I ask.

"The results of their experimentation were highly destructive and unexpected. It's not uncommon for scientists working on the fringe of tactile sciences—" she looks at Rain, "—who are laboring in the real world, rather than working out math problems or thought experiments, to meet their end when unexpected..." Her eyes flick back to me. Toward my growing despair. "Sorry. I'm being insensitive."

"But you're not wrong," I say, forcing myself to sit up straight and take another drink, to hide my awkward recovery. "They were messing with something they shouldn't have been."

"Shouldn't might be too far. I think the sciences are the most noble and natural pursuit in which a person can endeavor. They can be twisted and used for ill gain, but the human race has benefited more from those willing to push boundaries than it has been harmed. SpecTek was certainly not cautious enough, and the morally questionable way in which they conducted their research—" A glace at Rain. "—suggests that SpecTek cared more about 'could' than 'should.' It shows a disturbing lack of responsibility to the rights of the individual, not to mention the surrounding community."

I lean forward, pinching my nose.

Despite Reggie's insights, her long-winded logic is starting to overwhelm me. And she doesn't miss it.

"We can talk about this later." She places a gentle hand on my shoulder. "You need to sleep. Both of you. When you're rested, we can consider next steps."

"No offense," I say. "But your lab isn't exactly cozy. And sleep..." I shake my head. I'm not sure I'll ever sleep again.

"I was in Salem, remember. My car is fine. My house has power."

"I don't want to put you in danger," I say.

"Probably too late for that, right?"

"I'm sorry."

She gives my shoulder a squeeze. "I'm glad you came. And I'm happy to help."

"Even if it means dying?" I ask.

She shrugs and grins. "Quickest way to solve that ghost mystery, right?" She stands and motions for us to follow her. "C'mon. Better to not be here if they track you to the lab. Unlike you, they won't have a key, and I'll get an alarm if they kick down the door."

When I stand to follow her, Rain catches my arm. The intensity of her glare asks a single question, which I answer with, "We can trust her. I promise."

Given what I suspect happened to Rain, it wouldn't surprise me if she had a natural fear of scientists. Even if she can't remember what happened. But I've earned her trust. I'm not sure I'll trust *her* completely until she remembers who she is, but right now, she's still my one-and-only path to figuring out what happened, and whether there's even a slim chance of Morgan being alive.

"And she's right," I say. "Better to get out of Cambridge."

Reluctance falters and then fades. We exit the lab like three thieves tip-toeing out of a bank vault, checking every nook and cranny for watching eyes, before slipping out of the lab, back outside M.I.T., and to the street, where Reggie's vehicle awaits. I stop next to the short, lime-green Prius.

"This is your car?" Rain asks. She's short and thin, but still looks big beside the vehicle. "If they spot us—"

"They won't," I say with false confidence. "Also: shotgun."

Rain doesn't remember her life, but she seems to understand the etiquette of calling front-seat dibs. She rolls her eyes and opens the back door, sliding down into the vehicle. I have to adjust the seat to fit, but I manage to slip inside and shut the door, just as a helicopter thunders overhead.

We sit still and silent for a moment, as it circles the campus. On the outside, I look calm—I'm trying to, anyway—but my heart is pounding. When the helicopter heads to the North End, I say, "Slow and calm. Like you're not running for your life."

Reggie puts the car in drive and pulls away from the curb. Our drive east along the Charles River is slowed by traffic flowing in from Boston. Much of it is emergency services, but a large number of vehicles are curious people—mostly young people—heading across the river to learn what they can. The light show from Boston highrise apartment buildings must have been spectacular. Without working traffic signals, we're dependent on the mercy of others when we arrive at intersections, and since this is Boston... Well, it takes a while.

Ten minutes later, we're stuck at the intersection of Edward H. Land Boulevard and the Charles River Dam Road. The Museum of Science is to our right. Beyond that icon of my childhood is the nighttime Boston skyline. After three minutes of false starts, I say, "You're going to have to be more aggressive."

"Hard to be aggressive in a Prius," Reggie says.

I'm about to suggest that I drive, when I notice the car's interior growing brighter. I glance in the side mirror, expecting to see a vehicle approaching from behind, hoping it's not a black SUV. But I see nothing. I turn around the other way, intending to look out the rear window, but my eyes never make it past Rain.

She's glowing.

Bright.

I squint as her fear-filled eyes flicker to life and flare bright blue.

12

"Uhh," I say, and I take hold of Reggie's arm.

She turns to me. "What—" Her head swivels toward Rain. "Whoa..."

Screeching tires pull my attention to the intersection. Two cars collide. Nothing serious, but the drivers aren't shouting at each other, trying to place blame, or complaining about the damage. They're staring at the Prius. At the glowing woman in the backseat.

And their faces are cast in blue light.

Our car is shining like a beacon. If the helicopters know what they're looking for, we'll be easy to spot.

"We need to cover her up!" I shout, considering removing my shirt to throw over her.

"Behind your seat," Reggie says. "On the floor."

Rain might be glowing like a lightbulb, but she's still with us. Still herself. She bends down, plucks the folded blanket from the floor, and yanks it open. Sand sprinkles throughout the car, some of it in my mouth. While I spit the granules out, Rain cloaks herself beneath the blanket, leaving just a small slit for her to see through.

"Sorry about the sand," Reg says. "It's my beach blanket."

The light shining through the blanket strobes. Rain shouts in surprised discomfort, her voice sputtering in time with the flicker.

"Get us out of here!" I shout.

Before Reg can hit the gas, Rain leans forward and grasps her arm. "No! That way!" Her glowing gaze turns right, toward the Museum of Science. Toward Boston. "It's going that way."

"It?" I say.

"I think she wants us to follow a ghost," Reg says, eyes wide.

Rain coils in discomfort.

"It's hurting you," I argue. "We should get away—"

"I need to know," Rain says, her voice almost a growl. "What I am. Who I am. And you do, too."

"It's a compelling argument," Reg says. "Sometimes answers can only be found at the end of a breadcrumb trail."

"Or in an evil witch's candy house," I grumble, turning my attention to the Boston skyline. The city looks peaceful. Nothing intimidating there. No helicopters either. *Why not?* "Go for it."

Reg turns the wheel and hits the gas. The prospect of a scientific discovery eradicates her timidity behind the wheel. She lays on the horn, squeals tires, and tears past the Museum of Science like the hounds of hell are chasing us.

Once we're over the bridge and entering the city, Reg slows down. The police presence is intense. Patrol cars everywhere. They don't know what happened, and they're responding like it was a terrorist attack. If they see Rain's glow we might be stopped and searched.

What will they do when faced with a glowing woman who looks like she could explode?

God, I hope she doesn't explode.

Reg glances back. "What are you feeling?"

Rain shivers beneath the blanket. "It's...intense..."

"Figured that out already," Reg says, and then to herself. *"Don't be a snark. She's dealing with a lot. Fine."*

"I feel energy," Rain say, oblivious to Reggie's dialogue. "It feels warm...and cold...if that makes sense. It's moving through me. And...I can feel it in my head."

"Like pressure?" I ask. "A headache?"

She shakes her head. "Voices."

I'm frozen for a moment. Hearing her speak Norwegian was freaky enough. I don't really want to experience it again. But the more we understand about what's happening... "Can you hear what they're saying?"

"Him," Rain says.

"Him...who?"

"It's not a they. It's a him." Rain's light flickers again and then goes dark. She gasps and presses into the back of her seat. Then she lurches forward and points down Cambridge Street. "That way!"

Reg follows her directions, making a last-second left turn that takes us straight toward downtown.

Are we really chasing a ghost through Boston? I wonder. How does that even work? If it's a ghost in the traditional sense—a human spirit—how is it moving? I thought they haunted the place in which they died? And if it's an echo from the past, who the hell made this journey in a way that bent time and space? Paul Revere?

Okay, that would be cool, but how does it help us find out what happened to Morgan?

Where are you, baby?

I tune out the car, the city, and the sirens filling the air.

She was home just a few days ago. We had pizza. Watched *Back to the Future,* again. She has a thing for 80s movies, especially the lighthearted ones. She wore the footie pajamas I bought her for Christmas last year. I see her in the living room chair, feet up on the ottoman, popcorn in her lap. The way she laughed, more at her own running commentary on the movie, than at the movie itself. The night ended in bed. No sex. Just curled up together, me sleeping well.

A horn blare shocks me out of the past.

The Prius swerves left and then right, narrowly avoiding being T-boned by a large truck. I turn back. Our light is green.

Why did he run the red light? I wonder, and then I notice the city's lights, all around us now, are flickering.

As is Rain.

We're catching up to the ghost...and it's affecting the whole city, not just Rain.

With every light in the city turning off and on, it feels like we've entered the world's largest rave. And then everything takes on a blue hue, as though lit from above by a giant fluorescent bulb.

"Shit," I whisper, leaning forward to look up through the windshield. But the car is too small for me to look up past the skyscrapers blocking my view. So I roll down the window and lean outside like a dog. I'm struck by warm air and the smell of ozone.

Then I look up.

"*Shiiit.*"

Clouds swirl above the city, pulsing with the same blue light emanating from Rain's body.

It's happening again.

"Does SpecTek have another lab in Boston?"

The question was rhetorical. I didn't expect anyone to have an answer, but Reg says, "They have labs in Chicago and Austin. Cambridge was their only lab in the Northeast." When I give her a 'For real?' look, she adds, "Their work is secret. Their locations are not." She shrugs. "I keep up."

"I can feel him again," Rain says, voice quivering. "He's here."

"Here?" I ask, looking around the street. We're on State Street, surrounded by massive, flashing buildings. "I don't see—"

But then I do.

The memorial is so subtle that most people miss it. Only those walking along the Freedom Trail's red-lined path usually take note. The cobblestone circle is of immense importance, not just to Boston, but to the United States as a whole. It marks the location where the very first patriots gave their lives in rebellion against the British throne, four years before the more well-known Boston Tea Party. What started as a scuffle, with a single Red Coat, ended in a bloodbath that sparked a movement, which gave birth to a nation.

Is this the event that Rain is connecting to? If Reggie's chronological residue hypothesis is right, a massacre that shaped all of history since would surely fit the bill.

But Rain is sensing only one person. A him.

Not a them.

"Can you hear me?" I ask Rain, trembling beneath her blanket. "Can you hear him? What he's saying?"

I can't see her face, but the way the light flickers from within the blanket, I can tell she's shaking her head.

"Can you focus?" I ask. "Try to control it. Contain it."

"We don't know what it is," Reg says. "How can you expect her to—"

"I can try," Rain says, voice strained. Her body stiffens. She sits up straighter, revealing her face. Pulses of blue energy flow through her skin. Her luminous eyes are brilliant and pinched, as she furrows her brow in concentration. The light dulls, but it takes intense effort.

"It's..." Rain grimaces. "It's looking for an outlet."

"For what?" I ask.

"Rage."

As the word escapes her mouth, something moves through me. It's like a magnet has tugged on my soul for a moment. It's followed by a chill, and the hair on my arms standing on end.

A stunned Reggie stares at her arm, hair on end, too. "I felt that," she whispers. Louder, to me. "I *felt* that."

"Can you hear what he's saying?" I ask Rain.

"Turn right!" she says, and Reggie follows the instruction, taking us the wrong way down a one-way street. At the end, Rain says, "Left," and we follow the path as the storm above builds. Wind-swept trash spins through the air. While some people gather in windows, silhouetted by their flashing lights, others decide to get out of Dodge, some in vehicles, some on bikes, but most are running in the streets.

After a series of rapid-fire directions, Rain shouts, "Stop! He's here."

Reggie and I look out the windows. We're stopped in McKinley Square, at the base of the Custom House Tower, a five-hundred-foot-tall building that looks like a bell tower, sans the church at its base. Once upon a time, it stood on Boston's waterfront, looking out over the Atlantic, but the city's land reclamation efforts separated the building from the sea by several blocks.

I turn back to Rain, who's no longer hiding beneath the blanket, but also no longer glowing as brightly. I don't think the...signal, or whatever it is, is less intense here. If she's right, it's *more* intense.

She's just controlling the effect it has on her body. Or containing it. Who knows how it works. But the look on her face says it's not easy.

"Can you hear him now?" I ask.

Her face relaxes for a moment, and then twists with anguish. "I...hear him. He's... I can't understand. There's too much emotion."

"Can you let us hear?" Reggie asks.

I think that's a spectacularly bad idea.

Whatever is happening is powerful enough to affect the whole city. What's going to happen to Rain if she allows it to move through her?

Before I can voice my concern, Rain says, "Yes."

Her body goes rigid, her inner illumination is bright enough to make me squint. Her eyes are like a car's high beams, and when she opens her mouth, light emerges. I have flashbacks of a movie. *Big Trouble in Little China*, I think. What was his name? Lo Pan? The light streaming from his eyes and mouth. This is the same, but the sound...

It's unlike anything I've ever heard.

Rain screams. Her high-pitched voice becomes like the roaring of a waterfall. The volume of it forces my hands to my ears. And then, all at once, Rain and the city go dark.

13

The inky darkness around us inspires nothing but fear.

"This is not good," Reggie says. I'm about to respond when she does it for me, talking to herself again. *"No kidding. But what could it be? It's not atmospheric.* Not true. I saw the storm. But that's a byproduct. Like the lights. *So what's causing the—"*

Rain's light returns with the suddenness of a nuclear blast. I flinch back, hitting my head on the low ceiling. Reggie lets out a yelp that morphs into a scream, when the city shakes and the light show resumes.

The quake thumps once, jouncing the car.

Outside, chaos grips the panicked throng. People flee in all directions.

They don't know what they're running from or where to go, but if what happened in Cambridge is being reported as a terrorist attack, their frantic flight response is understandable.

What changed? I wonder, looking to the sky again. The clouds roil with flashing light, swirling around a dark core of clear night sky positioned directly above us.

Rain has led us to the storm's eye.

"I'm starting to think this might be a bad idea," I say.

"Wait," Rain says, struggling to contain her brilliance again. "It's getting closer."

"It?" I say. "I thought *it* was a *he?*"

Rain either ignores me or doesn't hear me. Teeth grind. Hands clench. Her light dims.

What the hell are you?

Rain makes a solid effort, but then loses the fight with a gasp that turns her face toward the ceiling. Her back arches. "Coming..." she says. "Here..." Then she lurches forward, glowing eyes staring past me and Reg, out through the windshield.

The car is thumped again, bouncing off the road for a moment.

"That's not an earthquake," I say, slowly turning to face whatever it is Rain is looking at. "It feels like..."

I see the impossible, slipping into and out of reality a few hundred feet away. But I'm not seeing the whole thing...just part of it.

Just...a limb.

An arm.

A two-fingered, emaciated hand the size of a house, knuckles down in the street.

The pale skin flows with long, luminous hairs that ebb and flow like they're underwater, but the skin looks dry, like someone came along with a giant peeler and partially peeled back flakes of flesh, exposing the luminous blue beneath.

The way the meat of it compresses and cracks suggest it's support-ing immense weight, but all I can see is an arm, tapering up a hundred feet and out of existence. Whatever it's connected to must be...massive. Hundreds of feet tall.

An ethereal cloud flows through the city. A living thing, flashing with thunderless lightning.

"This isn't possible," Reggie says. "This can't be real."

"Pretty sure we're all seeing the giant white arm," I say, and then I motion to the people outside the vehicle, now fleeing in a unified direction—away from the arm. "Mass hallucination?"

Reggie shakes her head. "It's not a real thing. Mass hysteria, sure. Happens all the time. This..." She motions outside the car. "This is real hysteria. Mass delusion. Even more common. Politicians and corpor-ations propagate mass delusion on a daily basis. But mass hallucination,

in which a group of people of different backgrounds, ages, living situ-
ations, beliefs, and preference in media—all of which affects what we
hallucinate—doesn't exist." She looks through the windshield again.
"We're all seeing the same damn thing...because it's real."

Her eyes flare wider. "And it's coming this way!"

The long arm lifts off the ground and swings forward, sliding a
hundred feet closer before slamming back to the pavement. A car
folds inward and explodes beneath the arm's weight. I follow the
flames upward. The limb is longer now, stretching high up into the
air, but I don't see a body.

"It's angry," Rain says.

"Shit!" I shout with a start. I'd forgotten she was there.

*How the hell do you forget about a glowing woman in the back
seat?!*

When there's a ghost-monster-thing stomping toward you, I respond to
myself, realizing that if I'd verbalized the debate, I would have sounded
a lot like Reggie.

"And afraid," she says. "It's confused..."

"Can you communicate with it?" Reggie asks.

Rain shakes her head. Fast little tics, side to side. I don't know if that's
a solid 'No' or an 'I'm not going to freaking try.' Either way, I think it's a
bad idea. The less attention we draw to ourselves the better. In fact,
I think it's time we make ourselves scarce. We're not going to get any
answers if we're pancaked in the middle of the street.

"Get us out of here," I tell Reggie.

"But look at it." Reggie is being guided by scientific curiosity. It's
making her overlook her own mortality. "This is going to change the
world."

"We won't be around to see a changed world if it takes another
step!" I shout. The upper end of the arm is leaning forward, like some
other hand somewhere is stepping forward.

And then I hear it.

The thunderous roar of a collapsing building. To the right, the
building behind the Custom House Tower crumbles to the ground
like it was kicked.

When I see a second, luminous white limb slam down amidst the debris, I know that's exactly what happened.

How is this possible?

I thought ghosts were intangible.

Shouldn't it be sliding through the buildings?

Shouldn't it be a shit-ton smaller?

Ghosts are supposed to be the spirits of people. As far as I know, they look like people, too. This...is something else. Or was. If it's a ghost at all.

Thoughts of the unreal are replaced by sobering thoughts of reality.

How many people were hiding in that building?

How many people were nearby when it collapsed?

My questions are erased when a billowing, gray dust cloud roars toward us between buildings. "Reggie!"

Reggie puts the car in reverse, lays on the horn, and hits the gas. She swings an arm over my seat and twists around to look out the back window. "What—get down!" she shouts at Rain, whose glowing face is blocking her view.

Pedestrians scatter away from the onrushing vehicle, clearing a path for us, even as they run for their lives. While Reggie looks back, twitching the vehicle left and right to avoid people, I turn forward and watch the thing we're all running away from.

Pulses of light shoot up through the limb, extending what can be seen, and revealing what *might* be a shoulder joint. The glowing hairs react to each pulse, fluttering as they pass.

Weight shifts and lifts away.

"Here it comes!" I shout.

The fingers rise from the ground, revealing a crater in the pavement, reaching from one side of the street to the other.

As the arm swings toward us, trailing a cloud of dust, I look up again, imagining the size and position of its unseen body. It's not there...but it is. And if it comes into contact with the physical world... My eyes drift higher. Custom House Tower is five hundred feet tall, much of it solid granite. Untold tons. It will all come crashing down, right toward us.

The horror I see next replaces those conjured by my imagination.

People run through the streets in our wake, trying to escape. Most are dressed for bed. All of them are screaming. And the lot of them are oblivious to the massive arm swooping through the air like a wrecking ball. I see flashes of what will happen to their bodies upon impact, but I reassess when the limb slides through the dust cloud ejected by the collapsed building without creating any wake or disturbing the flow.

Is it only material when it steps down? I wonder.

For a moment, I think the people it's about to strike will be okay. But then it reaches them.

No one explodes. That's the only positive thing I can say about what happens next. As the twenty-foot-wide, two-fingered fist swings down the street, each and every person it passes through falls to the ground with a wail of agony. Glowing blue wisps are yanked from their bodies. Pulled up into the beast's flesh.

It's taking their souls, I think, despite the fact that I don't believe souls exist.

When the bodies hit the ground, they're nothing more than desiccated husks dressed in loose fitting clothing.

I shrink into my seat, unable to speak or scream.

The fist slams into the ground just a few feet shy of the Prius. The impact bounces the car into the air.

A deep cold burns my skin for a moment. Then the tires return to the pavement and we screech away.

"Reggie..." I say.

"Don't want to know!" she shouts.

I look up as something high above flickers into view. A body? An eye? Many eyes? I see it for just a moment, but it's enough to let me know I never want to see it again. The brief flicker into reality is also enough to collide with, and knock over, the top half of the Custom House Tower.

14

"Faster!" I scream. There must be something in my high-pitched panic—the sound of a man who knows he's about to die—that resonates with Reggie. She slams on the gas and throws caution to the wind. It's do or die time. If she has to thump a few people on the way, I'm sure our future selves will look back on this moment with regret. But right now, in the moment, no one is analyzing choices, because they're not really choices at all.

They're knee-jerk reactions built into our DNA, meant to keep us alive. And if you want to get logical about it…no one, short of an Olympic sprinter, has any hope of outrunning the collapsing tower. And I don't see Usain Bolt anywhere.

Thankfully, Reggie doesn't run anyone over, or even bump anyone. Turns out my fellow Bostonians are smarter than the genius behind the steering wheel, or maybe they learned the real lesson taught by the movie *Prometheus*: when something tall falls toward you, don't run away. Run to the side. The street clears as people head north en masse, through alleys and side streets.

I nearly suggest we do the same, but my conscience catches up with me before the falling tower. Taking the car down one of those tight spaces would mean running over a large number of people to save just three. Not even Spock would agree with that logic.

We need to outrun the tower or—

Darkness.

The world shakes outside and inside my body.

I'm thrown upward and then wrenched back down, pummeled on all sides.

Metal shrieks. Snaps.

We didn't make it... We didn't—

I see light. It's bright. Hurts my eyes.

It's Rain in the backseat. The brightness cast by her face cuts through the dust now flowing through the car's interior.

I'm not dead.

But I haven't escaped the Grim Reaper yet.

Grit fills my lungs, forcing great heaving coughs from my chest. I lift my shirt and bunch it in front of my mouth, breathing and coughing.

When the dust starts to settle, the world remade coalesces around me. The Prius's hood has been crushed by a granite block, flattened like an empty tin can underfoot.

Debris surrounds the car. When the tower fell, it also came apart. While most of the building fell short of us, stones ejected from the collapse sprayed out into the street.

"You okay?" I ask Reggie.

She cricks her neck back and forth. "Shook up, is all."

I turn back to Rain and jolt when I find myself face-to-face with her intensely glowing eyes.

"Get out!" She gives me a shove. "GET OUT!"

When a giant monster is rampaging through a city and a skyscraper has just narrowly missed falling on your head, you don't think twice when a glowing woman screams at you to get out. I shove open the Prius door, flop onto my hands and knees, and then break into a sprint. As I bunny-hop through the debris, a quick glance to my right confirms that Reggie is with me, more fleet-footed than I would have guessed.

I look farther back, expecting to see Rain, but she's not there. The Prius's interior warbles with bright light, as she kicks at the back door, trying to get out.

Pebbles grind beneath my feet as I slide to a stop.

My moral debate team is working overtime today. Should I go back and help her? The argument against this course of action comes from a block to my right, where the second glowing appendage is kicking its way through another building.

How long do I have before the soul-sucking fist slides forward again? Seconds?

And what about after that?

Behind me stand six of Boston's largest skyscrapers, dwarfing the Custom House Tower, both in height and girth. If this thing plows through those with equal ease, there isn't going to be anywhere I can run...if I don't leave now.

Rain weighs in with an angry, "GO!"

When I see her slide into the front seat, heading for my working door, I obey. Reggie is a good half block ahead of me now. I don't know if she'll be able to hear me over the rumble of destruction and the cacophony of screams, but I try anyway. "Reggie! Head for North Station!"

Clear of the rubble, I look back again.

Rain is on her feet and on the move. I thought Reggie was quick, but Rain is like lightning, her legs a blur as she weaves her way through the debris field, propelled by Morgan's pink Swoosh Nikes. Dust billows out of alleys on the southern side of the street, kicked up by whatever building has just finished falling to the ground. But I don't lose sight of Rain. Her brilliance shines through the darkness.

It's staggering.

If not for the massive glowing leg rising up behind her, I might have stopped to watch.

"It's coming!" I shout.

Rain slips out of the cloud without missing a step. At our current paces, she'll pass me in ten seconds.

If she makes it that far.

The limb swings toward us.

A group of coughing and wailing people emerge from the debris cloud in Rain's wake. *They're following her light,* I realize...*straight toward oblivion.*

None of them see the two knuckles sweeping toward them. I suppose there is some mercy in that. They're alive and running and desperate, one moment. And then it moves through them, leaching their lives away with the quickness of a gunshot.

The shock of seeing that happen again is overwritten by the realization that Rain is next.

I open my mouth to shout a warning, but even as I do, I know it won't make a difference.

"Rain!" I shout, as the bus-sized hand swings through her.

I lose sight of her glow a moment later, as the limb continues its arc—straight toward me.

I bolt to the side, diving into an alley.

A chill grips my legs, but doesn't hold on. Behind me, the hand thunders down, filling the street. Shards of pavement jut up like crushed peanut brittle. Its weight is immense, even though most of it hasn't fully resolved.

But will it? I wonder, eyes wandering upward. Pulses of energy reveal a little more at a time, stretching not just up, but back. The creature is as long as it is tall, but I can't see its back side. It could end in more legs, or a slithering body, or tentacles for all I know. But it's there, wreaking havoc. I can hear it in the distance, wading through Boston.

Show yourself, I think in anger, afraid to voice it, in case the thing actually hears me.

A haunted howl rolls through the city, coming from far above. The monster's still-translucent head is present enough to roar. And it sounds...tormented.

For a moment, I feel bad for the thing.

And then a bright light on ground level catches my attention. It bounces and weaves a course around the giant limb, cutting through grime and smoke until it emerges.

"Rain!" I shout, wearing my befuddlement on my face like a neon billboard in downtown Tokyo.

"I know," she says, just as surprised by her still-living status as I am.

She bends over to help me up, and I find myself staring at her shirt—at Morgan's shirt, featuring the Queen of Monsters herself... I can't help but chuckle. "That has to be the most ironic shirt in the—whoa!" Rain yanks me to my feet.

"Go!" She shouts, giving me a shove. "It's not done yet!"

We flee through the city, heading toward North Station. Rain is faster than me, but without her memory, she has no way of plotting a course. Might not be able to if she *had* her memory. For all we know, she's from Florida or Ohio or something.

"How much farther?" Rain asks, when I reduce my pace to a cramp-slowed walk.

"Couple blocks," I say.

"Where are we going?"

"Train station."

"Will there be enough room?" she asks.

"Enough room?" I ask. "There's just the three of us." I scour the street ahead, looking for signs of Reggie. She's not a Bostonian by birth, but she's been here long enough to navigate her way to North Station...if she heard me.

"More than three," Rain says, motioning behind us.

In the glow of Rain's light, I see a throng of people following us. For them, she's a beacon. A sign of where to go. And they're going to follow us straight toward the train station. Hundreds of them.

I cup my hands. "Reggie!" I wait a moment, and then repeat, "Reggie!"

"I'm here," replies a faint voice. Reggie emerges from the throng, holding someone's dusty, petrified child in her arms.

Our reunion is cut short when Rain's body flickers and then grows brighter. She moans and staggers into my arms.

"What's happening?" I ask.

"I'm not..." She looks up.

The monster's massive body—four hundred feet tall and somehow even longer—covered in twisting, luminous coils, and loose, white skin shimmers into view. A long, thin neck leads to an emaciated head, covered by long, flowing white hair, all of it framing a face of eyeballs. There might be a hundred of them, ranging in size from basketball to SUV. And all at once, every single one of them turns toward us.

Not us, I think.

Rain.

"I think it's after you," I say, wondering how I can tell all these people to stop following us.

But Rain shakes her head and looks up, toward North Station.

Above North Station.

I stagger to a stop beside Reggie, whose jaw has gone slack.

"Well, fuck," Reggie says. "There're two of them…"

15

It's like seeing something in your periphery, but looking straight at it. There, but not. A hint of a thing not yet coalesced into reality.

While the first ghostly giant projects brute strength, this one flows. Wisps of it come and go. Luminous tendrils, like sheets in a breeze. I never see more than ten percent of its transparent form at a time, but slowly I put together a basic, headless picture.

And it's haunting.

Twisting coils of what look like living fabric flow around the creature and stretch out hundreds of feet. The...tentacles...for lack of a better word, delicately pick a path through the city. I can't see where it's stepping or the destruction it's causing, but I get the impression that it's being careful.

While the brute—*Just 'Brute,'* I decide—is indifferent to people, or perhaps worse, seeking people out, this new otherworldly being is...gentle.

Every neuron in my mind is firing off the same signal: *Run!* But this new monster instills no fear.

In me, at least. Everyone with me screams in horror, frantic for a new escape route.

Rain, like me, appears unfazed by the newcomer. Or perhaps she remains more concerned about the more immediate danger ravaging the city behind us.

"We need to keep going," I say, looking to...

Wisp.

"I know," she says, and she takes Reggie by the arm before she can bolt west. With the ocean to the east, a monster to the north and south, west is the only clear choice...unless you've got nothing left to lose.

"Hey!" Reggie tugs her arm, but can't escape Rain's firm grasp.

"Not that way," Rain points at Wisp. "This way!"

Reggie is about to argue, when a building crumbles behind us. The sound of it knocks the air from our lungs. The air itself shakes, sending a vibration through my body that's unnerving. I glance back at Brute, stepping closer, sucking up glowing blue souls as it passes through people on the street, trapped in buildings, or dying in the rubble.

"Now!" I shout, grabbing Reggie's arm and yanking her behind me, as Rain and I resume our course for North Station and toward Wisp—now heading straight for us.

We spill out into the large Y-shaped intersection in front of Boston's impressive Edward W. Brooke Courthouse. I've spent many hours inside the building, waiting to hear whether one criminal or another was going to walk free or head to jail. At times, the building felt more like my office than my actual office did.

I give the building a glance as we head across the intersection, dodging vehicles as they flee the scene. Had this happened during daylight hours, when the city's population swells from just over 600,000 to 1.2 million, it would be a chaotic deathtrap. That's not a lot compared to Los Angeles, or New York, but with only ninety square miles within the city limits, Boston is one of the most densely populated cities in the U.S.

The death toll is going to be in the thousands, if not more, by the time Brute finishes its tour of the city. *If* it finishes. What it's here for and how long the monster is staying are mysteries.

All I really know is that we need to get the hell out of the city, or we won't be alive to find out the answers. And you better bet your God-damned life I'm going to get answers.

An image of Morgan flashes in my memory. Its painful flare focuses me.

Face forward. Keep moving. Right toward Wisp.

The ghostly creature is rising up over the buildings in front of us. A block of shorter, brick buildings are all that separate us from Boston Garden. Some of these buildings have survived the past three hundred years. I have a feeling they won't make it through the night, though.

A roar spins me around. Brute kicks its way through the massive Government Center Garage, a lasagna of concrete and steel that should have been able to survive a nuclear blast. It's pulverized by the monster, whose many eyes seem to be locked on me.

Has it even seen Wisp?

Does it care?

I duck my head as concrete bits explode into the air. The fragments pepper the crowd of people still following us. Their numbers have reduced since Wisp appeared, but some of them still believe the glowing woman might know best. I'm not sure if their logic, or mine, will lead to death, but most of us are lemmings at heart. We follow whoever leads the pack and hope for the best.

Screams of pain ring out behind us, as people fall victim to flung debris. Their loved ones stop to help, but nearly a hundred people still follow us.

A haunting howl rolls out through the night. It's higher-pitched than the Brute's roar, and has a sing-song quality about it, but it cuts through me, right to my soul. Where Brute instills abject fear, Wisp projects great sadness and loss.

But Rain seems to be the only other person to feel it, and since she's a lightning rod for these things, and what they're feeling, her reaction is far more intense.

A sob barks from her mouth as her legs buckle. She falls to her knees, skinning them. When I reach her, she's weeping.

I get my hands under her arms and lift. I'm not a weightlifter or anything, but Rain is light. Ninety pounds, tops. With adrenaline's help, I get her back to her feet.

"Okay?" I ask, ready to keep running.

She looks me in the eyes, her glowing gaze burning into me, then flashing wide with a kind of recognition. She places a hand on my cheek and then flinches back to herself, shoving me away and shouting, "Keep going!"

The closer we get to Wisp, and the closer it gets to us, the more my feeble mind is able to comprehend its size, and that of Brute closing in behind us. They're hundreds of feet tall. Who knows how long and wide. But Brute crashed into the Custom House Tower, which is five hundred feet tall. Brute was at least another hundred feet up. Wisp is a little shorter, but much of its flowing body is spread out, supporting its impermanent weight on many limbs instead of on Brute's four.

I'm assuming it's four.

Twin high-pitched shrieks draw my eyes to the east. The sound grows louder, fast. Given the night's events, I expect to see a third monster flicker into view. Instead, I see the navigation lights of two jets streaking down from the swirling clouds. The planes are silhouetted by blue flashing above, helping me identify them.

A-10 Warthogs.

Tank-killers.

Designed for air-to-land combat, rather than dogfights. They pack a punch and scream like banshees.

I wince at the volume of their passage, drowning out the sound of crumbling buildings and horrified people.

Twin sets of missiles launch from each jet. Two streak toward Brute, and I hope they punch a hole in the beast's ghostly hide, sending it back to whatever hell birthed it. The other two cut a path toward Wisp, and I can't help but feel afraid for the creature.

Why? I wonder.

Because it's not here for us, I decide, which isn't a huge leap in faith, since I'm already running straight toward the thing.

I turn to watch Brute. The first missile strikes the monster's arm, as it slides into the courthouse intersection. There's a ball of fire, followed by a boom that knocks the wind out of me, and a shockwave that stumbles me. I manage to stay upright, and I watch as the second missile slips through the transparent upper arm, through the torso, and into the courthouse.

I flinch away from the explosion. I don't need to see it to know that the building's façade and a good portion of its insides have been destroyed—but not by the beast. Just before I turn forward again, I see the big arm slip through the fire and smoke. For a moment, it appears damaged, like its skin has been peeled back to reveal a blueish, gelatinous inside. Then the gigantic limb swoops through a crowd, sucking away their lives and replenishing the body's original appearance.

Pulses of blue streak up through the limbs, igniting the monster's upper torso, revealing what I think is a mouth in its chest...and the eyes above, partially concealed by the flowing hair...or what I think is hair.

A chill runs through my body.

It's watching me.

Or maybe that's what everyone sees when they look at it?

Or maybe it just has enough eyes to watch us all?

A third explosion turns my eyes forward in time to see the Garden's roof lifted up and cast away by a plume of fire.

The fourth missile misses both Wisp and the Garden.

Following the missile's trajectory, I realize it's going to strike somewhere in the West End, a densely populated area that includes Mass General, which is full of people unable to run away. I cringe when the missile's booming impact rolls into the already charged night sky.

"Oww!" I shout, when sudden pressure compresses my wrist. It's Rain, tugging me along. I hadn't realized I'd slowed down, and I pick up my pace.

"We don't have much time!" she shouts.

"Until what?" I ask.

"Do you not see the two behemoths about to collide?" Reggie shouts, nearly hysterical. "We're at ground zero, man!"

Before I can reply, a long tendril the width of a king-size blanket flickers to life beside me. It presses to the ground, the pressure of it sending a charge up through the long limb, exposing its flowing form as the tendril rises up into an undulating body, which is actually quite beautiful. *It's like an angel,* I think. Not the winged kind from pop culture, but the Biblical kind—both beautiful and horrifying in a way that instills the literal fear of God in people.

Other tendrils snap to life around us, compressing the streets, but somehow avoiding both people and structures.

It's protecting us, I think.

I hope.

As we pass beneath Wisp, and it passes over us, our band of Bostonian refugees falls silent. But it's not just that people stop screaming. It's like all sound is being absorbed, or deflected. I can't hear the jets anymore. Can't hear Brute, or the buildings crumbling in the creature's wake. I can't even hear my own breathing.

And for a moment, despite the horror, and the anguish—and the previous sadness I felt being projected by Wisp—I feel peace.

It moves through me, emanating not from the air around me, but from Rain's hand, still grasping my wrist. From the placid look on her glowing face, I know she feels it, too.

And then the world rushes back to life.

The screams return.

The crackling of fires.

The wail of sirens.

Brute's roar.

Acrid smoke draws raw coughs from my chest.

And then...the monsters collide.

16

Running for your life, while intensely drawn to look backward at what might kill you, is a dangerous recipe. If not for Rain's intense focus on survival, and her continuing grip on my arm, I'm not sure I'd make it out of the city.

But how can I *not* look?

This is on par with Moses parting the Red Sea, or the Hindenburg crash, or the World Trade Center's destruction. While I wasn't alive for the first two, I know for a fact that for every hundred people running away from the collapsing Twin Towers, there was one standing sentinel, head craned up, watching the impossible unfold. It's why there's so much video footage of the event, much of it from vantage points of immediate danger.

Just like there will be video of this.

You don't need to see it, I tell myself. *Just run.*

But I can't look away.

Wisp is a flurry of motion, its many ribbon-limbs flowing through the air, fluttering in and out of reality, pulsing with energy as they make contact with Brute. The long tendrils wrap around the larger monster's powerful arms, binding it, slowing it down.

Or, at least, attempting to.

Before the larger creature is completely immobilized, Brute swings a backhand into Wisp's body. While the flowing body is never fully visible, that doesn't seem to keep Brute from making contact. The creatures are only partially tangible in the physical world, but they seem fully tangible to each other.

Wisp's core falls back with a haunting wail that actually makes me feel sorry for it.

But why?

Because it's helping us, I realize. While everything about Brute screams anger, hate, and rage bred by fear, Wisp is very different. It's sad. And lost. But also peaceful. Maybe even loving, if something so horrifying is capable of love.

Wisp falls back, leveling several buildings. The creature's body shimmers from the souls it inadvertently absorbs. When it wails again, I think it's more for the lives it's just stolen, than for its own pain.

Brute takes another step, closing in on us as we race down the sidewalk running along the Garden's ruined side. The entrance to North Station is just a hundred feet ahead.

Wisp, who never relinquished its grasp on Brute, lifts itself off the ground, and in a surprisingly quick, fluid motion springs back toward its larger, more powerful foe. Tendrils wrap and squeeze like pythons.

Brute's pace slows, but all it needs to do to catch us is topple forward. Its six-hundred-foot height, laid out flat, would close the distance. Luckily, it doesn't seem smart enough to figure that out.

As Brute clears the buildings behind us, smashing its way through ancient brick, Wisp punches its tendrils into the pavement, anchoring itself.

Buying us time.

For what?

"Inside!" Reggie says, snapping me out of my observer's point of view. Suddenly back in my body, I stumble through North Station's open doorway, propelled by Rain, who's shoving me from behind. The door's window has been shattered. Did Reggie do that? Or was it already broken? *Doesn't matter*, I decide, stepping into the dimly lit entryway.

The throng of fleeing Bostonians follows us, diminished, but still nearly seventy-five strong.

I've spent more than my fair share of time in North Station, chasing stories as close as Revere and all the way out to Gloucester. It's the fastest way to get in and out of the city. And in all those visits, I've never seen the terminal empty. Never seen it quiet. If it's not rush hour, then there're school groups visiting the Aquarium or the Museum of Science, or art students visiting the MFA, or Red Sox fans ready to watch a game at Fenway. Even the ever-present panhandlers are missing. Then again, I've never been here in the middle of the night. The station is open from 5am to 1am, so there's just a four-hour window where the building is empty, save for night shift janitorial staff, but anyone who is supposed to be here has long since fled.

We file into the tall terminal, its old wooden, pew-like benches all empty. The Dunkin' Donuts is dark. The schedule of incoming and outgoing trains is empty. For a moment, I'm struck by a powerful sense of loss, of life once vibrant now missing.

Then I remember the true source of this emotion.

My wife is dead.

I'm sure of it now.

In all the insanity that's taken place since her phone call, I haven't had a lot of time to process. Haven't had a lot of time to even think. Or feel. And as much as it sickens me to say it, I've almost forgotten the fresh wound of her passing.

Almost.

Rain's presence is a persistent reminder of my wife's fate.

"Are there any trains?" I ask, as Reggie presses her face against the glass door leading out to the train platforms.

"Trains, yes." Reggie looks back, sullen. "Keys, conductors, or the knowledge to operate a five-hundred-ton locomotive? I'm afraid not."

A wall of people pushes up against the glass doors, looking for salvation like believers gathered for an Easter service at Vatican City. I slide my way to the left, moving down the line of parked trains.

And then I see it. A light.

It's at the far end of Track 8. A Boston T commuter train, the gray body and purple stripe are easy to recognize. I find the lock, give it a twist, and force the doors open. Then I'm outside and running like I've got a Pamplonian bull charging behind me.

The train is long. Nine cars. Easily enough to carry us all, but is someone here, or did a conductor accidentally leave a light on?

I'm out of breath by the time I reach the engine. The steady glow illuminates the conductor's cabin. I mount the stairs, peer through the small window at the top, and peek inside. It's hard to see, but I think there's someone inside, seated, head lolled back, earphones on.

I pound on the door. "Hey!"

No response. Not even a flinch.

Is he dead? Did he witness the events in Cambridge, fear the end was nigh, and have a heart attack?

I pound again, this time hard enough to wake the dead.

Still nothing.

People are starting to force their way onto the train, having faith that I'll get the thing moving in time to save their lives.

The moment it takes to look back at the train is all it takes for me to notice Brute again, looming up over North Station, still pressing forward despite the tangle of Wisp still tightening its grasp. The two giants are in a battle, but it seems more like a battle of wills, Brute wanting to catch us, Wisp attempting to prevent it.

"Running out of time!" Rain says, her face flickering with light. Her expression is hard to see, but easy to read. Whatever turmoil is being projected by the giants is reaching a climax that only she can feel.

I reach back my fist, ready to pound my way through the glass. I'm pretty sure I'll break my hand instead of the window, but I have to try. Before I can swing, Brute plants its big fist inside the Garden, pounding the ground hard enough to send a quake through the entire train.

The man inside stirs.

I pound on the glass with both fists. "Hey! Hey! Wake up!"

The train shakes again. Brute closing in.

"HEY!" I scream, and I manage to put a crack in the glass.

The man twists around, rubbing the sleep out of his eyes. He pulls a fancy noise-blocking headset away from his ears. Inside the train's insulated interior, with sound-blocking earphones, he might have slept through the last few hours of drama.

Confusion gives way to anger, when the man sees the cracked window. He picks up a wrench and heads toward me. I back away, descending the stairs. He opens the door and steps out into the night with all of Brute's rage, but none of its size. The gray-haired, mustached conductor is still in uniform, ready to fight in defense of his train.

But he never manages to shout an expletive or ask for an explanation. His eyes move from me, to Rain, to North Station and then up... up...up...

"What...da...fuck?"

"We need to go," I shout. "Now!"

The old man has trouble pulling his attention away from the skyscraper-sized WWE match coming our way, but he manages for a moment. Looks me in the eyes. Then back to Rain.

"The man said, now!" Reggie shouts, stepping up and shoving the conductor back inside his train. "Move, move, move!"

As the rest of our followers enter the train through a pried-open door, I follow Rain inside the engine. Reggie takes the seat beside the conductor. "Full speed ahead! Engage! Whatever you have to do to get this thing moving, now, do it!"

The conductor, freed from the spell of seeing real-life kaiju—giant monsters like Nemesis or Godzilla—slipping in and out of reality, is already hard at work attempting to preserve his life. The train powers up. The engine rumbles to life. The conductor looks back. "This is a big train. If you can uncouple the cars—"

"There are people on board," I tell him.

For a moment, I think he's going to ask me to do it anyway. Then he just frowns and starts the train forward. We accelerate at a cringe-inducing pace. Right now, I could outrun the train on foot.

A vibration rolls through the ground and the train. I hold on to a grab bar and catch Rain as she loses her balance. But I don't think it was the jolt that knocked her over. She's cringing, overwhelmed by the intensity of what she's experiencing.

"It's here..." she says.

"No shit," I say.

"...for me." She looks me in the eyes, and I immediately understand her intention. Since Brute laid its eyes on me, I've wrongly assumed it was here for me. But that egotistical view is shattered by the realization that those giant eyes weren't looking at me, but at the person by my side.

"No," I say, blocking her path to the side door. As noble as it might be to sacrifice her life to save all these people, I still need answers, and she's the only one who might have them. I'm not only egotistical, I'm also selfish, and right now, tonight, I don't give a shit. "No way."

I relax when she backs away, and I realize too late that instead of forcing her way past me, she's retreating to the back door connecting us to the other cars. When I catch her by the arm, she spins around and delivers a punch to my solar plexus, knocking the air from my lungs, and slamming my body to the floor.

By the time I look up, she's gone.

17

"No matter what," I tell Reggie, "you keep this train moving."

She saw Rain exit. She knows I'm going after her. The look in Reggie's eyes says she's willing to stop the train to help us, but no one here deserves to share in the fate Rain has planned for herself.

"Don't worry, buddy," the conductor says. "I ain't stopping for nothing or no one."

"Be careful," Reggie says, and then I'm out the door, headed back through the train. Between the engine and the first car, surrounded by the unmuted sound of the churning locomotive and the haunting cries of both Brute and Wisp, I'm struck by the visceral stupidity of what I'm about to do.

But I can't let Rain die.

Not until I have answers, and probably not after that, either. I don't know her well—how can you really know someone who doesn't know themselves? But our brief relationship has been forged in a hellish heat. She is a stranger.

And a friend.

I turn to the exit door. When I find it unlocked, I know this is the path she took. Rain's a small woman, but she's athletic in a way I've never been. If there isn't a ladder leading up to the roof, I'm afraid I'll never reach her.

I lean out into the warm night, choking on the engine's exhaust. There's no ladder, and when I look up into the sky behind us, I realize there's no time.

"Faster," I will the train. "Faster!"

While there isn't a ladder, there are two vertical grab bars on either side of the door. I can visualize how a gymnast might make the climb in seconds, but when I try to insert myself into the fantasy, I see myself falling to the tracks and getting run over. I know the physics of my imaginary death don't work. I'd fall away from the train. But physics don't matter when conjuring images of your own demise.

This is why sleep eludes me.

Don't be fancy, I tell myself. I'm strong enough to lift my own weight. But stamina isn't my strong suit...and I'm already exhausted from running, and the knock to my head, repeated adrenaline peaks and valleys, and from still having Ambien in my system...but well, screw it.

I grip the twin grab bars, plant a foot on the side of the door and monkey my way up, all while pretending there isn't a pair of translucent kaiju careening toward us. My feet have no trouble sticking to the rubber door seal, and the bars extend nearly all the way to the roof.

Nearly.

To finish the climb, I need to really Spider-Man this. I slap a hand on the train's smooth roof, extending my fingers and hoping that friction alone will support my weight. *One hand up,* I think. *And now...* I fling my left hand up and over onto the roof, doing my best chameleon impression. But my palms are growing sweaty. I start to skitter-slide back.

In a very not-heroic looking last-ditch effort, I fling my upper torso on the roof, letting the whole of my body, and its weighty dad-bod pudge, hold me in place. Hands extended again, I swing my legs up, roll to the center of the train's roof and catch my breath.

I smell the ocean, the city, the train, and fresh ozone.

The last in that collection of odors pulls my eyes open.

"Shit!" I shout upon seeing Brute. It's right behind us. If not for the still-clinging Wisp, it would have caught us by now.

The Garden fades in the distance behind us, a smoking ruin that matches a swath of Boston's North End. How many people died tonight?

For a moment, my own grief feels selfish.

Sitting in a train is often a bumpy experience. Standing atop one as it accelerates and follows the path of aging tracks feels more like surfing through choppy seas. Hands extended, legs splayed wide, I find my equilibrium. Only then do I see Rain.

She's standing at the end of the train. Her glowing arms are spread to the sky. Her blonde hair snaps in the wind, creating a strobe effect from her luminous head. She's glowing brighter than ever. No longer a beacon, but a sacrifice.

Are they gods? I wonder, looking up at the clashing titans.

Are we witnessing an actual End of Days, not envisioned by the prophets of any religion?

Brute's many eyes are locked on Rain.

The monster becomes desperate.

Frantic.

Its pulsing muscles strain against Wisp's coils.

And then, Brute loses its patience.

A loud buzzing fills the air, like an arc of electricity. Veins of bright light flow upward, exposing more and more of the creature's body, its gaping torso-mouth, its flowing hair, bulbous eyes, and its long, emaciated, sharply-bent back legs. If this thing stood on its hind legs, it would be at least a thousand feet tall!

But that's not what it does. All that flowing light cascades through Brute's body. An internal lightning storm. And then it flows back down to its two-fingered fists, which it lifts off the ground and slams back down.

In a flash, all that energy is released.

The brightness of it forces my eyes shut for a moment. When I look again, Wisp has been knocked away, its massive body spilling across I-93, blocking the fastest northbound escape route from a burning city.

But Brute... It's gone.

I race down the line of cars, leaping from one to the next like a bona-fide action hero. I nearly fall off twice, when the speeding train takes a long right turn—probably a lot faster than it's supposed to. I think the max allowed speed for a commuter train is 80 mph—if it's in a straight, unpopulated area. The train's actual top speed is probably double that, but I don't think we can achieve that speed without hopping the tracks. The path through and out of the city is winding.

"Rain!" I shout, as I leap to the final car.

She's still glowing with the brightness of a white dwarf star trapped inside a person. But the space behind her is empty now, and Wisp is fading into the distance—and out of existence.

"Rain, we're clear!" I shout at her, my voice whisked away with the wind. I put a gentle hand on her shoulder. "Come inside!"

She turns to face me, hair snapping around her face, so bright it hurts. "It's not gone! You have to leave! Let me do this!"

"You're not making sense!" I shout.

"It wants me!" she shouts. "I can feel it!"

"You can control it. The brightness. Turn it down! Let it go!"

She falls to her knees. "But it hurts!"

I hadn't stopped to consider that whatever is making her glow might also be burning her, but I don't think that's what she's talking about.

"It hurts!" she shouts again, but her voice is deeper now. Rumbling. Not her own.

"Let me go!" she shouts at me. "It won't stop until I—"

I take her hand, holding tight, like she did mine when she dragged me out of the city. "Neither will I!" And I mean it. What do I have to lose? "It takes us both, or neither of us."

She stares at me, an angelic being of pure light.

For a moment, I think this impossible person must exist for some divine purpose.

Then she says, "Both of us, then."

Brute flickers back into view as Rain's illumination flares brighter. Moving on all fours and not slowed by the inner-city buildings, the monster matches the train's pace. While it doesn't have a head, per se, its collection of eyes lean forward, shimmering with transparent brightness. Toothless chest-mouth open and ready to receive, its long, flowing hair stretches toward us, like hungry, electric whips.

I put an arm around Rain, consigned to my fate, and I lean my forehead against hers.

The moment of connection propels me into a memory.

George's Island off the coast of Boston. During a tour of the ancient fort there, Morgan and I snuck away, exploring the deep and dank tunnels running beneath the island. Upon resurfacing, we claimed to have been lost in the dark. Twenty years ago, in the days before cell phones, that might have been believable. Our guide knew better, as did every other person in the tour group, sheepishly smiling at the young couple who'd snuck off into the dark.

Do you think they 'did' it? I overheard a teenage boy ask a friend.

Hell yeah, we did. I didn't say that. Pretended not to hear the question. Pretended like everything was normal, though I couldn't hide my smile. It was one of my happiest days, and for a flash, I feel it again like I was there.

Rain gasps, snapping back from me, her pale blue eyes no longer awash with light.

She felt it, too. The memory. The love. And now she feels the loss.

Tendrils wriggle just a few feet away, reaching.

"I'm sorry," Rain says, then crushes herself inward like she's trying to contain the universe itself.

Her brightness dims.

Brute roars.

Rain screams.

Massive hands reach, as Brute fades out of existence.

I duck down in a self-protective orb, as the hands clasp shut around us. A sudden chill passes through me, but that's all. When I look up, all that remains of the kaiju is a twirling light-blue mist that twinkles out of sight.

The train takes a turn far too fast. The car actually tips to the side for a moment, nearly flinging us clear.

"You okay?" I ask Rain.

She looks up, clearly not okay, but she nods anyway. I help her to her feet and we walk to the nearest door with grab bars. Rain helps me slide down, hovering on the side of the train like a tree frog, blasted by wind.

Perched in place, I knock on the door.

A wide-eyed woman appears on the far side. After a stunned moment, she unlocks the door and yanks it open. I slip inside, stumble to the floor, and by the time I turn around, Rain is there, too, closing the door behind her. "How... Never mind."

I push myself up and lead the way back toward the front of the train, passing seats full of people watching Rain and me, like we're Greek gods reborn on Earth. Rain, I understand; but me? I'm just a broken man.

When we reach the engine, Reggie leaps up from her seat and embraces me. It's an awkward hug, mostly because Reggie is not fond of displaying affection, and I know that. It makes me as uncomfortable receiving it as it does her giving it. But the message is received: she's thrilled that I'm alive.

"You can stop," I tell the conductor. "It's gone." I turn to Rain, "It is gone?"

"I—I think."

"Keep going, Chuck," Reggie says, and then motions to the old man. "That's Chuck."

"I figured," I say. "Where are we going?"

"Salem," she says. "To see a friend. He might be able to help."

I've met a lot of Reggie's friends in the past. They're all nerdy types with doctorates, labs, grants, and research papers. "What kind of scientist can help with—"

"He's not just a scientist," she says, and then she looks disappointed in herself for revealing it. *"Don't tell him.* Have to. *He's not going to like it.* Doesn't matter." She gives me a smile that says, 'Thanks for ignoring my multiple personalities,' and then says aloud, "He's a Warlock."

18

What the hell are we doing? I think to myself for the hundredth time in the past hour. The world is coming undone. Morgan is gone. Boston is in ruins. And giant kaiju-ghost things are responsible, maybe for all of it. I didn't see a kaiju in Cambridge, but that doesn't mean they weren't there before I woke up.

Maybe the monsters were after Rain all along?

Maybe SpecTek was protecting her?

It feels like false hope. In my gut, I know it's not true. But I hope it's true.

Early morning in Salem should be full of commuters, but word of last night's devastation has spread. The streets are mostly empty. Salem is close enough to Boston that some residents probably saw the light show. Might have even heard distant explosions, or roars. But those who slept through it have seen the news by now. Probably huddled around TVs and refreshing news sites, waiting for the latest update. Hell, Nepalese Sherpas on Mt. Everest have probably heard the news by now: monsters are real, huge, and capable of destroying cities.

The world will never be the same.

During our walk from the train station, I haven't seen more than a handful of people. What I *have* seen is evidence of the city's claim to fame:

witches. I've never personally understood the appeal. I mean, despite the best efforts of modern-day Wiccans to present themselves as something closer to tree-hugging, flower-child pagans, most people still associate witches with the mysterious dark arts, rampant evil, and even Satan—who, like Jesus, doesn't play a role in the religion. Probably didn't help that the city's official witch claimed to have created the 1991 Perfect Storm—the one that killed George Clooney in that movie—with a curse. That's what I heard at the time, anyway. But the city of Salem went all in on the occult, and it reaps a multi-million-dollar tourist payday every year, as curiosity seekers and true believers congregate to the city's museums, shops, tours, and historical sites.

Most of those people don't know that neighboring Danvers was the true geographic epicenter of the witch trials—and Salem is happy to keep it that way. Every town needs their thing, I guess. Hell, Beverly is just across the bay, and they're famous for being the fictional home of the FC-P. If only Jon Hudson was real. We could use his help now. Instead, we're visiting a warlock.

A *freaking* warlock...

Ugh.

Like Boston, Salem has an old-world feel. Cobbled sidewalks. Buildings older than my great grandfather. Classic New England stylings dutifully maintained, rather than replaced. It looks the same today as it did thirty years ago, with the exception of new supermarket chains and updated museums in the nooks and crannies.

When we stop beside the bronze-green statue of Roger Conant, regaled in a cloak and wide-brimmed hat, looking ready to hunt witches, I fear our destination is the iconic building just beyond the grim-faced founder of Salem. While much of the old city is built from old wood and red brick, the old Gothic Revival-style church, once known as East Church, is an impressive stone building that is equal parts church and castle. But it's neither, now. The building is home to the Salem Witch Museum, and it houses a massive pentagram on the floor, arcane symbols, and a freakish wax-museum history of the Salem witch trials. While the narrated tour instills a sense of weirdness in the viewer, I'm not sure it would make a good home for a serious warlock...mostly because the witches of old Salem have nothing in common with modern witchcraft. Because all those young women murdered by the church were actually God-fearing Christians.

"We're not..." is all I manage to say, while looking at the museum.

"Of course not," Reggie says, turning me around and pointing to a small black sign hanging from what once would have been a home, but has been transformed into a small shop... Or rather a 'Shoppe,' as the sign says. The *Grand Pagan Shoppe.* A hand-painted sign. White text on black. The words are framed by a pentagram, a witch's hat, and a black cat.

My head hangs low, but I keep my groan contained.

Rain, on the other hand, seems taken in by it all. She reads the sign taped beneath the 'Closed' sign in the front window. It's handwritten. Sharpie on cardboard. "What is *CBD-infused tea?*"

"Nothing to do with why we're here," I say, patience thinned by the worst night of my life. I turn to Reggie. "They're closed, which isn't surprising, because I doubt anyone will be open for business today—and oh yeah, it's six o'clock in the morning."

Reggie gives me an 'I'm no fool,' look and then approaches the door. "Bjorn is an early riser." She gives the door a gentle knock. When she's done, I hear footsteps approaching.

She seems to know this Bjorn fellow fairly well...including what time he wakes up. "Wait," I say. "You and Bjorn aren't—"

Reggie grins. "We met online."

"Not eHarmony or something like that?" I say, about to downgrade my opinion of her.

She chuckles. The grin fades, replaced by a single raised eyebrow. "Tinder." The smile returns. "Smart people have primal needs, too."

The door swings open to reveal a tall, skinny man with Mediterranean looks, a dark beard, and pony-tailed black hair. He's wearing a hooded and a black cloak, and he's carrying a gnarled staff. Beneath the cloak is a pair of Homer Simpson boxer shorts and nothing else.

The man, whom I presume is Bjorn—perhaps named for Bjorn Ironside, the Viking made famous by modern TV more than the actual man's Norse exploits—lights up when he sees Reggie.

"Regalia," he says, arms open for an embrace. "You've come back!"

She returns his hug, squeezing his wiry frame, her head coming up to his bare, hairless chest. A Viking, this man is not. I'm pretty sure there isn't a single Danish gene in his body.

When his hands on her back start traveling south, she leans back and says, "We're not alone."

Bjorn's dark brown eyes snap up, seeing me and Rain for the first time. He glances over me, but seems taken aback by Rain for a moment, and she's not even glowing. "You're here for something, then?"

"Do you always carry a staff?" I ask, unable to hold back my growing sarcasm.

He lifts the staff up, revealing broom bristles on the bottom, and without a single chink exposed in his positive attitude, he says, "I was cleaning. Perhaps you're on a quest?"

I'm revolted by his light-hearted tone. For a warlock, he's not very good at reading people. While Reggie might be happy to see him, both Rain and I wear darkness and exhaustion like a mask.

Reggie steps back so he can see her face. "We were in Cambridge last night."

His smiles falters and then fades when he looks down at Reggie's face, only now seeing the grime on her dark skin and the tiredness in her eyes. "Oh..." he says. "*Oh.*"

Bjorn steps back and sweeps his hand into the shop. With the broom in hand, and the cloak rolling off his arms, it's like watching a young Gandalf welcome us to his own personal Shire. "Come in. Come in."

The shop is essentially a knick-knack emporium for the occult—herbs, incense, crystals, arcane books, and little skulls from various animals. But there are modern touches as well, including a whole rack of overpriced CBD products, Salem witch T-shirts, and games from Ouija to Dungeons and Dragons.

At the same time, I get the feeling that none of this is real. Bjorn is just another sycophant suckling on the popularity of modern witchcraft and Harry Potter. Then again, that's not all that different from Salem as a whole. I'm about to voice my negative assumptions and leave, when Bjorn gently places his hand beneath Reggie's chin and looks over both sides of her face.

"You're not hurt?" he asks.

"I'm fine," she says, "but..." she looks at me. "We could use a place to...rest."

"Of course," he says, maneuvering his way past me to deadbolt the shop door. "Whatever you need."

The angry bubble about to pop from my mouth sinks back down to my gut. I'm judging him too harshly. He's obviously a decent guy. But there's one thing I can't let go. "Bjorn's not your real name, right?"

"And you are?" he asks, extending his hand.

I accept his handshake and say, "Saul Signalman."

"Ahh, Dickens. I love it."

"What?" I say, baffled by his response to my name.

He turns to Rain and offers his hand again. She doesn't accept, but says, "Rain."

"Can I call you Freyr?" he asks, and when Rain says nothing, he adds. "The Norse god of rain. Very power—"

"No," Rain says.

"Okay..." He takes a step back to look at both Rain and me. He waves his hands toward us. "Your auras are—"

"Bjorn," Reggie says.

"Sorry. Habit. And to answer your question," he says to me. "The name my parents gave me was Emmanuel. It's the Romanization of the Hebrew Immanuel, which means 'God with us,' which refers to Jesus as God, living among us. It's not a bad name, really, but..." He motions to the occult shop. "My patrons wouldn't appreciate it, and my critics—the local church—would be incensed by a warlock named Emmanuel. So it is easier to go through life as Bjorn."

"That...makes sense," I say, and I force a smile. "It's been a long night."

"I'm sure," Bjorn says, and then his eyes flare a bit wider. "Signal-man..." He turns to Reggie. "This is your friend. The one you spoke of?" For a moment, I'm flattered that Reggie has told someone about me, but then he adds, "The man with the brilliant wife. I'd love to meet her, too. Is she with you?"

The question is directed toward me, and it decimates my attempt at looking like life isn't a dark and horrible thing.

"Oh..." he says. "God, I'm sorry. She was...last night? The explosion?" He turns to Reggie, desperate to be bailed out of his awkward faux pas.

She takes his hand and leads him toward a staircase at the back of the store. "There's a lot to tell. Just...try not to talk much until we've explained." She gives me an apologetic smile and leads Bjorn up the stairs.

I turn to Rain. "What do you think, Freyr?"

She bends over, looking at a glass case of small skulls, potions, and bongs. "I think we're in the wrong place."

I pick up a book that reminds me of the Necronomicon. Since it doesn't bite me, I open it and find myself looking at crude sketches of various monsters and calligraphic text that looks hand-written. "Maybe." I turn the page to more monsters. "Maybe not."

I wouldn't say I feel open-minded right now, but after last night I can't discount anything, no matter how ridiculous it seems on the surface.

Except for Bjorn's boxers. They're horrible.

"Let's go," Rain says, losing interest in the collection of curiosities. "Maybe he has some food that isn't cursed, or newts, or whatever." She gives me a subtle smile as she heads up the stairs.

As I follow her, the hairs on my arms spring up. Some instinctual part of my brain shouts, 'Behind you!' I whirl around, ready to fend off an attacker. But no one is there. The shop is empty.

I think.

Maybe.

If those things from last night really are supernatural, then maybe ghosts are real, haunting and tormenting the living. And if that's true, Salem is the last place on Earth I want to be.

19

Bjorn's apartment is the antithesis to the 'Shoppe' below, and a welcome relief. There are no dusty tombs, ancient symbols, or items that look like they were fashioned four hundred years ago, but were probably made in China—like everything else. The furnishings and décor are modern. The paintings on the walls are geometric and colorful. Morning sunlight flows through large windows and skylights.

We follow the smell of coffee to the sparkling kitchen with granite countertops and chrome appliances.

Reggie is there, getting out mugs with the honey and creamer already on the counter.

"Bjorn is dressing," she says.

"What..." Rain says, looking around, as befuddled by the apartment as I am. "This is..."

"I had the same reaction the first time I came here," Reggie says. "The dichotomy is fascinating, isn't it?"

"That's a word for it," I say.

"This," Reggie says, motioning to the apartment, "is a representation of his true self." She motions to the geometric painting, square lines inside of square lines, each a slightly different color, rotating and shrinking to create a sense of depth. "Of his true mind."

"And the 'shoppe' with an extra P and E? The cloak?"

"Before Bjorn opened the shop, he dabbled in acting on the side, most prominently in *Cry Innocent.*"

"I think I've seen that," I admit.

"It's a local play that allows the audience to judge Bridget Bishop."

A memory is sparked. I saw the play with Morgan. Five years ago. The drama starts in the streets and then moves into a courthouse, where the audience acts as a jury, freeing Bridget Bishop, or repeating history to condemn her. Morgan voted to free her. I, like the majority of people, voted to repeat history. I have a dark side.

"But acting isn't his true career," she says.

"And it still isn't," Bjorn says, stepping out of the bedroom, fully clothed and looking more human in dark blue jeans and a T-shirt. For a moment, I wonder if he's secretly a normal guy, then he opens his mouth again. "I was a nude model, too, but my forays into the arts have little to do with my true passion."

Rain and I stare at him, waiting for the grand reveal this former thespian has planned for us. He smiles at his audience, and then with a flare of his eyes, says, "Science."

Neither Rain nor I react.

After a moment, I blink out of my stunned state. "Wait, you're serious?"

"Bjorn is a brilliant theoretical physicist," Reggie says.

"A little too far on the fringe," he says.

"A warlock," I say.

Bjorn chuckles. "In a sense. I wrote a paper on Spectral Duality, the idea that when people see ghosts, they're actually getting a glimpse of a parallel world, particularly during times of solar upheaval. My hypothesis is that the increase in charged particles and solar radiation warps the frequencies of reality, allowing us to see, for a moment, what is normally hidden. It was just an idea, one of many, regarding what we still consider the supernatural. But publishing it? Well, it ruined my career. Universities wouldn't hire me, and no one would publish my papers. So I research in private and support myself with the shop. I might be a charlatan, but I'm probably the only person in this damn city with any hope of truly understanding the supernatural."

"Our own personal Dr. Venkman," I say, and I quickly worry that Bjorn's sense of humor will eventually tire of my jabs.

His response, "More of an Egon," puts me at ease.

I smile, sensing a fellow *Ghostbusters* fan in our midst. "Did you tell him about the Twinkie?" I ask Reggie.

"What about the Twinkie?" Bjorn asks, managing to get a slight laugh out of me.

"Uhh," Reggie says. "I don't know anything about a Twinkie."

"I think I like Twinkies," Rain says, hand on her belly.

"Do you have anything to eat?" I ask Bjorn. "Something without newts?"

"I think I have some dried bats around here somewhere," he says, opening a cabinet. When he joins us at the kitchen's island, he's holding a box of Dunkin' Donuts munchkins. "I'm afraid they're a day old."

"You're a saint." I waste no time pulling the box open and plucking an assortment from the mass of dough, lard, and sugar.

"Well, let's keep that to ourselves," Bjorn says, taking a seat, while Reggie pours the coffee.

I slide the box to Rain. She looks down like she's never seen a Munchkin before. "I know what they are," she says, "but I can't remember them." She plucks out a chocolate honey-dipped sphere.

"You can't remember if you've eaten a donut?" Bjorn asks, and then he squints at Rain. "You're not one of them Krispy Kreme weirdos, are you?"

"Bjorn," Reggie says, sliding coffee cups to everyone, "there's a lot you don't know. Maybe we should have a seat?"

Coffee and donuts in hand, we find seats in the living room, which is almost posh. Rain curls up in a chaise lounge, while Reggie and Bjorn claim a love seat. I find myself in a rocking chair, which seems determined to defeat the caffeine's effects. We debated sleep on the train ride to Salem, but ultimately decided to push through the day. There's too much to figure out, too much to process, to spend the day asleep. I'm no stranger to all-nighters, so this is nothing new for me. Reggie is coping with caffeine, and I have no idea how Rain will handle it. So far, she seems just as alert and on edge as she has been since I freed her.

Reggie breaks down the previous night's events—starting with my own—for Bjorn. It's an exhaustive account. I hear my own words about Morgan's fate, Rain's discovery, and our flight from capture, all regurgitated, sparing me from having to conjure those memories on my own. Of course, I do anyway, replaying events as she speaks, trying to eke out understanding. But at least I don't need to choke through getting the words out.

To his credit, Bjorn sits in silence, his coffee untouched, his face slowly morphing from interest to shock to horror and finally to skepticism.

"*That's* what happened in Cambridge?" he asks.

"There must be news reports by now," Reggie says. "You can confirm anything you want."

"I saw the news before you arrived," he says. "There was a blue light in the sky. Something about a transformer explosion. I assumed that's what happened to Mrs. Signalman." To me, "Sorry," and then, "People from neighboring cities got photos."

"Nothing with a glowing crater?" I ask.

He looks mystified by the question.

"They must be spinning the story," I say to Reggie. "Covering it up."

She's not buying it. "How could they possibly cover-up Boston?"

"I don't know." My impatience flares. "I don't even know who *they* are."

"Wait," Bjorn says, but we ignore him.

"Too many people saw it," she says. "There was too much damage. How could they hide that?"

"Reg," Bjorn says.

"They'll probably call it a terror attack," I say, "a chemical attack. Something psychedelic. A mass hallucination." I hold up my hand to keep her from explaining again that they're impossible. "It doesn't have to be possible for the government to claim it's real. Facts are optional, remember?"

"But the destruction," she says. "Won't—"

"Regina," Bjorn says, annoyance creeping into his voice.

We fall silent. He has our full attention.

"What..." He looks afraid to ask. "What happened in Boston?"

It's our turn to be dumbfounded.

Reggie flinches like she's smelled something foul. More than once. "You said you watched the news."

"There wasn't anything about Boston," he says.

I turn on the wall-mounted flat-screen and return to my seat, confident that any channel will have news on the partial destruction of a major U.S. city. I realize the fault in that logic when a woman from the Home Shopping Network appears, shilling a new way to peel an apple.

"I got it," Bjorn says, picking up the clicker and pointing it at the TV.

The channel changes to a local ABC affiliate. The news is on. But no panicked voices. No breaking announcements. No frenzied reporters. And something is off. The cityscape behind the desk-jockeys isn't Boston, or any other recognizable Massachusetts city. "Is that...Providence?"

"It is," Bjorn says, sitting up a little straighter. "Why would they be showing Rhode Island news? He changes the channel to NBC. It doesn't take long to figure out that the local news on this channel is out of New York. "What the hell?"

CBS is broadcasting out of New Hampshire. So is Fox.

"They're keeping people in the dark," Reggie says. "Why would they do that?"

"To obfuscate the truth," Bjorn says. "Clearly. But...what is the truth?"

"That ghosts are real." Rain punctuates the statement by popping the last of her munchkin feast into her mouth, and then saying, while chewing, "And they're fuckin' huge."

"Excuse me?" Bjorn says. "Did you say..." He turns to Reggie. "Did she say..."

Reggie nods. "It's our best hypothesis."

"Ghosts..." he says, sounding surprisingly doubtful for a paranormal scientist/warlock. "And they did what, exactly?"

"Picture Stay Puft," I tell him. "But six times as tall and about as cute as the ghost in *Poltergeist*, the one in the upstairs hall that roars like a lion. But with more eyes, a mouth on its chest, and not a puppeteer in sight. They destroyed a portion of the North End. One of them was chasing us. The other was, I don't know, trying to protect us. Or people in general. I don't know."

"And you all *saw* this?" I don't appreciate his raised eyebrow.

Nods all around.

"Why would a six-hundred-foot-tall ghost be interested in you?" he asks me.

"Not me," I say, and I turn to Rain. *"Her.* We think."

He swivels toward Rain as she chugs the last of her coffee. "Same question."

She wipes her mouth. Shrugs. "Best guess, they're just as offended by my presence as I am by theirs."

Bjorn's laugh is nervous. "Are you suggesting that you're somehow in contact with these...spirits?"

"Only when they cross my path," Rain says.

"And you can feel them..."

"She can do a lot more than that," I say.

Bjorn leans forward, more challenging than interested. "Show me."

"I don't think you'd like that."

"I think I'd like it very much," Bjorn says. "If it's true. If any of what you've said is real." He turns to Reggie. "I'm sorry, but I've been studying this subject for two decades, and I still have only hypotheses to show for it. What I can conclusively declare is that every medium I've ever encountered has been no more a conduit to the supernatural than I am a warlock able to cast fireball spells."

"It's just that he's already angry," Rain says.

"He—who?" Bjorn says, and then he turns to me. "He doesn't look angry."

"Aww shit," I say, scanning the room. "Someone's already here?"

"You felt him downstairs," she says.

I glance back at the staircase, where I felt the chilly presence. "How come you're not...you know?"

"I'm containing it," she reveals.

"You can shut it off?"

She shakes her head. "More like plugging a hole with a finger. The moment I forget about the hole, and my finger slips..."

"Move your metaphorical finger," Bjorn says. "Please."

"I warned him," she says to me.

"I heard you."

She closes her eyes.

After just a moment, Bjorn loses his patience. "If you start talking with an accent or something, I'm going to—"

Rain opens her eyes, blazing with white light.

Bjorn flails back, falling up and over the love seat. By the time he rights himself, Rain's skin is lighting up. She turns her brilliant gaze toward the door leading downstairs. "Here he comes."

20

"I don't understand," Bjorn says, eyes locked on Rain's glowing face. "H-how are you doing that?"

"We don't know how it works," Reggie whispers in awe, and then with a stern voice, "And I'm not sure this is a good idea. Rain..."

It takes just a moment for me to realize why Rain's ability has Reggie on edge. The giants seemed drawn to Rain, once she lit up and got close. Moths to a flame. I'm not sure activating that beacon is a good idea anywhere. For starters, we could end up inundated with normal ghosts, if there is such a thing, but she could also summon those giants again.

"Rain," I say. "If there's a big one—"

"Don't worry," she says. "It's just us and this guy." She motions to the door, like there's someone to see.

"I don't see anything," Bjorn says.

"Don't try to see him," Rain says. "Try to *feel* him."

I'm about to warn her off again when the hairs on my arms rise up from a chill. It's the same thing I felt earlier. There is something here... I glance to Reggie and Bjorn. "You can't feel that?" I ask, holding up my arm, so they can see the hair standing tall.

Their stunned expressions say they can't.

I'm no one special. I've never experienced anything like this before. Why would I suddenly be able to sense when ghosts are around? Everything about the idea is insane. And yet, it's far more believable than everything else I saw last night.

So what makes me different?

Maybe the better question is, what makes Rain different? She was at the epicenter of the explosion that removed SpecTek from the face of the Earth. But she was protected. Her exposure to the blue energy limited. Or maybe filtered.

But mine wasn't. I felt the frigid energy on my skin, for just a moment, as it rushed up into the sky. Maybe that was enough to grant me just a touch of what Rain can do? Enough to make me sensitive to spirits, or if Bjorn is right, another dimension of reality.

"Who is he?" Bjorn asks, sounding a bit panicked. "What does he want? How...how long has he been here?"

"I can't talk to them," Rain says, a trace of annoyance.

"Have you tried?" I ask.

Rain's high beams shift to me for a moment. I can't tell if I've annoyed her. Her expression is lost in the light. Then she says, "What's your name?"

We all hold our breath, waiting for, but not really expecting to hear, an answer.

"See," Rain says. "He's not going to—"

The painting on the hallway wall falls to the floor. It's subtle. Not really violent, but hair follicles where I didn't know I had any are rising as goosebumps.

A few feet closer, the leaves of a potted tree rustle.

Closer still, a chair slides, as though someone has absentmindedly walked into it.

"He's confused," Rain says, now grimacing, the deepening connection making her uncomfortable. "And angry."

"Angry at whom?" Bjorn asks, truly frightened. Seriously, this guy is the world's worst warlock. I can't help but like him because of it.

"Hold on," Rain says, standing up. "I'm going to try something."

She moves toward the approaching disturbance, growing brighter as she does. She reaches out a hand. "He's right here..."

I reach out and take her hand, intending to pull her back. There's no way this is a good idea. But the moment our hands make contact, my sense of proximity to the strange increases ten-fold.

For a moment, I see what looks like a shadow. Then it steps into Rain, enveloping her. It's not inside her, per se. Not inhabiting her. But she is immersed in it, the brilliance of her glow pulsing through the shade.

"Someone's here," Rain says with a gasp. For a moment I think she's talking about another ghost, or someone in the store below, but then I hear her deepened voice and a strange, old-world accent. "My spectacles. I can't see!"

Her voice becomes ragged, like that of an old man. Her body hunches with age. "No! No, stay back!" Her hands stretch out, defending. Cowering. "Please. No. Not my doubloons."

Fascination overrides fright. We are hearing the voice of a man who's been dead since a time predating the United States, when doubloons were a recognized currency.

"*Who is this?*" I ask, really to myself.

Rain gasps, spinning toward me, her old frame bending away in surprise.

"Who is that?" she asks, and I get a sense that the...spirit is no longer reenacting its end, but *reacting* to me.

"You can hear me?" I ask.

"Speak your piece!" the grumpy old man says. "I'll not have you delaying my...my... Where am I?"

Rain looks around, flinching as she seems to notice the apartment for the first time. "Who are you?"

"Saul," I say.

"Named for the apostle before his conversion?" Rain asks. "Your parents must have been cruel."

"For the king," I say, correcting him.

"Ahh, ye've been given a name from the Old Testament, then."

My heart races, blood roaring behind my ears. I want to let go of Rain's hand and end the conversation, but I'm rooted in place, my reporter's instincts kicking in.

"What's your name?" I ask.

Rain hobbles closer to me, her head craned to the side. "Name's Captain Joseph White, procurer of rare Earth elements."

"Joseph White!" Bjorn whispers with the force of a fog horn. Rain—or rather, the Captain—doesn't react to the outburst. I don't think he can hear it. Only my physical connection with Rain, and maybe my brush with the unknown energy at SpecTek, allows us to communicate.

"What kind of elements?" I ask.

A wide, glowing grin slips onto Rain's face. "People."

"People?"

"I trade in slaves, boy. Don't you—"

Repulsion snaps my hand back.

The connection is severed.

Rain's light flickers, and then dulls as she concentrates, her posture returning to normal.

When she speaks, it's with her own voice. "Well, I feel dirty now."

"He was a treat," I say, hands shaking.

"He was murdered," Bjorn says. "Almost two hundred years ago. He was bludgeoned, in bed. The mystery of his death, which was something of a scandal at the time—like who shot J.R.—inspired the writings of Edgar Allen Poe and Nathaniel Hawthorne."

Bjorn flinches, as his mind returns from the past. Eyes twitching with fear. "Is...is he still here?"

"Does your hypothesis about spectral duality make you afraid or give you comfort?" Rain asks.

"I'm not following you," he says.

"She means," Reggie says, "if there are people around us all the time, does it matter if they're in a parallel dimension or if they're spirits?" To Rain. "Is that right?"

Rain gives a nod.

"I...suppose." Bjorn finally works up the courage to walk back around the love seat and reclaim his spot next to Reggie.

Rain hisses through her teeth like he's just stepped in shit.

"What?" Bjorn says, ready to bolt. "What happened?"

"You just sat on him," Rain says, triggering an explosion of lanky limbs. Bjorn dives from the chair, trips over himself, and sprawls onto the rug.

For a moment, stunned silence. And then, laughter.

Rain has a peculiar laugh, almost like she's trying it on for the first time. Takes me a moment to realize she was screwing with him. And then I'm laughing, too, unleashing pent up tension from the previous night. Reggie joins in, too, bellowing like she does.

Bjorn chuckles along, but I can tell he's more embarrassed than amused.

As the laughter fades, Reggie turns to Bjorn and asks, "So, what do you think?"

He just stares at her, dumbfounded. "I...I don't know what to think. I mean, there are more questions than answers, right? Joseph White is a historical person, who lived and died in Salem two hundred years ago. That seems to discount duality...unless time moves differently in other dimensions."

"Which is extremely unlikely," Reggie says. "And if it did, our different Earths would rarely align in space-time."

"Then what we saw..." Bjorn's voice shifts from embarrassed to genuine awe. "What we saw was real evidence of the spiritual realm. And if ghosts are real, so is the afterlife! If we can get data on this...tangible evidence...then it would change the world."

His excitement is palpable, and intellectually understandable, but I don't share his enthusiasm. "What about her?" I motion to Rain. "What she can do."

"What you both can do," Reggie says, and I decide to let it go. If we can understand Rain, I should be easy to explain.

"I don't know..." Bjorn says. "I would need data from the explosion in Cambridge. Samples from what was left behind." He motions to Rain. "Bloodwork, obviously. But science isn't quick. It could be a long time before we understand any of this."

"How long is a long time?" I ask.

Bjorn makes eye contact with Reggie. He clearly doesn't want to field that question.

She sighs. "Years. But we don't have anything from Cambridge, aside from the two of you, of course."

The development is discouraging, but then I realize there is one piece of evidence from Cambridge that maybe no one knows about. "Would video help?"

"Video of what?" Bjorn asks, leaning forward.

"Morgan FaceTimed me from the explosion. To...to say goodbye." I take a moment to swallow my emotions. "I screen-captured the whole thing. You can see the lab in the background. And Rain. It cuts out just before the explosion."

"Yes, of course." He reaches out a hand. "Can I see it?"

"I don't have it," I admit. "It's still in Cambridge. In my bedroom. The EMP killed the phone, but the data should still be there."

The news sucks the wind from Bjorn's sails, but he's undaunted, lured by the possibility of scientific discovery. "We won't know until we—"

Bing, bing! His phone chimes.

He stands and heads for the door. "I'll send them away."

"Send...*who* away?" I ask.

He holds up his phone. "It's an app. Lets me know when someone has entered the shop."

"Bjorn, honey," Reggie says, voice tense. "You locked the door."

21

"Is it another ghost?" Bjorn asks Rain, his voice nearly a gasp.

"Pretty sure spirits don't need to use doors," I say, already on my feet. I turn to Reggie. "They must have tracked us to you. And you to him." I motion to Bjorn.

"Tracked you?" Bjorn asks.

"The government," I say. "Whatever agency or black op was overseeing SpecTek's work. They've been after us since Cambridge."

"Because of what you saw?" he asks.

"Because of what I took," I say, watching Rain tip-toe toward the stairs, moving toward danger rather than away from it.

At least she's not glowing.

Despite her readiness to fight, Rain doesn't reach the stairs fast enough, and the rest of us haven't really moved, our instincts closer to fainting goats than any kind of predator. A man emerges from the dim stairwell, a silenced handgun leading the way. He levels the weapon at Rain's chest, stopping her in her tracks. She's brave, but she's not stupid.

"Targets acquired," the man says. I can't see it, but he's obviously speaking into a live mic hidden on his body, which is clad in black from head to toe. Unlike the men chasing us last night, he's not dressed in armor and military fatigues. He's wearing a suit. The only splash of color comes from the bottom of his tie, which is dark red, like it was dipped in blood. A pair of cold blue eyes glare from the mask concealing his face.

He's not a soldier. He's a killer. A mercenary at best...an assassin at worst.

"Two primaries and two secondaries," the man says. "Advise."

The man waggles the gun toward me and speaks to Rain, "Back there. With them."

Rain hesitates.

"You don't want to push me," the man says, and I believe him.

"*Rain...*" I warn.

Her coiled stance relaxes. She backs away from the man, stepping closer to me, while keeping herself between the gun and us. I don't know much about Rain, but I do know she's brave as hell and a good person. I think she would take a bullet for us.

But I can't let that happen.

"What do you want?" I ask, trying to keep my voice calm and noncombative.

The man just stares at me, waiting for the person on the other end of the comm.

Rain's hands clasp behind her back, like she's hiding something. But her hands are empty.

And then they're not. A dull glow moves from her fingertips to her palms, growing brighter. If the room were dark, he'd have already seen it, but with the morning sun streaming through the skylights above us, the light just blends in.

What is she doing?

"Copy that," the killer says, and then he turns to me. "It's your lucky day. You're coming with me."

"W-why?" I ask.

"I'm guessing what they need from you is information," he says, revealing that he is, in fact, a gun for hire rather than an employee. "What they need from them is silence."

"I can be silent," Bjorn says, hands raised. "I won't tell anyone."

Reggie looks momentarily disappointed in him, but then Bjorn moves her behind him. "Please, you don't need to kill us."

"Afraid I do," he says, "but first..." He points the gun back toward Rain. "You are priority Numero Uno. Unfortunately for you, I've been told you're dangerous. So..."

I see the man's finger compress on the trigger.

Light surges up Rain's arms, exploding hot white from her face, blinding me, and everyone else looking at her.

There's a sound like a loud cough, coupled with an angry buzz that zips past my ear. It's followed by the sound of breaking glass.

The man fired, I realize, *and he nearly shot me in the head!*

I open my eyes, viewing the world through a green splotch the size and shape of Rain's head and arms.

She turned her body into a flash-bang grenade!

And she follows it up with an assault.

Her first two strikes connect, pounding the man's chest, spilling him back and knocking the gun from his hands. But the assassin turns the fall into a roll, returning to his feet in a fighting stance, no signs of injury.

Rain's next three strikes come as a lightning fast barrage. The man blocks each one and counters with a sudden backhand.

In my mind's eye, I see Rain take the blow and sprawl to the ground, unconscious. She's a skilled fighter, that's for sure, but she's still human. The man's sledgehammer fist could knock out most anyone in a single blow.

"Oh!" I shout in surprise when Rain leans back from another blow, arching her back, hands to the floor, to catch herself in a bridge, while simultaneously kicking out a leg.

Rain's foot drives into the man's crotch, and he's totally unprepared for the move.

He lets out a shout that is equal parts pain and anger. Rain has hurt him, but I take him for the kind of man who's been trained to push past injury.

Rain propels herself back like a gymnast, returning to her feet and taking a fighting pose of her own. Despite the man's size, skill, and clear history of killing for hire, it's Rain whose body language exudes confidence.

During the melee, I work my way to the kitchen, intending to get a knife. Using my fists, I'll be no help to Rain. A momentary distraction at best, but if I can get a weapon...

I'll do what? I ask myself. *Stab him?*

It's more likely that he'll simply disarm me, stab me with my own weapon, and then use it to kill the others.

That's when I see it, lying beside the kitchen island. The man's gun, flung there when Rain disarmed him. It holds my eyes for a moment, and the man notices me. I can't stop myself from glancing at the gun, gauging how long it will take me to retrieve it. The killer's gaze follows mine. He sees the weapon, too, and without any internal debate, he lunges for the kitchen.

It's a mistake.

Rain leaps into the air, kicking the man with both feet. He collides with the kitchen's door frame, sprawling to the floor.

It's not until he recovers again that I make my move. This time the man doesn't try to beat me. Doesn't even try to stop me. Instead, he turns his full attention to Rain and presses the attack.

He throws punches and kicks in rapid succession, using what looks like—to me—several different martial arts.

Rain dodges and blocks many of the strikes, but a couple connect, forcing her back and off balance. She backs into the living room, all that stands between Bjorn and Reggie, and the assassin.

I don't see what happens when I duck down to retrieve the weapon, but I hear it. Grunts of pain from both Rain and the man, a lamp shattering, and then Bjorn screaming in a way that would make his namesake cringe—or laugh. I rise in time to see the killer pressing a knife against Rain's neck.

I raise the weapon. It's heavier than I expected, but I'm not sure if I'm feeling its weight or the gravity of what it can do. "Stop!" I sound more pitiful than tough. "You don't need to kill anyone."

The killer ducks behind Rain, using her as a shield. "Boss says I do."

"Who's your boss?" I ask.

The man's blade draws blood from Rain's neck. There's pain in her eyes, but no fear.

"I *will* shoot you," I tell him, strengthened by rage.

"I won't die alone," the man says. If he's feigning indifference to the idea of his own death, he's doing a damn good job.

I'm about to plead with him again, when I notice Rain's lips moving. I missed the first word, but I have no trouble figuring out that she's counting down when I read her lips, "...two...one!"

Rain ducks her head forward and then slams it back.

The move is insane. Will probably get her neck slit. But it also works.

The back of her head connects with the man's nose. The crunch of shattering bone makes me ill, but there's no time to pity the man. In the moment the man's grip loosens, Rain drops straight down, slipping out of his grasp and leaving his body totally exposed.

The gun shakes in my hand.

I'm about to take a life.

You can't go back from this, Morality whispers in my ear.

He'll kill you all, Common Sense argues.

All life is precious, Morality counters.

I have always been in the strange, political crossroads of being opposed to abortion as birth control, opposed to the death penalty, and generally opposed to war when there isn't an Adolf Hitler to defeat. I've seen enough crime and death to know it is never good, even when it's the bad guys doing the dying.

Morgan is dead because of these people, Vengeance adds.

I pull the trigger.

The first round misses the man, punching a hole in the wall beside his head. Realizing I'm a poor shot, even at close range, I let a curtain of rage fall over my eyes, and I pull the trigger again and again. I'm aware of the man twitching, of the red splotches bursting on the wall behind him, and of him falling to the ground, but it feels like I'm in VR, simulating his death.

I'm disassociating from the act, my mind defending itself from trauma, and I'm totally cool with that. So when the gun clicks empty, I simply turn away and place the weapon on the counter.

I flinch when Rain's hand rests on my shoulder. "Saul..."

"I'm okay," I say, starting to shake. "Are you okay?"

"We're all okay," Reggie says, "but I think we need to—"

Bing, bing!

Bjorn stares at his phone, horrified.

Bing, bing!

Rain moves to the stairwell as footsteps thump across the shop's hardwood floor beneath us.

Bing, bing!

22

Rain steps to the stair entrance like she's got no reason to be in a rush. She moves to the side, hands raised and open, ready to grapple. As feet thump up the steps, she turns to me. "You might want to move back."

I make it just a few feet before reinforcements arrive. I'm a little surprised when it's a woman—which I suppose makes me sexist. Women can be contract killers, too. But this woman lacks the same 'cold-hearted murderer' vibe as the last guy. She's got a gun in her hands, but there's no mask concealing her face, her brown hair is pulled back in a pony-tail, and her blue windbreaker has three bright yellow letters on it.

FBI.

"Don't kill them!" I manage to shout, before the woman enters the apartment.

After a flash of concern in the woman's eyes, her lips begin to form the start of an 'F,' but she never gets to finish declaring her affiliation. Rain's hands snap out, catching the gun. With a twist, Rain redirects the weapon's aim and the woman's path—into the wall. The collision dents the dry wall and sends the FBI agent sprawling to the floor.

A man follows, weapon drawn and already swinging toward Rain. She kicks up hard, striking the gun so that the single, deafening round it fires punches a hole in the ceiling. Rain follows it up with a spinning kick that sends the man sprawling back down the stairs, where he collides with a third agent. The two men fall to the bend in the staircase, slamming into the wall. Before either can recover, Rain sets upon them, launching off the top step and descending with clenched fists.

I don't see what happens next, but it only takes a few seconds, and it's punctuated by two grunts and two bodies hitting the floor.

By the time I reach the top of the stairs, Rain is standing over the two men. "They're not dead." She digs into their pockets, withdrawing wallets. "Check hers."

"Damnit," I whisper to myself, trying to control the jitter in my hands.

We just attacked the FBI. Well, Rain did, but really, at this point, same difference.

I always hated that saying—*same difference*—but Morgan said it so much it became endearing.

The woman's wallet confirms my fears. Unless the now-dead killer travels with a trio of faux government agents, Jennifer Garcia, here, is FBI.

At least they're alive.

"I think..." Bjorn says, "we should go."

"Not without answers," I say, surprising even myself.

"If they wake up and we're still here..." Reggie lets the point hang. None of us knows what would happen, but I don't think it would be good. They might not be contract killers, but they could have been sent here by the same people. Allowing them to take us into custody might be the last thing we do.

"So we'll take her," Rain says, stepping back out of the stairwell. She flashes the two men's FBI badges and tosses them to the floor. "We can ask Garcia questions when she wakes up."

"I'm not sure adding abduction to our list of offenses against the FBI is a good idea," Reggie says. It's a reasonable point, but this agent might know something. I mean, they followed the same breadcrumbs the killer did. They knew to look for me. And for Reggie. And even Bjorn.

"I'm with Rain," I say. "We should take her. But...she's not who I was talking about."

Bjorn looks down the stairs. "What makes you think either of them will know something she doesn't?"

"Wasn't talking about them, either." I shift my gaze to the killer's bloody corpse.

"Oh," Bjorn says. *"Oh..."*

Rain steps over the unconscious agent and approaches the dead man. She doesn't reel back at the sight of blood. She just reaches into one pocket at a time, finding nothing. Then she stands and looks around the room. When she turns toward me, I see that her eyes are actually closed.

"He's still here," Rain says. "But...he's pissed."

When Rain starts glowing, Bjorn asks, "We have time for this?"

"Collect their weapons," I tell him. "Tie them up if you want. I want answers."

Rain's brilliance forces me to squint, but I don't look away from it. Instead, I step closer and take her outstretched hand in mine. The connection is quick, but less disconcerting than last time.

A little.

"What the fuck?" Rain says, her inflections matching the killer's. "Where... You..."

Rain grimaces, hunching inward. This might be easy for me, but it still hurts her.

"You okay?" I ask Rain.

"He's fighting for control," she says. Her voice. And then in his, "Going to kill you."

"Got news for you, buddy," I say, still pissed at the asshole who tried to kill me and my friends, and who was sent by the people who were somehow involved in my wife's death. "You're already dead."

Rain growls at me.

"Who sent you?" I ask.

"Fuck you."

"You have no reason to protect them now," I argue.

"I have spite," he says. "I have hate."

"Well, he's a horrible person," Bjorn says.

Reggie shakes her head. "He was a contract killer, dear."

"It's the right thing to do." Doing right is a flimsy argument to use on a contract killer's recently deceased ghost, but I don't have a lot of ammunition to fire at him. He had no scruples in life. How much more of a monster will he be in death?

Rain grunts. Falls to her knees.

"Is he trying to take over still?" I ask.

She shakes her head. "Something else."

She looks back with a gasp, but when she speaks, it's the killer. "The fuck?" She scrambles away from the empty door, a look of horror on her face. "Stay back!"

Bjorn's eyes widen. He looks to the door, sees nothing and backs away anyway. Though none of us can see it, we all know something is there. Something that scares a ghost.

Something that scares a murderer.

"It's coming for you," Rain says, every word a struggle. "You should have lived...a better...life."

His soul isn't lost...it's waiting to be claimed.

Her face morphs from determination to horror. When she turns to me, hope shines through her bright eyes. "There's a second lab. In Austin."

"Who's running the labs?" I ask.

"SpecTek," he says.

"Who is in charge of SpecTek?"

"DARPA!"

"Tell us something we didn't know," Reggie grumbles, and she's right. All of this is old news.

"You work for DARPA?" That doesn't seem likely. The Defense Advanced Research Projects Agency's mission is to fund scientific research on behalf of the United States, mostly for defense, and by 'defense' they mean 'a strong offense is the best defense' kind of defense. They don't hire assassins.

"It's a black op," he says through Rain, backing away, pulling me along. "The details are secret, even from DARPA. Please, help me. F-forgive me!"

"I don't think that will save you," I tell him. I have more questions, but it's clear the man's time has come, and I don't want Rain in contact with him when whatever is with us in Bjorn's apartment decides to take him. I yank my hand away, but Rain holds on tight.

"It wasn't supposed to happen this way, but that doesn't mean they can't regain control," the man says, nearly squealing in fright.

"Control of what?" Rain asks herself.

"Of the monsters," he says, and then shouts, "Of his wife!" Rain lifts a hand in fear. The man shouts, "No! Help!"

Rain's light flickers out and she leaps away from where she'd been crouched. The room is empty, but I can feel it. Something cold and heavy. Rain cringes, feeling a lot more than I can.

And then it lifts away, leaving a lightness in its wake. The killer is gone, this time for good, taken by something I don't want to think about. But his final words still haunt me.

Morgan is alive.

Maybe in Austin.

She must have escaped the lab with her coworkers and been whisked away to a second location. That she hasn't contacted me about it, and the fact that I'm being hunted, means she's probably being held against her will.

The information fuels me. Gives me clarity.

"You have a car?" I ask Bjorn.

He nods. "Garage in the back."

"Get it started."

"Where are we going?" Reggie asks.

"Cambridge," I say.

23

The drive from Salem to Cambridge isn't a long one. On a good day, without traffic, it can be done in 30 minutes. With traffic, an hour. But today, despite the roads being largely empty, we've been driving for an hour, and we're only halfway there. Normally, any sane person would take 128 to Route 1. But Reggie insisted on staying off highways, because 'They'll see us coming on traffic cams.'

I thought faster was better, so I pointed out the number of cameras watching storefronts and traffic lights we'd pass by taking back roads. Reggie agreed with my point, but not with my solution. And Bjorn is hers to command.

So now Reggie, Rain, and I are crammed into the back seat of a black Mini-Cooper. I'm in the middle, with my legs squeezed tight and my balls in a thigh vice. I attempted to man-spread just a bit, but neither Rain nor Reggie was having it, and I lacked the will to argue my case. We're ducked down low, but anyone passing us in a big SUV would have no trouble seeing us, so we're covered in the black sheet from Bjorn's bed. It smells like Axe body spray and patchouli.

Bjorn is driving, all crammed up behind the wheel. Beside him is the FBI agent, Garcia. Her unconscious body is seat-belted in place. Her FBI jacket has been removed, and her face is concealed by sunglasses and a Red Sox cap. Head lolled to the side, any passerby would take her for a snoozing passenger. I'm a little concerned she hasn't come to yet, but I'm also somewhat relieved. I'm not looking forward to that conversation. She's not gagged, but her hands and feet are bound with extension cords.

Overnight, I've gone from being a struggling blogger to a murderer, a witness, a fugitive, a medium, an abductor of a federal agent, and a widower. And I'm not even sure what label to put on what happened in Boston. Supernatural attack survivor?

Being proactive feels good. Feels right. But I'm not sure what it will accomplish. The small bit of video I captured on my phone won't reveal enough for Reggie to really understand what's happening. But if I can get it to the news, it might be enough to expose SpecTek, and maybe make killing me a waste of resources. It was also the last time I saw Morgan. Her final goodbye. And I would face ten kaiju ghosts to get it back.

"Hey, Bjorn," I say, attempting to adjust my nether region without making a spectacle of it, "you're what, six-foot-three?"

"Six-four," he says.

"Why the hell do you have a Mini-Cooper?"

"Uhh, because it's fuel efficient," he says.

"Bullshit," I say. It might be true, but Mini-Cooper owners are more interested in style than fuel-efficiency. If you really cared about fuel efficiency and didn't mind driving a Matchbox car, you could always get a Prius, like Reggie.

"It's because women like them," Reggie says.

"C'mon," I say, and then realize I'm talking to 1) a woman, and 2) the woman that is *with* Bjorn. "Really?"

"I don't see why this matters," Rain says.

"He's trying to distract himself," Reggie says, cutting through to my emotional core with a hot laser knife.

"From what?" Rain says. "We should be focusing."

"Well," Bjorn says. "His wife died last night, right?"

Bjorn opens Reggie's cut wider and dumps salt in it. Man, smart people can be socially awkward. As I sink in on myself, I'm only vaguely aware of the group discussing all the things weighing me down. Instead of listening, I picture Morgan's face.

For now, the freshness of her memory will keep me going. The mystery of her death. The giant monsters somehow connected to it. Distraction is the balm for my wounds.

So I remember her instead.

Sunday morning is the best time to go see a movie. The only other people at our local theater are a church group that rents one of the rooms for their service.

Two years ago, we went to see a Marvel movie. I don't remember which one. They're all kind of the same. We passed on the early morning popcorn—honestly, movie theater popcorn makes me feel depressed when there's a bucket of it in my gut, no matter what time of day it is—and I think that made us look like churchgoers. Or maybe it's that Morgan greeted everyone we encountered with a smile.

Despite pre-ordering our tickets and reserving seats, we arrived thirty minutes early—an old habit to ensure getting prime locations. Feeling mischievous, we decided to infiltrate the service, which turned out to be a simulcast of some church in California. As weird as that was, the music was great—old hymns made modern. When *Amazing Grace* played, Morgan was moved to tears. At the time, I didn't see why she would react strongly to 'Amazing Grace, How sweet the sound, that saved a wretch like me,' but now I've got some perspective. Her life wasn't as blameless as I believed.

I push thoughts about what Morgan might have been involved in out of my mind and focus on the memory.

We still made it to our movie with fifteen minutes to spare—thirty if you count the inordinate number of trailers, but those fifteen minutes of praise music to a God we didn't believe in remain one of the highlights of our marriage. There was something about it...some kind of connection between us that wasn't normal. Something I might now call supernatural, since I know it's not *all* smoke and mirrors.

Smoke and mirrors can't destroy cities and suck people's souls into the sky.

And with that thought, I'm back in the present, in time to hear Bjorn say, "It's amazing he's still functioning."

I know he's talking about me, that I should feel something, or say something, but mostly I just agree with him.

Why haven't *I cracked up yet?*

Because, as crazy as it sounds, I can still feel her with me. It's not a physical thing, like with the other ghosts we've encountered. It's more like a feeling. An instinct. Some kind of M. Night Shyamalan sixth sense. But I'm not about to say that, and I'm happy to let the conversation fizzle.

"Out of respect for your friend in the back seat," the FBI agent says, "I think you should probably shut the hell up." She turns her face toward Bjorn and looks at him over the sunglasses that have slid down her nose.

"Has she been awake for long?" I ask, bewildered that I was so far gone down memory lane that I missed her waking.

"I woke up about an hour ago," she says.

"We've been driving for an hour," I point out.

She raises her eyebrows at me.

"You've been listening to us this whole time?" Bjorn asks, sounding somewhat offended by the idea.

"Gathering intel on multiple suspected terrorists," she says. "Yeah, that's kind of my job."

"And why are you talking to us now?" I ask.

"Because you're clearly not terrorists." She motions to Rain with her head, "Aside from this little firecracker—nice moves by the way—I doubt any of you could last ten seconds in a fight with Minnie Mouse."

"Well, yeah," Bjorn says. "She's a cartoon."

"Quiet, wizard," the agent says, revealing she knows a lot more about us than I would have guessed. I mentally run through the last hour's conversation and realize she knows *a lot*. Really, everything there is to know about us, about last night, and the situation we're in.

"I'm not a wizard," Bjorn says. "I'm a war—"

"Qu-i-et," Garcia says, lifting a hand and pinching her fingers together.

"Hey," I say, leaning forward. Her hands are untied, the extension cord lying on her lap. "How'd—"

"You're all horrible abductors," she says, and she quickly unties her feet.

When she sits back up, looking somewhat casual, I say, "You don't seem angry."

"I'm not thrilled about being knocked out," she says. "But you're not who I thought you were. Not who I was told you were."

"Maybe we knew you were awake this whole time," Reggie says, "and have been manipulating you with—"

Garcia twists around in her seat. "None of you are smart enough to pull that off."

"I'm a professor at M.I.T.," Reggie complains.

"I know," Garcia says, showing her first sign of true impatience. "You've mentioned it like five times in the last hour. And here's the thing, all of your time in a lab..." She motions to Bjorn, "or his time selling false hope..."

"Hey," Bjorn says.

She ignores him, turning toward me, "Or your time being a washed-up crime reporter..."

Ouch.

"...isn't going to help you out of this mess. If the people responsible for Boston really are after you, they have deep pockets, and that dead assassin in the apartment won't be the last."

I feel like I've just been part of a Comedy Central roast, except it wasn't funny, and no one's watching. I don't think Garcia was even trying to be mean. She's just laying out the cold, hard facts. She could have just as easily said, "You're screwed," but someone would have argued.

"What about me?" Rain asks.

"You..." Garcia looks Rain up and down. "You don't even know your own name."

"But the things she can do," Reggie says.

"Mmm-hmm," Garcia says. "She glows, right? Talks to the dead?"

"I talk to them," I say. "She..." Garcia's lone raised eyebrow of doubt takes the fight out of me. "Never mind."

"I'm afraid that horseshit falls squarely in the 'I'll believe it when I see it' category. But...I believe you're not terrorists. I believe you saw something you weren't supposed to, and that people—powerful people—are hunting you down. And I believe your wife died last night." She loses a trace of her edge. "Sorry about that."

"Thanks," I say.

"You can thank me by telling me what you're planning to do about it," she says. "It's the only damn thing you all *haven't* talked about."

"We're going to my place," I say. "To get my phone."

"Your place," she says, cracking a smile. "Funny."

When I don't grin or even blink, she frowns. "You're serious?" A long sigh. "Your house is cordoned off." To Reggie. "Your lab, too." Back to me. "Why do you need your phone? You were in Cambridge last night. It's a brick, right?"

"The data is still on it," Reggie says.

"What data?"

"A video of what happened," I say.

"You mean the big blue explosion and the light shooting up into the sky?"

"You saw it?" I ask.

"I heard about it," she says. "In a briefing."

"And Boston?" I asked.

"The chemical attack," she says.

Reggie and I share an aghast look. Not even the FBI knows the truth about what happened? I decide to not discuss the kaiju, which we've apparently also left out of the conversation for the past hour. "The video is a screen capture of a FaceTime with my wife, from inside SpecTek when it exploded."

Garcia stares at me. "You're serious?"

"If we get the phone, we can clear our names and show the world that we didn't do what everyone thinks we did. And maybe we can figure out what happened to my wife."

"And who I am," Rain adds.

Garcia takes several moments to process, sighing several times. "Near as I can tell, the worst thing you've done is abduct me. Given the circumstances, I can't say I blame you. And if everything you said is true, the real bad guys are still out there."

"Are you going to help us?" Reggie asks. *"It sounds like she's going to help us."*

Garcia takes a moment to look each of us in the eyes. She lingers on me, and says, "I'm going to try. But the moment any one of you steps out of line, doesn't do what I say, or turns out to be anything more than good people in the wrong place at the wrong time..." She glances at Rain. "I will take you down." A second glance at Rain. "From a distance."

"Thank you," I say, and the earnestness of my gratitude seems to take her by surprise.

She gives a subtle nod. "Now, assuming at least one of you was smart enough to bring my badge and gun..." She reaches over the seat and holds out her hands. "I'm going to need them back."

24

"Do you think we can trust her?" Bjorn asks.

"I'm not sure I trust *you*," I say, watching Garcia walk down the street toward my house, gun on her hip, badge in her pocket, Red Sox cap on her head to cover the lump from when Rain slammed her into the wall. If all goes well, she'll be allowed past the guarded police tape and find the phone, where I left it. In the bedroom. Somewhere. Honestly, I can't remember where I left it.

"I have done nothing to warrant your distrust," Bjorn complains.

"Guess I just have a thing against warlocks," I say. I don't really mean it. I'm fairly inclusive. I'm just not interested.

"I'm not a real—"

"I also have a thing against hacks."

Bjorn clamps his mouth shut. Reggie gives him a pat. "He has other things on his mind."

That seems to sink in to the bubbling cauldron that is his mind. He turns around to face me. "Sorry. I'm being selfish."

"You're fine," I say, leaning to look around him, as Garcia reaches the police line, flashes her badge, and strikes up a conversation with one of the police officers guarding it.

Any second now, she's going to turn around, point out the Mini-Cooper, and send an army of cops after us. I'm sure of it.

And if that happens, we'll be running away on foot. She took her badge, wallet, *and* the car keys.

Then again, she could have turned her gun on us right away. Could have single-handedly subdued the terrorists. Could have built a career atop our captures.

When the officer lifts the yellow tape, giving Garcia access to my house, I remember to breathe.

"This is ridiculous," Rain says. Seated behind Bjorn, whose seat is all the way back, forcing her knees against the seatback. She might not have any memories, but she's come to understand that she is, and was, a woman of action. Sitting in this tiny car, waiting for someone else to do what needs doing is driving her nuts. More than the kaiju creatures, the supernatural revelations, or the fact that she is without history, this inaction triggers her ire.

"I don't disagree," I say.

"*You* let her go," Rain says.

"I..." It's then that I realize I'm in charge of this little band of would-be terrorists. The realization makes my heart skip a beat. Not because I have a fear of leadership, but because if something bad happens to any of them, I'm responsible. "I didn't see any other—"

"There're always options," she says in a way that suggests she's quoting someone she can't remember.

"I didn't see a better option," I say.

Rain's response is a grunt, so I ignore her and focus on the road ahead, hoping to see Garcia heading back our way. Though that seems unrealistic. She needs to sell that she's there for the investigation. Running in and out of the house might raise suspicions.

Stop overthinking it, I tell myself, annoyed at my own frantic thought process. *Just shut up and wait.*

When Rain grunts again, I nearly bark at her. Then I remember the other times I've heard her make that same uncomfortable groan.

I spin toward her, knowing what I'm going to see, but hoping I'm wrong.

Her fingertips are glowing.

"That's new," Reggie says, looking past me.

"Is there a ghost here?" I ask, looking around the car like we might have a stowaway.

"Maybe it's Joseph White, hitching a ride out of Salem?" Reggie says, and then counters with, "Can spirits do that? *Don't be silly. They stay where they died.*" She turns to Bjorn. "Right?"

"Most often," Bjorn says, twisted around, wide eyes on Rain's glowing fingers. "But there are several documented cases of spirits returning home, to where they feel most connected to the world. It's like a chain...no, that's too strong. Like a *tether*. They're bound to where they feel the strongest connection. It fuels them."

"Like an umbilical," Reggie says. "But, gross. 'Tether' is better."

A flare of light from Rain's fingers, coupled with another grunt, refocuses me. "It's not...*them* is it?"

She shakes her head, but says, "It is...but, not here. Not in Boston. I can feel them pulling me."

"A human ghost-compass?" Reggie said, sounding doubtful.

"I need a map," Rain says.

Bjorn digs his phone from his pocket. "I have Google maps."

"A real map," she says, grunting again. She's working hard at holding back the glow. "Before I lose them."

With my house so close, I mentally rummage through the closets, cabinets, and drawers. We could sneak in the back, maybe. Or send Garcia back for one. But like most of the modern world, I gave up on impossible-to-fold paper maps about a decade ago.

But my neighbor didn't. I reach past Rain, tug the door handle, and shove the door open.

"Where are you going?" Reggie asks.

"Randy's house," I say.

"Who is Randy?" Bjorn asks.

I slide to the open door, as Rain climbs out. "A friend."

"A *good* friend?" Reggie asks.

"I think so." I close the door and turn away from the police at the end of the road. To Rain I say, "Keep your head down and your hands covered."

She tucks her hands into her pockets.

The light shines through the fabric, but it's muted enough in the daylight to go unnoticed by men two hundred feet away.

"Just act natural," I tell her, leading her toward the front door of a home, whose owners I've never met or even seen. "Like you're supposed to be here."

"Are you talking to me," Rain says, "or yourself? Because you don't look natural, or like you're supposed to be here."

I glance at her, about to form a rebuttal, when I see how calm and casual she looks. I'm moving more like Elmer Fudd on a hunt for wabbits. I try to mimic her, but by the time I get it close to right, we're out of sight on the house's side. After a quick look around, to see if we're being watched, I crouch-walk to the back yard and head toward Randy's house.

The good thing about this part of Cambridge is that everyone has a back yard, most of them sporting big, leafy oak or maple trees. Our path to Randy's yard is clear of prying eyes. The bad thing is that each and every one of the yards is divided by a collection of fences. Some of them are short wooden affairs. Some are chain link. And two of them are six feet tall. Rain makes short work of them all, leaping the shorter fences, and climbing over the taller two by jumping onto the central support beam and heaving herself over the top. I'm somewhat more clumsy, but I run the gauntlet without falling or giving us away.

It takes a good five minutes, but we reach Randy's back door without being seen. Hands cupped, face to glass, I look through the living room window. Empty. There would normally be a sports game on the TV, even if no one is watching, but there isn't a single light on in the house. Then again, the power is still out.

I'm about to verbalize my debate over whether or not someone is home when Rain grunts again. Her cheeks crackle with light. We need to do this now.

Randy keeps a spare key hidden in his bird bath. It's under an inch of water and a 'smooth layer of bird turd.' He'd said so, when he showed it to me. Not even the most desperate criminal would look for it there. Looks like he was wrong about that. My fingers slip through the sludge, but after plucking the key up and giving it a shake in the water, we're good to go.

The key slips into the deadbolt. It snaps open, when I give it a twist. The volume of it gives me a start, but it's nothing compared to the high-pitched wail that nearly escapes my throat when Randy whips open the door and shoves a shotgun in my face.

For a split second, I'm sure he's going to kill me.

Then his eyes go wide, and the weapon lowers. "Saul, holy shit!" He embraces me, giving my back a hearty slap that knocks the wind out of me. "What they're saying about you, it's not true. I was with you last night. I didn't tell the suits that, but I can testify if you need it. For both of y—"

He's seen Rain. Seen her inner light shining through.

"The hell?"

"Long story," I say. "You still have your map up?"

"M-map? Yeah, but she's—"

I slip past him, tugging Rain behind me.

The home is strangely quiet. "Family is away?"

"My sister's," he says. "In Revere."

"Good," I say, and I push into Randy's 'office.' He doesn't work from home. I'm not sure he does any actual work in this room aside from yearly taxes and bill paying. It's wall-to-wall Boston sports memorabilia. Signed baseballs, footballs, and hockey pucks. Framed jerseys. Wall-mounted bats and hockey sticks. A football helmet worn by Tom Brady under glass. It's like a museum to Boston sports legacy, with the exception of a U.S. map mounted on corkboard and hung on the wall. It's covered in bright tacks representing all of the sports stadiums visited during the family's yearly RV trips.

"What do you need the map for?" he asks, when I move to the blinds and slowly twist them shut.

"I have no idea." I turn to watch Rain, as she approaches the map. "We're clear."

With the suddenness of fireworks, Rain's brilliance bursts into the room. Randy stumbles back, but he catches himself on the doorframe, averting his eyes from the light.

Rain places her fingertips against the map.

"She's going to catch it on fire," Randy says. He's clearly freaked out, but still a concerned home owner at heart.

"It's not that kind of light," I say, stepping closer, as Rain's hands move over the paper.

"What the hell kind of light is it?" Randy asks. "It looks like what we saw last night."

I nod in agreement. "That's exactly what it is." It's not an answer, but I think he understands that I don't really *have* an answer. Not yet.

"I can feel them moving," Rain says, her voice desperate. Pleading. Channeling what she feels. All the light in her body pulses and concentrates, first in her arm, then in her hand, and finally a single luminous finger, which is resting on Boston.

She closes her eyes.

Her hand moves across the map in a way that reminds me of a Ouija board, like some force other than her muscles is guiding her. Her fingers come to a stop. A spasm runs through her arm. The light extinguishes.

Rain opens her eyes. "They're following a tether."

I step closer. "They're?"

"I felt three."

"Three of *what?*" Randy asks, but neither of us answer him. I'm more interested in where this...tether...leads.

I get my answer when Rain lifts her finger from the map, revealing the text underneath, resting beside a red thumbtack.

Chicago.

25

"Chicago?" I ask. "What's in Chicago?"

"The fuckin' Bears," Randy says. "And the Bulls, obviously."

The Chicago Bulls, under Michael Jordan, is the only non-Boston sports team I've ever heard Randy speak positively about.

"If I knew, I wouldn't remember," Rain says.

It's not much of a lead, but it's something. And if Rain is right, we need to warn the city. I head for the door. "Let's go."

"Wait," Randy says, following me out into the hall. "You're not even gonna tell me what this is all about? I mean, it's chaos out there, right? I know you're not a bad guy, but you're mixed up in it."

"Better if you don't know anything," Rain says. "In case you're questioned."

Randy crosses his arms. "I know how to keep a secret."

"Not from these people," I say. I'm guessing that people who hire assassins, wouldn't have a problem with torture.

"I should probably knock him out," Rain says.

"What?" Randy is aghast.

"So they don't know you helped us."

Randy takes a step back, reassessing Rain. "Look, lady. I can handle myself, and no one knows you're here. Just go the way you came, and I'll keep my mouth shut."

Rain looks to me.

"We're not knocking him out," I say, despite knowing, in my heart, that she's right. But he's not wrong either. If we leave his house without being spotted, he'll be equally safe, sans a concussion. "But, you can't stay here."

"Can't leave my house unprotected," Randy says.

When he says, 'house,' what he's really saying is, 'My memorabilia collection.'

"No matter how much that Tom Brady helmet is worth, it's not as valuable as your life," I tell him.

"Not sure about that," he says.

He's half-joking, but he needs to sober up. "The people looking for us are killers. They already sent an assassin for us."

"An assassin?" He's not buying it. "How are you here, then?"

The twisting emotions on my face take all doubt away when I say, "I shot him. I killed him."

Rain puts her hand on my arm. "You saved my life."

"Oh, God... Holy shit."

Randy double-takes his house like an assassin might have followed us here. And it's not an unreasonable assumption. Which is why he needs to leave.

"Be with your family," I tell him. "They need you more than they need a baseball bat signed by Jim Rice."

"Wade Boggs," he corrects, and then he nods. "Okay. Yeah. I'll just—"

Motion in the living room window draws his eyes. A black SUV drives past, slowing to a stop. A moment later, Garcia walks casually away from the crime scene, glancing back at the vehicle. Then she's eyes forward, her pace a little too quick.

Randy leans to watch the SUV park in front of his house. "That's them, isn't it?"

"Could be," I say, and then I point to Garcia. "She's with us."

"And she is?"

"FBI," I say.

"You could have told me you were working with the FBI," he says.

"We abducted her," Rain says, much to Randy's horror.

"But she's working with us now," I clarify, moving toward the back door. "And that's our cue to leave."

Randy gives me a firm handshake and claps my shoulder. "Stay safe, buddy. I'll leave in a few minutes. We took a bus to Revere this morning. I came back with her sister's car. So I'm good."

I feel bad that I hadn't even considered how Randy would leave Cambridge while everything in the city is powerless, but I'm grateful he thought to explain.

"We'll catch up when this blows over," I say, but it feels like a false promise.

"See you around, Phillips," he says to Rain, and then he closes the door behind us.

"Does he think my name is Phillip?" Rain asks, as we climb the first fence.

"Phillips," I say, and I drop down into the Henderson's back yard. "It's a lightbulb brand."

"Oh," she says. "Ha. He seems like a nice guy."

We crouch-hustle across the yard. "He is."

"Hope they don't kill him."

"Thanks," I say, and I quicken my pace.

I'm proficient at fence-vaulting by the time we reach the last yard. We cover the distance in half the time it took us to reach Randy's house. But Garcia still beats us with enough time to practice the death glare she levels at me when we casually walk out into the open and climb into the Mini-Cooper's back seat.

"Are you two stupid?" she asks after Rain closes the door behind us. "Did you not see them?" She hitches her thumb up the road. Two bona fide Men-In-Black-looking dudes stand in the road, questioning a police officer.

"We had a situation," I say.

Garcia raises an eyebrow, waiting for an explanation.

"I was glowing," Rain says.

"Glowing..."

"We need to go to Chicago," I say.

"Chicago?" Reggie says. "What for?"

"Since I can't actually summon a cloak of invisibility," Bjorn says, "I think we need to get the hell out of here."

When he puts the car in drive, Garcia says, "Slowly...but not too slow. Like you live here."

"Right..." Bjorn starts a lazy three-point turn and ends up completing it in two, thanks to the Cooper's size and turn radius.

My body relaxes as we coast away from my house. It's only then that my mind clears enough for me to remember why we're here. "Did you get it?"

Garcia hands my phone back. Despite knowing it's dead, I try the power button. Seeing Morgan's final goodbye is going to hurt. A lot. But it's a pain I'll be spared a little while longer.

"Give it here," Reggie says. "I can fix it. *Need the screwdrivers. They don't know about the screwdrivers.*" She looks up at Garcia, who's now frowning at Reggie. Her self-conversations are disconcerting, until you learn that she's a genius.

"In the glove box," Bjorn says.

Garcia retrieves a set of mini-screwdrivers, amused by their size. She smiles at Bjorn, "Sorry, Bjorn, I'm not buying it. No way you're descended from Vikings."

"That's what I said," I say.

She hands the tools back to Reggie. "Go nuts."

Reggie turns her lap into a makeshift workshop, disassembling my phone with the efficiency of someone who has done it before. Wouldn't surprise me if she'd used iPhone parts for her creations. She's a regular Dr. Frankenstein of robotics.

"So," Bjorn says. "You know that black SUV from the house?"

He doesn't need to answer his question for us. Rain and I spin around to look out the small rear window. Garcia adjusts her side mirror.

"They must have seen you," Garcia says.

"Or the FBI agent, who's been reported as abducted by terrorists," I point out. She doesn't agree, but she doesn't dismiss it, either.

"Doesn't matter," Rain says, and then to Bjorn. "Take a left."

"I was turning left anyway," he says, panic rising.

"When I tell you, gun it," Rain says.

We take the left turn, and suddenly there's a house between us and the SUV, which is a good hundred feet back.

"Now!" Rain says.

To say the Mini's engine roars would be a gross overstatement. It whines. Loudly. But it also accelerates, probably a lot slower than it would without four passengers, but fast enough.

"Turn right!" Rain says.

Tires squeal as we round the corner, putting an extra layer of shielding between us and the SUV.

"One more turn," Rain says. "Next right."

The turn is just ahead. We're nearly there.

The roar of an engine—a real engine—pulls my attention back to the rear window. The SUV charges up behind us on a collision course. The beast of a vehicle has no trouble closing the distance. And if it hits us...

"Bjorn..." I say.

"I see it!" He cranks the wheel hard to the right, and we squeal around another turn, narrowly missing the curb. I think it will be impossible for the much larger, much faster SUV to make the turn at speed, but the driver is a pro. The big vehicle drifts around the corner, taking it faster than we did, narrowing the gap.

Out of the corner of my eye, as we blow through the stop sign for my street, I see a car barreling toward us, and Randy behind the wheel. Despite there being no real danger of a collision, he slams on the brakes, blocking the intersection. He gets out of the vehicle to shout at us, flipping us the bird as we peel away. When the SUV screeches to a stop behind him, honking its horn, he turns around and starts shouting at them, which in this part of the world is pretty standard behavior.

I lose sight of Randy and the SUV when we take another turn. Twenty more turns and ten minutes later, I'm pretty sure we've lost them. But how long until more vehicles join the search? Or helicopters?

"Got it," Reggie says, turning on her phone, which now contains the solid-state drive from mine. It starts up like new, loading as though it was my phone. Reggie wastes no time opening the Photos app, scrolling to my videos, and playing the most recent file.

Without warning, I'm propelled into the past, reliving my final moments with Morgan. While I'm somewhat traumatized by the fear in her voice, the chaos all around her, and the knowledge of how the call ends, Reggie views it through a different set of eyes. "Fascinating..." she says, as what I now think is the scientist's soul being sucked from his body stretches out behind him. *"Don't say that in front of him."* Then she turns to me. "Sorry." And then turns to Bjorn. "Take us to Logan."

"What's at Logan?" Garcia asks.

"Uhh, planes," Reggie says, like it's the dumbest question she's ever heard. "We're going to Chicago, right?"

"What's in Chicago?" Garcia is close to losing her patience.

"SpecTek's original lab," Reggie says, "and maybe a better understanding of this." She hands the phone forward and hits play for Garcia. I can't see the video from the back seat, but I can still hear the audio and the pain in my voice.

I tear up when I hear Morgan say, "Baby, you can do it. You can live. You can be bold. You don't need me. Never have."

Trying not to be reduced to a blubbering mess, I turn my eyes to the window and my mind to the near future instead of the recent past. But I don't know which is worse, because I'm pretty sure answers aren't the only thing we're going to find in Chicago.

26

"How is this possible?" I ask, standing in front of a private jet parked inside a hangar at Logan airport. The plane is sleek, shiny-new, and it sports a wavy blue design on its side. It shouts wealth and power. When we approached the gate, I was sure the TSA would search us, ID us, and arrest us, but Reggie's ID—not Garcia's—was enough to get us whisked past security.

What Garcia did do with her knowledge of FBI protocols, was call in a very convincing and anonymous tip about a terrorist threat to Chicago, citing the destruction in Cambridge and Boston as proof of what was coming. The general public might not know the extent of what happened in Boston, but the FBI certainly does. If they believed her, hopefully they'll get enough people out of the city to limit the death toll, should Brute or Wisp make another appearance.

"This is a Cessna Citation X," Garcia says. "It's one of the fastest private jets in the world."

The side hatch opens, stairs extending down. A handsome pilot— who looks like he spends equal time at the gym, the hair salon, and the beach—stands in the open hatch, smiling at us. "Good to see you again, Dr. Adisa. We received your itinerary. We're fueled up and ready to go."

"Thanks, Chuck," Reggie says.

"No luggage today?" Chuck asks.

Reg shakes her head. "Day trip."

"Very good," he says, and he slips back inside.

Somehow Reggie arranged all this from her phone, even after swapping out hard drives. While I don't understand the technical aspects of her phone hacking, I don't doubt her ability to do it. But the plane? The security pass? Captain Handsome? It baffles me. So I ask again, "Reggie, how is this possible?"

I'm not sure she's going to answer, but everyone—including Bjorn—waits to hear it.

She sighs. "I own a few dozen patents."

That's not really shocking news. I mean, a few dozen is a lot, but Reggie is an inventor. Patents are part of the job.

"Most of them are leased to corporations," she says.

"What corporations?" Bjorn asks.

"The kinds that require NDAs," she says. "But they're...not small."

"So, you're rich," Garcia says, and motions to the plane. "Really rich."

"She lives in a one-bedroom apartment in downtown Salem," Bjorn says to Garcia, with a nervous chuckle.

"She drives a Prius," I add.

"Drove a Prius," Reggie says, and she starts up the stairs into the plane. "I don't believe in leaving a big carbon footprint."

"Says the woman with a private jet," Rain says.

Reggie stops in the door. "I don't own it. I just...have it on retainer."

She disappears inside. We stand there, baffled for a moment, and then Bjorn heads up, followed by Rain.

Garcia gives me a side-long glance. "Carbon footprint, my ass." Then she heads up and inside the plane.

I used to spend days alone, just writing, by myself. For the past 24 hours, I haven't been alone other than the two times I've used the bathroom. So I take a moment to re-center.

I try to clear my mind, but I end up thinking about what we've experienced, what we've learned, all the things we don't understand, where we're going, and what we might find in Chicago. My thoughts are a chaotic jumble that quickly overwhelms me. As my chest tightens toward a panic attack, I close my eyes and picture Morgan's face.

I hear her voice. *You can be bold.*

It's like she knew I'd be faced with this moment.

Be bold.

It's like a whisper in my ear. Like she's right here with me, still...even though she's God knows where. Literally.

Unless the dead assassin was telling the truth... That she's alive. That SpecTek is trying to control her. But that doesn't feel true. As much as I feel her with me, I feel that she is gone. How could anyone survive that explosion? They couldn't. She couldn't.

He was just screwing with me, I decide, and I feel a measure of peace return. There is nothing worse than not knowing. She's gone, and it's time to listen to her advice. I take a deep breath, hold it, and let it out slowly, repeating the process five times.

When I open my eyes, I feel centered. Not exactly confident, or bold, but on task.

"Hey, asshole." Garcia stands in the open door. "You coming or what?"

I can't help but smile. Our resident FBI agent is pretty, but tough and merciless, in an old-school Boston kind of way, though her accent, tinged with Latina flare, is hard to place. I suspect she might actually be a New Yorker.

She waits for me at the top of the stairs. "Thanks," I tell her.

"For what?"

"Believing us," I say. "For seeing this through, despite—"

"Being knocked unconscious and abducted?"

"Yeah, that."

She hesitates. "The truth is, I know who you are. Who you were, I guess. You did good work, back in the day. I've been in Boston for eight years. You covered cases I worked on, and you even kept a few guys from walking. I know you're a good guy. If you weren't at the center of all this, I'd have already locked up your sideshow friends."

"Thanks...I think."

She smiles. "Just keep in mind, the moment I get a whiff of B.S. from any one of you..."

I raise my hands. "I get it. You'll take us to pound town."

Garcia's forehead is wrinkled on one side. She has a habit of raising a single eyebrow when she questions something, which she's been doing a lot of since we met.

Her eyebrow raises again, on cue, this time with a laugh. "Pound town?"

"Yeah...like, the town where you get beat down. Something like that. People say it. I didn't make it up."

"I know." She laughs again and steps aside, letting me past her. "Pound town isn't a place; it's rough sex." She pats my shoulder. "And you're not my type."

Embarrassment burns my face like I've been in the sun too long, but the plane's luxurious interior distracts me from my faux pas. There are eight plush, leather seats, four to a side. The chairs face each other, like four dining tables for two at a restaurant, except the tables here fold down, and the seats recline. Behind the seating section is a small kitchen and a wet bar, all of it built from shiny, red mahogany.

"Do I smell mint?" Bjorn asks, leaning back in his chair, enjoying the ample leg room.

Reggie sits across from him. "Helps calm the mind. There's a sprig of it in your ash tray."

Bjorn opens the ashtray built into his armrest, and sure enough, there's a little branch of mint leaves pressed inside, turning a stench receptacle into an air freshener. I make my way past them and sit in the back, across from Rain, who is already buckled in and looking out the window at the view...which is currently the inside of the hangar.

Garcia takes a seat across the aisle from Bjorn, from where she can look both Reggie and me in the eyes, and easily stop anyone heading for the door. She buckles up, tilts her head down, and closes her eyes.

When the engines whine to life and Captain Handsome announces that we're underway, I decide to do the same.

To my utter shock, I wake up at 30,000 feet.

Even though I didn't sleep a wink last night, and I've been running for my life, adrenaline waxing and waning, all while dealing with Morgan's death, I didn't expect to sleep without an Ambien or two. I nearly cheer, 'I'm doing it,' like a four-year-old learning to use the potty. If Morgan's watching, I know she's proud.

When I look up, it's Rain who's watching me, her blue eyes impossible to read. "How long has it been?"

I'm expecting to hear something that ends with, 'minutes.'

"Almost three hours," she says.

"Three *hours?* We must nearly be there."

"That's what the pilot just said. I think he woke you up."

I look out the window. The view is gray. I'm about to ask if it's a storm when lightning rips through distant clouds, flinching me away from the window. I haven't been a fan of flying in storms since the Twilight Zone episode with Captain Kirk and a plane-eating gremlin. I close the shade and pretend the storm doesn't exist.

I close my eyes for a moment, trying to calm myself. When my eyes snap open again, Rain's gaze is waiting for me. She already knows what I'm going to ask. "Is this..."

"Could be," she says. "I'm not sure."

"Do you feel them?"

"I've been feeling them for the last hour," she says, and she lifts her hand. Slowly, it starts to glow. Then she balls a fist and the light fades. "But it's definitely getting stronger."

"Any sense of why they're here?" I ask.

"You'll have to ask them," she says.

I smile, until I realize she wasn't joking. Unable to even respond to that idea, I turn to Garcia. *Is she still sleeping?* I wonder, but then she opens her eyes and lifts her chin at me like a bro, saying 'Sup?' Reggie and Bjorn are talking, voices quiet. Sounds like science stuff. I'm pretty sure Garcia was listening to them the whole time.

"We're making our approach now," the pilot says over the intercom, and the plane begins a rapid descent, leaving my stomach a few hundred feet above us. Wind and rain lash the jet, shaking us like a mixed drink, and then spewing us out into the lower atmosphere.

Rain looks out her window, eyes widening slowly.

At first, I think she's starting to glow, but then I realize the light is coming from outside.

"Holy Ereshkigal..." Bjorn says, face pressed to glass.

I lift my shade to find a massive, swirling storm similar to what first appeared in Cambridge. Lightning arcs across the sky above Chicago. The clouds are so thick it looks like night, the city cast in a wavering blue glow.

I hope they got the people out, I think.

Before I can ask Rain what's happening, the plane tips to the right and makes a sharp turn. Reggie stands in the cockpit door, clinging to its frame.

"What the hell are you doing?" Garcia says. She's angry, but also confused by what she's seeing outside. She wasn't at ground zero for what happened last night, and we haven't mentioned the whole ghost-kaiju thing yet. Probably should have, but I think we'd have lost all credibility with her, and we might have found ourselves being arrested instead of helped.

"Getting a closer look!" Reggie says, as the plane swoops in toward the city, breaking who knows how many laws. *These pilots must be paid a shit-ton of money to pull a stunt like this,* I think, and I wonder how long it will take the Air Force to shoot us out of the sky.

We're just a few hundred feet above the ground, as we fly past the city's outskirts, avoiding the downtown and the buildings that tower above us.

"Get this plane out of the city!" Garcia draws her handgun. "Now!"

Reggie steps out of the cockpit, hands raised. "This might be our only chance to—"

Garcia aims the handgun at Reggie. *"Now."*

Reggie is about to argue her case again, when Bjorn does it for her. "What...the...fuck..."

Bjorn wasn't with us last night either. He might believe what Reggie tells him, but he hasn't seen it. Hasn't lived it. Survived it. Then I turn and look out the window again, and I share in Bjorn's horror. "Oh... Oh, God."

Please let the city be evacuated...

I turn to Rain, whose now-luminous face is staring out the window. "There are *three* of them."

27

Chicago is screwed.

As we swing out over Lake Michigan, its choppy surface reflecting and fracturing the lightning above, the three spectral monsters come into view. Mostly. They shimmer in and out of reality, as they turn their attention toward the city's core.

Brute is among them, its long arms swinging. From a distance it appears to be moving slowly, but it's a trick of perspective. Each step moves the creature a hundred feet forward, destroying everything in its path. So far, that's mostly residential buildings, but it won't be long before skyscrapers are tumbling.

The second specter is like something out of a Salvador Dalí painting. Its three-hundred-foot-long, spindly legs swing over rooftops, each step carefully placed like a hunting crane. The creature's body, what I can see of it, is bulbous, like a hundred-foot-tall and long marshmallow that's been puffed up with air and then left in the sun too long. It's fringed with fans of stretched flesh over spines, like a Dimetrodon's back. The fans wave in unison, like they're helping the slender legs keep its immense weight off the ground. I can't see a face—just a mangled mass of bulging, twitching flesh.

They're not real, I think.

They're the stuff of nightmares.

Impossible creatures not confined by the laws of physics, and yet fully capable of interacting with the physical world.

And the third is the worst of them all. Its long, eel-like, translucent body, extreme underbite, transparent needle-teeth, and harsh, bug-eyed stare reminds me of a black dragonfish. Lines of bright dots and luminous stripes flare away from its jaws, undulating as it moves. Hundreds of short, stiff appendages dangle from its underside, wriggling as the body moves. It's like God handed over control of its design to H.R. Giger. But this thing isn't swimming through the ocean depths. It's cutting a path through the sky, held aloft by six-paddle shaped wings, each trailing luminous strands of hair. Its four-hundred-foot-long, undulating body, unhindered by the structures on the ground, will reach the inner city first.

But why?

What are they after?

Rain grunts, her inner light flaring against her will.

"They're angry," she says. "And lost."

Not exactly answers, but it's a thin foundation upon which to fling guesses. My personal theory is that SpecTek pulled these things from some other dimension of reality and into our own. But since they connect with Rain in the same way as human spirits, that suggests they're made up of the same supernatural stuff. A supernatural dimension.

Only two come to mind, and if anyone in the history of religion got it right, these things aren't from Heaven.

"They're demons," I whisper.

Rain turns her glowing eyes to me. I think she's going to argue, but then she sags a bit and says, "Could be."

Demons brought to Earth...by my wife. Lovely.

But what about Wisp?

While it destroyed a few buildings and sucked up a bunch of souls, that all appeared inadvertent. And Wisp protected us. Protected Rain, whose connection to the creatures is undeniable.

I seem to recall the Bible being full of angels telling people not to be afraid, of being almost monstrous in appearance to human eyes. If the others are demons, maybe Wisp is an angel ripped from the Heavenly realm?

Ridiculous, I think. Everything about all of this is just stupid.

But there they are: three behemoths about to destroy a major U.S. city.

"What the hell is this?" Garcia asks. She raps on the window with her knuckles. "Are these display screens?"

"They're not screens," Reggie says. "And you're not hallucinating."

"This is what happened in Boston," I say.

"Bullshit," she says, and then whispers, "This can't be real."

"I didn't believe you," Bjorn says. "I went along with it, but I didn't really believe you." He turns to Reggie. "I'm sorry, it's just so..."

"Fucking horrible," Garcia says, the toughness in her melting away.

I turn my eyes back to the view, heart breaking when I see wispy pulses of light moving up through Brute's arms, as they sweep through buildings. I have no idea if Garcia's terror threat had any effect, but there are clearly a lot of people still in the city. Maybe even millions.

I don't know what I was expecting. It's not like three million people can flee a city in a few hours, and there's no guarantee that the FBI believed there was a credible threat.

What I *do* know is that a lot of people are dying, and... "We need to do something."

"Do *what?*" Bjorn asks.

I turn to Reggie. "How brave are your pilots?"

"Money makes people brave," she says, and then she must realize what I'm thinking, because her tone quickly shifts. "Wait. No. No way."

"We can't let all those people die." I motion toward Brute, stomping along the lake's edge, a few long strides from reaching the first skyscraper. Unlike Boston, whose downtown is somewhat condensed, Chicago is a vast and sprawling collection of massive towers carved in two by the Chicago River. If all three monsters reach downtown, the destruction will be unthinkable: Hiroshima times ten.

"This is as close as we get," Reggie says. "It's not our job to protect—"

"But it's mine," Garcia says, stepping back from the window. She holds out her gun. "And bullets can inspire bravery, even when money can't." She looks to me. "What are you thinking?"

"You with me?" I ask Rain.

"You know I am," she says, and I'm struck by how strongly I feel for her. Not in any kind of romantic way—my heart is broken, not philanderous. It's like I've known her my whole life, like we share some kind of guiding force. Like we're connected. Twins or something.

"We need to get closer," I say. "So they know we're here."

"And then?" Garcia asks.

"They'll follow us," I say. "We can lead them out into the lake."

"Why would they—"

Rain interrupts Garcia's question by releasing her control over the effect that spectral proximity has on her body. The plane lights up like we're having a photoshoot.

"God damn," Garcia says, fishing out a pair of sunglasses and putting them on. "What...what are you?"

"Wish I knew," Rain says.

"Tell the pilots to take us through the city," Garcia says.

"Through the..." Reggie is aghast.

"A Death Star trench run," I say. "Right up the river. Out the back and right, around toward Brute and out to the lake. Hopefully Dragonfish will follow us, without flying into anything."

"You're...you're naming them?" Bjorn asks.

I quickly point out the three kaiju, one at a time. "Brute. Dalí. Dragonfish."

"Dalí?" he asks, and then he looks out the window again. "Oh, I see it."

"The fourth is Wisp."

"There are *four?*" Garcia leans down to look out the window.

"Wisp was in Boston. It's not here." I turn to Reg. "We need to do this now."

Reggie takes a steadying breath, while Garcia's gun grip tightens. One of them will give the order. I'm relieved when Reggie heads up to the cockpit. Raised voices filter back to us, and then Reggie returns looking dismayed. "I think you're going to have to ask them," she says to Garcia.

Gun in hand, Garcia storms the cockpit. This time, the plane banks toward the city almost immediately. Rain and I head for the front of the plane. I pause as I pass Reggie. "Sorry."

"I think we'll all be sorry soon," she says, followed by, *"Give it a rest. At least they're trying. What have you done?"*

"Better buckle up," I say, and I note that Bjorn is already buckled up and is praying to whatever shrubbery might help us. Then I remember he's a sham of a warlock. I'm not sure who he'd be praying to, but I hope he/she/it is listening.

When I reach the cockpit, I find Captain Handsome at gun point, and a far less good looking and much younger pilot with a wild look in his eyes controlling the plane. The cockpit is a modern marvel full of screens and sensor displays that are so user friendly I understand most of what I'm seeing—including a multi-spectrum view of the city and the surrounding landscape that displays information the human eye might not see, allowing the pilots to fly in pitch darkness.

What's not on the screens is Dalí. The towering, twisted thing, straddling the Chicago River at the city's far end, flares in and out of reality with every long step it takes. But on the screens, it doesn't exist. Whatever sensors the plane is utilizing to create its Predator view of the world—infrared, thermal, ultraviolet—the kaiju creatures are invisible to them.

"Where do you want to go?" the young pilot asks.

"Low and fast," I say. "Get us close, but try not to hit them."

"This is going to be awesome," he says with a grin, throttling forward and taking us to just a hundred feet above the ground. Alarms flash and chirp as we descend. The pilot flips a switch, silencing them. The plane rockets down the river, twisting and turning with its bends, framed by mirrored skyscrapers that reflect our luminous passage. I see my reflection in the buildings, looking out the cockpit window. The distance to my mirrored self shifts with every building we pass.

As we approach, Dalí lets out a shrill, chirping roar. I don't see an orifice from which the sound could be made, but it's loud enough to hurt my ears, even through the plane's hull.

It knows she's here, I think, glancing back at Rain. She's gripping the door frame, eyes clenched shut. "They're coming," she manages to say through grinding teeth.

To the left, Dragonfish swerves its way through the city.

It narrowly misses some buildings and clips others. I'm not sure it, or even Brute, is trying to destroy the city, or trying to purposefully consume people's souls. Those things are just a byproduct of their size, and their desire to reach a goal—in this case SpecTek's Chicago lab, and now...Rain's beacon.

When Dragonfish peels the top three floors off a thirty-story building, I cringe, but is the destruction born from malice?

They're confused, I think. *Desperate.*

Instead of outright fearing them, which is reasonable, I find myself pitying the creatures.

"Look out!" Rain says, her voice a mix of pain and concern.

She's sensing what we have yet to see: Dalí's mantis-like arms, which I hadn't seen flash into reality until now, are as long as its legs. The appendages slice down from the lightning-painted sky.

"Hold on!" our young pilot shouts, banking hard to the right and pulling back. G-forces fling me against the wall and hold me there, as we bank away from the river and down a street lined with towering buildings.

For a fraction of a second, I think we're clear.

Then Rain shouts, "Back!" Her glowing hands lock onto Garcia and me, yanking us out of the cockpit. I fall atop my female companions, my view of our two pilots perfectly framed by the cockpit doorway, as a blade of pure light cuts straight through the plane, doing no physical damage.

Again, I feel a momentary sense of relief. Dalí wasn't fully in our world when it attacked.

Then both pilots flop over in their seats, their souls sucked away.

28

"Umm," I manage to say.

It's a wholly inadequate expression for the hysterical fear consuming me. But I'm numbed by shock. Unable to speak or move.

Until someone tells me what to do.

"Take the controls!" Rain shouts, shoving me from behind.

"I don't know how to fly a plane," I complain, even as I throw myself back into the cockpit.

"Just keep us flying straight," she says. "If we get close to the ground, pull back."

"I don't think it's that simple," I say, leaning over Captain Handsome's flaccid corpse and taking hold of his control stick. When the pilots died, the plane was flying straight down the street, level to the ground. With the controls relinquished, the best private plane money can buy stayed on course.

I can do this, I tell myself. *I can do this.*

A gust of wind from a side street tips us to the left. It's just a nudge, but it's enough to redirect our course so that we'll crash into a building inside of four blocks. At our current speed, that will be just a few seconds.

Don't panic. I turn the control stick to the right, hoping it's the right thing to do. *Don't freak out.*

Captain Handsome slides out from under me, as Rain drags him away.

"We're descending," she says, calm as can be.

"Shit," I say. She's right. I'd been so focused on not crashing into a building that I forgot the ground. "Doesn't this thing have autopilot or something?"

"Not for navigating a city," Reggie says, unbuckling the younger pilot and wrestling his body to move it backward. *Why doesn't he know that? He does. He's just panicking. Can't say I blame him.*

I glance at Reggie. Her self-conversation is on rapid-fire. She's panicking, too.

"This was a mistake," she says, grunting as she drags the dead-weight pilot toward the door. "I belong in a lab, not in the field. Shouldn't have brought them. *They didn't give you a choice.*"

"Reggie," I snap. "Quiet!"

I have no idea if I've hurt her feelings, but she falls silent.

I slip into Captain Handsome's empty seat and focus on the view ahead. My stomach twists. The street below is full of gridlocked cars. People flee, ants through a maze, running away from the plane crashing toward them.

"Pull back on the stick," I say to myself, tugging back gently, afraid pulling back hard will put us into a full loop.

The nose comes up a bit, and as it does, I see something strange. The people running away from the plane stop in their tracks and start running *toward* the plane.

What the hell?

As the ground rushes up, I pull back harder, careful not to twist in either direction.

We level out just twenty feet above the ground, screaming over the heads of fleeing pedestrians. And then I see it. *Brute.* Sensing Rain's unleashed brightness, Brute has made a beeline through the city, cutting off our path ahead, charging straight toward us.

I lock up, unsure about what to do. I'm not a pilot, and I think it will take some kind of ace to maneuver through the city, or around the kaiju.

"Umm," I manage to say again, and then I wince as my brilliant co-pilot takes the seat beside me.

"Everyone buckle-up," Rain shouts, taking the controls on her side. To me, she says, "I've got it from here."

"You can fly a plane?"

"I have no idea," she says, "but I feel like I can."

"Great," I say, starting to feel a little punch-drunk. "Awesome. Channel your inner R. Kelly."

"I don't know what that means," Rain says, taking the controls. "You can let go now."

"You don't know *I Believe I Can*—whoa!"

The plane angles up into a steep climb that takes us straight toward Brute's head, six hundred feet up, a half mile out and closing.

"Okay, yeah, I suppose that could be taken the wrong way," I say, gripping my armrests. "I wasn't telling you to channel your inner sexual predator."

Rain shoots me a brilliant glance.

"Sorry," I say, pushing myself deeper into my seat—or is that the G-forces? "I'm nervous."

"Well," Rain says, still sounding calm. "You should be."

Brute's two-fingered hand reaches out for the front of the plane. I have no idea if we'll collide and explode or pass straight through and have our souls sucked away. Either way, we're about to die. I don't think Rain is suicidal, but if we pass through the kaiju, she'll survive. That was established in Boston. So maybe she's planning to save herself, and not the rest of us?

That doesn't really jibe with her character, though.

And she confirms it a moment later, twisting the stick to the left—and then we're upside down, pulling back hard. It's hard to describe what happens here. It's kind of a nauseating blur. But I'm pretty sure we've just twisted around the hand, dived back toward the ground upside down, then leveled out just above the street again.

My head spins for a moment, but it clears in time for me to see us pass between Brute's hind legs, which are something like a goat's legs, covered in long, thick strands of glowing hair that stretch out toward us as we pass. We clear Brute's far side and exit the city's core unscathed... not counting the pilots...

Then we ascend again, this time at a more reasonable pace.

Realizing Rain can not only fly, but can do so with skill, I say, "Take us out over the lake. Let's see if they follow."

"And then?"

I shrug. "We do circles until this blows over?"

"You're a tactical genius," she says, deadpan. When a hint of a smile emerges on her bright face, I can't help but laugh.

"How long was the attack in Boston? Ten minutes? Maybe there's a time limit for how long they can exist in the land of the living? That's my only idea."

"Well," Rain says, turning the plane toward the lightning-illuminated lake. "It's an idea."

I look out the cockpit window, straining to see the city to our right. What I can see looks mostly unharmed. But what I can't see are the kaiju.

Reggie returns to the cockpit, looking a little green. When she reaches for the control panel, Rain says, "What are you doing?"

"Rearview," Reggie says. "You *can* fly in a straight line without the fancy screens? *Of course, she can. She can do loop-de-loops in a city street.*" She pushes a few buttons and the screen switches to a multi-spectrum view of what's behind the plane. While she might not be able to pilot the plane, she knows her ways around the controls, which isn't really surprising. Hell, she might have designed parts of the Cessna.

The city is easy to see in the image, its digitally rendered buildings are stark against a simulated and stormless sky. But there's something wrong with the image. The buildings are intact—all of them. The system must be combining the camera data with GPS, radar, and who-knows-what else to create a live 3D map of the area. Which might be why the image also doesn't show any of the kaiju.

"Sorry," Reggie says, rapidly adjusting the image until all that remains is a visual display of what's behind us.

The dark sky flashes blue. In between lightning pulses, when the city is dark, the monsters behind us stand out, their shimmering bodies wavering in and out of the world. All three of them are there, storming after us.

With each step, Dalí and Brute slash their way through buildings. The destruction is immense, but at least they're not rampaging through the city's core. In a few seconds, they'll enter the lake. If they remain fixated on whatever energy Rain puts out, we'll do a holding pattern over the water until they fade back out of existence. We could lead them all the way to Canada, if we needed to.

"C'mon, assholes..." I whisper. "Come and get us."

"I'm not really sure taunting the monsters is a good idea," Reggie says.

"Are we clear?" Garcia says, on her feet again.

"For now," I tell her.

She tugs Reggie's arm, pulling her out of the doorway. "You can sit." Reggie is about to complain, but Garcia cuts her off. "I think your boyfriend needs a hug."

A buckled up Bjorn is fetal-positioned in his seat, his shade drawn. Reggie hesitates and then gives in.

Garcia takes her place in the cockpit doorway. "Nice flying. Where'd you learn to do that?"

"She doesn't know," I say.

"I don't know," Rain confirms, when Garcia calls bullshit with her infamous eyebrow.

Garcia notices the rearview screens. Leans in for a closer look. "What the hell are they?"

"Still trying to figure that out," I say. "But...this is going to sound insane."

"There are giant monsters destroying Chicago." She motions to Rain. "And she's a damn human flood light. Whatever you're thinking, it can't be weirder than that."

"They're ghosts," I say.

"Ghosts..." She cranes her head toward me, but the eyebrow isn't raised. "Great... Of *what*?"

"I can only guess," I say, "and my guesses are definitely weirder than the ghost part." She raises both eyebrows this time. I give in. "They could be demons."

Garcia flashes a faux smile. "Let's stick with ghosts. What makes you think they're...supernatural?"

I motion to Rain, "She can connect with them...feel them, I guess."

"A glowing ghost-magnet."

"Pretty much, yeah. And if she touches a ghost, they can speak through her."

"Like a medium," Garcia says.

"But real," Rain adds, piloting us out over the water.

"And..." I say, unsure about where her suspension of disbelief is going to hit a wall. "...if I touch her, while she's in contact with the ghost, *I* can talk to *it*."

"Have you tried that with *them?*" she says, pointing at the rearview and rolling with the freakshow punch like she'd heard it before. And maybe she has. I can't remember exactly what was discussed when she was pretending to be unconscious, but communicating with the dead was probably part of the mix.

It's my turn to raise a skeptical eyebrow in her direction.

"If they're ghosts, then they're here for a reason, right? They want something. That's the way it works in movies. Find out what they want, give it to them, and hello afterlife. Best way to get answers is to ask questions."

I try to find a flaw in her logic, but can't. What I do find is fear. A lot. To connect with one of the kaiju would mean Rain coming into contact with it, and me being close enough to touch her...putting me easily within soul-sucking range. I'm not sure I'm brave enough for that...even if I do have nothing left to live for. The problem isn't death itself. Now that I know there is some kind of life after death, I really don't want to be trapped inside a kaiju for all eternity. Maybe I'm wrong. Maybe they're just roaming the Earth, or in some kind of Heaven or Hell, but I can't shake the feeling that all those people now belong to the kaiju that extracted their spirits.

While I have zero information to back the hypothesis up, fear doesn't require evidence or facts.

"Looks like you might get your chance sooner rather than later," Garcia says.

My eyes snap to the rearview. As Brute pounds into the water, sending out a wave that will damage the lake's far side, Dragonfish soars up and over its unholy brethren, its deranged eyes locked on us, its long lower jaw—full of dagger-teeth—unhinged and ready to feed. Its broad, hairy wings beat at the air as its serpentine body writhes.

The monster is quicker than its legged friends, and judging by how large it's getting in the rearview, it's also faster than us.

Rain glances back at Garcia. "Better sit."

Garcia rushes to the back, telling Reggie to buckle up, fastening herself in and then shouting, "Punch it!"

29

I look for the Cessna's speedometer, assuming planes have speedometers. I don't spot a familiar car-style gauge, but I do find a digital readout in the top left-hand corner of the display screens.

965.606 kph.

Kilometers per hour.

This means nothing to me. I'm an American, after all. But I think it's fast. Probably close to the plane's top speed, though the digits are slowly climbing.

The plane shakes as strong winds roll off the lake and slam headlong into the Cessna. Dragonfish is still gaining. Whatever supernatural energy powers the thing has, it's got more punch than jet fuel, and I suspect the wind has little effect on a creature that can be fully part of the world, and then not.

Distance is hard to judge through the view screen, but we've got just seconds before it reaches us, whether it be five or fifteen.

"Any ideas?" Rain asks.

Her simple question nearly undoes me. At every turn, Rain has proven herself to be resourceful and knowledgeable. My very own Ethan Hunt, despite her lack of memory. That she's asking *me* for ideas means she's out of them.

"Uhh," I say.

I feel bad that my most recent contributions to our predicament have been a series of 'umms,' and 'uhhs,' but *shit*, I'm about as far out of my comfort zone as a hamster in one of those little runny balls...at the bottom of the Mariana Trench.

"Never mind," she says, and she yanks back on the controls. We're thrown into a rapid ascent that pins me to my seat. In the back, Bjorn groans.

Focus on Dragonfish, I tell myself. *Don't puke.*

The rearview is empty. I can see the lake's frothing waters reflecting the shimmering clouds above.

For a moment, I think we've out-maneuvered Dragonfish, but then its awkward jaws snap shut just behind us. A loud snap rolls through the plane, and the volume of those massive teeth clashing together is painful to hear.

The plane twists 180 degrees and then pulls back in a tight turn that shifts the view out the windshield from the lightning-filled sky to its reflection in the water below.

In the back, screams. I'm not sure who from. Maybe all of them.

On our way back down, Rain pilots the plane around the backside of Dragonfish's long body. Though the creature has turned to follow us again, its thousand-foot-long body is still rising. Not only that, it's still reaching for us.

"Damnit," Rain grumbles.

The tail tip sweeps toward us, on a collision course with the cockpit.

This is it, I think. *This is how I die.*

My soul will either be sucked away, or I'll be crushed in the air over Lake Michigan, destined to haunt boaters as a spirit, because I am not ready to die. Not until I know what happened to Morgan. Not until I have justice for her.

"Take my hand!" Rain shouts, reaching out. I can't see her fingers. They're lost in radiance.

I reach out, feel her fingers lock with mine, and I'm slightly comforted by the fact that I will not die alone.

The bright blue tail flickers as it swings into the cockpit, shifting out of the physical world and into the ether. It slips through the nose and console without damaging the plane. Then it strikes Rain, whose light goes supernova.

And then...

It hits...

Me...

I'm stretched out.

Time slows. I see my body below me, mouth open in anguish, eyes clenched shut, frozen in place. My hand is still touching Rain, who looks...angelic.

The light emanating from her is no longer harsh to my eyes. It's... beautiful. It calls to me, promising peace. I've never wanted anything so much in my life. I try to go to her, but I can't move.

Like my physical body, I am frozen. Locked in place.

I see my new self for the first time. I'm still me, but transformed. A being of light. Of energy. Like the kaiju. Like the light streaking into the sky at SpecTek. And I'm stretched out. Distorted, as part of me still clings to my mortal coil, part of me stretches for Rain, and the rest of me is yanked away by Dragonfish.

The moment I give the monster the slightest bit of attention, I'm washed in raw emotion. I feel confusion, rage, betrayal.

"I want to go home!" The voice is feminine. Desperate.

Is it Dragonfish or one of its victims?

An electric jolt courses through my soul, arcs through my body, and draws a scream of pain from Rain.

For a moment, I feel her hand squeezing mine. My real hand.

She is anchoring me. Resisting the monster's pull.

"Who are you?" I ask the monster, speaking without lungs, vocal cords, or mouth. It's more like pure thought, and it is heard.

"Arrgghh!" The voice booms, vibrating my spirit. Loosening Rain's grip. Anger. Burning. *"Pol-ash-kee!"*

Everything I'm experiencing supports my theory that these things have been ripped here from some other plane of existence. It wants to go home. Its name is otherworldly. And there's no way beings so large could have naturally evolved or existed on Earth.

Then again, it's speaking English.

Or perhaps that's just how I'm hearing it, the unspoken-yet-heard words understood by supernatural means.

Bullshit, I think. *All of it.*

"Where is home?" Rain's voice filters to me from the real.

I repeat the question with a thought. *Where is home?*

I'm struck by a series of images, each carrying the weight of turbid emotion.

A desk. Small. Inside a school. A pencil scratching over paper. Adventure.

I smell chemicals. There's glass everywhere. Liquids. Community.

A laboratory. Clean and brilliantly lit. A breakthrough.

I miss it.

I miss it so much.

Where are you?

These are not my thoughts. Nor are they the thoughts of a monster.

Another lab. Tension. Blue light. Screams. Betrayal.

A face. Out of focus. Full of sorrow.

She did this.

SHE DID THIS!

I wake from the dream, back inside my body. Just a moment has passed. The flickering tail tip slips away from me and out of the plane's nose.

I'm alive.

Rain saved me.

Again.

I turn to thank her when a vibration rocks the plane.

"It hit the wing!" Garcia shouts.

Alarms sound. The plane's nose dips down, as Rain pulls back on the stick.

We're going down.

"Is there anything I can do?" I ask.

"Get in the back," Rain says. "Put your head between your knees." For a moment, I think she's joking. Then she shouts, "Now!"

I unbuckle from my seat, but don't stand. "I don't want to leave you."

"Saul," she says, and I think it's the first time she's actually said my name. The light billowing from her face dims. I can see her eyes, blue and piercing, locked onto mine.

I brace myself for heartbreak. I have a sense that what she's about to say will be profound. Last words meant to motivate me. To spur me on to whatever finish line we might be running toward. "Get your *fucking* ass in the back."

I hesitate, caught between obedience and a smile.

"NOW."

I stand as the plane's downward angle increases. I rest a hand on Rain's shoulder. She smiles at me, and then...I leave.

The distance to the plane's rear seats is just thirty feet, but it's more of a climb than a walk, as our angle of descent increases.

I clutch seat backs, dragging myself past Reggie, Bjorn, and Garcia, who are all seated in the front half of the passenger's section.

Desperate and frightened eyes watch my progress. Bjorn looks broken. Reggie mostly looks pissed. Garcia seems resigned to her fate and is still capable of offering me a 'Nice knowing you' nod.

I push myself into the rear-most seat, facing the cockpit. Through the open door, I see the flashing lake through the windshield, Dragonfish pursuing us toward the depths, and Rain, pulling back even harder now.

The plane starts to level out.

She was using the speed of our descent to keep Dragonfish at bay.

I'm pressed into my seat as my body wants to keep falling, but the plane streaks forward instead of nose down. In the rearview, Dragonfish misses us and plunges into the depths.

A burst of flame outside the window draws my attention. The engine on the damaged wing has exploded.

Shit.

Shit, shit, shit.

My buckle snaps into place, just in time to keep me from sprawling forward, as Rain rapidly decelerates—no doubt trying to keep us from pancaking into the lake. At this speed it would be like driving a car into a concrete wall.

The plane groans.

Bjorn shouts in either despair or pain.

Something explodes.

And then—nothing.

30

I wake to the sound of voices—Bjorn's indiscernible whimpering and Reggie in a hushed, one-sided conversation.

"You have our coordinates?" she says. "Good, good. Make it fast."

I open my eyes in time to see her tuck her phone into her pants pocket.

"You're awake," she says, upon seeing me. "Can you move?"

My chest aches like I've been stomped on by an elephant, but I'm breathing and all my appendages can move. "I'm okay," I say, wincing as an intense flare of pain radiates from my right side. *Broken ribs,* I think. *Hopefully just bruised. You'll live. Just push past the pain.*

I grunt as I unbuckle and twist out of the belt.

My legs wobble when I stand, but I manage to move down the plane's aisle, holding onto seatbacks. "You called for help?" I ask, unable to imagine anyone brave enough to risk death by ghost kaiju to save us. The Coast Guard must have a station in the Chicago area, and probably routinely rescue people from the depths, but this...

They've already got their hands full. How many people need rescuing on the mainland? Thousands? Hundreds of thousands? Why would they come after the four of us?

I crouch beside an unconscious Garcia, intensely aware that the cockpit is dark. Rain's glow is missing. Every ounce of my body wants to go to her. To see if she survived, but Garcia is here because of me. I need to make sure she's okay first.

When I put my fingers on her neck to check for a pulse, she flinches awake.

"You're okay," I tell her. "We're on the ground." It's then that I feel the steady warble of the plane beneath my feet. "Well, in the water."

The panic in Garcia's eyes fades fast. She squeezes various body parts, doing a self-check. Despite being in obvious pain, she declares, "I'm good," and unbuckles. "What's our situation?"

"We're a mile out and going down," Reggie says, helping Bjorn to his feet. The man is broken, emotionally more than physically. "Rescue ETA in five minutes."

The plane tilts forward. The lake gurgles in through the cockpit.

I slosh through the ankle-deep water, entering the dark cockpit. By the time I reach Rain's side, the water is knee deep.

"Open the door," Reggie says to Garcia, somehow still calm. "Before outside pressure seals us in."

I check Rain's pulse. It's faint, but steady. *Alive, but unconscious.* Probably injured, but I have no way to assess that, and honestly, even if her neck is broken, I have to move her.

"Not until they're with us," Garcia says.

I unbuckle Rain, and pull her up into my arms. "Thank God, you're light." I let out a little chuckle as I hoist her into my arms, grunting when my elbow pushes against my ribs. "You're light. Get it?"

"If you don't open it now," Reggie complains, "we'll be sealed inside."

I step out of the cockpit with Rain in my arms. "Go."

Garcia pops the side door and has to shove against an onrush of six-inch-deep water to get it open.

"Step aside," Reggie says, and for a moment, I think she's been overcome by a primitive instinct to self-preserve at all costs. But then she tosses something into the water and yanks a cord. An octagonal life raft expands with a hiss of gas, growing to its full size in seconds.

Wind and waves quickly tug the raft away from us.

Garcia dives for it, landing half in the water. She yanks herself up over the side, her actions stuttering, lit by the strobe-light sky.

Then she's up, thin rope in hand. She tosses the line to the door, where Reggie catches it.

"Help me!" she shouts at Bjorn, who flinches, but then lends his muscle to tug the raft back in.

Rushing water roils through the shattered windows, flowing past my legs.

Reggie all but shoves Bjorn into the life raft, when it bumps against the sinking plane. Then she follows him out into the whipping winds and the lake spray. She turns around and reaches for Rain. "Give her to me!" Her eyes dart to the side. "Hurry!"

Knowing something bad is coming our way, I deposit Rain in the raft and then wait a moment, while Garcia and Reggie pull her away from the edge.

"It's coming!" Bjorn shouts, eyes turning slightly up.

It's the kaiju, I think. Despite Rain's light being extinguished, they're still coming for us. Which means this life raft isn't going to be nearly enough, and Reggie's rescue will come four minutes too late.

But I'll do what I can to live as long as I can. I owe my wife that much.

I'm about to dive out of the plane when it lurches down. Water strikes my chest, shoving me back inside the plane. I bump off the plush leather chairs on my way back, stopping when I'm slammed into a cabinet at the plane's rear end.

Fluid coughs from my lungs as I surface, treading water in a plane that is now nose down, held aloft by the air bubble allowing me to breathe. Cabinets and drawers open, vomiting their contents into the water. I'm about to dive down and swim for the exit when the diffuse light of lightning slips through the water and the windows, illuminating the debris in the water. The flare lasts just a moment, but it's enough for me to spot a familiar logo on fancy letterhead.

SpecTek.

"What the—" The rest of my revolt is cut short when water surges into my mouth and rises up over my head. The plane is going down.

I spin around in the water, plant my feet against the back wall, and shove off, ascending a little faster than the plane is going down.

Hands on the door frame, I pull myself from the wreck and launch off it.

Above me, the world is a lightshow. Lightning, distorted by the water, flashes blue and purple, mesmerizing. I hover there, my body freed from gravity, the pain in my ribs reduced. The abyss is peaceful. For a moment, I let go of my fear, and anger, and questions.

I wish you were here, I think to my dead wife. *Well, not* here. *But, with me. You know what I mean.*

I smile, knowing she would be smiling, too. Even when she was upset, me fumbling for words lightened her mood. I can write all day, but speaking coherently, including my inner dialogue, is sometimes a challenge.

My lungs remind me I need to breathe. I focus on the octagonal silhouette and kick for the surface.

Ten feet from the air, I stop swimming. Something is wrong. Like the world has turned upside down. I've been swimming toward the light, but now it's above *and* below me.

I look down.

Swirling blue water resolves into lines of energy that form a shape. A body. Dragonfish is here, in the water with me, and it is just as graceful in the deep as it is in the heights. Far below, its coiling body turns in my direction, its wild eyes locked on me—or is it the life raft?

Rain might be unconscious, but some kind of residue, or perhaps memory of where the glow and its attraction came from, still guides the monster toward her. I felt its desire to go home. Saw the places it felt at home—which makes no sense to me—and I remember how strong Rain's pull felt during my out-of-body experience.

A plan formulates, and I kick for the surface again, this time frantic and seconds away from drowning.

I breach the surface with a gasp, sucking in air with all the grace of a howler monkey. Hooked and desperate fingers squeak over the raft's water-slick surface. Stars weave patterns in my vision, as I attempt to take a second breath, but I find my muscles are too weak to fight the water and the weight of my soaked clothing.

I scrabble for a handhold, but find nothing.

Then one finds me.

Garcia's hands lock onto my wrists. "I got you!"

"Better hurry," Reggie shouts, as the depths around us begin glowing.

Garcia leans over to pull me up and sees the luminous water. "Hell..." With a grunt, she yanks me into the raft.

I flop to the wet floor, gasping for air the way a fish gasps for water. It feels like I've been tossed onto a tumultuous waterbed, each wave-driven thump keeping me from sucking in the air I need to speak. When I find my voice, it comes out as a croak. "Hold on to her!"

I wrap my arms around Rain, holding on tight, hoping that if everyone is in contact with Rain, and Dragonfish passes through us, Rain will somehow be able to anchor us in the land of the living—even though she's unconscious. When no one joins me, curiosity pulls my attention up.

"Oh," I say, looking at the fifty-foot-tall wave rushing toward us. Behind it, Brute and Dalí continue their charge through the lake. As the water beneath us rises, displaced by Dragonfish's body—fully present in the physical world for the moment—the light surrounding us intensifies.

We are at the confluence of life and death, surrounded by giant monsters, water to drown in, and lightning to cook us.

And in that moment, I hear Morgan in my memory.

Baby, you can do it. You can live. You can be bold. You don't need me. Never have.

I did need her. Still do. But I understand what she meant. Without her, I am less, but I'm not nothing, and I can be more.

I reach out for the rope around the inside of the life raft, take hold and haul myself and Rain to the edge. Arms wrapped around the rope, legs gripping Rain under her arms and around her waist, I try to channel all the strength I would feel if Morgan were here with me.

And then, confluence becomes collision.

31

Physics saves us. Or at least delays our inevitable demise.

Water displaced by the rising leviathan lifts us skyward, while gravity says, 'Fuck that,' and yanks us down the steep wall of water. By the time the onrushing wave reaches us, we are perfectly poised to surf its sloped surface. Instead of being flung or flipped, we slide up the crest and are carried out of Dragonfish's reach.

The behemoth, fully in the real world now, explodes out of the lake, its open jaws snapping closed in the spot we'd been just seconds before. Its ever-surprised, small-pupiled eye tracks us as we're propelled away.

We're canted at a sixty-degree angle. I can look forward and straight up. Dragonfish rises into the sky. Its long body slides upward into the lightning, rising up and above the fifty-foot wave carrying us. For a moment, I think it's going airborne again, but then its radiant body arcs toward us, breaching like a whale.

There is nothing I can do to speed our retreat, so I just hold on and watch the giant topple toward us.

Bugged-out eyes locked on us, jaws open wide in a sickly grin, Dragonfish lets out a bellow that hurts like hell. I nearly let go of the rope to cover my ears, but I resist the pain. If I let go, Rain and I will die in the abyss.

As the fast-moving wave whisks us away from Dragonfish, its bulging eye widens further.

It's just realized the same thing I have: it's going to miss.

I really want to flip the thing the bird, but I decide to never let go of this rope. When Dragonfish hits the water with its untold tonnage, the wave carrying us is going to grow bigger and faster. It might not crush us, but the creature is still ensuring our demise.

Then again... its body flickers from solid to translucent, just as the bulk of it crashes down. I'm not sure how far into the depths it plunges, but it fails to displace any more water. Our insane water park ride keeps plugging along, though, carrying us out into the middle of Lake Michigan.

As the wave moves farther from shore, it changes shape, stretching out into a faster moving, yet shorter wave. For a moment, we accelerate, but then the wave slips beneath the raft and carries on without us. As we slide down the back side, our speed rapidly decreases and then stops.

We spin in the flat water of the wave's wake. I stare up at the tumultuous sky, catching my breath.

"Is it over?" Bjorn asks, lifting his head. His soaked long hair and beard give him a wet-dog kind of look. His glasses are missing. I feel bad for him, as he looks desperately hopeful for our hellish experience to be over.

But he's looking in the wrong direction.

Dalí and Brute are just a mile off, sloshing through the lake to reach us. I don't know if it's good or bad, but every time they shift into fully tangible forms, they kick off another wave. In seconds we'll be struck by the first of several thirty-foot waves that will continue pummeling us until we're caught. They might carry us farther away, extending our lives by a minute or two, but they could also capsize us.

My glass is officially half empty, but the optimist in me—squelched since Morgan's death—whispers, *You made it this far.*

While that's true, I'm pretty sure the only thing optimism will accomplish is to make me slightly more disappointed in my fate, when my soul is sucked away. So I hold on tight, let the raft do its job, and repeat a mantra that feels more realistic than a lie: *We're going to die.* We're going to die. "We're going to die," I inadvertently shout, when the first wave strikes, lifting us up with stomach lurching force.

We ascend the wave, quickly reaching its apex. For a moment, I'm vertical. My fingers burn as all of my weight, and Rain's, tugs down. A finger slips, and then the raft falls backward. We drop twenty-feet before slapping against the wave's upward angle. The impact knocks the air from my lungs, leaving me coughing, as the raft settles once more.

"Just hang on," I hear Garcia shout. She's got one arm looped around the rope, using her free hand to haul Bjorn back to the edge. He must have lost his grip when we hit.

Reggie is there, too, and she looks concerned. But not about Bjorn's welfare. She's not even watching his struggle. Instead, her eyes are on the sky, searching.

Is she looking for Dragonfish? I wonder, but the flying kaiju hasn't emerged from the depths yet.

When I look at her again, the memory of what I discovered in the plane returns to the forefront of my mind. *The plane doesn't belong to her,* I remind myself. *It belongs to SpecTek.*

Reggie is a part of this.

But the assassin, I argue.

A ruse? Would he have killed us, or subdued us?

What about Bjorn? Is he aligned with her? Garcia is certainly not, but what about the theoretical warlock? Is he genuinely her lover? Or is he another co-worker Morgan kept from me? How long was Reggie working with Morgan? Who hired whom?

So many questions, but only one really sticks with me.

"Why?" I shout over the wind.

Reggie snaps out of her skyward vigil. The expression on her face is something like that of a teenage boy caught looking at the hosiery section of a Sears catalog. "What?"

"Why did you lie to me?" I shout. "Why didn't you tell me you were with SpecTek?"

She freezes up a bit, face locked in place, trying not to give anything away. Then she resigns herself to the fact that I know. She almost looks relieved. "I wanted to tell you," she says. "Honestly. But we needed to know—"

A wave scoops us up, lifting the raft high, and then tosses it down. Prepared for the impact this time, I brace, but I take the hit on my side.

My ribs scream. I turn the pain into anger, into strength, tightening my grip on Rain, though I now wonder if it would be better for both of us to roll into the water and drown.

"Know what?" I ask.

"What she could do," Reggie says, motioning to Rain. "And now... what you can do with her."

"You did this to her?" I ask.

"I played a part, but it was Morgan—"

"Don't say her name," I shout. "She would never be a part of this!"

I turn to Dalí and Brute, now a half mile away and looming above us.

"This wasn't the plan," Reggie says. "And she didn't conduct the experiment; she fucked it up. *That's too harsh. Don't make him angry.* She sabotaged the experiment, Saul. *That's* why she's dead. That's why five of my colleagues are dead. Why countless more in Boston and now Chicago are dead. So don't give me any self-righteous bullshit about Morgan. She was brilliant, but she was also a—"

Another wave strikes.

When the raft reaches the top, we're nearly thrown forward. If not for a gust of wind, we'd be upside down in the water, riding the same wave for a second time. Instead, we crash back down, my injured body taking another beating.

"Why would she—"

"Because of you and your damn bleeding heart," she growls. I've never seen her this angry, and I'd have never expected it to be directed at me.

My mind flashes back to the last time I saw Morgan.

I was up early. She was getting ready for work. Really distracted. A heavy heart. I asked her what was wrong, and when she didn't say anything, I poked and prodded until she presented me with a hypothetical situation in which a research bunny developed human intelligence. The scenario she presented was long and complicated, with a lot of unnecessary detail. Boiled down, she asked if it was okay to continue the experiment.

I argued it wasn't. I waxed about the sanctity of intelligent life. Hell, I had nearly convinced myself to be vegan by the time I was done.

What I didn't know at the time was that the bunny *was* human and that the human was Rain. As a result, Morgan did something to save Rain, but somehow doomed the rest of SpecTek as a result. But that doesn't really answer the question about what the kaiju are and where they came from.

Doesn't really matter now, I think, looking up.

Dalí reaches us first.

Its bulbous head flexing, its long mantis arms swinging down from the sky, reaching to stab and crush, or simply sweep through us and suck our souls away.

I clutch Rain, hoping she'll keep me from having my soul sucked out. And then—light.

Despite being unconscious, Rain begins to glow. It's subtle at first, but then it flares to sun-like brilliance.

"What's happening?" Bjorn shouts, safe again thanks to Garcia, who has heard everything that's been said and looks appropriately pissed.

"There's something else here!" I shout, looking for signs of Dragonfish.

And then I hear it.

A sing-song cry. It's mournful, and then angry, building in intensity.

But no one else can hear it.

"Can you hear me?" I ask.

In response, a massive creature flickers into the world, loose dangling bits of its gargantuan self drooping down around us. A single strand touches Rain's body, connecting me to it.

To Wisp.

Its flowering body opens in the sky above us, blooming with urgency. Long flowing ribbons shoot out, wrapping around Dalí's wrists, halting its attack with just feet to spare.

"You saved us again," I say, knowing it can hear me through Rain. I don't know if it can understand me, though. "Why?"

The answer comes as a pulse of energy, flowing through Rain's body and into mine. For a moment, I glow, too. It hurts like hell, but it also lets me see...lets me really see...Wisp.

The creature's dangling tendril slips away from Rain. The connection with Wisp should be broken, but it's not. If anything, it's stronger. A glowing blue strand stretches down from Wisp, pulsing with light, with feelings of love and comfort and closeness. And it's not touching Rain.

It's touching me.

The tether connecting me to Wisp pierces my heart.

Without having to ask or think, I know that it's always been there. For the past day, anyway. Ever since the explosion at SpecTek... Ever since I touched that cold blue light. And with that knowledge comes the realization that the kaiju aren't beings from another dimension—they're people. Used to be, anyway.

I reach a hand up toward Wisp. "M-Morgan?"

I'm infused with a sense of wellbeing and confidence, and then I hear two words that confirm my horrible suspicion and churn my insides.

"Run, Saul."

32

I'm undone.

Tears in my eyes, my body goes limp with shock. Sobs bubble up out of me. Here is the irrefutable proof that Morgan is no longer living. That she is no longer my wife. If that wasn't bad enough, she's not just dead, she's a ghost—a lost soul—roaming the Earth. As a damn monster.

Whatever she was involved in at SpecTek, she didn't deserve this fate.

As questions without answers pile up, my heart breaks. In life, Morgan was a beacon of love, hope, and beauty. In death...

I look up at Wisp and find it nearly impossible to think of the kaiju as my wife. But then I see past the sheer size and otherworldliness of the monster and see the same love, hope, and beauty.

She is here to save me.

She's been with me since Cambridge, watching over me, entering the realm of the living when the other kaiju close in. She is my protector.

I look for the tether connecting us. It's invisible again, but I know it's there.

I can feel it.

Can feel *her*.

And now, more than ever, she exudes power.

Before I can fully wrap my head and heart around this revelation, Wisp's dangling ribbons pull up into the sky above, just as a wave strikes and carries us beneath her massive form.

Rain's glowing body nearly slides from my now limp grasp. My body flexes, snagging her before she falls away.

The wave deposits us fifty feet behind Wisp's hovering body. While the petals and ribbons that make up the massive form flow, twist, open, and close, she has no wings to speak off. No way to fly in the real world. The laws of physics that require technology to defy them, no longer apply to her—or the other kaiju. I suspect that Brute and Dalí might be walking out of habit, perhaps not fully realizing that they are dead and capable of floating.

While the wave has moved us behind Wisp, we are far from being safe. If I could paddle, I would, but we are at the mercy of the waves.

Wisp's sing-song call fills the air. Instead of pursuing the raft, Dalí goes on the attack, reaching for and clutching onto Wisp's flowing body. Sharp, hooked arms cut through petals and ribbons.

The sing-song becomes an ear-splitting shriek.

The kaiju might be dead, but they still feel pain, at least from each other.

Brute lunges around the battle, its many eyes locked on us with rabid intensity, now that Rain is glowing again. Being unconscious, she has no way to squelch the power, as she did on the train fleeing Boston. Not that it worked earlier. She was dark and the kaiju still came for her.

Do they remember her?

Morgan remembers me.

I look up at my wife-turned-monster, enraged by her pain, but incapable of doing anything for her. Unless...

I pat Rain's cheek. "Wake up."

When she shows no signs of rousing, I give her a shake and shout. "Rain! Wake up!"

"What are you doing?" Garcia shouts to me.

"She can stop them," I say. "She did it before. In Boston."

Garcia looks me in the eyes, weighing the validity of what I'm saying against forcefully bringing Rain out of a concussion. Maybe worse.

"Do it," she says, as another wave picks us up and carries us a little farther away.

After being deposited in another trough, I give Rain's face another tap, harder this time. "Rain! Wake up!" I raise my hand to strike her a bit harder. Not enough to leave a mark, but it's going to sting. I swing down, but my open hand never reaches her cheek.

Rain catches me around the wrist, squeezing. "I'm awake."

"Thank God," I say, relieved.

"We're alive," she says, more surprised than observant.

"You saved us," I say. "And we need you to do it again."

She lifts her hand, looking at the glow. "How close?"

Before I can answer, we're lifted up and over a wave. On our way down the far side, Rain gets an upside-down view of Wisp battling Dalí, and Brute working its way around the action toward us.

"Can you shut them off?" I ask. "Like on the train?"

"I didn't *shut them off,*" she says, rolling over with a grunt and a wince. Her head is no doubt pounding, and her body must have taken a beating. "I...don't really know what I did. It was more like pushing. Denying."

"Then deny away, lady," Garcia says. "Or we're toast."

I notice that Reggie hasn't said much of anything. She's just clinging to the raft, waiting. For death or rescue, I'm not sure. But she is no longer *with* us, if that makes sense. Neither is Bjorn. While Reggie presented him as someone who might be able to help, I wonder if the man was really just a pawn meant to distract. Even if his background in paranormal science isn't a ruse, like his claim to be a warlock, he's been reduced to a blubbering mess.

"They're too strong," Rain says. "Too present."

Her eyes lock on Wisp. "Is that—"

"She's fighting for us again," I say.

"She?" Rain asks.

"Later," I say.

Brute rounds Wisp and Dalí, closing in. Desperate frenzy fuels it. Long ropes of glowing hair stretch toward us with static energy. Its long legs carve through the water, body shimmering with each lunge.

It will reach us in seconds.

Wisp crackles with light. It flows from deep inside and then bursts out through her myriad flowing limbs. With a burst of energy, she tosses Dalí to the side. While the towering monster falls, long ribbons jut out, wrap around Brute's front limbs and bind them together.

The four-legged kaiju topples forward, plunging beneath the waves, sending another tsunami in our direction.

"I hate to be that person," Garcia says, "But there were four of them, right?"

I lean over the raft's side, looking down into water that glows so brightly, I can see the bottom, several hundred feet below...and the creature giving off the light. Dragonfish swirls in the depths, swimming in a tight circle. It's only then that I notice that the continuing onslaught of waves is lifting us up, but not really carrying us away. It's impossible to see from water level, but I'm pretty sure if we could look down, we'd see the beginnings of a massive whirlpool, locking us in place.

I turn to Rain, intending to beseech her again, but she's no longer lying next to me. She's on her knees at the center of the raft, a heatless star.

"They're using up their energy!" she shouts. "Burning themselves out."

It's then that the toppling Dalí finally hits the water, the creature's bulbous body and head fully in the land of the living. I can't imagine how much kinetic energy the impact generates, but we're about to find out.

Brute rises from the water, flexing its arms apart until Wisp's ribbons snap, drawing a sing-song cry of pain from the thing that was once my wife.

The whirlpool grows faster, and as we swing around the outer edge, I see a basin form. Dragonfish doesn't need to surface to catch us.

We'll be sucked down to it.

I'm struck by an intense sense of wrongness, of being out of place, a mortal among gods. I have no business being here. A trespasser. But that's not the truth. It's the kaiju who don't belong. They shouldn't be here—including Morgan. Whatever the human spirit is meant to do after death, *this* isn't it. This is a perversion...and if we survive, I'm going to put a stop to it.

Somehow.

The sound of a fifth monster approaching from the sky dashes any hope of survival. Its thundering chop makes me cringe, not just because it's loud, but because it's close. I'm struck by a vibrating wind and stung by whipped water pellets. By the time I turn around to look, Reggie is already half way up the helicopter's dangling ladder. Bjorn is right behind her, missing every other step in his panic, but somehow matching her pace.

Garcia holds the ladder still. "Let's go!"

I have no idea if Reggie will have the helicopter peel away without us. We have just seconds to climb onto the ladder before she reaches the top. Before the tsunamis reach us. Before the kaiju creatures claim us.

"Rain!" I shout, yanking her glowing body toward the ladder.

"I'm close!" she says.

"We're leaving!" I shout, taking hold of the ladder and motioning for Garcia to go first. She's brave, but not stupid. She gives a nod and starts up.

I tug Rain to her feet, and put the ladder in front of her. She's in another world, experiencing who-knows-what, but she needs to get on this ladder. "If you don't go up the ladder, we're both..."

She's not really hearing me.

And I'm not leaving her.

So I wrap my arms around her and take hold of a rung. Then I slip my legs between hers, sit on a lower wrung and lock her in place. The moment her weight is added to mine it seems to increase ten-fold, testing the strength of my already worn-down arms, and my pain threshold, as her body presses against my ribs.

When I open my eyes again, the weight shift makes sense. We're being lifted into the air.

But is it fast enough?

Multiple waves bear down on us.

Brute is right behind them, despite Wisp's attempt to stop the creature.

The swirling light below rises toward the surface.

And all I can do about it is dangle like a worm on a hook.

The waves reach us first, slapping into us, trying to drag us away. It's a one-two punch of water, each one submerging us for a moment. The second, larger wave nearly breaks my bond to the ladder, but we emerge from its crest, still rising, swinging back and forth.

Brute lets out a roar, and I let the sound puncture my ears. Letting go means death.

The creature reaches for us, five hundred feet above the lake's surface, rising toward the lightning-filled skies, buffeted by twisting winds, heavy, wet, and cold.

Dragonfish explodes from the water, mouth agape.

If one of them misses, the other won't.

Above all the chaos is an almost sweet song, like that of a whale, but brewing with power.

Wisp.

Rain gasps out of her trance-like state.

"Hang on!" she shouts.

"What do you think I'm—"

An explosion of energy bursts from Wisp, pulsing through the sky. The clouds above bend away from its force. The waves below are flattened. The kaiju creatures flail, as though electrified. And the helicopter...it continues on its way.

When the wave hits me, I feel transformed. Renewed. Loved. The power of Morgan's life flows out and over Lake Michigan, wounding the spirits bent on destruction, while freeing the living from their grasp.

This is the Morgan I knew.

Rain grows bright one more time, squinting her eyes shut. "That did it!" She flickers with intensity, and now far below, the kaiju creatures wink out of reality, one at a time.

When they're gone, and Rain is dark again, I turn my eyes up to the helicopter, where Garcia looks down at me. I give her a grin and then see the logo painted on the helicopter's side. It isn't the Coast Guard who has come to our rescue.

It's SpecTek.

33

My soaked body shivers, but not from the cold.

The summer heat and the dry helicopter cabin are comfortable, but recent revelations and fading adrenaline leave me in a state of shock.

Morgan is dead, and is one of those...monsters.

Reggie has betrayed me.

We've been rescue-captured by the same people who might want us dead—or worse.

I wonder if the assassin was there to extract information without exposing Reggie. It's possible Reggie hadn't been in contact with SpecTek at the time, that the killer didn't know she was with us, that they were acting to contain without realizing Reggie was already doing that *and* hunting down answers. As much as I want to know what happened to Morgan, Reg wants to know what happened to the experiment.

Instead of turning us in, she made us allies.

Unwitting accomplices to her crimes.

Arms folded, I sit between Rain and Garcia, and across from Reggie and Bjorn, who are framing the entrance to the cockpit. The pilots are as much a mystery as the specters, their faces hidden behind helmets and visors. I can see them talking. Can see Reggie replying. But the sound-blocking headsets given to everyone aside from Reggie don't let us listen in or join the conversation. Reggie, on the other hand, has been talking the whole time.

She's taken control.

That's not true. She was *always* in control. The only difference is that now I know.

I glance down at Garcia's hip. Her weapon is still holstered there, so there is some hope.

But do I really want to escape?

SpecTek and Reggie have the answers I want. So there's that.

On the other hand, they'll probably kill me if I get those answers. Hell, they'll probably kill me for what I know already. Garcia, too. Maybe even Bjorn. The only one of us not headed to the gallows is Rain, and I suspect her fate will be even worse. Then again, Reg knows that I can commune with the dead via Rain. Maybe I'll share in her fate? Lab rats together.

I look out the side window. Chicago smolders, but the heart of the city has been spared.

A subtle grin slips onto my face. I can't guess how many people died, or how many millions, maybe billions of dollars of damage was done. But without us, it would have been worse. A *lot* worse. I take a small measure of pride in knowing that I played a part in saving an entire city.

Two cities.

We didn't understand what was happening at the time, but there's no telling how much damage Brute would have done to Boston had we not led it away.

Wasn't just you, I remind myself, and by 'you' I mean the living.

Morgan was there with me. The whole time.

I look down at my chest. I can't see it or feel it, but I know the connection to my wife's spirit remains, even though she might be in some other part of the world, even though she no longer resembles anything human.

As we circle around, O'Hare International Airport comes into view. I don't see any planes going in or out, but the terminals and runways appear undamaged. Looking for planes in the sky, my eyes drift up.

The storm has faded. The spectral blue glow is gone. All traces of the otherworldly have fled. But a swath of destruction has been left behind, along with millions of witnesses.

No way they're covering this up.

And maybe they don't have to. In Boston, the epicenter was Spec-Tek. The lab's destruction was a precursor to the attack on Boston. It didn't take a huge mental leap to connect them. But SpecTek doesn't have an active lab in Chicago, and the destruction was widespread. The kaiju might have been here because of some memory of a lab, but very few people know that.

Chicago is the perfect distraction for SpecTek, diluting attention from their clandestine actions, turning the facility's destruction into just one of many victims, rather than the cause. They might even get federal emergency funding to help rebuild...

I shake my head. That's a stupid idea. They already *have* federal funding. What they might not have is federal support. Black projects provide a layer of plausible deniability for the agencies involved. In this case, DARPA. But if we can expose SpecTek—show the world what they did—support might be withdrawn internally, the project dissolved. Those responsible might fade into the background—too valuable to scapegoat—but *maybe* the targets on our backs will fade, too?

For a moment, I think survival will be enough.

But I want *justice.*

I spent the better part of my life exposing criminals for who they were. It's been a while since I felt able to shine a light on the world's darkness, but now...

Give me a fuckin' spotlight.

Newfound determination chases the numbness away.

Just in time for the helicopter to land. Outside, the airport is lit in greens and purple, the wavy terminal roof, despite its size, looks small in the distance. We've landed in front of another private hangar.

Garcia gives me a nudge. She lifts a headphone from her ear and motions for me to do the same. When I do, she says, "How do you want to play this?"

"Why are you asking me?" I say. "You're the FBI."

"I'm as out of my element as you are," she says, and I understand. No one on Earth is trained to deal with what we've experienced. "But you know her." She glances at Reggie. "Your wife was involved."

Still is...

"And you and Lite-Brite over there—" She nods at Rain, who is sound asleep. "—have some kind of spooky otherworldly connection. So I'm deferring to you, because I'm feeling pretty clueless right now."

"There are more questions than there are answers," Reggie says. She's taken off her headset. As the rotor blades slowed and quieted, she heard some, if not most of our conversation.

I decide there's no room for error or nuance, so I decide to be blunt. "Are you going to kill us, or not?"

"If it were up to me," she says, "no one would be hurt."

"But it's not up to you," I say.

"Not remotely." She frowns. "Whatever hobgoblin you've no doubt imagined me to be, I assure you, I'm not. My part in all this is as a scientist. Nothing more. *That's not entirely true.* Quiet. Now's not the time." Reggie pauses to compose herself and silence her dissenting voice. "Look... I am happy to argue on your behalf. I owe Morgan that much. But I'm afraid that means proving your worth."

Reggie turns to Garcia. "Right now, you're the hardest sell. So, I suggest you hand over the gun, and keep that sassy mouth closed."

Garcia glares.

"There are men with guns outside," Reggie says. "What happens next depends on you, but the math doesn't work out well for you, or the people sitting beside you."

If Garcia is intimidated by the not-so-veiled threat, she doesn't show it.

Reggie sighs. "I'm not your enemy."

"Horse and shit," Garcia says.

"If I were, you'd already be dead." The cold tone in Reggie's voice makes me believe her.

It also makes me realize that I don't know her nearly as well as I thought.

It also pisses me off. "Why stop with Morgan? Why not make all of your friends into ghosts?"

Reggie leans forward. "If your wife was still alive, she would be sitting next to *me*." She reaches a hand out to Garcia.

Waits.

Rain leans forward. As calm as can be, she says, "Give her the gun."

I can't tell if she's confident or simply resigned to her fate.

Bjorn just looks on, muscles quivering, no use to anyone.

"They could kill us," Garcia says.

Rain shrugs. "I'd rather die and know why, than get shot in a helicopter."

"They're not going to kill you," I point out.

"My life is not in SpecTek's hands," she says, and then repeats, "Give her your gun. We're running out of time."

Reggie's head snaps to Rain. "Time until what?"

Rain smiles. "When we know everything, you'll know everything."

Rain is dangling an imaginary carrot. I'm not sure what good it will do us in the long run, but for now, she's increased her worth. Then she increases ours. "And if any one of these people is harmed, what I know will die with me."

Reggie stares at Rain, sizing her up.

Garcia interrupts by placing her weapon in Reggie's hand.

"Thank you," Reggie says. "You've all made the right choice." She lifts her mic, about to speak to whoever is waiting for us outside. Rain catches her by the wrist. For a moment, I think it was all a ruse, that Rain and Garcia are about to storm the cockpit, hijack the helicopter, and get us the hell out of here. But then she asks a simple question.

"Who am I?"

Reggie stares at her, breathing heavy.

Then she calms. "The man we left dead in Salem... He was your replacement." She offers a faux grin. "Me, you..." She motions to me. "His wife. We all worked for the same people."

They linger for a moment. Then Rain releases her.

Reggie opens the helicopter's side door. Three armed men in suits wait outside, their postures calm, but somehow still ready for action.

"Maybe they'll give you your old job back, though I'm not sure anyone will appreciate your new self-righteous attitude."

After Reggie exits, Garcia leans forward, looking around me to Rain. "Hey blondie, if things go south—"

"I'll die fighting," Rain says.

Garcia grins. "What about you, Gargamel?"

It takes Bjorn a moment to realize Garcia is speaking to him. Then he flinches and blinks a few times. "W-what?"

"Are you. Going to. Fight for. Your life?" Garcia asks.

I'm not sure Bjorn is capable of responding. Then he looks at Reggie, outside the helicopter, speaking to the three guards. His fear melts away, replaced by molten anger. He looks Garcia in the eyes…but says nothing.

"Good enough," Garcia says, and then she claps my knee cap. "Lead on, Leonidas."

"Leonidas died," I say, remembering the Spartan king whose last stand against the Persians at Thermopylae was made famous to modern generations by the movie *300*, and the comic book it was based upon. "Horribly."

"Yeah, but he died fighting. And," she says, "he knew why."

And with that, we have our two-step plan. First, get answers. Second, fight our way to freedom—or death.

"Great," I say, and I unbuckle my seatbelt.

34

Anyone watching from the outside would likely assume that we are spoiled VIPs. That the three men in suits are protecting us, rather than holding us captive. That the plush jet—a massive Boeing 747-8 this time—was sent to whisk us off in style to some high-powered meeting or tropical location. We're not manhandled, threatened, or even glared at. The three guards, whose weapons are mostly concealed, are polite, calm, and lack any trace of fear or anger.

Somehow that scares me more than if they were violent assholes. These men aren't compensating for anything. Their confidence is unnerving. I find myself listening to their requests. Hell, I even thanked the man who motioned me to my seat on the plane.

They haven't bothered binding us. The only hint of discomfort I've seen in the guards is when they approached Rain. Subtle body language suggested they were ready for a fight, but when she showed no signs of aggression, they relaxed.

We're seated separately. There won't be any theorizing or plotting on this flight to who-knows-where. Reggie has been silent, seated at the front of the cabin, speaking on a phone and working on a laptop. She walked by me once, on her way to the bathroom. When she returned—wearing a scarf for some reason—she looked uncomfortable and avoided my gaze.

While I haven't really gotten an evil villain vibe from her, I'm pretty sure I can't count her among my friends anymore, and I certainly can't trust her. I'd like to discover that I'm a good judge of character. I used to think I was decent at that—seeing the good and bad in people, even those determined to hide the truth. But Reggie had me fooled.

So did my wife.

Thinking of Morgan no longer fills me with an intense sense of loss. I mean, I still miss her. Still want to hold her in my arms again. To hear her laugh. But mostly I feel suspicious. Of who she was before she died. Who she really was. Like Reggie, she led a double-life, at least in terms of morality.

Maybe.

I think.

Reggie all but blamed Morgan for this mess.

And Wisp...my wife's deformed spirit, is fighting for us. I felt my wife in the monster's touch. Heard her voice. Felt her love.

The Morgan I knew wasn't a lie.

There was just more to her. And she kept it hidden from me—the crime reporter, whose job it was to expose the wrongdoings of others.

Maybe that's why she was so supportive of me leaving the *Globe*.

I look around the cabin, wishing I could bounce all this off someone. But I'm in a plane full of strangers, and old friends turned enemies. So what's a guy supposed to do?

I glance out the window. Fields crisscross the landscape. The terrain is mostly featureless. No cities in sight. No landmarks to speak of. We could be anywhere. My only clues are the sun's position and the amount of time we've been in the plane.

We've been heading south for a good three hours. So that rules out New England, and the western states—assuming we don't change course. So someplace in the South, which helps me about as much as knowing the stats for the World Bowling championship in 1985.

And then it hits me: Austin. Texas.

SpecTek's third location. That must be where we're heading. And if we're right about the kaiju, that they're drawn to significant locations associated with their lives, or maybe just with the circumstances of their deaths, maybe that's where they're headed, too.

Guesses upon unanswered questions. Creating a narrative based on either of those won't do me any good. So I opt for distraction. My therapist would call it avoidance, but tackling this particular problem head on might get me shot.

Tactical avoidance, I tell myself. *No reason to feel like a wuss.*

And like a good avoider, I focus on what's in front of me. There was a time when that would have been my laptop and whatever story I was working on. Now...it's the screen in the seatback in front of me.

I give it a tap. The display lights up, showing a menu of options ranging from meals, to movies, and even video games.

I tap on the menu out of habit. I like to eat on flights. Food calms my nerves. The selection is exquisite. Filet mignon. Lobster. Truffle raviolis. I have a Pavlovian response to the list of foods, but get stuck on 'Cheeseburger.' What can I say? I'm a simple man. I give it a tap, confirm I want fries with it, and select a drink: hard cider. Then I click 'Order' and have a little chuckle.

One of the guards seated at the front of the plane, facing me, leans to the side, eyes hidden behind sunglasses. He could be sleeping for all I know. But I'm not about to test the theory by sticking out my tongue or something. I switch over to the game menu, find Asteroids, and boot it up. I pluck out the little joystick embedded in my arm rest and go to town, channeling my inner ten-year-old.

Five minutes later, I'm dead.

And I have the high score. Unlike arcade games, this modern reimagining of a classic game doesn't have a limit on the number of characters I can input. So I use a classic Simpson's joke, Seymour Butts, and try not to chuckle again.

I'm getting a little punch drunk. Exhaustion is doing weird things to my mind. I barely feel nervous right now. I'm probably flying toward interrogation and death, but I've faced down supernatural kaiju.

Twice.

A gun feels...simple.

At least right now. When it's pointed at me, I'll probably piss myself.

But for now, I'm Lord Commander of the galactic empire on a mission to free space from asteroids. I fire up the game again, intent on beating the one and only high score. I die in minutes...but I still get to put in a new name. I type it in.

I.P. Freely.

Classic.

I'm about to start the game again, when I spot a name in the third-place spot of the mostly empty top ten list. With a score of thirty.

Only it's not a name.

YOU WERE FRIENDS WITH HER, RIGHT?

I'm tempted to stand up and look around. Figure out who else is playing the game. But that would be a dead giveaway. So I deduce, like Sherlock. It's not Reggie, who is still hard at work at the front of the plane, spreading out across a conference table. It's certainly not any of the guards, who are all sitting motionless. Bjorn is snoring. Rain has been silent, but she doesn't strike me as the type to play games, or even think about playing games. Which leaves Garcia. I don't know her very well, but like this question, she is straight forward and inquisitive.

Garcia, then, I decide. Or someone else on the plane I haven't seen. The 747-8 is a large plane. At the front is a conference room. In the middle, first class passenger seating—where they've put us. The sections behind the wings are walled off. The door leading back has been closed since we boarded. I have no idea what's back there or who's back there. So it's possible this is some kind of psy-ops meant to get information.

But I don't think so.

I start a game, career into an asteroid, and am brought back to the top ten list. 20 points. I type in my name.

GARCIA? YES. FOR A LONG TIME. I THOUGHT.

I wait and watch the list.

A new name appears. Third place again. 500 points.

I smile a bit. She's having trouble resisting the urge to destroy asteroids. It *is* cathartic.

THINK YOU CAN WIN HER OVER? GET HER ON OUR SIDE?

I throw another match, but only after getting 600 points, reclaiming third place.

MAYBE. I'M NOT SURE HOW MUCH OF IT WAS AN ACT.

The response comes a little slower. When it does, she's reclaimed third place with 2000 points.

I nearly laugh.

YOU'RE A NICE GUY. SMART. ACCOMPLISHED. AND YOU RESPEC-TED HER, EVEN THOUGH SHE'S A FREAK. SHE—

The rest of the message is cut off by the edge of the screen. I wait, knowing what's coming.

Third place. 2500 points.

SORRY. SHE LIKES YOU. SHE JUST NEEDS TO REMEMBER WHY. OR HOW MUCH.

I play my heart out as fast as I can. At 4000 points, I nose dive into a UFO.

My third place name is, I SEE HOW IT IS... SO, YOU THINK I SHOULD WHAT? TALK TO HER?

A long wait.

20,000 points. First place.

Damn.

BRING IT ON. BUT FIRST, TALK TO HER. NOW.

I sigh...

Not only have I been schooled at Asteroids, I'm being shoved out of my avoidance comfort zone. And I know she's right. If anyone has a chance of reaching Reggie, it's me. But I'm afraid...because if I talk to her, there is a good chance one of two things will happen. First, I could find out more about Morgan that I don't like. That seems likely. Second, I could lose my temper, which would probably result in a beat down. Maybe worse. I really don't know.

But it needs to happen.

If Saturday mornings taught me anything, it's that knowledge is power.

I'm about to stand up when the rear door opens.

A woman pushes a cart into the aisle and closes the door behind her. She's dressed in a form-fitting SpecTek-colored—white and light blue—stereotypical flight attendant uniform. She smiles at everyone who looks back. "Who ordered the burger?"

Ho-lee shit.

I raise a sheepish hand.

She smiles wider and brings the food to me, while the guards and Reggie look back at us with an almost amused 'Da-fuck?' look on their faces.

As I accept the tray of food from the flight attendant, she gives me a bemused grin and rolls her eyes. *She has no idea what is going on and who is on this plane,* I realize.

"Wait," Garcia says, seated somewhere behind me. "We can order food?"

"Sure thing, hon," the attendant says, flicking her hand through her long, blonde hair. "Menu is on the touch screen."

With that, she exits the way she came, and I can hear Garcia tapping her touchscreen already.

I take a deep breath in my lungs and then take my food tray in my hands. The guards stiffen when I stand and approach, but Reggie waves them off. They watch me like a hawk as I approach the conference table, but they don't move.

I take the seat across from Reggie, who's watching me over the top of her laptop screen.

"Hungry?" I ask.

She closes the laptop. Sets it aside. "I could eat."

There is a long list of sarcastic responses I could say or things I could do, but I opt for quiet kindness. The Bible says something about that, I think. From the depths of my past, the verse springs to mind, though I have no idea where in the Bible it can be found.

If your enemy is hungry, give him food to eat, and if he is thirsty, give him water to drink. For in so doing, you will heap burning coals on his head, and the Lord will reward you.

I unwrap the plastic utensils, take the knife and carve the burger in half. Then I move half the fries and half the burger to a napkin and slide the plate to Reggie. Next, I crack open the can of cider, pour half in the plastic cup, and slide that to her, as well.

She smiles at me, but her eyebrows are upturned. Wounded.

Hot coals poured, I think. *Now let's see how the Lord rewards me.*

35

I take a bite of the burger, trying to act casual. The juicy meat and gooey cheese hit my tongue as an explosion of flavor. I sag in my chair, actually relaxing as my hunger awakens. I'm pretty sure I moan and roll my eyes in delight, but I'm barely aware of it, as I take another bite.

When I emerge from my burger bliss to eat a fry and wash it all down with a sip of cider, I manage to say, "So good."

Reggie smiles at me, food untouched.

"You know," she says, "Morgan used to fret about you. She worried you'd never recover from... What was it? A nervous breakdown?"

My chewing slows. Is she mocking me, or just being honest? Either way, I decide to roll with it. Play it cool. Get some answers. "Something like that."

She waits for more.

"I spent too much time in the darkness," I say. "It broke me."

A nod is all I get, like she understands and doesn't need to hear more, which is good, because I don't want to relive that past. Breaking down in tears in front of these stoic guards isn't going to do me any good.

She takes a bite of her burger. It's more of a nibble. Then she places it back down. Over the years, I've interviewed hundreds of people charged with or convicted of crimes. I've built up something of a guilt radar. I can detect the difference between who is guilty, and who feels guilty. It might not seem like an important detail, but when you're seated across from a murderer, it's good to know if they're a sociopath or full of remorse.

And Reggie, she's torn up.

I just don't know why. Is it because we're friends? Because she was Morgan's friend, and apparently colleague? Or because the fate that awaits me is so horrible that she'd feel bad for subjecting a stranger to it?

"So," I say, chewing on another fry. "Can you tell me what's going on?"

"Why don't you tell me?" she replies.

"If I act clueless, will that change anything?"

Her frown is subtle, but says more than her words. "You're far from clueless."

She takes another bite, this time bigger, signifying that she's done speaking. It's my turn.

"Fine," I say. "SpecTek was developing something. For DARPA." My mood sours. "You fed me that information. You said you didn't work for them."

"I don't," she says.

"Right, you work for SpecTek."

"Consult," she says. "I'm an independent contractor."

"With access to their fleet of private jets," I point out.

She shrugs. "My contributions have been considerable." She rolls her eyes, but not at me. *"Don't brag.* I'm not. I'm enlightening."

My snicker pulls her out of the one-woman argument.

"What?" she says, irritated.

"I was wondering if that was real or an act," I say. "The talking to yourself."

"I imagine you've been wondering what is real since you awoke to Morgan's call," she says. There's a momentary staring competition, as I resolve to give her nothing, and she waits for me to break. Eventually, she says, "What else have you learned?"

"Those monsters... They used to be people. They're ghosts, but they've been changed."

"That was my hypothesis, too," she says.

"You didn't know?" I ask.

"It was not the intended outcome," she says. "They were not the intended subjects."

"Wisp," I say. "The flowery-looking one... It... *She*...is Morgan."

Reg lowers her burger to the plate, eyes locked on the table. She didn't know, and the news rocks her...though she's trying hard to hide it—maybe from me, maybe the men watching us.

I take a drink of cider and end up pounding down the rest of the can.

"How do you know?" she asks.

"I spoke to her," I say, "because, you know, I can do that now. Speak to dead people."

"But only when you're touching Rain."

"What's her real name?" I ask.

"No idea," she says. "I only ever knew her as Subject 005. But from what I understand, as bad as you think SpecTek is, she is worse."

"Was worse," I say.

"We'll see."

I don't like the sound of that, but I'm not about to let Reg psy-op me into not trusting Rain.

"What does it stand for?" I ask. "RAIN?"

She takes a pad of paper from beside her laptop. It's covered in scrawled math and crude drawings, none of which mean anything to me. She turns to a clean page and writes: Riesegeist Assault INitiative.

Assault and Initiative are easy enough to understand. But Riesegeist?

Sounds German. When I mentally break the word down, I recognize the word 'geist,' not because I've ever studied German, but thanks to the movie *Poltergeist.*

'Geist' means 'ghost.'

And it fits what I already know, so I don't question it. "What is Riese?"

"Giant," she says.

I close my eyes and sigh. "That's...the stupidest thing I've ever heard."

"I thought so, too," she says. "But Morgan convinced me. Showed me the potential—"

"To weaponize ghosts?!" I say, raising my voice. Down the aisle, Garcia leans over to check on me.

"Never mind the how of it," she says. "You wouldn't understand. Just try to imagine the *potential*. Souls not only exist, but they're also malleable. Easily changed into something...no longer human."

"A genetically modified human soul," I grumble.

"Essentially, though genetics have nothing to do with it." She eats another fry, hunger building as guilt gives way to the excitement of scientific discovery. I wonder if that's how World War II Japanese scientists in the horrific Unit 731 slept at night, focusing on the science rather than on the horrors for which their discoveries were being used. "With a Riesegeist, you could send it into an enemy stronghold, or city, and let it loose."

"And how do you do that?" I ask. "Send a ghost on a mission?"

"A beacon," she says. "Something that the spirit is connected to and will pursue to the ends of the Earth."

I remember the tether connecting me to Wisp. I am Morgan's beacon. She's been following me all this time.

"Ideally, that beacon is a source of great pain or rage—"

"Because what good is a killer ghost if it's not enraged?"

"You might think this reprehensible, but it's actually quite humane." She ignores my scoff and continues. "Do you know how many people lost their lives in the development of weapons you consider to be mundane and totally acceptable? All the bombs, and jets, and nukes? Thousands. The beauty of a Riesegeist is that you need only one. One sacrificial lamb."

"Rain," I say.

"Its victims die without pain, and our armed forces never set foot on a battlefield. There is no radiation to contaminate the land or prolong suffering. It's impossible to predict, or intercept—and best of all, no one would know who sent it."

"Them," I say. "There are four, remember? Cat's out of the bag now."

"There are five, actually," she says. "And while the destruction and loss of American life is regrettable, it also deflects responsibility away from us. Why would we attack our own people?"

I'm disgusted by her casual dismissal of the lives lost, American or not, but I focus on the first tidbit. "What do you mean, five?"

"There were five people at SpecTek that night. Six if you count Rain."

"Wisp, Brute, Dragonfish, and Dalí," I say.

"Silly names," she says.

"Says the woman who helped create kaiju-ghosts. Why weren't you there?"

She huffs a laugh. "I'm not stupid. I understood the risks. What I didn't understand was Morgan."

I wait for more.

"I know you want to blame me for this. Or SpecTek. But the burden of guilt for everything that happened that night rests on Morgan's shoulders. If not for her, we'd have one Riesegeist, and it would be under control. Now we have five on the rampage, and no clear understanding of what their beacons are, or even if they have beacons."

"What did she do?" I ask,

"I don't know how she did it, but she reversed the Riesegeist pulse so that it affected everyone *outside* the containment chamber, rather than the one woman inside it. As for why...she found out about Rain's beacon."

"What...is Rain's beacon?" I ask, not really wanting to hear, but knowing I must.

"A daughter," Reg says, eyes low. "She'd given the girl up when she was born. Rain wasn't a suitable mother, and she knew it. Imagine being raised by an assassin. Even worse, an assassin so dedicated to her country that she'd volunteer to become a perfect weapon."

"Until she found out you had her daughter," I guess.

"For the process to work, the Riesegeist pulse needed to be activated at the moment she felt the strongest emotion regarding her beacon. Her daughter's image, in the hands of SpecTek, would have accomplished it."

"And her daughter is where? In Austin?"

"I don't know where she is," Reggie says, looking dismayed.

I shake my head, disgusted.

"That's how you create the tether..." And then I understand. Tethers with the dead aren't just formed by rage, or loss, or desperation. Any emotion can get the job done. And in Wisp's case, it was forged by Morgan's love for me.

And now in death, as in life, she is doing her best to protect me from the world...and from her work.

"Yes..." Reggie says, squinting at me. "For most of the Riesegeists, Rain is a beacon, but only when she's in close proximity, and the connection between them seems more complex."

"She can shut them down," I say.

"But only when their emotional energy has been somewhat expended." Another fry. "It could prove useful. Other than that, it's clear the five souls feel a powerful connection to SpecTek and the labs they've all worked in or visited."

"Which is why we're flying to Austin," I guess.

"Unless Rain feels like repeating that map trick, it's the most logical assumption."

"And you'll do what? Contain them?"

"Ideally," she says, "free them."

"How do you do that?" I ask, but my mind is already hard at work, sussing out that mystery. Traditionally, ghosts are trapped on the mortal plane because something is keeping them here. Some kind of injustice doesn't let them leave. For the Riesegeists, that's SpecTek...and Rain.

"You're going to destroy the lab," I guess, and then I clench my fists beneath the table as I realize the full ramifications of what this means. "You're going to kill Rain."

Reggie says nothing.

"And Garcia," I say. "And Bjorn. They know too much."

She stares at me, waiting for more.

Damnit...

"But you're not going to kill me. And it's not because we're friends, or because you're a good person. You're not. It's because you already have a Riesegeist with a beacon you can control."

She smiles and takes another bite of burger. "Always said you were smarter than people thought. But you're still missing the point."

"And that is...?"

"*You* have nothing to fear. So, as my dear Bjorn would say..." She holds up her hard cider in a mock toast. "...Skål."

36

I return to my seat, still hungry and still confused. While I accomplished my mission—to obtain more information—what I learned has left me feeling powerless. Some small part of me feels relief about not having a target on the back of my head, but it's dwarfed by my concern for Rain, Garcia, and even Bjorn, who do. Rain still has a purpose—to lure the Riesegeists into SpecTek's containment trap—but I'm concerned Garcia and Bjorn will be killed the moment they step out of this luxury plane and onto the easily cleaned, polished concrete floor of a hangar.

At least Garcia is eating like she knows it's her last meal. The flight attendant has been coming in and out with samplings of the kitchen's meals, appetizers, and desserts. Even the stoic guards are smiling when the attendant returns with another tray. I don't know if they find it funny because they'll soon be killing Garcia, or because they respect her appetite.

I fire up Asteroids again and score a 10, intending to warn Garcia about her impending doom, but we've filled the top ten slots with decent scores.

So I'm forced to play again.

And again.

But my game is off. Exhaustion and despair are setting in. I'm losing my gusto for shooting digital rocks.

"C'mon," I grumble, crushing buttons and rubbing my eyes between levels.

My last life is taken by an aggressive UFO. I nearly shout a curse and toss the joystick like eleven-year-old Saul would have, but I rein in my emotions when I manage to snag the tenth place spot.

I AM SAFE. RAIN IS SAFE—FOR NOW. YOU AND BJORN ARE *NOT* SAFE.

Doesn't get any clearer than that, I think, and I send my high score message.

Her response comes just ten minutes later. A first-place score. My slack-jawed awe at how fast she decimated my high score fades when I see the response is just one word.

UNDERSTOOD.

What the hell does that mean?

I mean, on the surface, it means she understands. Obviously. But does the one-word answer mean she's resigned to her fate? I was expecting a plan. Or some hint at resistance, like 'WE'LL SEE ABOUT THAT.' But 'UNDERSTOOD?'

It's underwhelming, which is something I didn't expect from Garcia.

I want to prod for more, but I'm pretty sure I won't be able to hit the top ten again. Not when I'm this tired. So I exit the game—hiding evidence of our clandestine communiques—and I lean my seat back and close my eyes.

What follows might be a dream.

Or lucid thought.

Or maybe even real. Some kind of metaphysical experience. I'd love to scoff at that possibility, but my resistance to the concept of a supernatural realm is at an all-time low.

I'm seated, still in the plane. But there's a glowing umbilical extending out from my chest. It pulses with energy, sending sharp tingling sensations throughout my body, like my nerves are on fire.

The pulsing, I realize, is my heartbeat.

I reach out for the cord and take hold of it with my hands. It's warm to the touch. It's tangible, yet it slips through the plane's side without causing any damage. Simultaneously material and immaterial.

This can't be real...

But it is real. At least, my connection to Morgan is real. Or is it to Wisp? I'm having trouble reconciling the two of them being one and the same. Morgan might inhabit the monster, but she can't really *be* the monster. *Like Nemesis and Maigo,* I think, recalling the novel and the TV series. Together, but separate.

In my heart, I know it's not true, but there's no reason I can't pretend.

The tether moves, sliding closer and downward, like we're passing over—

I jolt upright, awake and aware.

"They're beneath us!" I shout, on my feet. I stumble into the aisle, trying to shake the tether's image from my mind. I glance at my chest. I can't see it, but I know it's there, sliding toward the back of the plane as we pass the Riesegeists, moving far below us.

The guards rise at my approach, but don't take action, and don't look to Reggie for guidance. They know my worth... And they don't really see me as a threat.

"What makes you think that?" Reggie asks. She's not doubting me, but as a scientist, she requires evidence.

"A dream," I say. "But I don't think it was a dream."

She raises her eyebrows, dismissive.

"How's the saying go?" I ask. "Any sufficiently advanced technology is indistinguishable from magic."

"That's not a saying. It's a quote from Arthur C. Clarke. And a dream is not technology."

"You used technology to open Pandora's Box," I say. "And now you're going to doubt what you find inside?" I have a little chuckle at Reggie's expense. "Despite all your brains and ego, you don't understand the supernatural any better than I do."

The cabin grows brighter, like the sun is blazing through the windows. When the guards look around me, I understand.

"Your evidence is behind me," I say, without looking back. I know who's there, and I know what's happening. I step to the side, letting Reggie have a good look at Rain's brilliance.

"They're beneath us," Rain says, calm as ever, confirming my claim.

"Ma'am," one of the guards says. "Are we—"

"We're thirty thousand feet in the air," Reggie grumbles.

"Actually," the guard says, "we're about to begin our descent."

Worry sneaks into Reggie's eyes. "We'll have to move fast. Once we're on the ground—"

A muffled trio of sharp pops interrupts from the back end of the plane.

"What was that?" Reggie asks.

The guards, like me, have no trouble identifying the sound of gunfire. In response, they draw their weapons.

"Swanson," the lead guard says, hand to earbud. "Do you copy? *Swanson?*" He motions for the other two guards to check it out.

"Move it," the first of the two growls at me.

I obey, sliding to one side of the aisle and glancing back. It only takes a moment for me to register the fact that both Garcia and Bjorn are missing.

The gunshots...

They were Garcia!

As the first guard passes, I extend my leg.

In a rush and focused on the rear door, the man doesn't see it. He topples forward and pancakes on the floor.

The second man's gun swivels toward my face. At the same moment, a luminous blur flashes by me.

Reggie and I have the same reaction. "Don't kill them!" we shout in unison.

While keeping Rain and me alive serves Reggie's purposes, she has no idea why I'd want Rain to spare the guards. The simple truth is that the moment Rain kills one of these men, the others will open fire. In the tight confines of the plane, I'm pretty sure not even someone with Rain's skill could avoid being shot.

But Reggie doesn't know that, and when our eyes meet, I can see that she has assumed I'm being protective of her.

And fine...yeah, I wouldn't want Rain to kill her. As much as Reg needs us, we need her.

I'd also like to think she might somehow redeem herself.

Rain drives her heel into the second man's stomach. As he pitches forward with an, "Oof!" she snatches the handgun from his hand, disassembles it with a quick jerk, and then tosses the pieces at the lead guard, striking him in the head.

The whole thing takes just seconds. In the end, two men are on the floor, and the third is holding a hand to his bleeding forehead.

Rain stands over the fallen men and raises her arms.

"Can I please shoot them?" the lead guard asks, aiming at Rain.

"What's your name?" Reggie asks the man.

"Burnett," the man says.

"Like Carol Burnett?" Reggie asks.

"Brandon Burnett, and I don't know who that is."

"Really?" Reggie asks, and gives her ear a tug the way Carol Burnett did at the end of every show.

"That supposed to mean something?" Burnett says.

Reggie rolls her eyes. *The man is a big brick.* I know. But there's nothing to be done about it." She looks at the guard. "From now on, I'm calling you B.B."

I nearly laugh at the man's scowl, but I'm distracted when Rain starts to flicker. We're moving out of range.

I'm about to ask how far we have to go. With our time, distance, speed, and position, I'm pretty sure Reggie would be able to figure out how fast the Riesegeists are moving and when they will arrive. But before I can speak, the plane shudders, as though struck.

"The hell was that?" B.B. asks.

My first instinct is that we're being attacked by Dragonfish. If the ethereal monster caught a whiff of Rain as we passed, it could have pursued us into the air. But I know that's not right, because Rain has gone dark. Whatever is affecting the plane is part of the real world, and with that in mind, there is only one possible explanation: Garcia.

Is she trying to bring the whole plane down? I move to a window, looking at the land far below. At first glance, I think we're shedding parts. A round, domed chunk of something falls away from the plane. Then a parachute emerges from the top.

"An *escape pod?*" I whisper.

Reggie looks out the window beside me. "Are you kidding me?"

"You should be happy," I say. "Bjorn's going to make it."

For a moment, she looks relieved. Then a darkness overcomes her. "You don't think that has a GPS tracker inside it?"

"Let me guess," I say, "You designed it?"

She shakes her head. "Common sense. They'll be caught on the ground."

"Reg, we're friends, right?"

She stares at me, either hiding her emotions or not having them.

"And you care about Bjorn. You can't hide that."

She doesn't. Her eyes dampen.

"There is more to life than scientific conquest, and now you know that there is more to death. If there *is* an afterlife, what we do in this life might matter. Really matter. Like, a lot. Your own science proves it. So maybe, instead of being an utter and total soulless asshole, you could acknowledge what your own science proves, and maybe—"

"You want me to repent?" she says, growing angry. "Get on my knees and beg an all-powerful being for forgiveness?"

"I don't know, Reg!" I shout back. "I don't know how it works! Maybe just *try* to be a good person."

"That's what your wife did," she says. "And look at where it got her."

I lean in close, my whispered anger warbling my voice. "If Morgan's final act in this life was to sacrifice herself for someone else, then I've never been prouder of her. But you... What are you going to leave behind? A path of destruction, blood, and misery, not to mention a man who believes you want him dead. A man you used and discarded like—"

"Stop!" Reggie shouts. Tears in her eyes spill onto her cheeks. She glares at me, shaking her head as she steps back, and then turns to B.B. "Give me your gun."

B.B. grins. "Finally." He hands the gun to Reggie, who then fires it six times.

37

"What the hell?" I say, standing frozen, as though under Medusa's control. My voice raises an octave. "What. The. Hell?!" And then a whisper. "Whatthehell..."

The three guards lie dead on the floor, each of them shot twice by Reggie. While she clearly had no real experience firing a weapon, the close range guaranteed that the defenseless guards stood no chance. B.B. went first, the poor lug. Two rounds to the chest. Then she dropped the other two before they could get to their feet.

And now I'm torn. On one hand, Reggie might have saved us. On the other hand, she was ruthless about it. B.B. was an asshole. A killer. But the look of abject fear in his eyes...when Reggie turned the gun on him. It was like looking at a little girl whose favorite doll had been dropped in a shredder. All of his machismo wiped away with the realization that he would soon be called to account for his shitty life. I suppose he had it coming...like the assassin I shot earlier, but B.B. was unarmed, and the other two guards incapacitated. I want to trust that she's with us again, but I feel even more like my long-time friend is a stranger. Or...she knows that every man left alive will be another hunting us down in the near future. A fragile justification, but I suppose it makes sense, especially given the stakes—which are far grander than just our own lives.

"Oh, don't look so torn," Reggie says. "It could have been worse."

"You *shot him* in the chest," I point out. "Twice."

"Well....he...he could have been licked to death by elderly cows," she says.

"What? Just...*what?*"

"*That* would be worse. Forget it. Here," Reggie says, placing the gun on the conference table and sliding it to Rain, who catches it and turns it on Reggie.

The cockpit door opens. A pilot steps out. "What is—"

The man freezes for a moment, wide eyes on Rain, then he ducks back inside the cockpit and locks the door behind him.

Reggie relaxes. "That was close."

"What the hell are you talking about?" I ask, nearly shouting, stomach churning at the growing scent of death filling the cabin.

Reggie motions to Rain. "They'll think she killed the guards."

"Why is that a good thing?!"

"Because," Rain says, "They'll believe she's still with SpecTek."

"But she *is* with them," I point out and turn to Reg. "You deceived me. Lied to me about Morgan. About your involvement. You led them to us in Salem. You took us on their plane, and now we're here because of you."

"All true, but—"

"But what? You think there is anything you can say to justify all of this, not to mention the three lives you just took?"

"What's three more lives added to the weight of the thousands I'm already responsible for?" She's heavy with remorse. "At least these three deserved it. Unlike all the other people's lives I'm responsible for ending."

"What...what are you talking about?"

"Morgan might have pushed the metaphorical button—the process is more complicated than that—but I'm the one who told her how." Reggie takes a seat. "She called me that night. Before she called you. She was distraught." She looks to Rain. "Over you."

Rain sits down opposite Reggie, and I am compelled to join them at the table though I mostly feel like pacing like a frantic meerkat. "Why?"

I know what's coming. Know the truth about Rain. And part of me wants to keep the truth from her, to spare her from that pain, but it wouldn't be right. I squeeze my fists and wait for it.

"You have a daughter," Reggie says. "They were going to use her to control you, after...you know..."

"I became a ghost-monster," Rain says, not a trace of emotion in her voice.

"A Riesegeist," Reggie says.

"Giant ghost," I mumble. "That's what it means."

"You knew this," Rain says to me. It's subtle, but I hear an accusation in her voice.

"For the last ten minutes," I blurt out. "I didn't have a chance to tell you."

"But you wouldn't have," she says. "You didn't want her to say it now." Rain is impossible to read. She could be angry, or indifferent, or broken-hearted. "Why?"

"Because I knew it would hurt," I say.

"You have been fighting to learn the painful truth about your wife's death," she says. "How would you feel if I denied you the truth?"

I stare at the table for a moment, aware that the plane is descending at a noticeable angle. We don't have much time. We need to come up with a plan. But that's not going to happen until we reestablish trust, or at least come to an understanding. "Angry. But...I would forgive you."

"Good," she says. "Because we've all been lying."

Reggie and I both sit up a little straighter.

Rain leans forward, elbows on the table, staring directly at Reggie. "I know who I am."

The pair stares at each other for a moment. Then Reggie says, "No, you don't. You're testing me. Seeing if I'll flinch and somehow reveal that I'm untrustworthy."

I'm about to say, 'You *are* untrustworthy,' when Rain drops a truth nugget she shouldn't know.

"The sixth person in the lab that night was my daughter."

I look from Rain to Reggie and back again. The stalemate lasts just three seconds. Then Reggie cracks.

"We never intended..."

My horror explodes as a shout. "You turned a little girl into one of those things?!"

Reggie punches the table. "We tried to save you!" She looks at Rain. "Both of you! *You didn't try hard enough. Or soon enough!* We did what we could! God damnit!" Reggie takes the laptop from the conference table and hurls it against the wall. She punches the table hard enough to hurt her own hand. The sting settles her back into her seat. After a moment of staring at the table, she says, "I'm sorry. Truly. Had I known…"

"I believe you," Rain says.

"You do?" Reggie and I say in unison.

Rain sits back in her chair. Ejects the gun's magazine. Glances at the remaining bullets. Slaps it back in. "Since we're being honest now, I don't really remember who I am."

"I knew it," Reggie says.

"But your daughter…" I say.

"I remember that night," Rain says. "Some of it. How I felt. Who I feared for. I remember having a daughter. I don't remember her name. I remember your wife. Her kindness." She smiles a little. "I remember you. On the phone. Your small, scared face. I remember thinking my life was a waste, because no one loved me the way you loved her."

"Thanks…" I say. It's all I can manage. My fears about my wife being secretly sinister have started to abate, which is a huge relief. I'm still disappointed in the choices she made leading up to that point, but in the end, she at least attempted to do the right thing. And now, it seems, so is Reggie.

"So," I say to Reg. "The whole truth, and nothing but… Why? The wild goose chase. The deception. The manipulation."

Reggie digs into her pocket and digs out something pill-sized and metallic. She places it on the table, rolling it to me. I catch it and look it over. It's mostly featureless, but speckled in red that rubs off.

"That's blood," she says, and I quickly wipe off my fingers. "My blood, to be specific." She unfurls the scarf around her neck, revealing a bloodied bandage. "It was in my neck."

"You took it out," I realize aloud. "When you went to the bathroom earlier. What is it?"

"Transmitter. Transponder. Vitality monitor. Among other things."

I can tell by the trace of pride in her voice that it was her design. I don't bother asking about it.

"Why didn't you destroy it?" Rain asks.

"It's activated by body heat. The moment I plucked it out, the transmission ended. *Just get to it already. You're almost out of time.* Fine. Look, the reason I kept this in, and kept you in the dark is... simple, but complicated."

"Makes total sense," I joke.

"I knew they were listening. And *they* knew I knew they were listening."

"Uh...huh..."

"By playing ignorant to you, they understood I was still working for them, even though it wasn't true. They also understood that I believed you and Rain would eventually help us understand what had happened."

"But you know what happened," I say. "You helped cause it."

"I didn't know the pulse would affect other people in the lab. I didn't know the whole place would explode. I didn't know Riesegeists would start destroying cities. And, I didn't know that Rain or you—you weren't even supposed to be there—would gain the ability to detect and communicate with the dead, or your wife would turn into..."

"Wisp," I say. "Just call her Wisp."

"I didn't have answers, and I needed to find them, while keeping your dumb ass alive. You saw what they would do to protect the project. What they'll still do... *Get back to it.* Right. Without the ruse, you'd have been killed and we wouldn't have had the resources we needed to chase down answers, which all of us still want... Agreed?"

A moment passes, and then I say. "Fine."

"Agreed," Rain says.

"So," I say. "What's the plan?"

Rain chambers a round in the gun and then lifts her chin toward Reggie's bandaged neck. "How's that patched together?"

"Tape," Reggie says, growing worried. "Why?"

Rain offers the kind of toothy grin that a killer might flash a victim, just before plunging a blade into their chest. "We need to make this look real."

38

"Put your weapons down!" I shout, "Or Doctor Spock here is going to get it!"

"Doctor Spock?" Reggie grumbles under her breath.

"I was trying to be insulting," I whisper.

"That's a compliment," she says.

"Move!" Rain says, giving Reggie a shove from behind, nearly knocking her down the stairs against the plane's side.

Below us, four SUVs form a semi-circle. Men in suits, weapons drawn, look down their sights. They waver like specters, distorted by the late-day heat rising from the sun-blazed pavement of the Austin–Bergstrom International Airport.

If just one of these guys flinches, we're all dead. Our only chance of survival is not just Reggie's worth, but also mine and Rain's.

They want us alive.

That gives us an edge...though their bevy of bullets levels the playing field. For all I know, each one of these men is a marksman capable of shooting out our legs. I suppose that's why we're holding Reggie hostage.

If they shoot, Rain shoots.

So, really, our grand plan depends on Reggie's worth.

And that is a total unknown.

What I do know is that Rain and Reggie are doing a better job selling our faux threat than I am. Rain has the practiced look of a killer who's not to be underestimated. And I think that means she's just acting like herself, or the self she was before her memory was erased.

And Reggie...she doesn't really need to act. Rain tore open the incision on Reggie's neck. As a result, she's covered in blood. Rain also has one of Reggie's arms twisted behind her back, and every now and then applies enough pressure to make Reg cry out in pain. Even I'm wondering if she still sees Reggie as the enemy.

The suits hold their ground, but don't lower their weapons. Dozens of guns track our progress toward the tarmac.

"They aren't backing down," I whisper.

"They're not shooting us, either," Rain says, hiding behind Reggie's head.

Before I can ask or guess at our next step, the back door of the closest SUV opens. A man in an impeccable light blue suit slides out. His styled white hair nearly matches his pale skin. He carries himself with the confidence and strut of a man in his prime, but the wrinkles on his face suggest he's in his sixties, if not his seventies.

He approaches with a steady, calm gait. Absolutely fearless.

When Rain adjusts her aim from Reggie to the man, he comes to a casual stop, grinning at the gun, like it's loaded with water, rather than bullets.

To say I'm unnerved by the man is an understatement.

And it only gets worse when he takes off his sunglasses and stares us down through light blue eyes that match his suit.

He's like a White Walker from Game of Thrones, I think. Cold-hearted, ancient, and quite possibly one step ahead. Or, at least, that's what he wants us to think.

Rain doesn't miss a beat. "We're taking a vehicle."

"It's good to see you again, Stephanie."

A moment of stunned silence lingers.

Stephanie? Rain's real name is *Stephanie?* It doesn't seem possible that at some point in her life, some loved one or friend called this living weapon, now imbued with supernatural ability, something like 'Steph.'

"Not anymore," Rain says.

"That's right. You go by 'Rain' now." He grins. "It's fitting I suppose, if not creative. You do know what it stands for, don't you?"

She doesn't. And I can see that gives the man some kind of perverse pleasure, like he's superior, simply for knowing more.

"Riesegeist Assault Initiative," I blurt out, defiant on Rain's behalf.

The man's dead eyes flick toward me and I nearly yelp.

"Mr. Signalman, your wife was valued. Do not suppose to share in—"

"Eat a dick," I say.

Reggie nearly laughs, but Rain cuts it short by twisting her arm and drawing a wince of pain.

The man glares at me, trying to intimidate me with his soulless eyes.

And yeah, it's working. I'm scared shitless. But this isn't the first time I've looked into the eyes of a man who had the power to end my life. This used to be my job, and I was good at it. The one thing that men like this are thrown by is a total disregard for the threat they present.

"Actually, why don't you eat a whole box of dicks." I say. "Shake them out into a bowl and nom, nom, nom them with some milk and sugar."

I'm laying it on a little thick, bordering on silly, but when the man's cheek twitches, I know I'm getting though. The only problem is that I don't know why. I'm kind of just acting on reflex here, coming to the defense of a friend who this man was trying to psy-op. Really, this is just a big, 'Fuck you,' moment. All we really need is for him to get out of the way and let us go.

Somewhere at the edge of my attention, I hear a distant, metallic crash and screeching tires. *A car accident,* I decide, and I move on.

Ice-man's eyes snap back to Rain. He thinks he's done with me.

"Hey," I say, snapping my fingers, until he looks at me again.

I'm so dead. "You might think you're the big man in charge. That you've got all the power. That I'm impressed or intimidated by your dead eyes and zombie complexion, but..."

Something in my mind tweaks.

I don't know what it is. Some kind of realization in the depths of my being bubbling up to the surface. I'm not yet aware of what it is, but my body reacts to it with a burst of tingling panic.

The subtlest grin I've ever seen slips onto the man's face.

I clear my throat and double-down. "But you are nothing without us. When the Riesegeists get here, your lab, all your work, and your lanky ass are all going to go the way of the velociraptor." The quiver in my voice and my lame metaphor don't do much to sell my insolence, but the message is on target.

"Actually," the man says, his voice like tearing paper. "All I need is you."

Rain tenses. She understands the message and is about to take action. But she doesn't have enough bullets to deal with all the suits, and Reggie's status is about to shift from shield to target.

The hairs on the back of my neck spring up, warning me of danger. For a moment, I think it's something supernatural, but Rain isn't glowing, and the sound is familiar.

An engine.

I spin around to find a teal 1966 Ford Thunderbird screeching beneath the plane. I'm not a car guy, but I recognize the vehicle from *Thelma and Louis*. While that ill-fated duo used the car to take their own lives, this one is being employed as a weapon.

Tires shriek, trailing smoke, as the car slides. The Thunderbird twists around, its back end swinging like a baseball bat in the hands of Manny Ramirez, whose name I know because Randy dresses as the former Red Sox slugger every Halloween.

Metal crunches as the heavy vehicle's back end collides with the stone-cold, still-nameless SpecTek exec. The man doesn't scream. Doesn't flinch with fear. He doesn't have time. One second, he's looming like an evil birch tree. The next, he's airborne, pinwheeling high into the air until he strikes the 747's underside and then plummets back to the ground.

I want to cheer, to joke, to exclaim my amazement, but there isn't time.

The car's acrid smoke billows past, revealing the vehicle and its occupants.

Garcia looks over from behind the wheel. "Get in!"

"What the—" I say. "Where did you get this?"

"We landed in a classic car show," Garcia says, and she gives her passenger a shoulder-slap. "Do it!"

Bjorn rises from the front passenger seat, letting out a battle cry his namesake would be proud of. And he's... He's holding an Uzi! He pulls the trigger, unleashing a torrent of bullets toward the suits and their vehicles, forcing them to take cover.

Reggie, Rain, and I waste no time leaping over the side of the convertible, landing in the white leather back seat. I push myself up as the car speeds off, peeking over the backseat. What I see—the SpecTek exec standing up and dusting himself off—takes my breath away. *How?* is all I manage to think before bullets ping off the car's back end. I duck back down, hoping the old vehicle's solid metal body will protect us.

It's not until we bounce over the airport's ruined gate and squeal onto the road that I sit up and help Rain extract herself from Reggie.

Bjorn pumps a fist in the air, whooping like he's at the end of an 80s movie, his long hair blowing in the wind. Apparently, his recent brushes with death either broke his mind, or loosened it.

He turns around with a smile on his face. Then he sees Reggie.

The smile descends into a deep frown.

He levels the Uzi at her. "What is *she* doing here?"

"Bjorn," Reggie says, but she's silenced when he shoves the Uzi in her face.

"Bjorn," I say, trying to sound calm, but failing, because I'm having to shout over the wind. "She didn't betray us." I struggle with the words, because I'm not 100% sure I believe them yet. Logically, I do, but a wounded heart takes a little longer to heal, or trust. "She was misleading SpecTek." His eyes ask the obvious question, 'How?'

"They had a listening device in her neck," I say. "If she had told us the truth, they would have known. It was the only way she could really help us without tipping our hand."

"And now?" he asks, still seething.

Reggie turns her neck, revealing the still bleeding, self-inflicted incision. "I took it out!"

Bjorn winces at the sight of the wound. And then softens. "You did that?"

"On the plane," she says. "With a steak knife."

"Bad ass," Garcia says, glancing back. "Nice to have you back on the team."

I smile at her last three words. 'On the team.' Is that what we are? Some kind of monster-fighting squad? An FBI agent, a genius, a warlock, a glowing assassin/kaiju lightning rod, and a criminal investigator who can talk to the dead.

Holy shit, we're a monster-fighting squad!

Bjorn lowers the Uzi. "Sorry."

Reggie places a gentle hand on his cheek. "It was deserved... And I'm happy to see you feeling..."

"Alive," he says, smiling again. "When we fell out of the sky, I thought for sure we were going to die. Again. But this time...I just felt, I don't know. At peace. Death has lost its sting. I don't understand it, but knowing there is more, that the story continues... I just feel fr—"

A bullet strikes Bjorn and knocks him into the front seat.

39

I'm frozen in shock, staring at the blood-spattered front windshield. Time moves slowly and doesn't catch up with me, until I'm flung to the side.

The Thunderbird screeches around a corner, up an onramp, and onto Route 71. The highway is flat and straight, framed by single-story car parks adorned with solar panels. The engine growls, picking up speed and coughing out a cloud of exhaust.

Reg leans over the front seat. "Bjorn!"

"I'm okay," the wounded man says, righting himself with a grunt. His shoulder is a bloody mess, but he's alive, and somehow not in a fetal position.

"You're *not* okay," Reggie shouts. "You've been shot!"

It's the most upset I've ever heard Reg. An hour ago, I wouldn't have believed it, but she really does care about the man.

"Tis but a scratch," Bjorn says, quoting *Monty Python and the Holy Grail* and scoring some brownie points with me.

Reggie climbs over the seat back as the classic car hits 80mph. She ducks down when bullets start flying again. I glance back. They're hard to see in the orange glow of the setting sun, but they're there. Two SUVs, a hundred yards back, gaining fast. The Thunderbird might have some pep to it, but it can't compete with the black beasts roaring up behind us.

"We can't outrun them!" I shout.

Garcia glances in the rearview. Then she holds up Bjorn's discarded Uzi. "Hey, Rain. You up to—"

Rain snatches the weapon from Garcia, ejects the magazine and frowns. It's empty. Before she can complain, Garcia lifts her hand again. This time she's holding two fresh magazines. "The guard on the plane was very helpful. Speaking of, what happened to—"

"They're dead," Rain says, taking the magazines and not revealing Reggie as the killer.

"Wait until we get close," Garcia says.

"Until we get *close*?" Reggie asks, looking up from tending to Bjorn's wound.

"We can't outrun them," Garcia says. "Can't outmuscle them, or out-gun them, either. Only thing we can do..." I brace myself when I see Garcia's eyes tracking a rapidly approaching trailer park entrance. "...is keep them off balance."

She yanks the wheel and hits the brakes, putting us into a sharp, sliding turn. Before we spin all the way around, she crushes the gas again and pulls the wheel the other way. The result is a perfectly smooth, high-speed turn into a maze of trailers positioned around dirt roads and separated by lush trees.

Dust kicks up behind us, obscuring our view of the SUVs, and their view of us. Garcia doesn't let up on the speed, despite the twisting turns. Instead, she takes every opportunity to cram the gas pedal to the floor, making the tires spin in the loose dirt, kicking up a never-ending cloud.

And then, we make a beeline down a straight-away. "Oh, shit," I say, as we approach a T junction at the road's end. "Oh, shit!"

Garcia swings out wide, hits the brakes, and puts us in a spin that fills the air with enough dust to make me start coughing. Before I can ask what she's doing, I'm pinned back in my seat, as the car rockets back the way we came—racing through the streak of dust.

"Get ready!" Garcia shouts.

Despite the sphincter-puckering intensity of Garcia's driving, Rain *stands* in the back seat like she's George Washington crossing the Delaware, and raises the Uzi.

But at what?

All I can see is brown dirt. Even the mobile homes on the sides of the road are hard to see now.

But then I hear them. The SUVs. They're barreling straight toward us, following the dust trail, assuming we're running away, rather than charging. Despite the Thunderbird being a metal titan of the 60s, capable of crunching the bodies of most modern cars without fear of damage, the tall SUVs will likely plow up and over us. Anyone sitting up will have their torsos crushed, if not torn clear off.

I want to duck, but curiosity and faith keep me upright. Garcia is good at this. Rain is better. And neither of them is suicidal.

A shadow slips out of the billowing clouds. A dark dragon with soulless eyes.

Rain lets it pass. I twist as the SUV careens past us. I make eye contact with one of the suits, whose look of surprise matches mine. There's a flash of red and a shriek of tires as the driver hits the brakes.

When the second SUV passes, Rain opens fire.

Rapid-fire bullets spray from the Uzi—and miss the driver. In fact, I don't see a single round strike the windows or spark off the metal body. For a moment, I think she's done a worse job of shooting the enemy than I would, but then the SUV's driver side front tire explodes, leaving nothing but metal rim.

Reacting to the spray of bullets, the second SUV's driver cranes the vehicle away from us, just as the tire bursts. The rim digs into the dirt road and sticks. While the front end of the vehicle comes to a sudden stop, the back end—propelled by Newton's first law of motion—shifts from moving forward, to moving forward...and up.

The SUV catapults into the air. I see it rise up, trailed by a column of dust, like a rocket blasting off toward orbit. And then it's out of sight, hidden by the cloud. For a moment, all I can hear is the Thunderbird's V8. And then, the sharp, grinding, metal-on-metal crash of two vehicles colliding.

"We got them!" I shout, turning forward. "We got them!"

Rain sits back down beside me. "We?"

I smile. "Hey, I didn't duck or cry. That's something."

She pats my knee, and slathers on the condescension. "Good job. What a brave boy."

She cracks a smile, and I can't help but laugh, as we burst out of the dust cloud and shriek back onto the highway.

We've dodged a proverbial bullet, but SpecTek's resources are vast. If they can black-out news of Boston's attack, what else can they do? Frame us for murder? Have every cop in the city looking for us? Track us through security cameras, traffic cameras, and satellites? We've escaped, but we're not even close to being out of the woods.

Hell, we're driving straight into the forest, and it's full of monsters.

"Stay to the right," Rain says, when we reach a fork in the highway.

"What's to the right?" Garcia asks.

"Downtown Austin," I say.

She gives me a questioning glance.

"South by Southwest," I say. "I've been a few times."

She rolls her eyes. "Of course, you have."

Before I can ask her what that's supposed to mean, Rain says, "That's where the SpecTek lab is."

Reggie finishes patching up Bjorn. The bandage, made from her scarf, is crude, but his bleeding has stopped. Her neck, on the other hand, is still oozing blood. It's slowly congealing, blood cells doing their job, but the wound is deep and will take a long time to heal without stitches, especially while she's moving around. She looks back at Rain. "I didn't know they brought you to this facility."

"They didn't," Rain says, and she lifts her glowing hand.

I look around, half expecting to see kaiju-ghosts slipping out of the sunset behind us.

"Far side of the city," Rain says. "They haven't resolved yet, but...it won't be long."

Garcia speeds up, racing us toward the horrific unknown.

Bjorn grunts as he pushes himself up a little straighter. "I know I'm not as experienced in these things as some, but can I suggest developing a plan before rushing headlong into the unknown?"

"Rushing headlong into the unknown is what we do," I say, loving the way it sounds when it comes out of my mouth. Like Bjorn, I feel like

I'm coming into my own, rising above my fears and anxiety, believing for the first time in a long time that I am capable, strong, and bold—without Morgan around to prop me up.

Though she still is here, isn't she? I think, looking down at my chest, where the invisible tether still links me to her monster-self. *In a way.*

All four other people in the vehicle turn to me, incredulous.

"If you say anything that corny again," Garcia says, "I might slap you."

I purse my lips, happy I didn't express my earlier 'monster fighting squad' realization. "Okay," I say, recalling that I'm somehow the de facto leader of our ragtag group, "let's head toward the lab, but keep a safe distance. We know that SpecTek is going to try containing the Riesegeists, which would probably work out best for Austin. If they do manage to contain the kaiju, then we'll... We'll find a way to destroy them. If the trap fails, we'll try what we did in Chicago—lead them out of the city and try to shut them down."

"There're untold variables you're not considering," Reggie says.

"And part of your plan is, 'Find a way to destroy them,'" Bjorn adds.

"That's what you smart people are for," I say.

"And what are you for?" Bjorn asks.

"Inspirational leadership," I say with a grin, "And I'm a real-life Haley Joel Osment."

"*What?*" Bjorn asks.

"He can talk to dead people," Garcia says over her shoulder. Off Bjorn's blank stare, she says, "C'mon, man. You're a warlock. *The Sixth Sense?* Bruce Willis?"

"Is it like *Die Hard?*" Bjorn asks.

After a moment, Garcia says, "Yes... Exactly like *Die Hard.*"

The off-topic conversation continues, but I don't hear it. I sit back in my seat, thinking about the fact that I can speak to the dead. And not just to Wisp.

"What are you thinking?" Rain asks, sitting back next to me, while the others continue talking in the front.

"I'm thinking that SpecTek can't be trusted to solve this—not in a way that's good for anyone."

She nods. "And?"

"That you and I need to stop running away from what we need to do."

"And that is?"

I look into her pale blue eyes. "Say hello."

Silence pulls my eyes forward. Reggie and Bjorn are staring back at us. Garcia is watching through the rearview. Somehow, they heard the new plan over the rush of wind and their own conversation.

"That's crazy," Garcia says. She flashes a grin. "But I like it."

40

During the ten-minute drive to Austin, we fall silent. I don't know about the others, but I spend the time contemplating my life and how I feel about it ending. Within a minute, I shift from fear to acceptance, to 'What better way could there be to die?' I mean, I could live until ninety and die in a hospital bed, or I could meet my maker at the hands of a ghost-kaiju while trying to solve the riddle of my wife's death, and while protecting the people of Austin and foiling a nefarious government program that tortures and weaponizes human spirits. Dying of old age because I feared to risk my life for something noble feels...wrong.

To be clear, I don't want to die. I'd much rather come out of this with my life intact. But I'm not about to let fear control me. Bjorn already came to this conclusion. With evidence of an afterlife, death has lost its sting. If I survive, I'll have to look into what all this really means, and where religion comes into play, but for now, I'm satisfied with shedding the fear that comes from the concept of post-mortem non-existence.

"Exit here," Rain says. Her hands are lit up. I can tell she's containing her radiance, which means the kaiju are close...but they have yet to make their presence known.

We exit Interstate 35, turning right toward downtown. The tall buildings blaze orange in the sunset. In twenty minutes, the sun will be gone, but I suspect it will be dark before then. Storm clouds are swirling into reality above the city, dark and ominous.

The late day streets are mostly empty and easy to navigate, but there are still a million people living in the city, and another million in the congested suburbs surrounding downtown. As with any city in the U.S., the appearance of six-hundred-foot-tall Riesegeists will exact a massive toll on life, not to mention terrorizing the nation, and the rest of the world.

We haven't tuned in the outside world. I don't know if people know the truth about Boston—they *must* by now—and I don't know how much footage has snuck out of Chicago and onto the web. But as we turn past a dark IHOP, its parking lot empty, I think people are staying huddled around their TVs, waiting for the latest news about the two decimated cities.

Are we still terror suspects? I wonder.

Do people have any idea about what's going on?

I look out the window, looking at apartment building windows as we pass. Most are dark, shades drawn.

They've left, I hope. With two attacks on U.S. cities, maybe people are hitting the road and getting out of town?

There's no way to know for sure.

Feeling as internally prepared as I can be, I turn to Reggie, who has returned to the back seat, and ask, "So, who was that guy with the white hair?"

"I'm not sure what his official title is," she says, "but he's the man in charge. Name's Frank."

"He goes by his first name?"

"Mr. Frank," she says. "It's his last name. I believe his first name is Matthew, but I never heard anyone call him that. His full name was on my NDA. He's not worth concerning yourself with now."

"Why not?"

She looks at me like I've just pooped out a baby dragon. "Because Garcia ran him over."

My stomach twists with the realization that I have yet to tell anyone that Mr. Frank not only survived being hit, but walked away from it.

Reggie's forehead creases like an aerial view of a World War I battle-field crisscrossed by trenches. "What?"

"He's not dead," I say.

"Impossible."

"I'm telling you, he got up and brushed it off." I replay the image of Mr. Frank spinning through the air, striking the plane, plummeting back down, and then casually standing back up. "He wasn't even hurt."

Reggie holds her breath for a moment, and then lets it out as a long, slow, "Shhhiiiiiittttt."

That's not a good 'shit.' Or even a mild 'shit', or a 'shit' that says, 'We're all going to die.' That's a 'I know something horrible, and I might have had something to do with it' shit.

"What did you do?"

"It was a hypothesis," she says.

In the front seat, Bjorn's head rises at the word.

"What hypothesis?"

Bjorn's head cranes around. *"What hypothesis?"*

The guilt in Reggie's eyes tells me the hypothesis was Bjorn's, and that Reggie gave it to SpecTek.

"I'm sorry," she says to Bjorn. "I thought it was bunk. I never thought it would work."

"Thought *what* would work?" Rain asks, leaning around me. The tension in the car has attracted everyone's attention, and once again, Reggie is in the hot seat.

Reggie's mulls over the question, and then to herself says, "I knew his hair looked grayer. *And his eyes. The blue.*" She leans forward and looks at Rain. "You used to be a brunette with brown eyes and a some-what darker complexion, thanks to an American Indian mother."

I can't help but stare at Rain, mentally dyeing her hair, her eyes, and her skin in shades of brown. It's only then that her high cheekbone struc-ture hints at her genealogy.

"What the hell did you do to her?" Garcia asks.

"She was touched by death," Bjorn says, "But left alive."

"In the same way it affected Mr. Frank," I surmise.

"Not exactly," Reggie said. "Not if what you said is true."

"Because he's dead," Bjorn says. "Still."

"That's why getting hit by the car didn't kill him," Reggie adds. "Probably."

"I'm not a fan of *probably*," Garcia says. "Or of bullshit, so this better be legit."

Reggie clears her throat. "No one knew how it would affect the human body—"

"Or mind," Bjorn adds.

"So," I say, "You made a zombie."

"Closer to a vampire," Bjorn says. "Without the need to suck blood. In essence, his body has been fused with the supernatural energy that surrounds us, drawing power from it. Drawing life."

"Like The Force?" I ask.

"The dark side," Bjorn says. "Something like that."

"Doesn't sound like Spectral Duality," I note.

"It's not," he says, sounding grim. "My work on Supernatural Fusion predates that of Spectral Duality. It was never published. Never shown to *anyone*." He turns to Reggie. "We weren't really a Tinder match, were we? After I turned them down, SpecTek sent you to steal my work."

Reggie says nothing.

The tenuously placed bandage on their relationship is being slowly torn off.

"Aren't you going to say anything?" Bjorn asks.

Reggie's mouth parts, but then her eyes go wide and she sits up straight. "We're nearly there."

"Where?" I ask. We didn't have a specific destination in mind. Rain has been guiding us.

"The lab," she says, leaning to look down a right-turn street as we pass. "It's just a block that way."

"Then they'll be coming through here, right?" Garcia asks. "Maybe we should—"

"Keep going," Rain says. She points. "There. Across the bridge."

I follow her finger forward and to the left, across the Colorado River to what looks like a massive Big Top tent with the top cleaved off.

I've been there…

I can't remember the name, mostly because there is a mishmash of buildings built around circular patterns, all of them involving the arts to some degree or another. I attended an outdoor concert there during *South by Southwest*. Electronica. I think most people enjoyed it more than me because they were high. The music was okay, but the true highlight of that night was fried chicken strips in a bacon cone. Pure magic.

And now, it seems, the site will be host to dark magic. Or science gone awry that *looks* like magic. I'm pretty sure they're the same thing— science and magic.

A scent catches in my nose, instantly recognizable, transporting me back in time. Night-blooming jasmine. Morgan grew it in our first apartment. Come night, the whole place would smell of the fragrant flower. I loved the scent, but when we got busy with work, our mildly green thumbs turned brown, and the plant died. But I have identified that smell with Morgan ever since.

"She's close," Rain says, when she catches me looking around, and up. "You can feel her?"

I grin. "Smell her."

"What does she smell like?" Then she holds up a hand. "Wait. Night-blooming jasmine?"

The others are staring at us, but I don't care. "That's her."

"Or we drove by a plant," Reggie says, somehow still managing to be a skeptic.

"So, ahh," Garcia says, as we cross the bridge over the Colorado, "we're almost there. I get that you two want to make like AT&T to reach out and touch someone, but the rest of us aren't exactly immune from soul sucking kaiju-ghosts—"

"Or being crushed," Bjorn adds.

"Right," Garcia says, "So..."

Reggie leans forward. "Plan B."

"What's plan B?" Garcia asks, and I'm glad she does, because I don't know what it is either.

"If they're here for SpecTek," she says. "We remove SpecTek. Maybe that's all it will take?"

Garcia glances back. "What do you mean, '*Remove* SpecTek?'"

"I mean," she says. "We blow it up...if no one is inside, of course."

It makes sense in a ghost-movie kind of way, assuming the Riesegeists are seeking out the SpecTek labs out of a sense of revenge. Removing their target could free them from whatever is binding them to the mortal plane. Then again, these aren't normal ghosts. They might just stick around and destroy stuff. And with SpecTek being gone, that will make Rain the one and only thing attracting them.

Fun...

Garcia raises a thumbs up above her head. "If we're spotted, I don't think my job will be waiting for me when I get home, but if we can stop these things, and keep SpecTek from making more, count me in."

Bjorn nods, an eager gleam in his eyes. "Hell, yes."

Garcia pulls to a stop beside a building whose architecture is hard to describe aside from modern, round, and concrete. The top of it is a giant circle, like Xena's chakram, and within it, a rectangular building with multicolored windows. "First stop," Garcia says, and reads the sign beside us, "The Joe R. and Teresa Lozano Long Center for the Performing Arts. Geez, that's a freakin' mouthful."

I point to a second sign that simply reads, *Long Center.*

"That makes more sense," she says with a grin. "Now, get out."

Rain and I hop out of the car. While Rain strikes out for the staircase leading up under the giant disc, I turn back to the others.

Garcia reaches out her hand. "If I don't get to see you again..." I shake her hand. "You're a brave man." And when I give her my version of her skeptical eyebrow, she gets serious. "Braver than me."

Coming from Garcia, that's a high compliment, and I'm not sure how I feel about it. It's certainly not how I've felt the past few years. But I *am* about to face down a horde of spirit monsters. So, I guess I've made progress.

"Saul," Reggie says. "I'm sorry. Truly."

She's near tears. Like Garcia, she's somewhat convinced that this will be our last goodbye.

I take her hands in mine and squeeze. "Just...make sure they can't do this again."

She nods.

"And thanks," I say. "For being a good friend."

Her tears slip free as she sits back, unable to speak in the face of forgiveness. Part of me feels angry at her still—and at Morgan—but showing someone grace feels good.

"Bjorn," I say, giving him a wave. "It's been weird."

"Nice knowing you," he says.

I take a step back from the car, glancing up as a shadow falls over us and the temperature drops by a few degrees. The storm is coalescing above. The setting sun is still sneaking beneath the clouds, casting them in fiery light, but soon, it will be gone and only darkness will remain... and not the kind that inspires me.

Tires squeal as Garcia does half a donut and speeds off the way they came.

Alone for a minute, I breathe in deeply, hunting for the smell of night-blooming jasmine. Detecting only the acrid odor of burned rubber, I turn and run after Rain, catching up with her at the top of the stairs. She's moving quick. No time to catch my breath as I match her pace.

"How much longer?" I ask, when we leave the building behind and step out into a large, empty field. There's no one around. No reason to be here. *This is good,* I think. *This will work.*

And then my eyes turn up, as something massive flickers into reality for a moment. Something bigger and scarier and more horrific than anything I've seen before. And while I don't understand what it is, I know who it was before...

Rain's daughter.

41

"What the..." I crane my head up, following the tangle of glowing tendrils. In some ways they're reminiscent of Brute's hair, but the mass of wriggling limbs support the weight of a body a thousand feet in the air.

Far above, the swirling clouds flash with blue light. Mixed with the blazing orange of a low-hanging sunrise, the view is, for a moment, beautiful. And then the others resolve out of the ether.

Brute. Dragonfish. Dalí.

They look almost small compared to... I don't know her name. I decide on 'Storm' to compliment her mother's current moniker.

Brute wades through the Colorado. When his body slips into the mortal plane, water gushes out into the city.

Dragonfish undulates in the sky, its massive wings beating only occasionally as it flies lazy circles around Storm.

They're on the move together, but what is their relationship? Are the former human adults protecting the larger, but younger soul? Or are they simply moving together, mindlessly toward SpecTek, like a horde of zombies toward a honking horn?

Dalí lets out a roar, its long legs sweeping forward as its bulbous body wriggles about. Its spiny fins, front to back, undulate. Almost calmly. A distant building crumbles. Billowing dust and debris fill the air around its lower limbs. Drawing the kaiju to the park surrounding the river will help minimize the destruction, but these massive creatures can't really be contained. Not completely.

Not by us, and not by SpecTek. Even if they have the means, it's a power no one on Earth should have. If we can stop that from happening, we will.

Storm's body is segmented, like an insect larva, but glowing white. The creature is covered in little mouths, each of them snapping at the air with big, blunt teeth. *But they're not really little,* I realize. Each mouth is probably large enough to consume a bus. Storm has no eyes to speak of. No hints of having been human, or a little girl. Brilliant blue light flashes from its underside, slipping out through gaps in its tendril limbs as they wriggle forward.

"Are you ready?" Rain asks.

I turn toward her. "Not remotely."

She reaches her hand out, and I take hold of it. Her hand is small, warm and clammy inside mine.

"Neither am I," she confesses.

I understand her trepidation. Never mind the 'Holy shit, we're going to be killed by kaiju-ghosts' aspect any sane person would feel in our situation. But we've both got personal connections to these monsters now. Me—the wife I'll never forget. Rain—the daughter she can't remember.

She laces her fingers with mine. "Don't let go."

"No matter what," I say. "To hell and back. We're in this together."

"I'd like to think we would have been friends," she says. "Before. But...I don't think you would have liked me."

"You remember?"

She shakes her head. "But the things I can do. What people have said about me, about..." She looks up at Storm. "About her."

"I'm calling her Storm."

Rain grins. "About Storm. I don't think I was a good person."

"Maybe," I say. Tip-toeing around the person that Rain used to be won't do her any good. She might have been a master assassin with hundreds of deaths on her hands. But that person is gone, stripped away by the power of death itself. "You're a good person now."

"You sure about that?" she asks.

"I know what it feels like to look the worst of the worst in the eyes," I say, staring into her light blue eyes, where traces of light are starting to flicker. "You're not one of them."

Her hand squeezes mine. I squeeze back.

"You're a good friend." Her eyes flare to life, forcing my gaze forward. She can't hold back the light much longer.

We stand, hand in hand, for a silent moment. In the distance, screaming. Buildings crumble. Water crashes. Sirens wail. The people who decided to remain in the city are now regretting their choice. Across the river, cars speed down the street, headed toward the setting sun and safety.

In front of us, the Riesegeists loom larger, their glowing bodies slipping in and out of reality, the lightshow above growing violent behind a swirl of dark clouds. A cool wind whips against us, carrying the scent of night-blooming jasmine.

"Morgan's with us," I say.

Rain's fingers adjust and clamp down on my hand. "Then let's say hello."

Star-like brilliance explodes from Rain, illuminating the grass around us in stark white.

Dragonfish is the first to react, flinching in mid-flight and turning its googly-eyed stare straight at us. With a twist of its coiling body, it redirects its flight path in our direction. Moving up and down, the creature's body slides in and out of the world, strobing toward us.

I don't think the Riesegeists need to eat. They're dead, after all. And I don't know if they have any memory of eating, but Dragonfish—and the person it used to be—opens its underbite jaw, intent on swallowing us whole.

To the left, Dalí flinches away from Rain's light, tumbling over its own long limbs like a drunk giraffe. It levels entire neighborhoods as it attempts to stay upright. A massive explosion rocks into the sky beneath it. The fireball offsets Rain's brilliance for a moment. The light took a fraction of a second to reach us. The shockwave is still coming.

I brace myself just in time.

The boom draws a shout of pain, and the shockwave feels like a slap to the chest from a sasquatch.

I manage to stand my ground and remain upright, but Brute follows up the explosion with a trumpeting roar and a stomp of his powerful, flaking forearms. The ground trembles as water explodes from the Colorado River, rushing up over the concrete banks. I'm driven to one knee by the volume of its roar, but Rain doesn't bow to it, or let me go.

"Here we go," she says, and I look up just in time to see Dragonfish's sharp-toothed maw snap shut around us.

I expect to feel the sudden, almost painless transition to death, but then I'm inside Dragonfish's body, still alive, still thinking, still standing. The monster's spectral form moves through us as it arcs back up into the air.

Rain disappears in a nuclear blossom of light.

This is it.

Time to say, "Hello!"

Nothing.

"What is your name?" I shout into the ghost.

"What do you want?"

A loud, angry scream billows around me. It's not coming from the monster's mouth, and I doubt anyone other than me can hear it.

This is the voice of its soul. Pain and suffering. Anguish. Rage. Despair.

It knows it's not supposed to be here.

It knows it's a monster.

But it's stuck in a loop of sociopathic rage toward...

"Who are you angry at?" I shout.

I don't hear anything, but I *feel* its anger reaching out, spreading toward the SpecTek lab, and then beyond...out into the world, to every single person.

The living. It wants to kill...everyone.

There is a desire among humans, to not suffer alone. Misery really does love company, and apparently, Dragonfish's fellow Riesegeists aren't enough.

The moment SpecTek is gone...

...they're going to attack the whole damn world.

If Reggie, Garcia, and Bjorn succeed before we've made some kind of progress, and these things head out into a defenseless world, humanity's days will be numbered. With no way to contact the others, I need to just try harder.

"Answer me!" I scream into the rushing, cold wind that is Dragonfish's soul. "Tell me what you want! Why are you angry?!"

The wail of pain that replies isn't in any language, human or supernatural. It is pure emotion, lacking any kind of logic. The Riesegeists are beyond thought. Beyond hope.

"We can't stop them," I say, Dragonfish's despair sneaking into me.

Ankle-deep water from the Colorado rushes past my feet.

"Don't give up!" Rain shouts from inside her cocoon of heatless light. I can't see her at all, but I know she's there because she's still holding my hand, still connecting me to the supernatural.

"You can be free!" I shout.

A wail high above draws my eyes upward, just as Dragonfish's body slips past us and back into the sky. Somehow, Dalí heard my shout and understood what I was offering enough to be offended by it.

Several hundred feet of praying mantis limb reaches out and snaps down.

Even if it slips past us, the ground is going to take a beating.

I step into Rain's light, eyes clenched shut, and hold her against me.

The impact's shockwave nearly knocks me unconscious. For a moment, I feel weightless, and then gravity tugs me down.

We fall together, landing five feet lower than we'd been. The impact is jarring, but not enough to pry us apart.

With the attack over, I roll out of Rain's light—never releasing her hand—and I look up as Dalí's spiked limb rises back up into the flashing sky.

Water rushes into the impact crater. I pull Rain up while diverting my gaze from her blinding brightness. We scramble up the muddy embankment, hands linked.

I'm dazed, partially blinded, and my ears are ringing from the explosive volume of angry kaiju roars. While they seem to be incapable of tangibly interacting with Rain and me while we're in contact, I'm not sure how much more I can take.

A wave of water rises over the river's banks, surging out into the field, threatening to knock us off our feet and sweep us back into the crater. Brute charges up the Colorado with the primal ferocity of a silverback gorilla, its many eyes locked on me, long luminous hair flailing about.

Round three...

Here we go.

I don't think I'll be able to get through to Brute, any more than I did the other two, but I'm going to try.

I brace myself for the kaiju's attack, but I get distracted by the rhythmic thump of helicopter blades. The already rushing wind picks up, whipping water into my face, just as the river surges past my knees, nearly knocking me off my feet.

Fifty feet above us, the helicopter hovers, lit in the fiery sunset's light, and silhouetted by the dark clouds above.

Brute swings, aiming for the loud, new arrival.

The two-fingered hand swipes through the helicopter, tearing two bright souls out of the cockpit.

What kind of idiots would—

The helicopter rotates, out of control, revealing a logo: SpecTek.

As the helicopter careens toward the river, a sole figure leaps out.

For a moment, he appears frozen in the air, arms outstretched, face seething anger, blue eyes cutting into me. It's Mr. Frank. Then he falls toward the ground, no trace of fear in his eyes. He lands with a white splash of water and just...disappears beneath the surface.

I'm about to proclaim his demise a victory of pure luck. Then he stands back up, dripping water from his suit. He cracks his neck one way, and then the other, indifferent to the monsters around us. He locks his eyes on mine, lets a one-sided grin slip onto his face, and sloshes through the water, headed straight toward me.

42

Brute's massive stride ensures that he gets dibs on who gets first crack at pummeling us into the earth. While its many eyes don't have eyebrows or a furrowed forehead to express emotion, the creature's body language is pure rage. And its gaze is unrelenting.

I squeeze Rain's hand a little tighter, knowing what's coming. Despite having survived both Dragonfish's and Dalí's attacks, my history with Brute in Boston makes him feel even more dangerous.

Or perhaps it's my own anger seeping through.

This asshole destroyed my hometown.

As his giant two-fingered fists swing down toward us, I feel no fear.

Glowing, flaky skin slides through us, unable to make contact with our bodies, even while it pummels the world.

"Stop!" I shout, as my body braces for the booming sound and shaking ground that will follow.

But the world goes quiet.

When I open my eyes, we're encased in Brute's shimmering closed fist. Rain is impossible to see, swallowed up in light.

"This is not okay!" I shout. For some reason, I'm talking to the dead man-monster like I would a toddler or the elderly—loud and simple. "You can't just kill people. You can't destroy entire cities!"

A wave of confusion and rage flows from Brute to me.

A non-verbal rebuttal.

"I don't give a damn how you feel. Your emotions are not an excuse to hurt people. We don't need to share your pain to understand it. Just... *tell* me what you need, and I will make sure it happens."

I roll my eyes at everything I've just said. *Geez, I sound like Brené Brown.* I've never been a self-help kind of person, but her book, *Rising Strong,* carried me through some tough times. I suppose rising strong is what I'm doing now—the gladiator face down in the dirt, picking himself up, ready to rumble with what needs to be done.

Doubt sneaks into my psyche. How is scolding a kaiju-ghost going to make a difference?

Pain lances through me, a gift from Brute. But it feels wrong.

I mean, all pain feels wrong. It's literally the body's way of saying, 'Something is wrong!' But this emotional turmoil...burning my skin and churning my insides... It doesn't feel like Brute.

While he's a beast of rage, the emotion I'm feeling is desperation— like I'm reaching for someone hanging over a cliff, but can't quite reach them without falling over the edge myself.

I reach a hand up into the wavering light that is Brute's fist, imagining myself as a kind of lifeline to the dead.

"Just let go," I say. "You don't need to take any more people with you."

My hand starts to glow. It's painless, but it fills me with trepidation.

How did that *happen?*

What does it mean?

And then I see them, swirling and shrieking through Brute's body, trapped by his ethereal form—souls of the dead.

Men, women, and children from Boston and Chicago, pulled up into Brute's body, trapped in a prison of rage.

I reach for them with my luminous hand, fingers outstretched.

"C'mon! Hurry!"

The swirling mass of spirits churns with frantic energy, racing toward me and the promise of an outstretched hand they can now see.

It's horrifying in every sense of the word. I can feel their confusion and their sadness. Their desperate hope at the sight of my hand brings tears to my eyes.

Brute's fists lift from the ground.

"No!" I shout. "Wait!"

A child-sized soul springs ahead of the writhing mass. Its face is stretched out, agonized. Its brittle arms, reaching as though to a parent, are nearly impossible to make out.

Its fingers brush mine.

The connection knocks a sob from my lips and me nearly to my knees.

As Brute's fists continue to rise, I close my fingers around the small hand, and feel the connection slide through me and into Rain, anchoring both of us.

There is a familiar tug, not on my body, but on my soul, as Brute's rising form attempts to carry off the tender spirit. It feels similar to the blue light rising from SpecTek, threatening to pull me away, but Rain and I resist it.

The child-spirit slips through flaky skin, emerging like a wriggling larvae.

"You can do it," I shout, as desperate to free this single soul as I am to put a stop to the Reisegeists. "Almost there!"

Nearly freed from its prison, the spirit's supernatural weight increases. What felt like pulling a car with one hand becomes a 747. The impossible mass stretches me, and for a moment, my spirit-arm slips out of my physical arm. I'm losing my grip on myself.

"Rain!" I shout, understanding that Brute is about to add me to its collection.

"I know!" she says from somewhere in the light, and I feel her ferocity counter-balancing the pull. She screams in pain or exertion. I can't tell which. My soul slips back in place like a popped joint.

"You can't have them!" I shout. "They're not yours!"

I'm cut loose, sprawling back as Brute's hands rise back up into the sky. I hit the ground hard, eyes clenched shut. For a moment, I'm lost. Confusion grips every cell of my body. I don't know what I'm feeling. It's like I'm standing in a crowded hall, surrounded by tightly packed people, all of them talking. My thoughts get lost in the noise, until I open my eyes again—

—and see them.

Hundreds of spirits, all grasping onto each other, flow out of Brute's arms, tapering down to the small child still grasping my arm. As the last of them flow free from the beast, a great pressure is lifted away. The chorus of supernatural voices rises in volume. What they're saying—individually— is impossible to make out, but I feel the message resonating from each of them, transmitted to me by the child whose haunting eyes now look at peace.

"You're welcome," I say, and then the mass of souls disperses into the sky like a flock of birds, several hundred strong, bursting from the leaf-cover of a wide-limbed tree. I turn my head up, watching them flit toward the clouds, avoiding the massive monsters around us.

Dragonfish pursues the spirits into the sky, but gives up when they enter the storm and disappear into the flashing blue light.

Eyes turned up, I take in the apocalyptic scene around us. The surrounding city is in ruins, some of it burning. Drawing the kaiju to the river helped contain the damage, but the monsters' sheer size ensures the damage done will be vast. What I'm not seeing are souls being pried from buildings. The people who chose to remain in the city are getting clear, and fast.

Dalí has circled to the left, its long legs cutting through the tent-like performing arts building. The Riesegeist seems apprehensive, like it's afraid to lose its grasp on the souls contained within its supernatural shell. But it remains solely focused on Rain and me, moving steadily to block any possibility of retreat.

Brute reels back, wounded by the expulsion of souls. It slips back into the river, thrashing in anguish and sending cascades of water up over the shoreline.

And above it all, Storm. The colossal being of tendrils and gnashing mouths glides toward us on its many limbs. It seems indifferent to the plight of Brute, the actions of the other kaiju, and the freed souls. It simply moves steadily forward, destroying everything in its immense path.

The brightness of its cloaked underside is like a white star, hidden behind a curtain.

What's under there? I wonder, and I quickly decide I don't need to know.

All that's important is that this...monster, used to be a little girl—Rain's little girl—and we will do whatever is necessary to set her, and Morgan, free.

"That was interesting," a cold voice says.

My upturned head snaps back to level ground. Mr. Frank stands over me, a smirk on his face. He's as indifferent to the Riesegeists as the monsters are to the plight of the living.

They have no power over him, I think, *because he's already dead.*

Or something.

I have no idea how Bjorn's vampiric hypothesis works, but the look in Mr. Frank's eyes says he's got no soul left to lose.

He glances left and right. "Where are the rest of your friends?"

On the upside, he doesn't know where Reggie, Bjorn, and Garcia are. That means they've got a chance at succeeding. On the downside, he's talking to just me. I glance back and find Rain, her light extinguished, lying on her back. She's submerged in water deep enough to cover her ears, arms, and legs. If Brute sends another deep-water surge our way, she'll drown if I can't move her.

My gaze flits to her hand resting on her stomach, no longer linked with mine. Mr. Frank isn't the only danger for me.

As the kaiju destroy the city around us, I turn back to Mr. Frank. He's stronger, faster, and deader than me. I'm not sure I could win in a fight against a tweenage school girl, so I decide to strike first and fight dirty.

I kick out hard, foot snapping out of the water and striking Mr. Frank's kneecap. I cringe when the blow connects, because I'm sure it's going to invert his leg and cause great pain. Despite Mr. Frank being as close to pure evil as I've ever seen, I can't keep myself from feeling empathy for the anguish he's about to feel at my hands.

But that's not what happens.

Pain radiates from my foot and up my leg. I feel like I've just kicked a Redwood.

Before I can recover or even shout, Mr. Frank reaches down, clutches my leg, yanks me from the water, and tosses me away. I flail and twist through the air, looking for some sign of hope, but only seeing a confusing kaleidoscope of kaiju, city, water-covered ground, and then nothing.

Water rushes up over me, cushioning my impact. I sit up, back inside the pool shaped like Dalí's limb, coughing and sputtering. Unsure of what I can do against Mr. Frank, or the kaiju, now that I've been separated from Rain. I scramble up the slippery mud wall and drag myself, like a migrating salmon, through the water still rushing down into the pit.

When I reach the top, exhausted, I find Mr. Frank standing over Rain's body.

He wasn't trying to kill me. Not really. Because he still wants me alive.

But Rain... Will he kill her or use her to control the kaiju?

I climb to my feet, feeling smaller than ever, yet somehow bolder than ever, and shout, "Hey!" It's not very intimidating. Lacks any kind of real threat. Like a Chihuahua's yip. But it gets Mr. Frank's attention. For a moment, anyway.

He looks back at me, the same confident grin on his face. "What are you going to do?"

I clench my fists, swelling with anger.

The moment his furrowed brow digs in a little deeper, I know something has changed. But I don't know what until I raise my fists for a fight.

They're glowing.

Like Rain.

But without Rain.

And that's when I feel her—my wife—standing behind me, whispering into my ear. "I'm with you."

43

Mr. Frank's confident strides cut through the water. Fists clenched. Smile on his face. He is absolutely unnerving. But he doesn't know what I do—that I am not alone.

Go get him, I think, assuming Wisp can hear my thoughts like I did hers.

But nothing happens.

Mr. Frank closes in. I step away, but am forced to stop, teetering on the edge of the water-filled pit.

"Where did all your confidence go?" Mr. Frank asks.

I have nothing to say...because it'll probably just sound like a whimper.

"You're in over your head," he says. "Have been since Boston. You know, I was angry at your wife. For what she did. Now I understand it was a gift. An accidental ramification of her betrayal, but a gift, nonetheless. Turning Stephanie into a Riesegeist was always a risk. Even with her daughter, controlling her was a gamble. But now..." He turns to look up at Storm's colossal form. "Using mother to control daughter..." He smiles. "The idea is so inconceivable that it never even occurred to me, but as long as there have been mothers and daughters, the elder has guided the younger. It's a more natural fit."

"Rain will never—"

"She will for you," he says. "Just as your wife will—"

"My wife is dead," I declare, fists growing brighter. I feel a kind of strength flow through my arms, like they're not mine at all.

Mr. Frank stops, just a few feet away. He eyes my fists, more curious than afraid. "And what will you do with those?"

I take a swing. I know it's what he wants, but I've never felt the urge to punch someone like I do right now. I miss by a good foot.

Mr. Frank's grin never slips.

He doesn't even duck back.

He simply lets me come up short and stumble past him.

In doing so, he doesn't see what I see.

Doesn't realize what I do.

When he turns to face me, and finds me smiling back, his confidence falters.

I take a step back.

And then another.

"There is nowhere for you to run," he says, glancing left and right. To my back, Storm's approach continues. To my left, the river and Brute—the beast recovering from its loss of souls. To my right, Dalí continues plowing through the arts building, heading past us. With Rain unconscious, her light diminished, the kaiju will head for SpecTek. I glance up, looking for Dragonfish, and I find the flying giant already half way across Austin.

Hurry up, guys, I think. If Dragonfish reaches the lab before it's destroyed, their lives and souls will be in danger.

"I'm not running," I say, stepping farther back without taking my eyes off Mr. Frank. "I'm making room."

He squints at me, about to make a move.

I raise my glowing fists, feeling power beyond my own—beyond the realm of the living or the natural.

I swing a back-handed punch.

It's a little dramatic, but it feels good, even though I'm sure I look like an awkward teenager making a homemade lightsaber battle video.

My glowing fist slips through the air, a trail of light stretching out behind it.

Mr. Frank is baffled by my action, until Wisp's long, ribbon-limb flickers into view between us, a mirror of my swinging fist.

His eyes go wide, and his body twists back. He moves with speed beyond comprehension. His hand taps the submerged ground, balancing his body as Wisp's tendril whiffs over him. Then he bounds back to his feet like some kind of Lady Gaga backup dancer. I half expect him to drop and spin in a series of breakdance windmills.

Instead, he just grins at me, pleased by the revelation that Wisp and I are acting in concert. I'm not sure how it's possible, or if it's repeatable, but I can tell it was a concept neither he, nor Morgan, nor Reggie, nor anyone else working with SpecTek had imagined.

"Crap," I say, and I follow my back hand with an awkward left-handed punch. As ridiculous as I look and feel, Wisp's ribbon-arm follows my swing with much more power and grace, slipping into reality and through the air. It whooshes over my head and swings at Mr. Frank.

This time, he doesn't duck.

He jumps.

Like a mountain lion, he springs twenty feet up, clearing the ribbon and landing with a splash.

"All that power," he says, moving toward me again. "And no real understanding of its potential. You're a small man, with a small mind and miniscule ambitions. No wonder she wanted to leave you."

He's trying to unnerve me, I think. *Trying to get under my skin.*

But maybe he's right.

Maybe he knew Morgan better than I did.

She kept all of this from me. What else was she hiding?

The light in my hands flickers.

He's trying to sever our connection, attacking my mind instead of my body.

And honestly, I have no argument against him, or any of my fears. I have real reasons to not trust my wife. But I know I love her, and I know —despite the secrets—that she loved me.

But more importantly, I've learned over the past few days that I am enough on my own, that I can be bold, and brave, and powerful without her.

I clench my fists tighter. The brightness flares.

I swing at the air and Wisp's tendril flows with me.

He dodges, leaps, and runs. An impossible target, and he's not losing steam, while I'm swinging at the air and starting to feel tired.

I'm rope-a-doping myself.

So I stop swinging and start imagining.

And the attack continues. One at a time, the ribbons strike, and one at a time, they miss. I nearly catch him off guard, striking with both limbs at the same time, but he still moves faster than I can attack with the two arms.

But I have more than two arms now.

Show yourself, I think.

I don't bother looking up. I know Wisp is above me. I can feel her massive form towering above me, filling the flooded field, her flowery form unfolding, her many limbs wriggling in the air like a child's drawing of the sun.

When Mr. Frank's eyes snap up toward the kaiju, I attack again, this time with dozens of arms, all striking out as fast as I can imagine.

Mr. Frank sprints across the field, leaving a wake behind him. He dives and jukes like a running-back as Wisp's limbs pound the ground, always where he'd just been standing.

And then he does the unthinkable.

In the face of an overwhelming attack from a ghost-kaiju controlled by a man, he charges.

One punch will do it, I realize. The moment I'm unconscious, I'll lose control. But that might not be the end. Wisp would still defend me.

I think.

It's also possible that without Rain or me actively awake and invoking whatever these strange abilities are, that Wisp—who isn't tethered to SpecTek—would be unable to act.

I launch a multi-armed attack, aiming for his legs.

And finally, Mr. Frank makes a mistake.

He jumps.

Unless he has wings under that suit, or can turn into a bat, his trajectory is set in stone.

Knowing that I'm bad at baseball—sorry Randy—and that Morgan was worse, I swing out with six arms.

The first three miss, as Mr. Frank folds his body into a ball and flips.

The fourth swing makes contact, but tips him higher. A foul ball.

Mr. Frank unfolds above me, eyes gleaming, still smiling, still confident. He cocks a fist back.

Then I wipe that smile off his face with a strike from behind he never sees coming.

One moment he's there, the next he's toppling through the air, across the Colorado River. I watch him sail away, losing sight when he crashes into and through a building.

I'm about to pump a fist in the air and cheer when I spot Dragonfish in a dive, headed toward the ground behind the building Mr. Frank just crashed into.

I cringe. *That must be where SpecTek—*

A ball of orange light bursts into the air, silhouetting buildings in front of it and drowning out Dragonfish's glowing blue form. As a shockwave moves through the city, glittering glass bursts from windows and twinkles toward the ground.

Dragonfish peels up out of the fire, underbite jaw open wide, aghast eyes looking back at the fireball.

The shockwave races across the river and strikes. The slap to my eardrums knocks me down. Gasping and struggling to right myself, I'm assaulted again, this time by the roars of monsters from another plane of existence. Hands clutched to my ears I fall forward, face submerged, the water helping to muffle the bellowing beasts. But the sheer force of their voices tears through me, shaking my insides and stealing my breath.

Nearly my consciousness.

And then, all at once, they stop.

I push myself up out of the water, and my first thought is of Rain.

She's still unconscious. Still lying on her back, but the water level has fallen some. For the moment, she's safe.

I glance up and find Brute's many eyes locked on me.

Not on me, I think.

I turn to Rain again, expecting to find her glowing.

But that's not what I see. She's still out.

Which means...

I turn back to Brute.

Yeah, he's looking at me.

As is Dalí. And Dragonfish is on its way back, double-time.

I lift my still glowing hands.

How the hell do I turn this off?! I wonder, and then I tremble as a high-pitched wail cuts through the sky. It's Storm. The monster is a quarter mile off, but the sheer size of the kaiju makes it look like it's right on top of me. I turn my head up, following its long tendril arms up to its mouth-covered body.

Before I reach the top, its many limbs part like a curtain, revealing its luminous underside. For a moment, I squint at the light, unable to clearly see what's been revealed. Then my eyes adjust.

"Ohh," I manage to say. "Oh, God..."

44

It's the face of a girl—a scared little girl, staring down from Storm's under-side, looking through the curtain of undulating limbs for the one thing it holds dear—its mother. Though Storm wasn't raised by Rain, something supernatural must connect them. She doesn't know Rain, but knows who she is. The luminous face is turned up in fear. Like the other kaiju, it is not destroying the world of the living because it is evil, but because it is confused, and frightened.

The Riesegeists shouldn't be hated...they should be pitied.

Like the people they're inadvertently killing, they're victims. The blame for all of this resides on SpecTek and Mr. Frank, whose punish-ment has already been doled out. Morgan and the other once-human SpecTek scientists aren't absolved of their involvement, but none of them signed up to be unliving monsters.

The only true innocent in all of this is Storm, whose real name I don't even know, but whose anguish I recognize even though I'm not a father.

I remember what it was like to be a kid. To be lost. To feel like I would never see my family again. I'd been left behind at a lake, sure I had been forgotten. Tears in my eyes, I wandered until a stranger picked me up. After a few minutes driving, covering more ground than I could on foot, I spotted my parent's station wagon. While I'd been searching for my family, they had been searching for me. I'd been lost for just ten minutes, but it left a mark on my psyche that lasted into adulthood.

What Storm must be feeling...ripped not just from her mother, but from her own body and reality? If she remembers anything of who she was...

Tears come again, like at that childhood lake, but the desperate sadness I feel now isn't for myself.

It's for the colossal monster about to smear me into the ground before it destroys Austin, and maybe the world.

She needs her mother...

But Rain is still unconscious. How will she feel when she sees Storm's face? Will she remember the girl that once was? Will she experience the profound pain of realizing someone you love isn't just dead, but an abomination? For the first time, I wonder if Rain's amnesia is a blessing.

The ground trembles as Dalí swings around toward me, small explosions erupting from the tips of its long limbs as they carve buildings and vehicles in half.

Brute lifts its powerful arms out of the river, pounding them on the shore as it pulls itself free.

Dragonfish has nearly returned, swooping up and down, showing no signs of slowing.

And Storm... The poor child's eyes have locked on to the tenuous beacon supplied by my glowing hands, but I offer her no relief or hope. I'm just a stranger, but maybe like that man at the lake, who offered me help, I can guide her to her family?

I reach a hand out to Storm. "She's here! Your mother is here!"

There's no way she can hear me over the rumble of explosions, heavy foot falls, and kaiju vocalizations, but maybe she can sense the message?

Several of Storm's thousand-foot-long tendrils jut out, piercing buildings on both sides of the river. The appendages tear through concrete, steel, and glass like they aren't even there.

The monster wails. While the many mouths on its upper body roar into the sky, the mouth on its youthful face lets out a sob.

My heart breaks.

I lift up my other arm, no longer offering a helping hand, but an embrace.

It's stupid. Insane. Makes no sense, but I'm being guided by instinct here. Somewhere in that quarter-mile-tall monster is the soul of a child who wants to be found and comforted.

My hands glow brighter, and I let go of my fear, reaching up and out with all of my being, eyes closed.

The rumbling around me stops.

The growls and barks of angry kaiju die down.

All that remains is the distant grind of crumbling buildings and the wail of sirens, which fade into the background of my consciousness.

The momentary peace startles my eyes open.

Far above, the swirling storm clouds have gone still. Soundless lightning continues to flash, filling the now-night sky with blue light, but the strong winds have died down along with the kaiju.

They're all connected.

Long ribbon arms reach up high above me, flickering in and out of the world as they stretch toward Storm.

It's Wisp, many arms open for an embrace. The Riesegeist that was once my wife extends my offer of comfort and mercy to the child.

You're safe, I will Storm to hear. *You're not alone.*

Storm's outstretched tendrils snap back, but don't cover her massive glowing face. The girl is looking at me now, and at Wisp.

The hundreds of long limbs supporting Storm slide out to the sides as the massive body lowers down.

Wisp's flowery body blooms, opening itself to the colossal monster. I don't know if the Riesegeist can be killed again, but the gesture leaves Wisp defenseless—to Storm and the other three kaiju. They're holding their ground right now, curious about what's going on, but that could change at any moment. With SpecTek destroyed, I'm the one and only thing drawing them. The moment they remember me, I'm toast.

The young face attached to the underside of a monster squints at me. She's not buying it.

Or not feeling it.

While Wisp is still mimicking my movements—or is guided by them—we are still separate, pulling Storm's attention in two different directions. Toward the strange man with glowing hands, and the even stranger once-was-a-woman who looks like a giant, ghost-flower.

How can we possibly hope to comfort this...thing?

She's a girl, I remind myself. *A scared little girl.*

And you're not doing enough.

Be bold, I think, or was that Wisp? *Step into yourself.*

I step back, toward Wisp. The Riesegeist's body hovers just behind me, held aloft on a bed of ribbons and extended petals. My hands slip inside the body and the connection slams into my gut.

For a moment, I share in Morgan's pain. Death is uncomfortable. Unbearable. At least, for a Riesegeist. I push back on the discomfort, letting my love for Morgan cut through.

"Are you here, baby?" I ask.

With you. I feel the words. **Love you.**

"I know."

I feel her spirit lighten. **Okay, Han.**

I can't help but laugh. This is definitely Morgan, and not just some small piece of her. It's all of her. Speaking might not be easy, given our existence on two different planes of reality, and our current circumstances, but our little *Star Wars* homage is enough to confirm that every part of this monster is my wife.

Proud of you.

I stand frozen for a moment, in part because Morgan's words have moved me, but also because I'm looking up into the glowing blue eyes of Rain's daughter. The face hovers a few hundred feet above, angled to look down at me, its long limbs twisting to accommodate the posture change. She's not impressed.

Wisp's ribbons extend farther, reaching slowly for the child's face.

A single ribbon traces a gentle path over the smooth, luminous skin.

I feel nothing.

No connection.

No understanding.

"It's not enough," I say. "I need to reach her."

I take another step back, my body just inches from Wisp's. My hands, glowing like Rain's, are immune to the effect of touching a Riesegeist, but I have no idea what will happen if I step inside her. I could be lost forever, trapped inside a monster that was—and still is—my wife. Or I could be protected by the power granted to me at the SpecTek explosion.

I feel Wisp tense behind me. She's unsure as well, and clearly understands the risk.

"I don't see any other way," I say, closing my eyes and stepping back. "I'm the only one who can—"

A hand clasps mine, fingers locking.

"Morgan?" I ask, opening my eyes to find Rain standing before me, soaked and serious. Her glowing hand is locked with mine, inside Wisp.

Light arcs between us.

"She needs her mother," Rain says, her body and face flickering to life and then exploding with light.

Protected by my connection with Rain, I step inside Wisp.

Rain follows.

Light flows around us, growing brighter. I attempt to close my eyes at the brightness, but I can't—they're already closed.

My skin tingles with cold energy.

Gravity falls away. My stomach churns as my feet leave the ground.

I open my eyes to find myself hovering in a growing cocoon of light, hands interlocked with Rain's. She's hard to look at, every part of her—even her hair—shines with the brilliance of life itself.

"Rain, what's happening? What are you—"

Before I can finish my question, the cocoon is pierced, and we are no longer alone.

The newcomer is the antithesis to Rain. Where my newfound partner exudes life...the thing with us looks like death. A ragged soul with an emaciated face and a tattered, legless body. Where there should be arms, there are fluttering, chunky ribbons. It glows an ethereal blue, like the Riesegeist...

Because it *is* a Riesegeist...

My heart breaks for it. For *her*.

"Morgan..."

45

Morgan's spirit hovers around us. On edge. Suspicious. Confused.

"It's me," I tell her. My instinct is to let go of Rain's hand and embrace my wife, even in her current hideous state—*because* of her current hideous state. My heart breaks for her, but Rain's grip remains tight.

If I let go, I'll be here forever.

Hollow eyes glare at me, outraged by the intrusion, perhaps offended by Rain's radiant life.

"Talk to her," Rain says. "Get her closer."

"Morgan, it's me. It's Saul."

She slides closer as the cocoon of light grows brighter, blue sprites swirling.

Something is happening. We don't have a lot of time.

What the hell is Rain planning?

"Remember..." I search the past for a distinctive memory. Something that's impossible to forget, even in death. Years of memories flit past. Passionate encounters. Arguments. Destinations. Events. I'm not sure why I land where I do, but I'm speaking before I really evaluate it. "Remember when we went horseback riding?"

Her stare remains blank.

"They gave me the white horse. The one who'd been carting around a...how can I say this politely? Hell, its just us. A heifer." While I'd never call an overweight person a heifer—I'm not an asshole—something about the image of a cow riding a horse, always resonates with Morgan when we recall the story.

"That poor horse was tired and grumpy. Bucked me every step of the way. Scraped me up against trees like I was a tick. And to make matters worse, the saddle was freakin' loose." A chuckle rises from my throat. This is always where I laugh, because from my perspective, it was somewhat frightening. "I swear to God, when I started sliding to the side, I thought I was a goner. I didn't know what to do."

So you just held on...

Morgan's dead mouth doesn't move, but I hear her voice.

A nod. "I held on. I thought my grumpy steed would crush me if I let go. In hindsight, I think that might have been preferable, because around this time is when that horse decided to push out the motherload of horse-shit. Dangling from my upside-down saddle, there was nothing I could do to stop it."

"You didn't," Rain says. I'm surprised to see an attentive smile on her glowing face. Despite all that's happening and all that's at stake, she's allowed herself to give my tale her full attention.

"I did," I say, turning back to Morgan. "Every mound and nugget of hay-filled shit smeared and rolled across my face. Did you know that fresh horse poop is actually hot? Like a hundred degrees. It was like—"

I remember.

Morgan glides closer.

"Take her hand," Rain says, and I reach out.

Looking at Morgan's emaciated hand, covered in peeling skin like Brute's, something in me recoils. Death, to the living, is abhorrent. But if people in Indonesia can exhume the dead, bring them home for a scrub and a change of clothes, then I can take the hand of my dead wife's spirit.

For some reason, being connected to Wisp didn't bother me as much as this. Maybe because I had no choice, or because while I knew Wisp was Morgan, the giant, flowering spirit is actually beautiful in a haunting kind of way.

But now...this is Morgan in death. There's no way to make this picture pretty.

But she is my wife, who I love, so I stretch my hand out to her.

She hesitates.

"It's me," I repeat.

I know.

Her blank eyes turn down to her ragtag body. While there is no life in her shimmering form, I sense her shame.

"You're still you," I say. "No matter what."

It's not what I am, I hear her say. **It's what I did.**

"You did what you had to," Rain says. "To save me."

Morgan's gaze shifts to Rain for the first time. **You... But... What happened to us, to your daughter, is worse.**

"It's time to make it right," Rain says, holding out her hand, a mirror of mine.

You must hate me.

"I don't even remember you," Rain says.

I remember you, Morgan says. **All of you.**

She glides closer, dead hands reaching for ours.

Okay, I think. *Now wha—*

Morgan's hands feel like cold coconuts—rough and brittle. A shiver rolls up through me as her fingers wrap around my hand.

The sheer horror on her face fades a degree when I squeeze back.

"Missed you," I say.

What I think is a smile stretches onto her gnarled face. Then she reaches out and takes Rain's hand, connecting the circuit. Light flares from Rain's body, flashing through mine and then striking Morgan's. White hot pain arches my back and turns my head up.

For a moment, I'm lost in eternal nowhere, and then...memories.

They come in a flood.

A childhood, lonely and full of pain. Desperate aloneness, and abusive parents.

Teenage years come with parties, drugs, alcohol, and violence. Fights, jail, rebellion.

Years in the military follow. Grueling boot camp. Face in the mud. Mockery and degradation. Followed by pushback. A tidal wave of effort. Rising above peers, instilling them with fear, and then respect.

Then freedom. Old habits return. Violence and trouble. Killing for money.

Assassin.

A blip in the painful character arc flares to life, revealing love, and vulnerability. A child. A daughter.

This is Rain's life. Every single moment of it.

The blip of love explodes into darkness. Death and pain follow. A return to darkness, and the giving up of life and hope. *Better off without me,* I hear Rain's words and pain.

I flinch at the face of Mr. Frank, his then-brown eyes still filled with an otherworldly confidence. He makes an offer. Money and protection. *She'll have the life you want for her.*

Acceptance and then betrayal.

SpecTek. The lab. Morgan's face. *I won't let them do this to you! I won't let them take you from her!*

On the far side of a glass wall, Rain's daughter, hand reaching for her mother as she's dragged away.

I feel myself in Rain's body, reaching back, desperate and broken. "Kate."

Cold blue light surges up and around. The explosion. The moment her memories were taken. All of it is back. My connection to Rain feels different now. She's not the same person I knew. She's herself—her true self—again. And she is pissed.

But not at me.

And not at Morgan.

And that's good, because I've seen the bodies left in the wake of her life as a career killer—for the military, for the depths of the U.S. government, and then for SpecTek. Being on her bad side is a very bad place to be.

I can't see anything other than light, but Rain's voice cuts through it. "Still friends?"

"Always," I say, and it's true. The Rain I got to know, free from the tortures of her past, was a kind, fiercely loyal and brave woman I'm honored to have known.

"You have a plan?" I ask.

"Always," she says.

"Am I going to like it?"

"Never."

I laugh.

"Going to miss you," she says.

"Wait, what?" My good humor drains away. "Are you saying good-bye? Why are you saying goodbye?"

Her face slides out of the light, electric blue eyes burning with intensity. "You are everything you need to be, and have always been. You didn't need Morgan, and you don't need me. But Kate does."

I understand her points, but I have no idea what she's really saying.

"This is going to be weird," she says. "At first, but you'll get used to it." She smiles. "And you'll never forget me."

"How could I?" I say. "But what are you—"

She leans forward, kissing my forehead. "Saul the brave. Saul the bold. It's time for you to come into your own. It's time for you to save her."

"Save *who?*"

She steps back into the light, disappearing from view. "Your wife."

She lets go of me.

Gravity reasserts itself. I plummet to the ground, falling out of Wisp's body and landing in several feet of water.

My first thought is that I touched Wisp's body and nothing happened. My soul is still intact. Then I see Wisp above me, a ball of blue light building inside her transparent body, and I forget all about my ability to touch the kaiju without consequence.

The light builds in a series of strobes, each one brighter than the last.

Around us, the four kaiju watch as though dumbfounded, all of their rage and fear interrupted by a spectacle that befuddles the living and the dead.

Light explodes out of the kaiju and then fades. Wisp's glowing form remains, but something inside it falls toward me. I dodge to the side, avoiding a collision while looking back. Rain's limp body is expelled by the kaiju and thrown into the water beside me.

"Rain!" I stab my hands beneath the muddy, churning water. I find an arm, grasp hold, and yank her up out of the pond like a pastor baptizing the faithful. She sucks in a lungful of air the moment she breaches, eyes wide.

Brown eyes wide.

Her complexion is darker.

Her straight hair is black.

The energy that changed her body back at SpecTek is gone.

But there's something else different about her eyes.

"Saul?" she says, arms around my neck, as though she can't believe she's seeing me, as though she didn't expect to survive.

And that's when I see it in her eyes.

Hear it in her voice.

A sob chokes my voice for a moment, and then I manage a single-word question.

"M-Morgan?"

She smiles.

I'm bordering on full-on blubbering now. My wife has been returned to me, maybe not in body, but definitely in soul. And that means...

I turn my eyes up to look at Wisp.

At Rain.

Oh, God... Rain... What did you do?

"Saul," Rain...Morgan says. *"Saul."*

My wet eyes shift back to...hers. She's fading, losing consciousness. "Your friend gave me a message for you."

I blink back tears and smile.

Of course she did.

Morgan's eyes flutter and close. "Run," she whispers. "Run..."

46

Above me, Wisp roars.

It's a new kind of sound, anger lacking the confusion of death. Rain stepped into this willingly. With a purpose. Where the other Riesegeists are caught in the confusing turmoil of having been both killed and turned into abominations, Rain knew exactly what she was doing, and she knows what she has become.

Wisp's body rises up, the ribbon-limbs spasming as though in pain.

It's not working, I think. The form of Wisp is rejecting Rain. Really, I have no fucking idea what is happening, but that's the only thing I can come up with.

Then, as she often did in life, Rain proves me wrong.

The flower-shaped body of Wisp folds in on itself. All the petals and ribbons twist into the core of the massive body, like a black hole is drawing them inside. Then all of that spectral mass comes out the other side, transformed into something new.

Two legs emerge first, flashing in and out of the world, slender but strong and human—toes and everything.

The others were lost when they became Riesegeists. Their confusion, rage, and desperate sadness turned them into monsters. Wisp was different because Morgan had been focused on me. On our love. Rain is fully herself and is transforming with that sense of self—and her humanity—intact.

Mostly.

Her luminous body is lined with spikes and serrations. An undead weapon. This is how Rain saw herself in life, before she lost her memory.

Fully formed, she emerges from what once was my wife...and drops to the ground.

I lower myself over Morgan's new and unconscious body as Rain lands. The ground shakes from the force of a several hundred-foot-tall ghost-woman dropping fifty feet.

Above us, Rain casually looks at the kaiju surrounding us, each of them growing more agitated by the moment.

Do they know who she is? Do they know that Morgan—the woman ultimately responsible for them being Riesegeists—has escaped their fate?

Rain turns her head down, frowning at me, as her luminous hair flows out around her face.

"Right," I say, like she can hear me way up there. "Run. I'm running."

I hoist Morgan-in-Rain's-body over my shoulder and scramble out of the watery pit. When I reach the top, the kaiju creatures' patience has boiled over. Brute pounds the ground and huffs out a bark.

Why aren't they leaving? My hands are extinguished. So is Rain's body. SpecTek is destroyed. So what's keeping them here?

Bright light casts my shadow thirty feet ahead of me.

It's Rain.

Even in her massive form, she has retained the ability to attract the dead.

High in the sky, Dragonfish bellows, bulging eyes on Rain.

Dalí lets out a bellow, raising its long limbs and smashing them down, its gelatinous body shaking like a deflated, water-filled balloon. Then it charges, straight for Rain, which also happens to be straight toward me.

But there's no other direction to run. To my left is the river, and Brute. To the right, vast destruction and Dragonfish, swooping down for a low approach. And behind me... Well, I'm not even going to look. At least there's a chance Dalí's long stride might miss us.

"You can do this," I tell myself, running toward Dalí. The only thing separating us is an open field. The arts center has been decimated.

I'm as close as I can get to a sprint with Morgan over my shoulder, my side already cramping up. And yet, for every twenty strides I take, Dalí's long gait halves the distance between us with a single step.

I shift to the left, hoping to skirt between Dalí and the river, but the monster's wide stride puts a stop to that. A long limb crashes down directly in my path, knocking me back and nearly to the ground. I stagger, off balance thanks to Morgan's weight.

And then I slip.

I'm going to hit hard. Going to be hurt.

How the hell am I going to get out of here?

Despair turns to confusion when my fall is arrested at a forty-five-degree angle. I'm pushed up from behind, back onto my feet.

I should run. But I can't stop myself from looking back for my rescuer. A glowing ribbon slips away, twisting back to its source, high above.

It's Rain, but it's not just Rain. The petals and long, flat tendrils that made up Wisp's body now flow from Rain's back, like wings.

"Like an angel," I say.

Rain flares like the sun, lighting up the whole city.

Dalí wails and charges, lunging past me and toward a patiently waiting Rain.

"Run," I tell myself, repeating Rain's final message to me. "Run!"

I feel pitifully small and slow, but I manage to push past the cramp and the exhaustion, and I break into another sprint.

Behind me, behemoths clash.

Dalí's anguished roar rips through the air, as Rain drives her foot into the long leg, bending it in the wrong direction.

A shift in the wind draws my eyes back again.

Dalí, its leg ruined, has twisted around and fallen to the side... straight toward me. There's no outrunning it. No dodging it.

"C'mon," I will my hands, trying to ignite the brightness that might make me intangible to the dead, and prevents my soul from being sucked away. But nothing happens.

Long, fleshy ribbons jut out from Rain's back, wrapping around Dali's limbs, keeping the kaiju from plummeting atop us.

I want to stop and thank my friend for continuing to save my life, but before I can speak, Brute thunders up from the river, tackling Rain from behind. Now, instead of one impossibly huge Riesegeist falling toward me, there are three.

Just run, I tell myself. *There's nothing else you can do.*

My legs burn and shake. I can't go on like this much longer.

The ground quivers from an impact. I stumble as the earth beneath my feet becomes about as stable as a vibrating bed.

Wavering blue light and a cold wave of pressure alert me to the presence of a Riesegeist descending above me. I don't bother looking. If the end comes, I'd rather not see it.

Another jarring quake knocks me off balance, the energy it takes to keep myself upright nearly makes me collapse. I drop to a knee, take a deep breath, steel myself, and then push myself back up. I'm still determined to not look up, but I don't need to.

The world around me has been transformed into an ethereal forest. Glowing, wriggling strands, like spectral anacondas, hang down from a luminous ceiling. I stare up into a shifting, blue membrane that is both there and not. Inside, trapped souls, mouths agape, claw in a futile attempt at escape.

A scratching spins me around. One of the tendrils, which I now recognize as Brute's long hair, snakes toward me.

"Gah!" is all I manage to say, before it strikes like a snake.

I'm struck from the side, wrapped and constricted.

My desperate shout becomes muffled as I'm lifted off the ground. Then it explodes into the night air as I'm freed—by Rain's ribbon. I see her long appendages twisting out beneath the fallen kaiju body, bearing its weight, assaulting the living hair, protecting me, and clearing a path.

"Thanks," I say to Rain, hitting my top speed—a slow jog—in just a few steps. In terms of gratitude, it's a pitiful representation of how I actually feel, but there's no time for me to recite the number of ways I'm grateful for Rain.

All around me, snaking hair reaches out for me, trying to suck away my soul. But I run with confidence, knowing that Rain still has my back. Ribbons flank me, deflecting attacks and tangling the hair. I duck and weave, legs threatening to give way.

Somewhere, a kaiju roars. The sound shakes the air from my lungs.

I can't make it...

I'm not going to make it...

My legs become unstable stilts. I waver. And fall.

And am caught—again.

A ribbon lifts me off the ground, wrapping Morgan and me in a gentle embrace, carrying us toward safety as the 'ceiling' above us lowers toward the ground. Even if I'd been at full speed, not carrying someone over my shoulder, I couldn't have escaped in time. But lifted up by the body of Wisp-turned-Rain, whom I can still touch without consequence. Then I'm propelled like a rocket.

The end of my journey comes as quickly as it began. The ribbon unravels just before it's pinned under the bulk of Brute's body. I roll to a stop beside Morgan's limp form, struggling for air and trying to push myself up. My arms get me halfway there, but my legs are Jell-O.

I shout in frustration. I can't let Rain's sacrifice be in vain. I get one leg under me and push. It wobbles, and fails me, but I don't fall.

Pressure wraps around my arms, and for a moment, I think Rain is still carrying me.

"I got you," Bjorn says. His nervous smile is brilliant through a face soiled dark gray. His teeth are gritted against the pain of using his wounded shoulder to support my weight.

"I'll get Rain," Reggie says, flinching when she sees brown hair instead of white-blonde. "What happened?" she asks.

The ground shakes. Dust billows around us. I don't know what's happening behind me. Don't want to know. Not yet. Right now, I just want to honor Rain's last request.

"Later!" I shout. "We need to run!"

"Run?" Reggie says, waving her hand to someone. "Screw running."

Tires squeal and an engine roars—for a moment. I lose the sound when a kaiju's bellow drowns out the engine. But it's impossible to miss the Thunderbird skidding to a stop in front of me. The side door flings open, revealing Garcia, equally as dust-covered as Bjorn. "Get in!"

The door swings open all the way, and then bounces back, closing in our faces.

All of my anxiety bursts out as hysterical laughter, cutting through my tension and the group's. We pile into the car, afraid for our lives, but still smiling.

"What happened to her?" Reggie asks, looking down at Rain's unconscious body lying between us in the back seat.

"This isn't Rain," I say, looking back at the ongoing battle...and then up. "*That* is Rain."

47

Brute is flung up and away, stumbling back and then toppling into the Colorado as the sidewall gives way. A wave of water rolls up the river, enveloping the bridge Garcia was about to drive across. She hits the brakes, and then forgets all about fleeing. She looks back with the rest of us, watching our friend-turned-Riesegeist rise into the sky.

Rain stands up, body shimmering like the other kaiju, but also burning with an inner light, the way she did in life. The way her daughter's face does in death. Rising to a six-hundred-foot height, she stretches her arms back, lifts her face to the flashing, stormy sky, and lets out a battle-cry. It's more human than the other kaiju roars, but there is still something haunting about it.

Arms outstretched, fingers hooked, the part of her that once was Wisp stretches out as well, spreading wing-like to the sides.

She is beautiful, even in death. A true force of nature. But is she still her? Is she still Rain? Or is she lost like the others, twisted by death into something confused, angry, and guided by misunderstood desires?

Drawn to the light still radiating from Rain's body, Dragonfish swoops down, sharp-toothed mouth stretched wide and rushing toward the back of Rain's head.

"Look out!" I shout, though I'm sure she can't hear me.

Rain's eyes open wide, blue light burning out.

She knows.

In life, she had the situational awareness of someone with actual eyes in the back of her head. In death...hell, maybe there *are* eyes in the back of her head?

Either way, she knows Dragonfish is coming.

She hasn't moved because she's waiting. She's planning.

I think.

Please be waiting.

I do not want my dead friend to be hurt—which is an insane sentiment. I'm pretty certain that she's the only one who can deal with the Riesegeists.

If she can't stop them...

Rain twists to the side. Ribbons explode up from her back, entangling Dragonfish's body. She reaches out with her massive hands, catching the open jaws and prying them apart.

She braces her legs.

The earth beneath her feet compresses.

Rain's arms lock, shoving up and down, forcing the already wide jaws farther open, to the point of breaking. For a moment, I see the shake of exertion in her arms and legs, and then Dragonfish's momentum is transformed into pressure on the gaping mouth.

To say Dragonfish's jaw breaks is an understatement in the extreme. Before its entire mass comes to a stop, the creature's head splits in two horizontally. Carried forward, the body comes apart like two halves of a banana peel.

I cringe, expecting to see an explosion of bone, blood, and guts, but the only thing that emerges from the undone kaiju is light...and then swirling wisps that soar up into the storm—spirits escaping to wherever they were meant to go upon separation from the body.

Dragonfish's body comes apart in Rain's hands, disintegrating into sparkling dust.

Dead again.

Or perhaps set free—along with all the souls it had trapped.

A blur of motion catches me off guard. Rain, too. The sharp end of Dalí's leg juts out, piercing her chest.

I'm no assassin, but I've seen enough gunshot and stabbing victims to know it's a kill shot.

Rain takes hold of the leg with both hands, and then in a show of impressive strength, withdraws it from her chest. It hurts. The pain etched onto her giant face can be seen from miles away.

A flash of white light blooms from the open wound when she withdraws the limb. There's no blood. No gore. Just light, and then nothing at all. The wound is healed. Or perhaps it never really existed.

With a quick twist of her hand, Rain snaps Dalí's long leg.

The beast wails and attempts to scramble away, but like a wounded spider, the attempt is somewhat pitiful.

But Rain takes no pity on the kaiju. She reaches down, taking both broken limbs in her hands.

Behind her, Brute rises from the water, as enraged as ever, thrashing about before leaping back on shore.

Rain leans back, twists her body. She yanks.

Ribbons shoot out, taking hold of Dalí, adding their strength to Rain's arms. The wounded kaiju dredges what's left of the arts center away, and then lifts off the ground.

Rain spins, swinging Dalí like she's a hammer-throw champion, leaning back as she comes around.

Brute sees it coming, but there's nothing to be done when a skyscraper-sized bat is swung in your direction.

The impact of the two kaiju creates a shockwave strong enough to lift our vehicle onto two wheels for a moment. As I recover from the blow, I watch the energy slide through the city, kicking up an expanding circle of dust and burst window glass.

Brute is once again thrown backward, rolling to a stop at the base of Storm's many tendrils. The giant, girl-faced kaiju stares down, a look of concern on her face, but unmoving. The long limbs bend and twist, but the many mouths covering its strange body remain clamped shut.

Dalí returns to earth with a crash that shakes the world and sloshes the river about. The bridge we were going to cross shakes, cracks, and falls away. No one else in the car notices, and I don't bother pointing it out. We're watching this show until the credits run.

Rain steps over Dalí, and without a moment's hesitation, she shoots her many ribbons into Dalí's bulbous head-body. Her hands go in next, and then all at once, she pulls.

The head stretches for just a moment, and then tears like a rotten orange.

Light spills out, followed by thousands of freed souls.

This isn't just a brawl, I realize. *She's setting those people free, and she knows it.*

"Yes!" I cheer, now standing in the backseat.

A bellowing roar announces Brute's return to the fold, but there's no time to react to it.

Twin forearms swing up and into Rain's torso.

She's lifted up off the ground and flung.

Toward us.

"Uhh," Garcia says, looking forward and seeing the bridge. "Guys…"

Even if she'd hit the gas, escaping would be impossible. We're too close, and they're too big.

Everyone still conscious in the car ducks down, fully expecting to be crushed. Everyone but me.

I just watch, a smile on my face. Because I know her. Because there is no doubt in my mind. Rain won't allow me to be harmed.

Ribbons stab into the pavement all around us. They flex as her massive weight follows. Her body slows to a stop, the bulk of her head misses us by just twenty feet. She glances in our direction for a moment, and I swear I see her glowing eyes roll in a 'You moron' kind of way.

Then the ribbons thrust her back up onto her feet, and then beyond. She's airborne when she meets the charging Brute head on, driving her knee up under his head of eyeballs.

Long glowing hair billows around the gnarly head, the eyes wide and bulging. The vertical mouth on its torso shouts in pain before eating the ground.

The kaiju slides to a stop just short of us. For a moment, its many eyes stare out, blankly, like the creature is stunned or unconscious, but it has no eyelids to close. Then the eyes dart around, looking in all directions, many of them landing on me, still standing in the back seat.

A muffled growl shakes the ground, but it turns into a surprised bark as the Riesegeist is dragged away.

Brute flips over and kicks out with both legs, catching Rain off guard again. The beast is faster than he looks and absolutely fearless. Rain falls back, landing in front of Storm.

For the first time since Rain became a Riesegeist, mother and daughter look into each other's eyes.

Then Brute arrives, leaping through the air and landing atop Rain.

His meaty, two-fingered fists rise up and pound down, again and again. It's like watching the final round of a Rocky movie, only Rain isn't ducking and weaving, shouting, 'C'mon!' and welcoming the abuse. Caught off guard by her daughter's face, she's stuck beneath Brute, arms and ribbons pinned by his long body.

"We have to do something," I say, but I know there's nothing to be done. Even if I could get my hands glowing again, even if I could make contact with Brute, without having my soul sucked away, what could I do? Tell him to use his words?

But I'm desperate to help.

And I'm not alone.

White hot spears pierce Brute's body, striking from all directions. The giant is helpless against them.

Then he's lifted up, suspended like a marionette with too many strings.

Storm hoists him up in front of her face, brow furrowed, mouth downturned. The girl screams.

The sound of her voice drives me down, hands to my ears, but I don't look away.

Brute's body vibrates between the real and the unreal, patterns of energy rippling across his body.

And then, all at once, he explodes into supernatural glitter.

Souls cascade up and away, fleeing into the sky.

Storm pays them no attention. Instead, she looks down at her mother, whose body is consumed in light.

Be okay, I will, which again, is an admittedly odd thing to think about someone who is now dead. At least in as much as we understand it.

Please, be okay.

The brilliance fades and flickers away.

Rain rises from the ground, leaving a divot in the shape of her body behind. She stands, dwarfed by the thing that is her daughter. She looks up into the massive face, and then reaches up a hand.

The touch is gentle. Affectionate. A mother's reassurance. The light inside Storm dulls to a soft glow. Her long, slender arms snake out and wrap Rain in an embrace. Her massive body lowers down once more, forehead tilting forward. Mother and daughter rest their heads together, and for a moment, they just stand there.

Rain's shoulders sag. The ribbons flowing out from her back retract.

I can't tell if they're talking, or communicating in some way we can't comprehend, but the fight is over. Rain poses no threat to the world, and with mother providing direction, neither does Storm.

I smile when I realize that their names together are RainStorm. Fitting, I suppose. A force of nature, potentially deadly and world-shaping, but at the same time, a source of life and relief. I can't say for sure which one they'll be, but I have a pretty good idea, and...honestly, I don't have much say in the matter.

Rain turns her head back. I feel her stare in my gut.

I wave my hand furiously.

She gives me a cool nod in reply.

And then mother and daughter vanish.

The actual storm above us stalls and dissipates.

Two fighter jets rocket past overhead, twisting as they seek out unreal enemies no longer to be found. I can feel the pilots' relief from here.

Below me, the new Morgan, stirs. "Saul?"

She pushes herself up in the back seat, blinking awake.

I take her hand. "Morgan..."

"M-Morgan?" Reggie is shaking when she looks at my wife. "Is it you? Really you? *Impossible. There's no way.* Quiet."

"Reggie?" Morgan says. "What..."

"Quickly," Reggie says. "Who do I think is the sexiest man alive?"

Morgan's brow furrows, and I'm unnerved by the sight of my wife's eyes. I mean, they're still Rain's eyes—what Rain's eyes looked like before I met her—but Morgan's soul is shining through them.

"David Hasselhoff," Morgan says.

Reggie barks a laugh and wraps her arms around Morgan, while Bjorn lets out a somewhat dejected, "Heeey."

"So, ahh," Garcia says from the front seat, looking back. "Mrs. Signal-man. Nice to meet you. I'm sure you're lovely. But..."

To the right, a building crumbles. Dust billows toward us, chemical and choking. All around, the fringe of the city surrounding the park is in a similar state. It's all coming apart. If we don't leave now, we might be stuck here for a long time.

"Where are we headed, boss?" Garcia asks me.

I'm torn like a kid about to leave summer camp. I don't want to leave, but I know I have to. Rain is gone. I still feel her nearby, but I'm worried that if I leave, that lingering connection will be lost.

What if she needs me?

What if she's stuck?

We're fine, I hear her say in my head. **Take care of yourself.**

I smile. "We passed an IHOP on our way here."

"Oh my God, yes," Garcia says, putting the car in drive.

Bjorn objects. "We can't just break in and cook our own food."

"Look around, Love" Reggie says. "No one's going to care if we help ourselves to a Grand Slam."

"Grand Slams are at Denny's," Morgan says.

Reggie smiles at her. "Back from the dead and already a pain in my ass."

Tires squeal, as Garcia swings us around and then reenacts the Death Star trench run scene, as we flee between crumbling skyscrapers.

I lean back, holding Morgan in my arms, calm despite the lingering danger. Like my wife, I've been reborn.

I'm a new person, whole, bold, and unafraid of what the future might hold.

EPILOGUE

"How's this?" Morgan asks.

We're cloaked in darkness so absolute that my eyes are starting to play tricks on me, blue-green phosphenes ebbing and flowing like tidal waters.

"Dark," I say. "But...it might work."

It's been three months since Austin. In that time, Morgan and I have reconnected, despite the lingering sting of her secrecy. NDA be damned, she should have told me about what SpecTek was doing. Should have revealed her struggle and allowed me to share the burden.

But we have yet to be...intimate.

When I look at her, I still see Rain. She has Morgan's eyes—somehow—but the rest of her is Rain. Then again, the Rain I knew was a luminous, albino version of her half-American Indian self. And now, that self is gone into the ether, replaced by the spirit of a woman who was equal parts British, Scottish and Irish...which feels wrong.

But here we are, reunited through impossible means, alone in the dark.

And I don't find it as welcoming as I once did.

My imagination once wandered in the darkness, conjuring stories and fantasies, free from the world. Now... Now I know that there is life after death, and sometimes it hides in the dark. Or, at least, that's the way it feels. The truth is that the dead are all around us, all the time. The position of the sun or the heat of a lightbulb have no effect on lingering spirits.

I try to put the dead out of my mind. The best way to honor Rain's sacrifice is to live my life, as best as I can. And that means accepting that she knew I might eventually be intimate with my wife, living in her body.

I shake my head in the dark. *This is so freaking weird.*

"Hey," Morgan says. Her hand finds my arm in the dark. Squeezes. "We don't need to do this. Maybe this was a bad idea? The first time was spontaneous. Maybe it can't be recreated?"

"I'd be the first guy in history to pass up sex with his hot wife." I feel guilty the moment I say it. "Sorry."

"For what?" she asks.

"For...you know. She's not you... I mean..."

"Saul," she says, hand rising to my cheek. "This is me now. And just so you know, my new body is way more flexible than my old body."

My barked laugh echoes in the pitch black, stone tunnel. When I picture people standing by the tunnel's end, somewhere else in the rambling underground maze that is George's Island, I laugh harder. They're going to think *I'm* the ghost.

If there was light to see by, I know my face would be bright red. The heat on my cheeks feels like I've been downhill skiing without a mask. "Oh, man. You..."

"We'll try again later," she says, patient as ever.

"I think, maybe, we just need some light."

"I left my phone in the car," she says.

I did, too. Taking a break from the world was part of the deal today. Things have calmed down as of late, but constant reminders of our ordeal are unavoidable. Boston is being rebuilt, as are Chicago and Austin. The world is starting to relax since a Riesegeist hasn't been seen since Austin, and multiple witnesses saw, and recorded, the destruction of Dalí, Brute, and Dragonfish, as well as the non-threatening behavior of Rain and Storm. Wild theories abound about what they were—aliens, interdimensional beings, devils and angels—and about what they wanted, but none have been close to the truth.

But, like Fox Mulder's poster said, *The truth is out there.*

Or rather, it's being suppressed. Supported by overwhelming evidence, Garcia blew the lid off SpecTek and their involvement. But the government and DARPA denied any knowledge of the black operation, its laboratories, and experiments—despite the money and resources that had been given to the shadow organization. The official word is, 'It didn't happen.' The truth, which has been relayed to us via Garcia is, 'Thanks for what you did, but don't talk about it.' There was never an 'Or else,' but I think it was implied. Garcia was ready to talk about it, but I convinced her to stay quiet.

SpecTek is gone. The Riesegeists are gone. Revealing the truth to the world would not only destabilize the U.S. government, it would also let every nation and scientist lacking scruples know that weaponizing the dead was possible. I'm sure DARPA won't forget, but SpecTek's labs and research have all been destroyed. And they don't know that Morgan is alive. Reggie's involvement wasn't insignificant, but all record of her and Morgan's participation has been destroyed, and Garcia didn't give them up.

Reggie's back to work in her lab, focusing on tech that will benefit humanity. She's enlisted Morgan to help, both of them toiling to redeem past mistakes. Bjorn splits his time between helping Reggie and attending seminary. I'm not sure he's a convert, but he's seeking the truth about what we experienced in his own way. Garcia has become my close friend and confidant. She's back at work protecting people, but checks in on the weekends. She takes time to play board games with our small group of truth-knowers and keeps us up-to-date on the investigation and the search for Mr. Frank's remains...which have yet to be discovered in Austin.

"I don't need a phone," I say, making a fist.

Light flickers from my fingers, and slides back through my hand, filling the tunnel with a supernatural glow. The ancient stone of the old fort is damp and oozing history.

Morgan is just a foot away, smiling up at me. "Show off."

"What good are superpowers if you never use them?" I ask.

She steps closer, wrapping a hand around my waist. "C'mere, Lightbulbman."

She stops, and chuckles, and then corrects herself. "Signalman. Close enough."

I lean in to kiss her. As my eyes close and my lips pucker, a blur in the corner of my eye makes my hair stand on end.

My eyes dart to the side, landing on a figure hidden in shadow.

I suck in a gasp and step back. "Shit."

My arms tingle with a sense that someone is behind me.

I spin around and nearly shout at the glowing blue face of a man, staring at me, his face a mirror of the shock I feel. But he's not surprised by me, he's stuck like that forever, still surprised and confused about being dead. From the look of him, he was a confederate soldier held at Fort Warren—a pentagonal stronghold built on George's Island during the Civil War. It served a role during the Spanish-American War, World War I, and World War II. The place is primarily a tourist location now, and home to more spirits than just the infamous Lady in Black said to wander the island.

I could talk to him. Same with the guy behind me, and the dozens of other dead inhabiting the tunnel.

"What is it?" Morgan asks. She knows, of course. My ability to see and speak with the dead hasn't faded. I've attempted to set some free of their bond to the mortal plane, but I have yet to succeed. And I don't think my breakthrough will be with this motley crew.

"Confederate soldiers," I say.

"Holy shit. Really?" She's more fascinated than afraid...probably because she can't see them. "Guess we had an audience last time, huh? They're probably wondering why you're back with a new lady."

I smile.

"That's just the way I roll, fellas." A dozen confederate eyes turn toward me, their blue gaze unnerving. They hadn't really noticed me until I addressed them—and they heard my voice—their first contact from the land of the living in two hundred years.

"Gah!" I say, and my hand goes dark.

"Okay," Morgan says. "So, no old forts. No cemeteries. Or morgues."

"Or murder scenes," I add.

"Well, geez, where is a couple supposed to—"

"How about we start with the bedroom," I say, "and if we need to spice things up, we'll move to the living room."

"Or the basement?"

We've moved. To Beverly. Home of the fictional Fusion Center-Paranormal...who would have been handy to have around a few months back. Randy wasn't happy to see me go, but I couldn't let him see me with Morgan in Rain's body. Too many questions with unbelievable answers. Easier to just move on. The new house is recent construction with a concrete basement. No burial grounds. No ancient battles. No past murders. No ghosts.

"If we finish it."

We exit the tunnels slowly, hands brushing walls in the dark, following the path of turns we memorized on our way in. When we emerge from an old door bearing a 'Do Not Enter' sign, two little boys scream in surprise and bolt. We're still smiling as we exit the fort's rear, ocean-facing door, and we suck in a breath of cool, autumn air.

My smile plummets straight down to Hades when I spot the pale-skinned man in a fancy suit standing on the retaining wall, crashing waves at his back.

Mr. Frank.

When I tense, Morgan says, "That's him?"

She has vague memories of her time as Wisp. Knows she protected me from a pale man. But she doesn't remember what he looked like. Only what he felt like. But, when she answers her own question, it's clearly enough. "That's him. How did he find us?"

"Doesn't matter," I say, stepping forward.

"Are you sure that's a good idea," Morgan says.

"Been waiting for this moment," I say, and I give her a smile. "I'll be fine."

I give her hand a squeeze and step toward the undead man.

"You don't seem nervous," he says, when I stop ten feet short of him.

I smile at him.

For a moment, it's grin versus glare, you pay for the whole seat, but you only need the edge. Then he cracks, brow furrowing, wondering what the hell I know that he doesn't.

"You should have stayed in whatever hole you've been hiding in," I say.

"Bold words, from a small man."

"A small man, with big friends." I light up my fists.

Mr. Frank laughs at that. He knows I'm not a threat.

"FYI," I say. "I wasn't referring to *my* fists." I glance down when the tether snaking out of my body flares to life.

Mr. Frank's eyes widen.

He definitely didn't know.

The tether streaks into the sky like a lightning bolt, flaring wide when it strikes its far end. A body shimmers into the world, feminine and haunting, ribbons rising on her back.

Rain.

Behind her, the flash of light continues skyward, illuminating a second spirit, its massive, feminine face downturned in anger.

Storm.

They've been hidden from the world since that fateful night, but they have been my constant companions since. We don't chat, watch movies, or play UNO, but I am always aware of them, and the protection they offer—mother and daughter.

Mr. Frank turns from the Riesegeists, his mouth slightly open in surprise.

"Oops," I say.

Rain's hand snaps down, snatching up Mr. Frank. And then, she squeezes. I'm impressed when Mr. Frank resists. His strength is supernatural, but it's no match for Rain. I cringe when his bones begin to break, and I look away when blood oozes from between her fingers.

Then she turns away, sliding out to sea with Storm, taking the corpse of Mr. Frank with them. No one will ever find him, and hopefully, what remains of SpecTek will die with him.

Morgan slides up next to me, taking my hand, watching RainStorm fade from view, along with the tether connecting us.

They don't look back or say goodbye. Don't need to.

No matter where they go—or where I do—they'll be with me, in this life and the next.

AUTHOR'S NOTE

"Well, that got weird," is the reaction I'm expecting from most readers upon finishing *Tether*. As is usual for me these days, I started this novel with a loose concept: a woman's spirit is twisted into the monstrous form of a kaiju. With that in mind, I just started writing. I didn't know who Saul Signalman would become. I didn't know Rain would be found at the lab. And I didn't know that an M.I.T. professor, FBI agent, or a flippin' warlock would be coming along for the ride. Every chapter was a surprise. I was just along for the ride, transcribing what my imagination conjured. The result is a kaiju ghost story featuring some freakish ghouls, Matt Frank as a villain, and hopefully a very original story and a refreshing addition to the genre.

If you enjoyed the ethereal strangeness that is *Tether*, please help spread the word by posting reviews on Amazon and Audible. Every one helps a lot, and it might take some convincing to get new readers to take a chance on a giant monster horror novel...because, whose ever heard of such a thing? You have, that's who!

And for that, I owe you a huge "thank you!". Without the support of my core readers and listeners, I wouldn't be able to let my imagination run wild. I'd probably be writing sordid romances. And if this was your first time experiencing one of my stories, there are a lot more where this one came from! Check out my other 60+ novels at my monster-themed website www.bewareofmonsters.com, and sign up for the newsletter, or connect with me on Facebook at www.facebook.com/sciencethriller.

Thanks for reading!

—Jeremy Robinson

ACKNOWLEDGMENTS

Despite being a fan of giant monster stories my whole life, it took a long time for me to realize I could introduce the genre to novel readers. Not bound by the constraints of what men in rubber suits can do, or the budget dictated by a Hollywood studio, I've been able to create strange and bold stories that are as much about the human characters as the monsters they face. Big thanks to Kane Gilmour, for helping me realize giant monsters deserve a place in novelized fiction, and for his edits of this, and all my books. And thank you to Roger Brodeur, Kyle Mohr, Chris Anstead, Dustin Dreyling, Dan Delgado, Jeff Sexton, Becki Tapia Laurent, Heather Beth, Kait Arciuolo, Julie Cummings Carter, Jennifer Antle, Donna Fisher, Dee Haddrill, Kelly Tyler, and Liz Cooper. Your proofreading makes me look like I know how to spell and type.

Thank you to Matt Frank, kaiju master extraordinaire, for his illustration found at the story's end, and for doing so much to make giant monsters mainstream in the U.S.

Finally, extra special thanks to Truls Osmundsen, for Norwegian translations—and even audio samples to help Jeffrey Kafer out with the audiobook. Much appreciated. *Takk!*

ABOUT THE AUTHOR

Jeremy Robinson is the international bestselling author of sixty novels and novellas, including *Apocalypse Machine, Island 731*, and *Second-World*, as well as the Jack Sigler thriller series and *Project Nemesis*, the highest selling, original (non-licensed) kaiju novel of all time. He's known for mixing elements of science, history and mythology, which has earned him the #1 spot in Science Fiction and Action-Adventure, and secured him as the top creature feature author. Many of his novels have been adapted into comic books, optioned for film and TV, and translated into thirteen languages. He lives in New Hampshire with his wife and three children.

Visit him at www.bewareofmonsters.com.

CPSIA information can be obtained
at www.ICGtesting.com
Printed in the USA
LVHW041842071019
633430LV00004B/782/P